Acclaim for
WINDWARD SHORE

"Like its predecessors in The Dancing Realms series, *Windward Shore* features fascinating worldbuilding undergirded by a spirituality that's as deep as its ocean universe. Populated by startling enemies and unexpected allies, and liberally sprinkled with memorable moments, this book will linger in my memory."

—KATHY TYERS, *New York Times* best-selling & Christy Award-winning author

"This heartfelt conclusion to The Dancing Realms is pitch-perfect. I was swept away by Sharon Hinck's imagination and touched by the depth of her spiritual themes. *Windward Shore* absolutely sparkles."

—LINDSAY A. FRANKLIN, award-winning author of *The Story Peddler*

Acclaim for
THE DANCING REALMS

2020 Christy Award Winner – Visionary
Hidden Current (Book 1)

"Hinck's intertwining of Christian theology and fantasy renders a thought-provoking tale, and readers will be challenged to question their convictions. Recommended."

—SCHOOL LIBRARY JOURNAL

"Both fantastical and a commentary on blind faith, Sharon Hinck's exquisite *Hidden Current* kick-starts a magical new series centered around the power of dance and staying true to yourself."

—FOREWORD REVIEWS

"Sharon Hinck's fantasy dances to the rhythm of our Creator's heart... the story moves well to the rhythm of an organic and necessary theme: the ultimate purpose of creative gifts, in a world that's guided not by human movers in a disordered Order, but by a divine and prime Mover."

—LOREHAVEN MAGAZINE

"Hinck's creative imagery takes readers into a world with a unique view of what it means for something to be evil, and how evil takes hold of innocence... Recommended as an excellent YA crossover, appealing to fans of the Christian genre, fantasy, romance, and adventure."

—LIBRARY JOURNAL

WINDWARD
SHORE

Books by Sharon Hinck

The Secret Life of Becky Miller
Renovating Becky Miller

Symphony of Secrets

Stepping Into Sunlight

The Sword of Lyric Series
The Restorer
The Restorer's Son
The Restorer's Journey
The Deliverer

The Dancing Realms Series
Hidden Current
Forsaken Island
Windward Shore

WINDWARD
SHORE

THE DANCING REALMS

BOOK 3

SHARON HINCK

Published by Enclave Publishing, an imprint of Third Day Books, LLC

Phoenix, Arizona, USA.
www.enclavepublishing.com

ISBN: 978-1-62184-167-8 (printed hardback)
ISBN: 978-1-62184-169-2 (printed softcover)
ISBN: 978-1-62184-168-5 (ebook)

Cover design by Kirk DouPonce, www.DogEaredDesign.com
Typesetting by Jamie Foley, www.JamieFoley.com

Printed in the United States of America.

to Flossie and Carl
who face every adventure with kindness and courage

"Deliver me
from sinking in the mire;
let me be delivered from my enemies
and from the deep waters."

—*Psalm 69:14 (ESV)*

WHERE COULD HE BE? I SQUINTED TOWARD THE HORIZON, where stormy sky met turbulent sea. Brantley had planned to be back by midday, but the primary sun was already lowering beyond the churning waves. Not a good sign. Wind howled from the ocean, and the ground bobbed. A gust slapped into me, rippling my tunic and forcing me to lean forward to keep my footing. My toes dug into the tangleroot.

Shielding my eyes against the subsun, I hoped to spy the silhouette of a herder balanced on the sleek back of his stenella, his determined form rising behind the graceful curve of the creature's neck. Surely he'd seen the storm moving toward our island. Why hadn't he raced home? Had he gone out too far? His new mount, Makah, was young and early in her training; she wasn't as skilled and reliable as Navar had been.

The island's rim lurched, forcing me to retreat. I could dance a pattern to change the wind's course and coax the storm away, but I had no idea where Brantley and Makah were. My interference could send the storm straight into them. A sigh ripped out of me. All I could do was wait.

My arms cradled the gentle swell of my belly. I'd hoped news of a babe on the way would cause my husband to take fewer risks. I shook my head, letting the wind tug my hair free from my braid. I didn't truly want him to change. But I did wish he had a more experienced stenella. Brantley still grieved Navar's loss. So did I.

The clouds broke open, and rain sheeted down, driving me to seek shelter. Our home welcomed me with warmth and light. High windows under the eaves let in the glow of the setting subsun that penetrated even the storm, and torches brightened the wall by the hearth, competing with the flickering fire. A smoky scent curled through the air.

I added a log, grateful for the refuge. A home like this was a luxury I'd never dreamed to experience. Shelves lined one wall, filled with food staples, tools, parchment, and neatly folded fabric. Through a low doorway, I could glimpse the cheerful quilt covering our bed. Spare tunics and cloaks hung from pegs.

I brushed moisture from my shoulders and rested on a bench near the table in this main room. Our bonding cup held a place of honor in the center of the table. Delicate carvings embellished the polished sides with images of land and sea, stenella and forest hound, and a man and woman. A rolled parchment rested against it as if in opposition. I pressed my lips together. As much as I longed for Brantley's safe return, I dreaded the confrontation that simple missive would bring.

Restless again, I rose and slid a full pot closer to the flames, sprinkled herbs into the seawater, and inhaled the comfort of brewing tsalla. Amazing how tastes could change. Hard to believe I once preferred rainwater to the sweet citrus tang of the sea. The rim dwellers may yet make a true rimmer of me.

After settling into a bent-willow rocker Brantley had built, I stretched my feet toward the hearth, savoring the warmth. I drew circles with my feet, rolling my ankles, willing suppleness into my bad leg. Ginerva's potions had brought some improvement in the past months, but the tendon severed by High Saltar Tiarel's knife still couldn't bear my full weight, and might never again. The scar throbbed at odd times—like now when a windy downpour disturbed the air. I pulled my foot into my lap, grateful I hadn't lost my dancer's flexibility.

Maker, I could serve You so much better if You healed me, I prayed for the thousandth time. I massaged my ankle and rewrapped the bandage, then stretched my foot back toward the warmth. My hands traced the curves of my belly and the signs of new life growing within. Only a year had passed since our bonding, and already we were blessed with the joy of a coming child. *I have so much to be grateful for. Thank You for Your blessings.* My brow furrowed. "Please bring Brantley home safely. Teach me to live in trust instead of fear." A log popped, drowning out my soft voice.

The door crashed open, and I jumped.

Brantley surged inside and wrestled the door closed, then shook his head like a wet hound. His fair curls were dark from rain and plastered against his head. "Whew! That storm snuck up on me. And I misjudged Makah's speed. Took longer to get home than I'd planned."

Another pang speared my ribs. Makah could never replace Navar. Even though we didn't speak of what happened anymore, it cut between us like a small crack in a tree limb. And like a landkeeper wrapping linen around that branch, I poured every kindness I could on him, hoping one day the seam would heal.

Brantley brushed water from his bare chest and mottled leggings. Then he unbuckled his belt and took time to dry his longknife before striding over to kiss me. "Were you worried?"

I forced a bright smile. "Of course not. How was the fishing?"

He sank onto a low stool and held his hands toward the flames. "Saw a great school of copper fish but . . ." He shrugged.

"Let me guess. Makah ignored your directions and chased them away."

He rubbed the back of his neck. "She'll figure it out eventually. She's still young."

"How long before I can ride with you?"

His head snapped up, ocean-blue eyes alight with pleased surprise. "She's big enough but tends to be erratic. I'd hate for you to take a tumble into open ocean." His gaze moved to my arms folded across my middle. "Especially now."

I ran a hand through my tangled hair and glanced at the parchment that seemed to glow in the firelight. "How about the river?"

His eyes narrowed. "I'm happy you're eager to ride a stenella. But what brought on this sudden interest?"

I squirmed. If I told him, his easy smile and clear gaze would change. Worry—even anger—would crease his forehead. I eased the pot from the fire and dipped a mug for him. "The tsalla is ready. You need to warm up. The waves looked cold."

He wrapped both his callused hands around the mug and inhaled the steam. After savoring a sip, he raised a brow my direction. "So you *were* watching the sea. Admit it, you were worried about me."

"If you had the common sense the Maker gave a flea, I wouldn't have to worry." This was what I got for bonding with a man so reckless. How was it possible that one of the qualities I loved most about him was also the one that most frustrated me?

His grin warmed me to my toes. "Have I mentioned that I cherish you, dancer?"

I pretended to search my memory. "Not in the last few hours."

"I need to remedy that." He moved to crouch beside me, giving me another lingering kiss, then planting a light kiss on my belly. "I love you, Carya. On this world or another."

His words soothed my heart in the same way Ginerva's ointment eased my wound. "And I love you, husband." Then I playfully pushed him away. "Get some dry clothes on. We need to talk."

He backed off as if he'd found prickly lanthrus in his porridge. "Nothing good follows that statement." But he strode into our bedroom.

I moved to the table and settled on the bench, picking up the rolled parchment and then setting it down again.

"News from Saltar Kemp?"

I jumped, then managed a tense laugh. "Stop sneaking up on me."

He had toweled off his hair, which curled out in all directions like golden whitecaps. He wore a loose linen tunic over dry trousers. The standard garb for the Windswell villagers, but the casual attire made him look wild and untamed. Especially since the knee of his pants needed mending again. He was as careless with his clothes as he was with the risks he took. "What makes you think the letter is from Saltar Kemp?"

He tilted his head. "There aren't many with the means to use parchment or pay a runner to deliver a letter. Besides, you're nervous as a minnow. Bad news?"

"Depends on how you look at it." I handed him the parchment.

Sure enough, his forehead creased as he read. Or perhaps that was just evidence of the concentration it took him to make out the words. Rimmers had little use for reading and writing. Another reminder of our differences. And Saltar Kemp was frugal, so she wrote in tiny script to conserve parchment.

He read through it twice, then tossed the letter back onto the table, the cause of his frown no longer in question. "No."

"That's all? We can't discuss it?"

"There's nothing to discuss. We promised to walk this life *together*, remember?"

I stared at the scallops carved along the rim of the bonding cup. So many ups and downs. "Of course I remember. That wouldn't change." I rested my hand on his, willing him to understand.

He lifted his gaze, and I shrank from the hurt in his eyes. "Everything would change."

2

"SHE NEEDS ME." OUR ARGUMENT HAD CONTINUED INTO supper. I pushed aside my bowl of stew, unable to eat much with the tension twisting my stomach. "I wouldn't consider leaving now, but she says I'm the only one who can help her. This doesn't sound like some small problem. She wrote that the safety of the Order is at stake."

Brantley chewed, swallowed, and glanced at me as if he were about to respond. Instead, he scooped up another spoonful of broth. His silence formed an angry wall between us.

Subdued, I angled my chair away from the table to watch flames dance in the fireplace. "Maybe another island has drifted into view."

His frown deepened. "You can't think that you'll go explore another world. Not again. Not now."

I scrambled for another explanation to appease him. Saltar Kemp's letter had sounded desperate but was very short on details about why she needed me. "Perhaps Saltar River is stirring up trouble. Think of all the ground that would be lost if she convinced people to return to the old ways."

He growled, then slid my bowl to his side of the table. "Done with this?"

I nodded.

He finished the rest of my supper, then took our dishes outside to wash at the shore. The rain had passed, but I wished for the howling wind's return to cover the deafening silence that filled our home.

When he returned, Brantley stopped just inside the door, jaw working as if a fishbone had stuck between his back teeth. Rubbing his temples, he closed his eyes, probably tamping down his temper by silently reciting fish species or rim villages and their herders.

It must have helped, because he was gentle as he led me to the rocker near the fire, then settled on a low stool near me.

"I understand the need," he said at last. "But why is she so cryptic? She hinted that the need is dire because she knows you. She knows you always feel compelled to help. Do you understand that I can't leave Makah? Teague won't be back from Undertow for days. He promised to help their new herder until Makah is able to adjust to another rider."

"Of course."

Clouds scudded across his brow. "That means I can't join you in Middlemost."

I nodded. The last thing I wanted was physical distance. But he had to understand there were times our responsibilities drew us away from each other—like the many hours he spent out at sea.

The shadows darkened over his expression. "You're that eager to be apart?" His lilt made the question playful, teasing. But hurt flickered in his eyes.

I leaned forward, cradled his face, and touched my forehead to his. "Never." I kissed him, offering reassurance in the language he most appreciated.

When we eased apart enough to breathe, his crooked grin brought an answering smile from me. "You'll make this impossible for me," I said.

"That's the plan." He sank back, his shoulder pinching and causing him to wince.

I motioned for him to turn so I could rub the knots from his neck and back. "Brantley, nothing in me wants to go. Now of all times. I love the dancers and enjoyed helping Saltar Kemp design new patterns, but she always understood my visits were temporary."

His muscles tightened under my hands, and I pressed my thumbs deeper.

"Ow!" He pulled away and stood to face me.

I raised my hands. "Do you really think I want to leave? My place is here. With you."

"But you're going." Accusation? Resignation? I couldn't read his tone.

My spine curved, weighted by conflicting responsibilities. "No. Not if you think it's the wrong thing to do."

He groaned and raked a hand through his hair. "We both know you're needed there. Maybe I can get a message to Teague. If he can come back and take over with Makah, I could go with you for at least a few days. If the Order is really at risk . . ."

"So is all of Meriel." I studied him. "You're truly all right with me staying there until things stabilize?"

He shrugged, then winced again and rubbed his shoulder. "I just didn't want you to be happy about it."

A startled laugh burst from my throat. After rising, I nestled into his chest and wrapped my arms around him. "I promise to be miserable every second we're apart."

His deep chuckle rumbled. "That answers one concern."

"What's the other?" I tilted my face up.

He touched my cheek, kissed my nose, then let his hand rest on my stomach. "The danger. To you both."

"I know. But the whole world is struggling. Maybe I can help."

He pulled me close again, squeezing with a hint of desperation. "Can't the Maker let someone else help?"

I smiled, resting against his chest. "He has. You, for one. We've served Him together."

He huffed out an exasperated breath. "Fine. We'll try Makah on the river tomorrow morning. If she manages that, we'll travel up to Middlemost. Maybe I can continue her training along the river and stay nearby while you help Kemp."

My heart lightened enough to make me feel like I was floating. "Can the villagers manage without their herder driving fish in to shore for a few weeks?"

"Thanks to your dances, the village's gardens and orchards are producing more food. And it's not as if my herding has provided much in recent months."

No hint of bitterness sharpened his voice, but the words stung. I burrowed against him so he wouldn't see my hurt. Another reminder of the amazing partnership he lost with Navar. Because of me.

"I didn't dare hope you'd come with me. I know the Order isn't your favorite place on Meriel."

"Someone has to keep you out of trouble. Whatever the danger, you'll need a man with a longknife."

"Oh, I'm sure there won't be any violence." Now that we had a plan and were on the same side again, my appetite returned. I rummaged the shelves across from our fireplace for a saltcake. "Saltar Kemp probably only wants me there to reassure the novitiates and dancers—reaffirm the truth and the Order's new direction. Perhaps a few heated debates, that's all."

He looked unconvinced. "You hate debates."

I offered a rueful smile. "I grew up learning to avoid any hint of conflict. There was no room for disagreement in the Order. But sometimes hard things need to be spoken."

"True." His eyes held a challenge. "So tell me what's been bothering you."

I blinked. I'd done all I could to hide my worries, my self-blame. Dare I tell him that regrets from the forsaken island still haunted me? That I longed for his reassurance? He'd insisted he held nothing against me, but I couldn't forgive myself for the pain I'd caused him. I opened my mouth.

Crash! Something hit our door, rattling the whole cottage.

3

ORIANNA BURST INTO OUR COTTAGE, FINE HAIRS POKING out of the braids that wrapped her head like a crown. Most days Brantley's niece was golden sunshine set in gangly limbs and carefree songs, but tonight her eyes were wide, and her chest heaved. Her over-large tunic, made with room to grow by her practical mother, canted off one shoulder. "You're needed," she gasped.

I cut my gaze to Brantley and back to her. "Which of us?"

"Both." She bounced on her heels. "It's Grandma."

That was all we needed to hear. Brantley tossed me my cloak, strapping on his knife belt while heading out the door. I reached for my walking stick and Orianna's hand as we followed him into the darkness. "Has she taken ill?"

"It's her breathing. Mama says Grandma will be all right, but her eyes looked scared. She didn't want me to bother you, but I convinced her."

In spite of my worry, I smiled. Orianna could charm a honeybird to her finger, and Brianna stood little chance against such a determined daughter.

Brantley ducked under a low branch, his long strides carrying him ahead of us. The wet earth beneath my soles made an uneven squishing sound as I limped as fast as I could. "How long has Fiola been sick?" I usually crossed paths with her during daily errands around the village but hadn't seen her in a few days. I should have checked in on her.

"Not long. But today it turned bad." Orianna was about to pull my arm from its socket. "Mama tried lanthrus, but it's not helping."

Brantley sprinted ahead. By the time I reached the cottage, low light spilled from the open doorway. On his knees beside his mother's pallet,

Brantley pressed a hand to her cheek. "I'm here," he said. Brianna wrung out a cloth and leaned past him to place it on Fiola's forehead.

His mother's frame was sunken into her bed, as if both illness and bedding were swallowing her. Her skin was almost the shade of her gray hair. My breath hitched. Not many months ago, I'd knelt by my own mother as she battled illness. And lost. Was Brantley thinking of that?

Fiola's eyes fluttered open, and she frowned at her son. "What are you doing here?" The words were reassuringly normal, but her voice was wispy, and as she drew a deeper breath, it rattled in her chest. "You have your own family to be caring for. Brianna has been fussing enough." Her gaze traveled past him and landed on me. "You're here, too? How is my new grandbaby-on-the-way?"

"We're all fine." My hand rested over the curve of my belly. I turned to Brianna. "What can I do?"

Exhaustion drew rings around Bri's eyes. "Stoke the fire. And see if you can make sense of her herb jars. The lanthrus broth didn't help, but . . . " She gestured helplessly.

I shot Brantley a worried glance, but he was fixated on his mother, whose eyes had closed again. With my arm around Bri's shoulders, I guided her to a chair. "When did you last eat? Or sleep?"

She rubbed her forehead. "Not sure."

"Well, let's see to that now. You'll do no one any good if you fall ill too."

She sagged, too weary to argue. After stoking the fire, I brewed Bri a mug of tsalla and peeled a persea for her. I knew she wouldn't leave Fiola's side, so the only way I'd coax her to get some rest was making up a spare pallet here. Orianna helped me.

As I guided Brantley's weary sister-in-law to the waiting ticking and blankets, she clutched my arm. "You'll stay?" Her words slurred.

"Of course. Now rest."

"And Orianna."

"I'll look after her."

While Brantley murmured soothing reassurances to his mother, I fed Orianna and then systematically opened each jar of herbs on Fiola's cluttered shelves. I found nuggets of an astringent resin that made my eyes water. That might help her breathing.

Fiola curled on her side as coughs wracked her body. She inhaled—a tight wheeze—and sweat beaded her face. Brantley helped her to sit up, supporting her as another round of coughs shook her.

I worked faster, hands shaking while I crushed the resin into a bowl of steaming seawater.

"Can she drink?" I asked Brantley.

Lips pressed, he gave a small shake of his head.

"All right. Help me hold this. Fiola, try a deeper breath. Breathe in the steam."

Her head lolled, but she drew in the fragrant mist. She coughed a few more times, but the next inhale went deeper into her lungs.

Relief slackened her features, and eventually she breathed more freely. "Thank you," she whispered.

Brantley eased her limp frame back onto the pallet. I set the bowl next to her head and fanned more scented air over her face.

A hint of a smile tugged her lips. "Believe I'll rest a bit." Her drooping lids closed.

Brantley tucked a blanket up under her chin and sank back on his heels. "I've been out training too much. I should have checked on her."

I rested a hand on his back. "This isn't your fault. I could have looked in on her. I had no idea she was ill. It must have come on suddenly."

He scowled. "Why didn't Brianna tell us?"

I glanced at the pallet where Orianna now also slept—a round egg in the nest of her mother's arms. "She probably thought she could manage."

"She should have asked for help." His irritation surfaced. Typical of Brantley to mask his worry with crankiness.

"The way you always ask for help?"

He scoffed. "Not the same."

Together, we kept steam filling the air near Fiola and replaced damp cloths on her forehead. She woke again, eyes glassy, her unintelligible mumbles triggering another coughing attack. I touched her cheek, which burned like a hearthstone.

"Fever is doing its work." I wished I felt as confident as I sounded. "Do you think this is what it will be like with a babe?"

Brantley's eyes widened, as if he'd never considered the possibility of sleepless nights or illness with our child.

I hurried to reassure him. "I'm sure she'll be healthy."

His jaw jutted. "*He* will be strong and hale. And go out herding with me."

Now my eyebrows rose. No child of mine would go out on the tumultuous seas.

Fiola stirred, drawing our attention. She plucked at the blanket's hem, then stilled again. Brantley leaned forward, tension gripping his spine. "I think this is meadow blight."

I shook my head, still hoping it was a simple fever and cough. Meadow blight could linger for weeks and turn nasty. "Whatever it is, we'll help her."

Brantley's eyes, bleary from the long night and astringent steam, met mine. "Except you can't."

I sagged. Saltar Kemp needed me at the Order. But how could I leave now? Fiola had become like a mother to me, helped me share the Maker's letter with Windswell, rejoiced over my bonding with her son. I glanced at Brianna and Orianna. They all needed me. Brantley needed me by his side.

"I'll send word I can't go."

Brantley stroked my face, buried his hand in my hair, and pulled me toward him until our foreheads touched. "You have to go. We'll be all right. And when Mother recovers, she'll want to know that the Order hasn't chained Meriel again."

I touched the bristles along his jawline, breathed in the scent of his skin, let my hand move to his chest and the strong rhythm of his heart. "But we'll be parted."

"I know." Sorrow flared in his pupils, or perhaps it was firelight. He rubbed the back of his neck. If he felt conflicted, he buried it quickly. "I'll bring you upriver to Middlemost and then return. As soon as Mother has recovered, I'll join you."

He was matter-of-fact, and I tried to match his stoic acceptance, but inside I screamed. *Dearest Maker, why do we keep facing these paths that we would never choose?*

HOURS LATER, BRANTLEY AND I BALANCED ON THE EDGE of the tangleroot shore. He whistled, and Makah approached. The moods of a stenella are hard to read, but she looked as if she answered him grudgingly. Moving slowly, she stayed a few feet from the rim. When Brantley made a tight circle with his hand to rotate her, she moved closer but didn't turn her body.

He repeated the motion, and her lids closed partway like those of a sullen child. After a long pause, she spun but flipped her tail fin and splashed us.

"She's about as excited about this journey as I am." I reached out to stroke her long neck, but she angled away.

"Maybe she'll perk up when she sees we're heading upriver. It's something new, and she's easily bored."

Like her herder. Whereas I craved routine and a stable life here in Windswell.

Brantley stepped onto Makah's back and offered his hand. With his help, I settled close behind her neck, in the same way I'd often ridden Navar. Her broad back offered ample room, and my feet rested lightly on her tucked-in side fins. Floppy ears swaying, she twisted to look at me, aghast at the unfamiliar rider. "You're a beauty, aren't you?" I crooned.

She truly was magnificent. Even though she was still smaller than a fully-grown, working stenella, graceful lines curved as she lifted her back fluke, then splashed it down impatiently.

Brantley chuckled. Training Makah had been irritating, but he was starting to bond with her. I hoped their partnership would deepen and help heal the wounds he carried—especially for Navar's loss. He remained standing and whistled a staccato command.

Makah surged forward, nearly jarring him off. Only an expert herder's balance kept him on his feet. I squeezed my legs against the stenella's flanks and kept one hand against her neck to steady myself. We traveled past the main part of the village. A few children waved as we went by.

When we reached the mouth of the river, Brantley gave a hand signal for her to turn, but she wasn't watching for his direction and swam beyond the opening. His short whistle pierced the air, and Makah pulled up hard like a rearing pony. It took a few more tries before he was able to steer her upriver.

I'd made this trip several times on Navar before we'd traveled to the forsaken island. The journey that took weeks of hiking was now but a half day by river. Part of me wished it was not so convenient. I wanted the Order to manage without me.

Makah swerved, startled by the shadow of a tree limb drooping out over the river. I ran my hand over her hide. "You're doing fine. Just think how jealous your pod will be that you had this adventure. Few stenella have traveled upriver."

Makah's ears flexed, round lobes swinging. She didn't look back at me, but I believed she understood the gist. Brantley scoffed, but didn't say anything. He scanned the waters ahead for any obstacles or dangers.

A log floated into sight.

I sensed Brantley tense behind me, but he kept his voice calm as he called, "Hang on."

Except there was little to hang on to. Makah stretched her neck forward, so I couldn't wrap my arms around it. I wished that herders used reins or saddles, even though I understood why it wasn't practical. None of the stenella had been pleased with the harnesses used to transport things from the foreign island. When Brantley had worked with Navar, subtle shifts of his weight communicated through his feet. A sharp whistle or hand gesture augmented those directions.

Brantley whistled, but Makah didn't respond. Instead, she bucked and writhed. "Lean left," he told me.

I tilted to a more precarious line, gripping with my legs until the muscles trembled. The approaching log twisted in the current, blocking the right half of the river. Makah chirruped her agitation.

Brantley's rising whistle sliced the air. Makah tossed her head, ears swinging. The log was nearly on us, moving quickly. Before I could prepare myself, our stenella dove, whooshing beneath the log. I sputtered as my face met the water. Out of instinct, I kept my grip and ducked my head down against her withers. Makah swam deep, and my ears ached from the pressure, because unlike a normal river, there was no bed beneath the water here. Just fathoms and fathoms of ocean, stretching for unknown depths. At last we shot upward again and finally broke the surface. Gulping lungfuls of sweet air, I looked behind me for Brantley.

He had disappeared.

I WAS ALONE. TERRIFYINGLY ALONE AND PILOTING AN immature stenella in a river full of hazards.

Tempted to yell at Makah for tossing her herder, instead I pushed wet hair from my face and stroked her neck. "Clever girl. You avoided the log your own way. But now we have to stop."

What was the signal for stopping? I patted her back to get her attention. "Please stop. We have to go back for him."

She raised her chin and turned her head, then blinked a few times when she realized Brantley was missing. Her lustrous eyes narrowed as if accusing me. But at least she stopped, fins shifting only enough to keep us in place.

"Don't blame me. You're the one who dove while he was standing. I'm no herder, but even I know stenella aren't supposed to dive until the herder is seated."

She stretched out her neck and ignored me. I eyed the shores, which stretched about three cottage widths apart and rose too steeply for me to climb. A slight bend blocked my view of the channel behind us. "Brantley!" I shouted.

Makah flinched, but still didn't move. "We're here! Can you hear me?" What if Brantley had hit his head on the log when Makah dove? Was he even now sinking into the ocean depths that churned beneath this seam in the island? He'd been worried about me making this trip but never gave a thought for his own safety.

I tried to whistle, but panic had left my mouth dry. Only a breathy sound emerged from my pursed lips, my effort mocked by easy birdsong from nearby trees. I shouted again, but that made Makah wriggle, and I feared being cast off.

Reining in my uneasiness, I studied my petulant mount. Perhaps I could build a relationship with this young stenella through dance as I had once with Navar. Makah's head swept side to side in the water, powerful neck muscles serpentine and smooth. In spite of my fear, I had to admire the beauty of her motion. I didn't dare stand, but I began to echo her actions with swaying. She wasn't watching me, but perhaps she felt the shift in weight as I built on the fluid motions. Imagining a stenella craning to view the world, I lifted my arms overhead. Then, with arms at shoulder level, I stroked the air at one side as if turning in water. A deep and slow drumming filled my head. All dances followed a rhythm. Every pattern we learned at the Order connected us with that part of the Maker's world. But we'd never learned a pattern for stenella. Now I found the beat of the sea creature and joined in.

Her muscles tightened, and she turned to look at me, head still resting on the surface of the water. I kept dancing with my upper body, seeking to understand her, to embody her. Offering her love and appreciation. Could she feel it? Did my efforts to emulate her mean anything?

At last, she deigned to lift her head, her neck creating a curved arch. She looked at me again, and her side fins stirred the water. As she copied my awkward motions, we turned in the river. Now my arms swam us forward, as if dancing through heavy mist instead of air. With a few clicking sounds, she glided downriver. I hugged her neck and crooned my thanks, then squinted ahead for any sign of Brantley.

In minutes I spotted him, stroking strongly toward us. Relief surged through me. "Whoa," I said softly, leaning back as I'd seen herders do. To my surprise, Makah stopped.

Brantley lifted his head, tossing water from his hair in one sharp gesture. Even frustrated and waterlogged, he was a beautiful sight.

As soon as he reached us, he climbed onto her, jaw tight. In a practiced motion, he pulled his feet under himself in a crouch and then stood. Irritation pulsed in the tendons of his neck, and Makah chittered nervously. Whatever rapport they'd built began to slip away.

"How did you get this stubborn creature turned?"

"Don't call her names. She returned me to you." I stroked her neck, hoping to soothe her again.

"She only had to return you because she threw me off. I'm supposed to be grateful?"

Behind his anger at Makah, I sensed his fear for me. He needed soothing more than the stenella. "Everyone is safe. She's doing her best. I'm sure she's sorry."

"Sorry?" His voice rose in pitch.

"Yes." I looked up at him with pleading eyes. I'd been just as frustrated with the young stenella moments earlier, but now I coaxed him to forgive her.

Makah swiveled to face him, and his mouth twitched. "How do you both manage to have the same expression?"

I felt some of the tension ease from Brantley and a corresponding softening of Makah's muscles beneath me. Instead of berating her, Brantley raised his fist and drew a tight circle. Makah instantly pivoted in place. At his crisp whistle, she resumed swimming upstream.

I smiled my thanks to Brantley for being gentle with her. He would be a wonderful father—if he managed to stay alive until our child arrived.

He raised a brow. "Seriously, how did you get her to turn? Or was it her idea?"

"I tried to bond with her by mimicking her movements."

"And she let you guide her? Makes me wish I had a bit of dancer training. You have an uncanny ability to connect to . . . well, everything."

I laughed. "When Fiola is better and you come up to the Order, I'll see if they'll let you in the first form novitiate class." I sobered. "I don't like leaving while your mother is so ill. You'll send someone with news if you want me to return, won't you?"

If only it were that easy. Until Teague returned to Windswell, there was no one in the village able to ride a stenella upriver, and even then, Makah wasn't an easy mount. Another wave of remorse rolled over me. If only Navar were still with us. If only I hadn't asked Brantley to call her to the lake. If only I hadn't opened a path for us to venture onto that forsaken island where she'd given her life to save us. "I still wonder if I should be staying to help you and Bri."

"Let's not chase a broken school of fish again. Saltar Kemp clearly needs you for something important. Just don't ask me to be happy about it."

"So as long as we're both miserable about being apart, we'll both be happy?"

His laugh was rich and deep, and my heart lifted. Whatever challenges we faced, if I could bring him laughter, maybe the shadows of guilt would eventually recede.

The warm air slowly dried our clothes. We avoided a few more obstacles, and Makah seemed more responsive to Brantley's directions. When a low limb stretched out from the bank, a quick shift of position and whistled code sent her hugging the opposite shore, carrying us safely past.

"Aren't you clever?" I patted her withers. "First time carrying two people. First time on the river. This must be overwhelming for you."

"Dancer, you recall how the novitiates are trained?"

I threw back my shoulders. "Of course."

"Did the saltars lavish praise on you?"

I glared back at him. "No. But that doesn't mean a little encouragement would have gone amiss."

"Carya, let me handle the training of my stenella, all right?" There was no harshness in his tone. In fact, his lips quirked with something like appreciation. But I got the point. He was the herder. Being able to train a stenella was a point of pride.

His next words affirmed my thoughts. "And could we please not mention to anyone that Makah threw me off?"

"Of course." Maybe it wasn't only the stenella who needed a bit of praise. "You've done something amazing. Very few herders take their stenella upriver, let alone one this young and willful. The village already recites sagas about your courage in braving the foreign island. Next they'll be composing stories about your skill with your stenella."

He snorted. But the last bit of tension left his jaw, and his body rode the shifts of balance with softer knees and more of his usual grace.

THE PRIMARY SUN SOON SANK BEHIND THE EDGE OF THE rock walls that had risen higher and higher as we neared Middlemost, the town that encircled the Order like unfolding flower petals. In deep shade that made me shiver in my wet things, we continued straight to the river's end under the cliffs formed by the riven gash. Brantley whistled the code for Makah to wait and helped me to the steep path. He carried both our damp packs and my walking stick. I needed my hands free to climb the many stories from sea level here in the center of the island where the land was thickest.

I touched a porous rock face. "Such a marvel, how the Maker broke open this path."

"Some say He split the island in anger."

"I believe He did this to create a means to connect the rim and the Order."

Brantley supported my back and helped me clamber up to another rock. "It has been useful. Although few herders have dared the trip yet." He paused and scanned the length of the river, checking on Makah.

"You can go back to her. I can make my way from here."

He chuckled. "I have no doubt of your strength or your courage. But if you think I'll let you walk into the Order before I assess the dangers, you're daft."

My heart warmed at his concern, but I stiffened my spine. "I survived the Order for most of my life. Long before you came along."

He nodded. "And I'd not see you suffer like that again. Come on." He guided me up another steep boulder.

My ankle throbbed, and I was grateful for his presence behind me. I never knew when the severed tendon would refuse to support my weight—a risky venture when climbing this way. But his fears about dangers in the Order were unnecessary. So much had changed. On each of my trips here since Meriel was freed, I'd been welcomed and respected. In fact, the pleasure of designing and teaching new patterns to the dancers had made me feel torn between my work for the Order and my life back in Windswell.

We reached the top, and I hugged Brantley. "I promise to be miserable while I'm helping the high saltar."

He laughed and kissed me thoroughly. "Thank you. But you can savor your work, as long as you don't put yourself in danger. Now let's go find Saltar Kemp."

We entered the paved courtyard where marble planters held carefully contained examples of plants. Thirsty calara reeds bent in the slightest breeze. Delicate alcea perfumed the air. Prickly lanthrus threatened any who dared touch it. During my years as a novitiate I often sought solace among the orderly trees and flowers. Now they looked too formal, too contained. I preferred the haphazard fields and cluttered forests covering the rest of Meriel. The Order wasn't the only thing that had changed since the discovery of the Maker's letter. I was a different person.

I smiled as we walked past two soldiers into the hall of polished marble. Drums rang from the middle ground—the open-air field of daygrass that the many-storied Order encircled. The sound made my legs flex, eager to join the dance. A contrasting rhythm, played on hollow sticks, bounced like raindrops from one of the smaller studios. I peered inside the open doorway. Rows of fourth-form girls jumped from side to side, feet pointed like swords in the air, bodies light. Some of the saltars had feared that reforming the Order would lower standards, but these girls looked every bit as skilled and dedicated as my class had been. Scents of polished stone, herb-washed tunics, and clean sweat stirred a happy familiarity.

But along with nostalgia came tight coils that twisted in my stomach. How could one place stir both love and terror? I had truly loved learning to dance—the challenge, routine, and sense of achievement. I saw it as a sacred service to our world. Yet the relentless push for perfection, relying on no strength but our own, and the pride of believing we could control the universe—it had wounded so many and tormented my heart. Each time I entered the Order, I grappled again with this mix of emotions.

Brantley cleared his throat. "Saltar Kemp?"

I nodded and pulled myself away from the classroom door. We continued along the hall, past the largest studio. I longed to step inside and watch the blue form rehearsing but walked past to the offices. Saltar Tangleroot sat behind a desk, chewing her lip as she studied a map. Her white headscarf tamped down her thick black hair, but a playful strand curled at her cheek. When she saw me, she sprang up and embraced me. "Thank the Maker you're here."

"What's wrong?" Brantley asked before I could.

"I'll let High Saltar Kemp explain."

I turned to say goodbye to Brantley, but he took my arm and aimed us both toward the high saltar's office.

"Brantley, you should get back to your mother. I'll be fine."

He gave a low growl. "After I hear what the dire need is and how they plan to keep you safe."

I shook my head. His protectiveness made me feel cherished, but he worried far too much. The Order wasn't a danger to me. Not anymore.

Engulfed by her formal gown, Saltar Kemp stood by the inner office windows overlooking the center ground. One arthritic hand pressed the glass, supporting a body as badly bent as her finger joints. Out on the daygrass, dancers in simple white tunics and leggings spun past. One of the harvest patterns. I shifted my focus back to the high saltar.

"We've arrived," I said brightly.

Saltar Kemp turned and straightened with visible effort. "Thank you for coming." Her voice rasped like gravel from all her years of shouting instruction over the drums. She glanced at my belly. "This isn't a good time for you to travel. I'm sorry."

"I promised to help you. I know the transition has taken a toll."

She left the window and took a seat behind her desk. Compasses and sextants weighted down piles of parchments. "We had no choice. Our world was heading for self-destruction." Her pursed lips sent multiple tiny creases across her skin.

Brantley shifted his weight. "Your message mentioned an urgent need. How can Carya help you?"

"I'm not even sure she can." The strong, unbendable saltar I'd long admired—the woman who now led our world—buried her face in her hands and wept.

THE HIGH SALTAR'S FRAIL FRAME, BENT IN DESPAIR, BROKE my heart. I hurried around the desk and knelt beside her chair. "Whatever has gone wrong, I'm here to do what I can. We can face anything with the Maker's help."

She raised her face from her hands, her tear-rimmed eyes meeting mine. A small, brave smile flickered across her lips. "Dear child, I'm glad you're here, but I shouldn't have called you."

Brantley crossed his arms and shifted his weight back to his heels. "Perhaps we should leave."

"I don't know how to stop this." Saltar Kemp thrust a flat parchment from her desk toward me.

Illustrations of Meriel filled the page. Soft colors of meadows and woods. Tidy drawings of villages and landmarks. This was a new map, because it included the river piercing the island from Middlemost to Windswell. Red circles marked several villages. My fingers traced a path down through the midrim villages to Undertow—the place of my birth—then along the rim. "I don't understand."

"It began with Foleshill. They refused to give their taxes for the season. I wasn't concerned. We knew many villagers still harbored bitterness because of the Order's past."

I nodded. The former high saltar, Tiarel, had sent soldiers to decimate villages that questioned her. Regaining trust would take time.

Brantley scuffed a foot over the marble floor. "How did you handle it?"

She sat taller and turned her gaze toward him. "We did nothing. We want support of the Order to be voluntary. Those who embraced the Maker's letter saw the value of the dancers' work. But then . . ."

"Let me guess." Brantley's jaw hardened. "More villages withdrew support."

I studied the map again. "But . . . you marked Salis. I know their matriarch. This makes no sense."

Saltar Kemp sank further into her chair. "None of it makes sense. We met with all the rim leaders after your confrontation with Tiarel. I knew there would be a time of adjustment, but we achieved unity. Agreement. And then the herders brought back seeds and crops from the strange island, kindling renewed hope. Now village after village is refusing to support us. No matter how hard we work, the Order can't survive without the tithes."

Brantley had hovered just inside the doorway throughout our conversation, but now he strode forward and snatched the map from my hands. Frowning, he scanned it, then handed it back to Saltar Kemp. "There's more going on here. These villages wouldn't stand against you without cause."

She nodded. "I plan to send a representative of the Order to find out their concerns. Not just a soldier or prefect. Yet it's hard to spare anyone. A third of our dancers left—some with Saltar River, and others to their home villages. Everyone here is dancing extra shifts to bring healing to our world."

Tiny spider legs of anxiety skittered up and down my back. Saltar Kemp's intent became clearer. "You need a dancer to explain the value of the Order's work."

"And remind the villages why it's important to trust in the Maker. To renew their hope that the damage caused by the years of rotating in place will change now that we are riding the currents again."

Brantley glowered. "You can't be serious. If a village has already refused their tithe, they aren't going to react well to a dancer's arrival. And all that traveling."

I shot him a fond smile. "I can ride a pony, so it won't tax my bad leg."

"And I'll send a few soldiers to protect her."

He raked a hand through his hair, and I fought the urge to reach over and smooth the curls down. "Carya, if I could go with you, it might work. But—"

"You're needed in Windswell. I know. But I can do this." I had to make him understand. I'd served an Order corrupt with lies. I'd devoted myself to its purposes when they held our world captive. Now that I knew the truth, I wanted to atone. I wanted to do all I could to help heal our land. I touched his arm. "This will be like the visits I made to villages when I shared the Maker's letter. And much safer now that more people know the truth."

"But I was with you then." He looked at the map again. "There's a dark current here somewhere. A reason for this chain of villages to all suddenly oppose the Order. There's a pattern."

Saltar Kemp rose. "Which is why we need a representative to find out what is happening. That's all. She won't be trying to collect tithes, simply gathering information."

Brantley rocked side to side, a clear dance of indecision. Before he could raise more objections, footsteps pattered through the outer office.

A wild-haired woman skidded to a stop inside the room.

"Starfire!" I squealed and opened my arms.

She ran to hug me, talking at a gallop. "Ginerva heard you'd arrived. I've been helping her care for the dancers. They offered me a place dancing in the center ground, but it takes too much discipline. I like assisting instead. Now, what is this about a secret mission? Can I come with you?"

I beamed and cut into her breathless words. "Would you? I'd love to have your company." I turned to Saltar Kemp. "I'm sure it would be helpful to have more than one representative from the Order."

Saltar Kemp paused, then nodded. "I couldn't spare one of the center ground dancers, but Starfire is fully trained. She might be a good companion in representing the Order."

"Can Middlemost spare enough mounts?"

She tilted her head with an affectionate gaze toward Starfire. "For this vital task, of course. I'll speak to the tender myself."

Starfire waved off that suggestion. "He still owes me favors from when

I worked down there. I'll be sure we get the best ponies."

I turned to Brantley, who wore a bemused expression. My enthusiasm slipped a bit, and I stepped closer to him. "I promise to have no fun until we're together again," I whispered, but this time he didn't laugh.

"As soon as my mother is well, I'll join you." His tone brooked no argument.

I firmed my chin. I'd caused him enough disruption. He was needed in Windswell, for his mother but also because the whole village relied on his leadership. "I'll be fine. A few quick visits playing ambassador of the Order and I'll be home before you know it. Don't keep Makah waiting. You want to reach Windswell before subsunset."

He frowned, then softened, worry swimming into pools of tenderness in his eyes. "I don't like parting this way."

I took his hand. "I know. I'll walk you to the upper cliff."

Starfire raced off to pack, promising to meet me down in Middlemost. Saltar Kemp settled back into her chair, a tenuous relief lightening some of the strain from her features. She was putting so much faith in me. I had no clue what I would encounter or whether I could help this situation, but I had to hide my self-doubt, or her despair would rise up again, and Brantley would worry for me even more.

Before my protective husband would return to the river, he insisted on meeting the two soldiers Saltar Kemp had chosen to accompany me. Belgor was perhaps ten years older than us, with the grizzled look of experience, yet still full of vitality. Aanor was young and earnest, dark brows curved over large brown eyes. Brantley fired questions at them and threatened dire consequences if any harm came to me. Viewing the inquisition from behind my husband, I offered a sympathetic smile to the two men.

When at last Brantley grudgingly accepted they would do all they could to protect me on this mission, I took his arm, and we walked slowly toward the river. As much as I'd loved the quiet life in Windswell and the small dances I could use to serve their orchards and gardens, a new fire kindled in my heart today. Those times when I'd stood in village halls reading the Maker's letter to hearers who had never known the words had been exhilarating and rewarding. Despite opposition and danger, I'd felt the Maker's blessing over me. His touch.

I tamped down my excitement and patted Brantley's arm. "I'll be careful. I promise. You can trust the Maker to care for me when you can't."

He drew to a stop at the ridge. Below us, Makah splashed her tail and circled impatiently. "I'm trying to believe that." He pressed his forehead to mine. "But you insist on expecting the best of people. Please, at least try to stay on guard."

I kissed him lightly and then leaned back. "I will."

He tugged me in close again and kissed me more thoroughly. "And miss me just a little."

"Every moment." My toes tingled. My head spun. I clung to him until I was steady enough to step back with a sigh. "You take care of Fiola."

A harsh chittering rose from the water below. I laughed. "And take care of Makah. I think you'll be in far more danger than I will."

His lips quirked in a crooked grin. "Makah and I will come to an understanding. Eventually."

He bounded down the rough stairway of boulders, leapt onto Makah's back, coaxed the rebellious stenella to turn, and headed downstream.

After they disappeared from view, a cloud passed across the primary sun. My confidence wavered. *Dearest Maker, I've relied so much on Brantley, perhaps I've forgotten to rely on You. Give me the strength and wisdom I'll need. Heal our world.*

THE FIRST TWO DAYS OF TRAVEL FELT LIKE A RARE NOVITIATE holiday. Starfire and I caught up on each other's lives as the two soldiers who accompanied us hung back. The trail from Middlemost to Foleshill—

our first destination—was well traveled, and although we sometimes heard the spine-tingling howl of a forest hound or the rustling of bog rats beyond the circle of our campfire at night, I felt secure.

Starfire had coaxed the tender in Middlemost to provide us with four excellent ponies, surefooted no matter the terrain. My muscles protested after the first long day of riding, but by the second day I was savoring the freedom of being in a saddle again. I barely needed my walking stick during the short breaks we took, and I relished the luxury of saddlebags to carry our supplies instead of wearing a heavy pack.

We brought ample food, in case the people of Foleshill begrudged our gathering tubers or hunting game near their town. I also had ten precious copies of the Maker's letter to distribute among the villages in case they had not been productive in creating their own copies.

The morning we approached Foleshill dawned cloudy and grim. The town rode a small rise, the gentle slope providing a foundation for the homes silhouetted on the hill's crest. We rode past a withered grain field, aiming for the cluster of buildings where puffs of smoke rose from chimneys and joined the gray sky.

We tied our ponies to trees on the outskirts. A few children were digging for tubers and gathering mushrooms near the village's border. When they saw us, they grabbed their baskets and ran into town.

"No element of surprise for us," Belgor said grimly.

I pulled a formal robe from my pack. "We don't need to surprise anyone. We're simply here to listen. To understand their concerns." I wouldn't let the weathered soldier's dour mood dampen my hope. Whatever misunderstanding had occurred, I would smooth the waters and bring back helpful information to the Order.

Still, both men looked skeptical, and I found their unease worked itself into my thoughts. I wished Kemp had sent someone with more age and wisdom than me. Or someone who understood trade negotiations.

Starfire dusted off her sleeves and glanced down at her dark leggings and coarse tunic. "Do I look all right?"

"More appropriate than I do. I wish the high saltar hadn't insisted I wear dancer garb."

My friend shrugged. "Sends a message, I suppose."

"I hope it's the right message." My white leggings and tunic stood out like a beacon of elitism, and the finely embroidered sleeves of my robe might seem to mock the villagers' poverty. Then there was my bandaged ankle and my walking stick and my limp. Would the people be offended that the Order had sent a defective dancer? I nervously tucked a strand of hair under my white headscarf. What if I said the wrong thing?

Starfire punched my arm lightly. "Don't go fretting now. I've never visited Foleshill. Come to that, I've never visited anywhere. Let's see what it's like."

Her irrepressible spirit helped subdue my qualms. I led the way past cottages toward the town's center. Most of the homes faced us with closed doors and shutters, and few people lingered on the streets. Woodsmoke curled from chimneys, and the breeze carried a hint of pine from the surrounding woods. I smiled and called a greeting to the men and women we passed but received only frowns and silence.

At the lodge, my cane thumped on each step leading to the long wooden building's open door. We paused on the threshold. "Hello?"

A gruff voice emerged from the shadows within. "Who approaches the Foleshill matriarch?"

"Carya. Sent by the Order to seek audience."

Murmurs rose inside the lodge, like early rumbles of an approaching storm. Sounds of argument, then abrupt silence.

"Enter," said the same gruff voice.

I gestured for my soldiers to wait on the porch. With Starfire by my side, I limped through the doorway, blinking until I adjusted to the dim torchlight. The Foleshill lodge had no windows, so the air was not only dark but also stuffy. My lungs struggled to work properly, and I scanned the room with a caution that Brantley would have appreciated.

The matriarch sat at one end of the long room, a dozen or so men and women scattered on benches facing her. A few aides and a couple of soldiers stood at her side. One of the men glowered my direction. "Visitors, approach the matriarch Grast of Foleshill."

Grast? She hadn't been matriarch when I'd visited here last. I walked down the center aisle, suddenly reluctant to venture deeper into the lodge. Even when I'd planned to see a familiar face, I'd been nervous about this mission. Now my instincts told me to turn and run. "I bring a gift from the Order." I pulled a bound copy of the Maker's letter from the pouch hanging from my shoulder. The soldiers tensed, as if expecting me to draw a weapon.

Grast waved to one of the men, who took the package from me and handed it to her. Her long dark braid draped in front of her shoulder, resting against a simple tunic of rich, deep blue. Her eyes were hard, her features sharp, and she was much younger than other matriarchs I'd met on my travels.

I hoped my smile would ease the tension throughout the room. "When I last visited, Silika was matriarch."

Grast sniffed and unwrapped the fabric around the precious bound parchment. Her frown deepened when she saw the contents, and she tossed the book to the floor. "Yes, when you came here to spread your lies. She was foolish enough to listen, but things have changed."

My mouth opened in dismay, and I moved to scoop up the book from the dusty floor.

One of the soldiers stepped in front of me, sword raised.

"I don't underst—"

"We support the true Order." Grast stood, torchlight casting writhing shadows on the back wall. She seemed to grow taller. "False dancers are no longer welcome here. Begone."

False dancers? What was she talking about? My gaze returned to the precious copy of the Maker's letter. My impulse was to somehow dart around the soldier and recover the manuscript. Starfire tugged my elbow and whispered in my ear. "We've overstayed our welcome."

She was right. A confrontation would only add to the rift. I dipped my head toward Grast and dared one last question. "May I ask what has brought this change?"

She laughed darkly. "Oh, you and your kind will know soon enough." The villagers on the benches drummed their fingers against the wood in approval, and her guards advanced, forcing us back. "And if you dare enter Foleshill again, we'll burn more than just your foolish manuscripts."

Back out on the porch, I released a breath I hadn't realized had caught in my lungs. "This makes no sense."

Starfire puckered her lips and swished them side to side. "They're madder than a fountain fish in a soup kettle."

More guards poured onto the porch, arms drawn. From inside, an angry chant rose up. "Destroy the false Order! Restore the old way!"

"Retreat to the ponies," Belgor ordered. Both men bristled like the ruff of a forest hound warning of impending danger. Aanor stepped closer and took my arm.

"But we haven't learned anything," I protested. Even as the men hustled me up the street toward the edge of town, I scanned in all directions for someone who could answer my questions. Danger or no danger, I wasn't leaving until I got some answers.

"WAIT!" I PLANTED MY WALKING STICK, FORCING AANOR TO stop or risk dislocating my shoulder. We had reached the outer rim of homes, our tethered ponies in sight beyond the village's edge. I scanned the shuttered windows and side alleys one more time, playing it safe. Apparently, Brantley's habit of cautious observation had rubbed off on me. A curtain stirred in a small cottage that was tucked off the main street.

"There." I pointed. "Let me try talking to someone before we leave."

Belgor frowned. "Grast's men will be watching."

"This won't take long."

Starfire bobbed her head in agreement, mop of auburn hair bouncing. "It's why we've come."

Not waiting for Belgor's approval, I headed for the tidy log home. Before I could tap on the door, it flew open, and a woman pulled me into a hug. I struggled to free myself. As abruptly as she grabbed me, she let go, looking in both directions with birdlike bobs of her head. "Quick, come inside."

I paused. She seemed not to mean us harm, but who was she? Could she give me the answers I needed? Before the soldiers could interfere, I stepped over the threshold, Starfire and our men crowding in behind me. The door swung closed.

Enough light filtered through her curtains to reveal a tidy room. The woman rounded on me, eyes wide and eager. Yet her hands fluttered as she spoke, betraying her tension. "Carya! You came back."

"We've met?"

Her voice dropped to a whisper. "You introduced us to the Maker we had all forgotten. He is my daily joy."

Ah. Now I understood. The woman was one among a sea of faces from my travels around Meriel. I breathed a silent thanks that all my effort had made a difference—at least for one person. "What's happening here? Grast demanded we leave Foleshill."

A shudder moved her shoulders. "She exiled our matriarch and took power."

"How?"

From the direction of the central lodge, the chanting grew louder. The crowd must have moved outside.

"We need to hurry," Aanor said quietly.

I frowned. If he would stop worrying me with warnings and interruptions, I'd be able to learn something. "Why did the village support her?"

"Our crops were stricken with disease. Before we could send word to the Order for help, a group of dancers arrived. They used their gifts to reverse the blight. And they convinced the leadership that the problems had been caused by the rejection of the 'true' Order. They said the recent reforms will ruin our entire island and that we should fight for a return to the old way."

None of this made any sense. High Saltar Kemp would have told me if she had sent a band of dancers out to help a local village, and those dancers certainly wouldn't have spoken against the reforms of the Order. And Grast's animosity was so unfounded.

I squeezed my forehead. "I don't understand. Our world is healing. I know it's taking time, but the Order is working as hard as they can. The damage was caused by forgetting the Maker, by chaining our world to one place against His design."

The woman glanced nervously around and leaned forward. "Grast demanded we burn our copies of the Maker's letter, but I hid one. Those who believe meet in secret. But we are the minority. Hungry bellies speak louder than truth."

Starfire peeked through the curtains. "Grast's guards are coming. We can't stay."

I had so many more questions. But we couldn't endanger this faithful woman. "I'll remember you to the Maker. Be safe." I squeezed her hand, and we slipped out her back door and hurried toward our ponies.

We mounted and rode out to what I hoped was a safe distance from the animosity of the village. As we fled, my sense of failure chased me. For the first time, I was glad Brantley wasn't with me, because I didn't want him to witness my shame. My hapless efforts had only inflamed more trouble.

At a crossroads, we stopped, and I unrolled my map. Another midrim village had been circled by Saltar Kemp, indicating their opposition to the Order. "Let's try the next village. It can't go worse than this visit."

In front of me, Belgor turned his pony to face me. "Can't it? The rebellion is more established than we realized. It would be safer to return to Middlemost and warn the Order." Worry creased Belgor's brow, and I noticed the smudge of weariness under his eyes. The men had taken shifts guarding our campsites each night, but I'd given little thought to the toll it took.

Aanor circled us as we talked, scanning the surroundings like a harrier bird, one hand on his sword hilt.

Still feeling guilty for how little attention I'd given our two protectors, I coaxed my pony toward him. "Aanor, where are you from?"

He frowned. "The Order."

"Before. Where is your family from?"

"Middlemost." He dipped his head in respect but then straightened. "We really should return."

Starfire wheeled her pony around, confronting Aanor. "We follow Carya. Give her a moment to decide our course." Then she leaned forward and squinted at him. "Middlemost, eh? I've seen you there. I used to work at the tender's."

His lips quirked. "I know."

"You remember me?"

Color tinged his cheeks. "You make an impression." Then he rubbed a hand over the sparse whiskers on his chin. "Not that we ever spoke. But I noticed you."

Now her freckles darkened. I hid a smile. There would most likely be new conversations around the campfire tonight. I returned to the map, studying the string of marked villages. Brantley had been right. There was a pattern at play, but I had too little information to figure out what was happening or how to fix it. My diplomatic efforts at Foleshill had totally failed. And the animosity was worse than the high saltar had expected. Perhaps it would be wiser to hurry back with that information and get reinforcements. But Saltar Kemp was counting on me. I'd been the one to challenge the prior Order and proclaim truth. I couldn't slink back in defeat now.

"We can't return to the Order yet. We need to learn more. Let's see if we can reach Salis by nightfall." I rolled the map and tucked it in my saddlebag.

Starfire thrust her chin forward, as if daring Aanor to disagree. He gave a terse nod and tapped his heels against his pony's ribs, leading us up the trail. Starfire and I followed, with Belgor bringing up the rear. I slowed so he could pull alongside. "I should have sought further advice from you. Do you really believe this path is unsafe?"

Belgor's chuckle rattled in his chest. "You ask now that we're on it? Ach, the young pup is nervous. Understandably." He dipped his chin. "But our orders are to protect you. The decision is yours."

I nodded, glad he'd reconsidered his original opinion. "I appreciate your candor, and I'm grateful for your service."

Belgor managed a formal bow from his saddle. "As our world is grateful for yours." He leaned closer and lowered his voice. "My entire family follows the Maker now. He's changed us all."

I blinked sudden moisture from my eyes. "He changes everything, doesn't He?"

"Indeed."

THE PRIMARY SUN HAD ALREADY SET WHEN WE ARRIVED AT the outskirts of Salis. I dismounted and rubbed my back. The babe in my belly was growing big enough to cause some strain, and weariness tugged at my limbs. Fiola had explained that was common for new mothers. My throat tightened. What would I do if we lost Brantley's mother? Her warmth and wisdom had helped me settle into life in Windswell when everything was unfamiliar and new. Was she recovering? What if I returned home to find she had—

No. *Maker, help me trust You and not invite the eddies of worry.*

"Do we enter?" Aanor leapt from his pony and offered a hand to Starfire, as if she were a frail grandmother.

She looked down her nose at him and ignored his help, showing off her dancer-trained agility as she sprang off. The young man would need to find other ways to win Starfire's interest. My friend had little patience with feigned shows of respect. After all she'd endured while working for the tender in Middlemost, she had little trust for men and no patience for solicitude.

Aanor eased back, confusion and hurt swimming in his eyes for a heartbeat. Then he braced his shoulders and turned to me. "Shall I venture ahead to reconnoiter?"

I sighed. "It's been a long day. Let's rest and enter the village at first light."

"Good plan," Belgor said, already unrolling a tarp and spreading it under an outcropping of stone. There'd been no rain all day, but he set up camp where we'd have protection from any unexpected downpour.

After a meager supper of saltcakes, Belgor took first watch while Starfire and Aanor sat by the fire arguing about the best chandler in Middlemost. I curled under my cloak and closed my eyes, surrendering to the weariness that had dogged me all day.

A gasp from Starfire startled me, and I bolted upright, heart racing. "What?"

Grinning, she sprang up and pointed overhead. "Look!"

Beyond the tree limbs, stars pulsed and swelled, pregnant with light that was ready to multiply. Despite my exhaustion, I stood and joined her. "Remember how often we would sneak out to the Order's gardens during a star rain?"

One of the lights burst, showering us with glitter—vibrant yet cool to the touch. Bits landed on Starfire's upturned face, adding freckles to her cheeks. I reached up to catch the sparkles from the next one, then fling them skyward. Then I kicked off my shoes. "Let's dance."

Starfire chewed her lower lip and slid off her shoes slowly. "Out here?" Then she shrugged and giggled. "I forget how much has changed. If you will, I will too."

Timidly at first, and then with more abandon, my friend kicked up the inert sand of the star rain and spun, casting rainbow light in all directions. I swayed, arms overhead, savoring the light and beauty that reminded me so much of the Maker's love.

On the periphery of my awareness, Belgor continued pacing the rim of the clearing and ignored our play. But when I glanced at Aanor, I caught him staring at Starfire, lips parted and silent. He quickly turned away and rummaged in his pack, unearthed a cloak, and moved off into the shadows to rest.

Perhaps we should have rested too, but while the sky danced, we echoed its patterns, until at last the rhythm of the stars quieted, and we both sank down beside the campfire.

I warmed my hands by the feeble flame, which flickered dully after the vibrant star rain. A night harrier cawed a warning deep in the forest. "This reminds me of all the times Brantley and I made camp when we were traveling across Meriel telling the villages about the Maker's letter."

Starfire shook her head. "How were you so brave? The whole Order was furious."

"It helped having Brantley along. I could face anything when he was with me." I picked up a stick and poked at the logs, frowning. "I hope he's remembering to eat. He's probably wearing himself out keeping vigil beside his mother. And I wish I could get his opinion about what is happening in Foleshill." My throat clogged. "I miss him so much. Maybe too much."

My friend glanced around and leaned in. "Do you think it's wrong for us to long for another to share our life? I mean, the Order always said . . ."

I shook my head. "The Maker knows how precious human love can be. He created it. Those bonds are a fragile echo of His great love. A gift to cherish."

As long as I remembered to cherish my Maker foremost. *With Brantley or away from him, help me trust You first.*

Starfire stared at the campfire, pensive. Was she longing to establish a family beyond the Order? Should I encourage her or warn her how difficult it was to overcome a lifetime of indoctrination? Before I could say more, she stood. "You need rest," she said firmly. "I wasn't much help in Foleshill, but at least I can remind you to take care of yourself."

As I settled under the tarp, I prayed silently for her, and then for Brantley, for Fiola's health, the people of Foleshill, the dancers of the Order toiling so hard for our world, Saltar Kemp, and the unknown that we would face in the morning.

My muscles softened, relaxing into the ground. But I missed the lively roll of the rim to lull me to sleep. Here in the midrim, the motion of the earth was barely discernable. I sighed and shifted to my other side.

In the misty realm of half sleep, memories painted images behind my eyelids. I was back in class. One of the younger forms. The tunics around me were the pale yellow of a fading subsun. Sticks tapped out a tight pattern. Lanthrus. I pressed my right foot off the floor into a sharp point and quickly back down. "Faster!" Saltar River glared down her hooked nose. Tall. Rigid. Harsh. Fear joined our class like a tether as we all fought to escape her notice. No errors. No flaws. River walked up and down our rows, sticks clacking. Cold sweat beaded on my forehead. "Other side!" My left foot obeyed, peeling up and pushing back into the floor over and over. I stared resolutely forward, my face in the perfect blank expression. Then a shadow colored my vision. The white robe of the saltar stopped directly in front of me and silenced the rhythm. "Novitiates, stop. Gather round. Watch this." Heat crawled across my chest, and my heartrate doubled. She made me repeat the pattern with everyone else watching, as she berated me. "This novitiate will never graduate to the next form. Look how lazy her feet are. And her posture." She poked at my shoulder. "Useless."

Hot tears burned in my eyes, but I refused to let them fall. I repeated the pattern over and over. My feet screamed. My calves spasmed. My joints locked. I kept doing the steps while she rained down abuse on me until the bell rang for lunch. The other students fled, afraid to glance my direction. Only Starfire cast me a sympathetic look. River leaned forward, her mouth so close to my ear I heard the pop of her lips parting and then the derisive hiss. "Ignorant rimmer. You're hopeless."

I jerked awake. It had been months since a nightmare about my early days at the Order had tormented me. I rubbed my arms.

"Stop! State your purpose." Belgor's shout brought Aanor to his feet beyond the campfire. I sat up, squinting, while Starfire clambered from her blanket beside me.

Cackling, an old woman limped forward, listing to one side. "She's here, isn't she? The wind told me." Another rasping laugh. The figure stepped closer to our fire, flames catching in her wild eyes.

Dancer Subsun!

I scrambled to my feet. "Belgor, it's all right. I know her."

"Who is she?" Starfire took a step forward, fists clenched as if she didn't trust our guards to protect us and was ready to pummel any threat.

"She's a friend." I eased away from the others and reached a hand toward the woman. The lonely shack where she lived wasn't far from here, but what had brought her out in the night? "How did you find me?"

"The Voice. The Voice whispered to me."

Goosebumps lifted on my arms. Had the Maker sent her? I had been longing for help or reassurance. Was this His answer?

Dancer Subsun cavorted in a tiny circle, then pointed at me. Her tangled hair looked as if it hadn't been braided in decades. Her tunic and leggings were dirty and tattered. The first time I'd seen her, shock and pity had overwhelmed me. Now I felt kinship. I had joined the ranks of the castoff, the hobbled.

Her gaze traveled to my wounded ankle. "I warned you." She pinched her forehead and winced. "Didn't I? I meant to." Then her expression cleared. "Ah, but it speaks more gently now. It's free!"

She spun again, arms wide.

Belgor moved himself between us. "What is she talking about? What is free?"

"Meriel. She used to hear the cry of our world's bondage."

Subsun shrieked and skipped in a strange pattern. Belgor bristled. "She's touched. Demented."

I rested a hand on his arm and shook my head. "The previous high saltar sent her into the center ground over and over, demanding that she control the world. It broke her mind. But she's not dangerous." *I hope.*

He grudgingly edged aside, and when Subsun stopped whirling, I opened my arms to her. Laughing, she skipped into my embrace.

"The Maker does not forget His children," I whispered against her ear.

For a moment, her tension melted, and sanity flowed across her eyes. Then the torment of her years of suffering and loneliness again turned her gaze wild. She waved her arms, sketching a frantic design in the air. "Flee! The refuge is now a trap! Beware the river!"

I tried to soothe her, but she only grew more agitated. Nearby, Starfire's face paled. She took my arm, trying to tug me away.

Subsun's agitation built. "My existence insults them. They've tried to end me, but I hide." She stirred her arms in the air again as if conjuring a mist. Broken chuckles shook her thin frame, her focus vague. Then she noticed me again and poked a finger against my chest. "Run. Run while you can. New dangers rule here."

Cold dread shivered up my spine. Salis was known as a place of refuge for castoff dancers. When Alcea Blue was hobbled and rejected, Brantley had given her a map and urged her to make her way here. Of all the places in Meriel, these people were the most likely to support the reforms and stay loyal to Saltar Kemp because they *knew*. They'd witnessed the atrocities of the prior Order firsthand. If even they now fought the changes, all was lost.

7

SUBSUN CONTORTED HER BODY IN A PARODY OF DANCE, then scampered awkwardly into the forest. With her words of warning still ringing in the air, Aanor cast a protective arm around Starfire, and she didn't shrug it away. Belgor pulled me back toward the fire, head tilted and listening for approaching enemies. But my focus wasn't on Subsun's vague cautions but on her suffering.

My heart broke for the woman. *Maker, grant her comfort. Ease her pain. Cast off, vilified. She needs Your love.*

I picked up my cloak and tossed it over my shoulders. "Maybe I should go after her."

Belgor growled low in his barrel chest. "We should break camp and return to Middlemost immediately."

I drew up my spine as tall as I could to confront him. "You acknowledged the decision to continue or return is mine."

"Did you hear what she said?"

I sighed. I'd definitely heard. But if I showed any fear, Belgor would haul us back to Middlemost, and I would have accomplished nothing. "She's confused. I met her once before when I was fleeing the Order. I understand her—to a point."

The white-knuckle grip on his sword hilt eased a fraction. "You're saying it's all nonsense?"

I would have loved to lie, to offer an easy reassurance. "No. Her thoughts can be distorted, overwhelming to her. But we can trust the core of what she says."

His jaw thrust forward. "Then let's be gone."

"Agreed." Aanor strode away from us and tore down a sheltering tarp.

I shot a glance toward Starfire for support.

She wrenched the tarp from Aanor's hands. "Carya tells us when to retreat."

He grabbed it back, and I rolled my eyes at their ridiculous tug-of-war.

"Belgor, I trust you and Aanor to stand guard. If danger approaches and you order it, we'll flee. But right now, we know nothing about what is happening in Salis. And our ponies are too exhausted to travel tonight." I chose not to mention that I was too tired to travel any more, as well. The babe growing inside me demanded rest. Already my responsibility to care for this little one was at war with my longing to bring peace to Meriel and succeed at this mission for the Order. "Please. Let's rest and make our plans in the morning."

Belgor appraised my drooping form and nodded. Starfire threw Aanor a triumphant look and tossed him her end of the tarp. He fumbled with it, tangled his arms, and finally freed himself.

I choked back a laugh. It wouldn't do to hurt the pride of a young soldier, especially in front of the girl he sought to impress. I limped over and helped him reattach two corners to tree limbs. "Thank you for keeping us safe," I said quietly.

With a terse nod, he huddled near the fire, leaving us to curl under the tarp. In spite of the disturbing events of recent days, I surrendered all my worries, imagining the Maker's wings shielding us in place of the fabric, the tree limbs, and the night sky.

THE NEXT MORNING WE SIPPED TSALLA AROUND THE EMBERS of our campfire. The night had passed uneventfully. In the light of the primary sunrise, I felt refreshed, strong, and ready to discover what forces were conspiring against the new Order. "I'll go into Salis on my own."

"Never." Belgor brushed saltcake crumbs from his armored tunic.

"The sight of soldiers might intimidate them. They're used to hobbled dancers and will trust me more if I don't arrive with guards."

"We can't protect you if we can't even see you." Belgor's jaw clenched.

"I'll go with her," Starfire offered.

Aanor scoffed, and she frowned in his direction.

I sighed. "This isn't a battle to be won with swords and force."

"I promised Brantley no harm would come to you." Belgor lurched to his feet. "We can leave Aanor here to guard the ponies, but I'm coming with you."

The young soldier's forehead bunched in dismay. Starfire snickered. An angry flush mottled Aanor's round cheeks. "Wait a minute—"

"If things go badly, we'll need the ponies ready." Belgor's tone held a sharp edge. "Have you the nerve to guard them on your own?"

Nostrils flaring, Aanor answered with only a terse nod. I shot Starfire a warning glance. If she kept mocking him, we'd waste time with more arguments.

"All right." I pushed to my feet, feeling every joint protest our recent rigorous days. "Belgor, you can follow at a distance. Give me a chance to greet people without them feeling threatened."

A wolfish grin pierced his bristled face as he stood and buckled on his sword belt. "Nothing threatening about me."

Great. This was going swimmingly.

Starfire patted my back. "Let's get on with it." She skipped ahead as if we were on a class outing in third form.

Maker, thank You for a friend. Thank You for her laughter, her spirit, her ability to lighten my heart.

I smoothed my long braid and tightened my head scarf, then brushed at a smudge on my white tunic. If I kept traveling in dancer gear, I'd soon look as tattered as Dancer Subsun. But I drew in a deep, strong breath and followed Starfire toward the village.

Salis was a sprawling collection of homes, much less compressed than other villages I'd visited. Perhaps their love for space and individuality is what had made them a refuge for castoff dancers over the years.

We'd only moved a short distance from Aanor and the ponies when from behind a tall pine came a loud, "Psst!"

I froze.

Starfire swiveled, her eyes wide. She tiptoed back toward me. Now that she wasn't trying to impress Aanor, some of her bravado slipped away.

"Psst! Over here!" Fallen needles scuffed.

I squinted into the shadows under the tree. Had a bog rat been given the gift of speech? After all the strange occurrences in recent months, it would scarce surprise me.

A darker shadow broke free of the others and stepped toward us. Belgor drew his sword.

A squeak answered.

"Hold!" I hurried forward, peering at a pale, fine-featured face under a dark hood.

The figure lifted her chin and offered a tentative smile.

"Alcea!" My heart skipped at the familiar face. We hadn't even entered the village, yet we'd found an ally.

"Shh!" She cowered deeper into her cloak and cast furtive glances around.

Starfire charged past me and threw her arms around Alcea. "How are you? Tell us everything. I've never forgiven the saltars for casting you out right before our final test."

Alcea shuddered in my friend's arms. When Starfire released her, our former classmate took in my walking stick and awkward posture. "You too?" Grief leached from her words—a sorrow I understood and lived with each day.

But the wound wasn't her only problem. She'd been living hard. She wore a mottled brown dress, the long tunic of an attendant or servant. Her bare legs displayed scratches and bruises. No bandage protected her ankle, so the angry red scar was visible even in the shadows under the trees.

I touched her arm. "I tried to find out what happened to you after that last time I saw you outside the Order."

She gave us a wobbly smile. "Brantley saved me. He told me where to find help, and I built a life here."

"He saved me, too," I said quietly. Although to be fair, I'd rescued him just as many times.

"Now everything's changed."

I straightened. "That's why we're here. After all the reforms, all the improvements and hope, some of the villages seem to have concerns. I came to find out—"

"Concerns?" Bitterness twisted Alcea's lips. "That's one word for it."

"Well, I'm going into to town to speak with the leaders and see if we can resolve this."

She leaned back, eyes wide. "Are you mad?" Then a sigh seemed to draw the last remnants of emotion from her. Her mouth flattened. "You understand nothing."

I took her hand. "Explain it to me."

"Only if you promise to flee after you've heard."

I couldn't make that pledge until I knew the details, but we'd grown up together, studied together, moved up through the forms together. I trusted her and longed to help her. "Come with us when we leave."

She trembled. "If only I could." A single tear traced a line through the dust on her cheek. Anguish swam in her eyes.

Holy Maker, help her. Help me to help her.

I settled on the ground in front of her and drew her down next to me. "Tell me."

Starfire settled beside Alcea, wrapping an arm around her. We could almost have been three young girls again, talking about the hard patterns we'd learned in class that day or arguing about whose turn it was to put oil in the torches. Showing each other calluses caused by mortaring the cracks in the walls. Whispering about the novitiates in older forms and placing guesses on which of our class would make it to the position of dancer. But the woman who sat between Starfire and me was a fractured shadow of the girl she'd been.

Alcea sniffed. "I hardly know where to start."

I mustered a smile, willing myself to patience. "The beginning?" Footsteps rustled as Aanor paced a distant perimeter around us. Belgor crept closer to the buildings at the edge of town and then back again. The soldiers' uneasy movements frayed my nerves.

She nodded. "Since I'd been taken to the Order so young, I had no memory of my rim village, but the people of Salis were so kind to me. Then I met Habsom. He was a blacksmith here in Salis and cared about me in spite of . . ." She gestured vaguely toward her leg.

My brows lifted. I wondered how much her life paralleled mine. I'd fallen in love and found a home too. "You love him."

She gnawed her lower lip. "We were bonded and had a child."

I gasped. "That's wonderful!" I hugged her, but when I felt the tension in her back, I released her.

"That's why I can't leave. Even now. Even when my life is in danger."

"We can take you all. Your husband, the baby. Get you somewhere safe."

Her shoulders caved in even more. "Habsom won't leave. When the village forbade dancers, he voted along with them. When one of the castoff dancers tried to plead her case, she was mobbed and killed. The rest have all fled."

In my worst nightmares, I couldn't picture Brantley standing against me, banishing me from my village. Even when the Gardener's spores had made him cold and cruel, some part of him still tried to protect me.

"If Habsom no longer wants you in Salis, why not take your baby and leave?"

Her chin shot up. "He took her from me. The village agreed. I've been hiding in the wilds ever since, slipping into town to watch over her from a distance."

Her pain pierced me. I smoothed my loose tunic. My babe was only half-grown within me, but already I knew losing my child would be a kind of death.

She shivered and grasped onto both of us. "If you go into the village, they'll kill you. Both of you."

Starfire shook her head. "There are truly no more dancers allowed in the village?"

"They'd not even give you a chance to speak."

Frustration clenched my muscles. "But why? What changed?"

She rubbed her red-rimmed eyes. "Saltar River."

I stiffened. "What does she have to do with this?" When reform came to the Order, she had stormed off with a group of dancers loyal to her, but after the wonders the Maker had performed that day, I hadn't expected her opposition to gain much following.

Belgor strode over to us. "We shouldn't stay in one place too long if there is a threat here. Are we going into the village?"

Alcea paled. "Only if you seek a certain death."

Belgor's gaze shifted to me. "That bad?"

I nodded. "So it seems. Give us a moment more, but stay alert."

He left and conferred with Aanor, who threw a worried gaze toward the three of us before continuing his patrol.

"Please let us help you get away from here." Starfire plucked the hem of her tunic. "We have ponies. We could rescue your baby."

"Salis has skilled riders. If we flee with the baby, Habsom will rally others and pursue us to the rim and back." Alcea managed a weak smile. "Don't worry about me. Although if you have spare supplies, they wouldn't go amiss."

"Of course." Starfire sprang up and raced toward the sacks on our ponies.

A few saltcakes would be small help to Alcea. I imagined limping into town and demanding her baby. But I couldn't jeopardize this mission for one woman, no matter how dear. I tightened the scarf covering my hair. "I don't like leaving you behind, but we came for information, not conflict. If you can help us understand what's happened, we'll bypass Salis."

She nodded. "Our crops had begun to improve after the island floated free. But then one day, right before harvest, mildew poisoned the fields. The next day limbs fell from the best trees in our orchard. There had been no storms, no wind, no explanation."

I rubbed my forehead, which lately felt permanently puckered by worry. Windswell was too remote to get news of every scattered midrim village, but I was surprised I hadn't heard about these problems. Saltar Kemp obviously hadn't either. She could have sent a group of dancers to help or changed the patterns of the center ground in response. "Did the village leaders send word to the Order?"

Alcea shook her head. "They didn't need to. A group of dancers arrived the day after the disaster."

That made more sense. "Weren't they able to help?"

"Oh, yes. The patterns they danced almost immediately banished the mildew and coaxed new growth from the crops."

I tilted my head. "Yet the village turned on them?"

"Not those dancers. Their leader was Saltar River."

ALCEA'S NEWS ROCKED ME LIKE A MASSIVE WAVE. I clutched the daygrass on the ground where we sat to steady myself. I had believed that I'd come to terms with the past and moved on. Years of harsh training, the terrifying confrontation with the saltars, the high saltar's remorseless hobbling. Those events didn't control my soul. We were in a new era with a reformed Order. Our world had left this all behind.

Yet every old dread rushed back into my heart. My injured tendon throbbed, and I rubbed it. I couldn't battle all this again. The Maker couldn't ask that of me, could He?

Alcea's gaze pierced me. "You understand why we aren't safe. You especially. She sees you as her greatest enemy because of the way your dance shook the Order and broke our world free of the dancers' tether."

"That was the Maker, not me. He just asked me to share the truth. Traveling the currents is what will save Meriel. All the damage was because of the Order trapping our world in place and forgetting Him."

Starfire nodded. "I was there. What happened was far beyond any dancer's ability."

Alcea's lip quivered. "I can only tell you Saltar River and her dancers healed the fields and orchards around Salis. They convinced everyone that your reforms caused all the problems."

Saltar River. Dancer Subsun's eerie warning rang through my mind. "Beware the river." It must also have been River's group that had visited Foleshill and convinced them to turn away from truth. I wasn't sure how she was showing up at the exact moment her dances could assist a village, but she was using their appreciation to spread poison and lies. Anger burned like a coal in my chest. The Maker's letter taught forgiveness, but how could I ever let go of my anger toward all the pain she'd caused when she was continuing to instigate even more turmoil on our world?

Aanor completed another sweep of the perimeter, and I waved him over. "We're returning to the Order to warn Saltar Kemp."

Relief softened his features, and he reached a hand to pull me up. Starfire helped Alcea to her feet.

I hugged her. "Come with us. Please. We can keep you safe at the Order."

Her chin lifted. "I won't leave my baby."

"We can't take on a whole village with two soldiers." Aanor braced his shoulders. "When this is resolved, we'll send help."

Her eyes were dull, but she nodded. She clearly held out no hope. But at least we had restocked her supplies. If she remained hidden, she'd be able to watch over her baby from a safe distance.

It wasn't enough. Failure weighted me again, but I rolled my shoulders and headed to the ponies as Alcea slipped into the shadows under the trees. I'd been sent to discover why villages were rebelling, and I'd finally done that. Now we needed to hurry back with the information.

Before we could mount up, a sharp whistle shrieked a warning from the outskirts of Salis. A distant voice shouted, "Enemies approach! Riders, to me!" One of their scouts must have noticed our presence.

"What do we do?" Starfire's voice quavered.

I swung onto my pony. "Outrun them."

As we sped up the trail, Belgor wheeled his pony around and drew his sword. "I'll slow their pursuit. Ride hard for Middlemost."

Aanor nodded and galloped forward, but I gestured to Starfire to slow, then reined in my mount and slipped to the ground. "Belgor, I'm not leaving you here. Starfire, help me dance."

She sprang down, but paused, looking at me with uncertainty. The taboos against dancing anywhere other than the center ground of the

Order would continue to take time to overcome. But the sounds of approaching soldiers convinced her. She bit her lip, then pulled off her shoes and joined me in a pattern for mist. Fog lifted quickly from the ground around us, obscuring the path.

"Keep going." I changed to a wind pattern, coaxing the growing mist toward our pursuers. As always, I had to ignore my awkward gait and endure the pain of using my hobbled leg, yet somehow our efforts worked. The clang of tack and ring of armor grew muffled and soon changed to muted shouts of confusion and the irregular hoofbeats of milling ponies. The path before us was clear, and I prayed the mist would linger long enough to stall the soldiers from Salis.

Finishing the wind pattern, I turned toward my companions. Starfire was grinning, her face an odd mixture of awe and terrified excitement. But Belgor's sword arm shook, his eyes flaring white. He'd been ready to face a band of soldiers alone, yet our fog and wind rattled him. The Order's center-ground dances didn't produce such specific and immediate results. The first time I'd tested a pattern away from the Order, I'd been startled too. And exhausted, as I was now.

When I put a hand on his arm, Belgor lowered his sword but remained alert. "My thanks, dancers." He waved us toward our ponies. "Waste no time."

My legs shook as I remounted. Dancing took a toll on a whole and strong dancer. For me, the cost was often uncertain and painfully depleting.

Starfire didn't seem as spent. Her spine was tall and strong as she gathered up her reins. "I could get used to this sort of dancing."

We met Aanor on the trail returning toward us. His pony tossed her head in confusion at being urged forward and then back again.

"We delayed them." I panted. "But not for long."

He nodded and jerked the reins of his poor pony yet again. I followed Aanor, with Starfire close behind me and Belgor protecting our backs.

Leaning forward, I breathed in the comforting scent of trail dust and sweat on the pony's neck and whispered to her. Her ears flattened, then flicked forward, and she stretched her canter into a vigorous gallop.

As we drew close to Aanor, his pony reacted to the pursuit and sped up too. We didn't dare slow until our mounts were exhausted.

Finally, when all four animals were blowing hard, Aanor reined his pony to a walk. "No sounds of pursuit."

Belgor dismounted and guided his pony onto an intersecting game path. "The beasts need a break, but let's not stay on the main trail."

We followed him into the underbrush. My pony's head sagged, but her labored breathing began to slow. "Maybe we should leave the trail completely." I swiped the back of my hand over my forehead. "Travel cross-country."

Belgor frowned at the tangled bracken ahead of us. "We'd have to go on foot." His gaze slid to my bandaged ankle.

Shame heated my skin at the burden I added to this mission. The others had a better chance of evading capture without me. Our news had to reach Saltar Kemp. "Perhaps we should split up. You could head for the Order, and I—"

"I hear a stream. This way." Belgor led his pony deeper into the underbrush, and we followed, keeping to a faint, wandering trail created by some forest creature. By the time we emerged along the banks of a rain-fed creek, our ponies were breathing normally, their flanks cool and beginning to dry. Starfire and I dismounted, and our animals eagerly lowered their muzzles to the water.

"We should probably split up," I repeated.

Belgor straightened from examining his pony's hoof, leveling a fierce frown at me. "Our duty is to protect you. No need for more talk about choices. When the ponies are rested, Aanor will scout behind us. If it's clear, we'll continue on the main trail as before."

"And if not?" Starfire's pale face had lost the flush of exertion, but her eyes sparked with enthusiasm for even this frightening adventure. If Brantley couldn't be by my side, I was grateful the Maker had given me such a bold friend to fuel my courage.

Aanor knelt and splashed water over his face and head, then tossed back his damp hair. "They'll be content with chasing us away from Salis. I doubt they'd follow us halfway across Meriel."

He had a point. Threatening visitors away was one thing. Pursuing us through the midrims and toward the world's center was a different thing altogether. Though after what I'd learned from Alcea, nothing would surprise me.

My legs cramped, the extra tension of our wild ride finally taking its toll. I lifted the knee of my bad leg, then unfolded the leg upward. After resting my foot on my pony, I stretched forward.

"Good idea." Starfire kicked one leg up, then held it suspended with the control of her years of training, before lowering it onto her pony. She sighed as she laid her torso flat over her leg. Then she turned and stretched to the side, bending her standing leg to deepen the stretch.

Aanor's gaze flitted toward her, away, and back again. The hand he'd been using to loosen his saddle girth fumbled, and the strap swung free.

Belgor cuffed his shoulder. "I'll tend your pony. Go check the trail."

THE NEXT SEVERAL HOURS PROVED AANOR RIGHT. NO further pursuit beset us that day. We spent several more nights camping and long days in the saddle before nearing Middlemost. I'd have enjoyed the journey under other circumstances. Discovering new flowers nestled beneath a copse of ferns, dancing encouragement to a berry bush that provided breakfast, seeing the Maker's hand in the bold stone ridges, slim silver creeks, and pines whispering in the breeze. If Brantley had been with me, I would have snuggled beside him at our campfire and talked of our dreams for our coming child.

Instead, we could never linger, always alert to approaching danger. We detoured widely around villages, not knowing whom we could trust. The threat dogged our steps, and the injustice of what Saltar River was doing burned in my chest.

The Maker had freed our world and promised to heal the land. Many fields and orchards were improving. The seeds and cuttings we'd brought to Meriel from the foreign island—at great risk and sacrifice—had also helped. Yet River and her group were convincing whole towns to turn against the work of the Order. If she ousted Saltar Kemp, if she took over the center ground, our world would be trapped in darkness and suffering again.

That fear rode with me through Middlemost and up the hill to the serene courtyards of the Order, and as I limped down the hall to the high saltar's office.

Saltar Kemp seemed to read my face. "The news isn't good?" She motioned toward a chair near her desk, then came around to sit beside me.

"First, has there been word from Brantley? How is his mother?"

She shook her head. "I'm sorry. No news." She rubbed her hands as if drying them, an unconscious sign of her worry. "Now, what have you learned?"

I didn't want to add to her burdens. It seemed wrong to deliver such a disheartening report without offering answers or recommendations. If only Brantley were here. He understood strategy.

Beyond the glass of her office's inner wall, dancers leapt and spun like leaves cast airborne by a wind gust. Drums beat a soothing rhythm, enabling me to take a steadying breath and fill her in on what we'd learned at Foleshill and Salis.

Shadows gathered in her eyes at the news of Alcea's plight. She herself had sent the novitiate away for a small mistake in the final days before our testing. Had she known about High Saltar Tiarel's policy of hobbling exiled dancers? Or had it been a secret kept even from other saltars?

I concluded my report. "As you suspected, Saltar River is behind the rebellion."

She frowned. "How did she convince them to turn so quickly against the reforms? All of Meriel witnessed the improvements following our island's return to nourishing currents. We distributed every resource fairly. Our dancers are exhausted but keep working day and night." Her words grew faster and tighter in her dismay. "Why would they reject the Maker's will so suddenly?"

"She manipulated them." I reached for her hands—a daring breach of etiquette I would never have taken as a novitiate or dancer. "River shows up with her band of dancers to save villages on the brink of losing their harvests. Desperate people are easy to deceive."

Saltar Kemp's shoulders rounded forward in a posture that would have garnered a sharp reprimand in any technique class. "I don't understand why Salis was struck by blight. And how did River arrive at such a convenient time?"

I'd weighed those questions often on our journey. "I can't be sure, but I suspect . . ." I could scarcely force the words past my lips. "What if River's group caused the disease so they could gain power over the village by fixing it?"

Saltar Kemp recoiled. "How could River twist the Maker's gift into such an abomination?" She passed a hand over her eyes as if to rub away the image conjured by my report. "I only wish I knew what to do."

Exhaustion made me blunt. "I don't know either. The Order can't spare the number of dancers needed to win each town back through service. But sending soldiers to force the issue would play into River's hands."

I rubbed my temples. "Let me send for Brantley. Either his mother has recovered by now or she . . . hasn't." I couldn't think about that now.

Saltar Kemp nodded and leaned back. "I'll send a harrier bird downriver with a note and hope he can come. You need rest."

I reached forward again and squeezed her hand. "So do you. Let's place this situation in the Maker's hands."

Her head lifted. "Yes. I forget that, don't I?"

"We all do."

We sat quietly, heads bowed, as the rhythm of furrow and field rose from the drums. Perhaps when our efforts fell short, it served to remind us that we were not the Maker. We needed Him. In spite of the fear battering my mind, my heart warmed with gratitude for that reminder. *We need You so much. And You are always with us. I trust You.*

THE NEXT DAY, STRENGTHENED BY A FULL NIGHT'S SLEEP on a soft pallet and a nourishing breakfast, I offered to teach one of the younger form's classes. The Order's remaining dancers and saltars were stretched thin, and I needed to stay busy while we waited for Brantley.

The third form, with girls about Orianna's age, was tiny. Only six had remained after Tiarel's policies were stopped. The others had returned to the families from which they'd been stolen.

I smiled at the eager young faces, the tight braids they hadn't quite mastered, the crisp tunics and clean leggings. At least these girls were here by choice. Saltars no longer drilled lies into young minds, and prefects no longer glared from the doorways, watching for infractions. I would do anything necessary to keep River from gaining control over their training once again and terrorizing them the way she had terrorized me.

I passed out parchment and willow pens. "Let's work on forming our letters as beautifully as your body forms patterns when you dance. When you're older, you'll be entrusted with reproducing the Maker's letter, until every person on Meriel has a copy."

Sitting cross-legged on the classroom floor, they bent to the task. The subsun chased the primary sun in a gentle arc, casting warm rays through the windows as I moved among the young novitiates, helping them.

The frantic clanging of a bell ruptured the silence. Some of the girls dropped their pens. A few stood. One ran to the window and peered out.

I limped to the hallway. An attendant came running up the stairs.

"Dancer Carya, Saltar Kemp needs you."

My pulse speeded. This had to be news from Brantley. "They're working on letters. Could you watch them, please?"

He nodded and stepped into the classroom. I leaned on my cane and worked my way down the stairs. I hadn't gotten far when Saltar Kemp and several other saltars met me on their way up.

"Do you have word from Brantley?"

"No. One of our watchers spotted something strange. We're heading to the telescope."

Good thing they'd caught me before I'd made it down too many flights of stairs. As it was, my ankle protested as I retraced my route, following the saltars up a few more stories to the Order's wide roof. From this highest point in the center of the island, the telescope allowed the saltars to monitor shifts in weather, currents, or even problems on land.

But today the watcher at the telescope had it focused out to sea. She stepped back and beckoned to High Saltar Kemp who bent, peered in, and gasped.

"Carya, you've traveled off island. What is that?"

Was the troubled island that Brantley and I had visited floating into view again? That was the last thing we needed with all the turmoil we already had to deal with. I squinted into the eyepiece. A smudge on the horizon certainly looked like an island. I nudged the scope a bit, adjusting the focus.

Not an island. Many islands. Fragments of lands glided into view, like potatoes floating in a stew.

"What is it?" Saltar Kemp asked again.

It was hard to judge size from this distance, but none of the islands looked as large as the one Brantley and I had visited. Unless it had broken apart.

"Possibly islands, but I can't tell. I wish we were closer."

One of the attendants took my place and studied the far lands. "The currents are pulling them this way. Soon we'll be traveling on a parallel path, and close as a few stones' throw to the islands. We'll know more then."

"Or perhaps we should have the dancers move our world away." Saltar Kemp's throat sounded hoarse with worry.

Another saltar smoothed her white robe. "The dancers are focusing on healing our crops. And they're already exhausted."

High Saltar Tiarel would never have tolerated debate, but Kemp seemed to welcome others' ideas. She nodded and turned to me. "Do we push our world out of its current to avoid whatever is approaching?"

Why did she look at me with so much confidence and hope? I had no clue about the wisest course. I'd once turned down the role of high saltar specifically because I didn't want this responsibility. I wanted to live a quiet life in Windswell, nurturing my baby and loving my husband.

I stepped closer to the parapet, resting my hands on the smooth stone surface. Dappled light from the suns made the trees look as liquid as the sea. The world I loved, in a faint echo of the Maker's love, stretched before me in every direction. Fields, farms, villages. The people in those towns wanted the same things I did. Peace, safety, love. If I could help them, I must.

Maker, guide us. Warmth engulfed my heart, deepening my trust that He would.

"In the past, we got into trouble by seeking to take control," I said slowly, feeling my way. "But the Maker placed Meriel in the current that *He* ordained."

One of the saltars paced toward the stairs and back. "Yes, but what do we do?"

"Carya?" Saltar Kemp's lips pursed, drawing tiny lines around her mouth.

I stared through the scope again. Dread made my muscles clench. The bits of land looked less like potatoes and more like the dark shadows of storm clouds. I almost expected to see lightning spark from them. The fearful part of my soul wanted to run, but I knew that wasn't the Maker's will.

"Don't fight the current. We made that mistake for generations, and it nearly destroyed our world."

Saltar Kemp nodded. "Right." She lengthened through her spine and smiled at the others. "Back to work everyone. We'll post two attendants up here at all times so one can carry messages about any change. For now, we'll wait and see what happens."

Like a scattered flock of birds, the gathered saltars and attendants fluttered off to their duties.

I took another look at the distant lands and echoed the high saltar's words. "Now we wait and see."

9

"YOU DID WHAT?" BRANTLEY GRABBED MY ARMS WITH A little too much force, and I winced. He'd arrived just before lunch with the welcome news that his mother was improving. But when he heard about the danger we'd encountered on our expedition, his temper flared. He pulled me from the Order's entryway to an empty room.

"We never expected Salis to send soldiers to chase us away. But we're all fine. Stop fussing."

"Fussing? I'm not—" He groaned in frustration and pulled me closer, kissing me with a passion and desperation that made my head spin. As his arms encircled me, his lips grew gentler, seeking reassurances I wished I could offer. How could either of us promise to be safe when so much turmoil threatened our world?

I rested my head against his chest. "We need your advice about River's rebellion. And we have a new problem."

"Of course we do." I expected another groan, but instead he chuckled.

Pulling back to watch him, I raised an eyebrow. "And this is funny because?"

He shrugged. "I knew you were trouble the first time I met you. When you thought I was hurting Alcea and you told me off."

My lips quavered, half rueful smile and half shame at my former foolishness. "You knew the truth of what was happening in the Order. I didn't understand."

"And even so, you wanted to help a friend. Even at risk to yourself." He caressed my face. "Now, let's go meet with your High and Mighty Saltar and take a look at the maps. If we have to raise an army against River, we can count on loyalty from the rim villages."

Relief flooded me as he guided me toward the saltar offices. He'd help us make a plan. I was no longer shouldering these problems alone. Yet darker, worrisome threads knotted around my heart. Once again I was dragging him into danger. He'd lost so much because of me. And before that, he'd lost a brother because of the Order. Some days it was still hard for me to believe he held no lingering resentment against me for having been a dancer. I would spend my whole life serving his village to make amends, but it would never be enough.

Saltar Kemp looked up when we entered her office. Parchments covered her desk, and she pulled out the map we'd seen days earlier. "Another report. This time from a rim village."

My heart sank. How quickly people forgot what life had been under the former Order.

Brantley strode forward and snatched the map from her. Circles marked each village refusing to support the new Order, cutting a clear swath across our world. "I can't believe she gained the support of any rimmers."

I peered over his shoulder. "We need a plan."

Saltar Kemp stared past us to the dancers laboring in the center ground. "Perhaps it's time to disband the Order."

My knees buckled and I sank into a chair. "What? You can't be serious." Facing outward opposition was one thing, but this spirit of defeat from the woman I admired leached the strength from my bones.

Sadness painted shadows across her face. "We have so few dancers left, and they're exhausted. The novitiates are so busy growing food they aren't getting enough training. Where will the new dancers come from? Especially if the villages no longer send girls to be trained."

"But our world needs the work of the dancers. The patterns honor the Maker and help protect and nurture the land."

She finally met my eyes. "It sounds as if River's team is doing that."

My face heated, and I pounded my walking stick against the floor. "No. If she were just bringing patterns to each village to help them, I might agree. But she's also convincing them to burn the Maker's letter. To turn away from truth. I don't how she is manufacturing benefits, but she's deceiving people. Our people. We cannot abandon Meriel to her lies." The words rushed out with more force than I'd intended, but when I glanced toward Brantley, his eyes gleamed with admiration.

He rested a hand on my shoulder and confronted Kemp. "Carya's right. River would love you to forsake the Order and disband. She'd swoop right back in, and all the gains of the past year would be lost. Now is not the time to surrender."

Shoulders bowed from months of struggle, High Saltar Kemp closed her eyes and massaged her forehead.

My chest contracted. I should have helped more. I should have seen the toll on the dancers and saltars. I should have visited more often. But I also had a home, a husband, a life in Windswell. Would I be torn between two loyalties for my entire life? I had no idea how to be free of regrets when the consequences of my choices stared me in my face.

As if reading my thoughts, Brantley squeezed my shoulder. "We're here to help. What would you—"

An attendant skidded into the room. "They're getting closer. Much closer."

Saltar Kemp's chin lifted, the invisible mantle of high saltar settling back over her. "Thank you. I'll come soon."

"Who's getting closer?" Brantley's fist closed over his longknife, every muscle alert.

I laid a restraining hand on his arm. "We spotted other islands in the distance."

He groaned and sank into a chair. "Again?" Then his head snapped toward me. "Did you say islands? More than one?" He pulled me to my feet. "Show me."

Without waiting for Saltar Kemp, he scooped me into his arms and strode toward the stairs. He bounded up two at a time and didn't set me down until we'd reached the roof. Although my ankle appreciated not having to make the climb again, heat crawled up my neck as the two attendants at the telescope witnessed our arrival.

"Is it aimed in the right direction?" Brantley asked, wasting no time in elbowing his way past the two men, who stepped back quickly. He stared through the lens and carefully adjusted the focus, sliding the scope to the side in incremental movements. Then he let out a low whistle. "I don't see barrier trees like those on the foreign island we visited before. This is something new."

I tugged his arm for a turn. In the past day, the collection of islands had moved much closer. I'd first spotted them beyond the river's mouth, a good distance from Windswell. But as Meriel had rotated in the currents, they now approached the coast of Whitecap. "I wonder if the local herders have spotted them." Few rimmers owned telescopes, and certainly none as powerful as this one atop the world. But those living along the shore might be close enough to see the islands with the naked eye.

Brantley nudged me aside and studied the view again. "If they have, they'll think it's another source of supplies. I hope no one heads out there unprepared."

A cold finger traced a line down my spine. Brantley and I had learned firsthand the threats that could lurk on a new world.

"Hard to make out, but it looks like there's smoke rising from one of them."

The chill spread to all my limbs. "Inhabited?"

"Could be," he said. "We need to hurry home. The current is pulling those islands in fast. It will take us most of the day to reach the rim. And with the turn of our world, it looks like they'll come closest to Meriel a few days' journey from Windswell."

"I can help with that." Saltar Kemp lifted a brass instrument to measure the wind. "The dancers can change the rotation."

I murmured an objection. The Order had caused massive damage by using patterns to hold our world in place.

With a new gleam of energy brightening her eyes, Saltar Kemp faced me. "Don't worry. We won't leave the current. I'll simply have them rotate our island on its axis. That way Windswell will face the islands as they come into range. There's no one else I'd trust to meet them. Just send me word as soon as you know if they are friend or foe."

Her swift determination startled me. "So no more talk about disbanding the Order?"

She braced her shoulders. "That was a moment of lost faith. Forgive me. It is our privilege to serve the Maker, and we can trust His purposes. We'll do all we can. Now hurry."

Brantley didn't wait but lifted me again and raced down all the many flights of stairs. After a detour to collect my pack from my room in the dancers' quarters, he carried me out the entryway and toward the cliff without a backward glance.

"I can manage." I tried to sound grumpy, but being cradled in his arms felt so wonderful, my protest was feeble.

He didn't release me until we reached the steep face. After setting me on my feet, he picked his way downward. I looked back. The drums had already changed their rhythm. The smooth walls of the Order rose up and surrounded the holy center ground. *Maker, give them strength for this work. Guide all our steps.*

Using my walking stick and my free hand to grab rocks, I picked my way down toward the channel. When I paused to look down at the surface, I gasped. "Where's Makah?"

Brantley looked up at me. "There's a pool a small way downriver. I told her to wait there."

I found his casual trust encouraging, but I didn't share it. What if she hadn't waited nearby or didn't come when called? It would take ages to reach Windswell over land. I clambered down the rest of the way and sat near the water.

Brantley signaled for Makah with his whistle, then settled on a rock and stretched his legs.

I twisted my fingers together in my lap. "There are too many problems hitting us all at once. Even though we know why some villages have stopped supporting the Order, we still don't know how to stop River."

"Cheer up, dancer." Brantley leaned back on his elbows. "My mother is better, you've returned in one piece from your scouting mission, and soon we'll have you safely home. And I'll have new lands to explore."

Of course. A dangerous adventure. Just the thing to bring that enthusiastic gleam to Brantley's eyes.

I shook my head, about to remind him of the horrible things that we'd endured that last time we'd explored a new island, but a splash interrupted my thoughts.

Makah's head poked above the surface. Her long lashes blinked water from her eyes, and she twisted her serpentine neck, treating us to a gurgling coo. Brantley gave her a hand signal to call her in. She swam directly to me instead of to him, but he only grinned. "Looks like she's bonding with you more than me. It's a start." He helped me settle astride her, then stepped onto her back and whistled.

She made a languid circle and began swimming downstream. I patted her silky neck. "Clever girl. You're making good progress."

She chortled and sped up.

A COOL EVENING BREEZE CARRIED FROM THE SEA AS WE neared the rim. I could tell by the changing position of the suns that Saltar Kemp had been successful in shifting the rotation of our island. Brantley guided us a short way out into open sea, but we still couldn't see the approaching islands around the massive curve of Meriel's rim.

When we went ashore, I headed straight to Fiola's cottage while Brantley stayed behind to reward Makah with some choice copper fish.

Orianna was skipping about in front of the cottage. I recognized bits of a pattern I'd taught her. When she saw me, she squealed and threw herself into my arms, nearly toppling me.

"How is your grandmother?"

She slid down. "Much better. She scolded Brantley for letting you go off on an adventure alone. I'm so glad you're back."

I smiled. "I wasn't alone. And he wanted to stay near his mother."

"Of course." Orianna nodded sagely. "But she still gave him a talking-to."

We both giggled as we entered the house.

Fiola was out of bed, sitting at her table and peeling tubers for a pot of stew. A smile lit her face when she saw us, and only the pallor of her cheeks testified to how close she'd come to death.

"Let me help with that."

She waved me away. "You've been traveling all day. And I'm almost finished. You and Brantley are staying for supper, and I won't hear a word of argument about it."

I longed to get back to my own cottage after all the days away, but I also wanted to reassure myself she was fully recovering. "Only if you let me help."

"Fine. Fetch some berries for dessert."

"I'll help." Orianna grabbed a basket and scampered ahead of me out the door. "Yesterday I found a patch along the shore, past the cove."

"Slow down." I laughed, trying to keep up. The walk made my ankle throb, but my thigh muscles thanked me. Gripping the sides of a stenella all afternoon had left me stiff. As we neared the shoreline, I breathed deeply of the fresh, astringent air.

Some distance along the rim, Brantley was reviewing signals with Makah. I waved and pointed to Orianna and he nodded.

We lost sight of him as we rounded the cape.

"It's just a little farther. I've been practicing the fruiting pattern you taught me. Maybe I can coax extra berries. Will you watch and see if I'm doing it right?"

"Of course." Fondness coated my chest. Orianna loved to dance, but I was grateful we'd rescued her from the harsh Order where I'd been raised. This little girl knew dance the way it was meant to be. Joyful, free, and serving the world the Maker had given us.

She pushed aside a prickly bush to rummage deeper into the undergrowth.

"Careful, there might be stinging lanthrus under that—"

Zing! Something stirred the wind past my ear and thudded into the nearest tree.

I froze, confused. A smooth stick had lodged into the bark, as if the trunk had suddenly sprung a new branch—but a branch peeled and sharpened.

"Ho there, Ratinger," a deep voice shouted. "Don't kill her. We need her alive."

I spun, looking for the speaker, and two men sauntered out from behind the trees. Strange garb. Rough features. Hard eyes.

"And lookie here," one of them said. "You were right. She don't look barren."

These men weren't rimmers. They weren't from Meriel at all.

Bruising hands grabbed me, and I screamed. "Orianna! Run!"

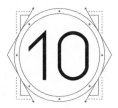

A HAND THAT SMELLED OF ROTTING FISH CLAMPED OVER my mouth, and a beefy arm crushed my chest, dragging me backward. I gagged and squirmed, but the man just squeezed me tighter. When I dropped my weight, hoping to slip from his grip, the other man grabbed my legs, and together they swept me off, farther away from Windswell. My shouts were muffled, and their long strides, though bumpy and clumsy, were eating up the ground. My hands were still free, and I pried at the fingers covering my mouth. No progress there. Bucking and twisting, I only managed to tangle my headscarf around my face. I wrenched it away, and the fabric fluttered to the ground behind us.

Exhausted and short on air, I stopped straining against them. Better to conserve my strength for later when I had a better chance to escape. In spite of my terror, I needed to think strategically, as Brantley had so often told me.

Brantley. Had he heard my scream? Were there more of these brigands about? Had they captured Orianna, or had she managed to run back to warn the people of Windswell?

"Hey, Ratinger. She ain't moving. Is she dead? Mander won't like that."

Something sharp poked my ribs, and I moaned.

"Naw. She's still breathing."

I squeezed my eyes shut and prayed.

When I opened my eyes again, the men were carrying me straight toward the rim. They were going to throw me in the sea! I bucked and twisted again, but they ignored my feeble efforts.

The man holding my legs seemed to step right onto the water. I blinked a few times, scrambling to make sense of what was happening.

They lowered me into something like a large wooden tree that floated on the water. From a pole in its center, a huge curtain of fabric snapped in the wind.

Relief lasted only a moment. I wasn't drowning, but Ratinger untied the hollowed-out log, and we shot away from shore faster than a stenella.

"Anyone following?" the man near my feet asked.

"Naw. Even if they noticed this one disappearing, they ain't got no veskals. Wait, what's that? I see a ripple."

"One of the blasted sea creatures?"

Both men tensed, then relaxed. "Just a school of copper fish."

Sea creatures? They were worried about stenella? I prayed for a glimpse of Makah—or any other stenella. Sitting in the center of the carved log my captors called a veskal, I rubbed at my face, trying to scrub away the feeling of filthy fingers that had dug into my skin.

Forcing my panicked breathing to slow, I lengthened my back and leveled my gaze at Ratinger. He wore an open vest that exposed a chest as hairy as a forest hound. His porcine eyes peered at me from a heavily bearded and pockmarked face. "My name is Carya of Meriel, and I'm no danger to you. Please return me to shore."

His face scrunched. "Hey, Wizzle, she talks. Fancy like, too."

"Sure she's not from one of the foelands? Mander won't like it if we bring a gal from the wrong place."

Ratinger grabbed my chin, examining me. "Don't look like no foelander to me. Besides"—he poked toward my belly—"she ain't barren. A rare find no matter where she's from."

I wrapped my arms protectively around the gentle swell of my middle. Little warmth or intelligence inhabited his features, so I turned toward Wizzle. He was a wiry man, ropey muscles revealed by his sleeveless tunic. Small stones studded the neckline and shimmered from the fabric. His pale hair was chopped unevenly, shaved to the skin on one side and tossed by the wind on the other. When he grinned, sharp points of his teeth flashed in the setting subsun.

Maker, help me. "Please take me back. I can negotiate trade to help your people. Just return me to shore."

Wizzle licked his lips. "Think she likes me."

Ratinger reached past me and cuffed him, jostling the veskal. "Don't go getting ideas. Mander said—"

He lurched up, pulling out an arched length of branch from behind his back. "Don't let them see her." Wizzle pushed me down, but I could just see over the rim of our veskal. Another tall pole with bright red fabric had glided into view. In a practiced motion, Ratinger launched a narrow stick. It released with the same twang I'd heard back in the woods.

"A few arrows should hold them back," he said.

I struggled to breathe. Would the people sailing toward us launch more lethal sticks in our direction? I covered my head with my arms as if that would shield me.

To my relief, the other craft changed course and soon disappeared into the distance.

Wizzle pulled out a telescope and squinted in all directions. "Mander was right. The other foelands will try to find all the best on the newland before us." He sneered at me. "Hope she's worth it."

I shifted on the uncomfortable bottom of the veskal. It wasn't actually a hollowed tree as I'd first thought but constructed of wooden slats like a cottage. Riding low in the water placed my line of sight at sea level. It felt too much like swimming—not my favorite activity in the best of circumstances. My stomach knotted, though I told myself it wasn't from fear but hunger. I'd never gotten a bite of Fiola's delicious stew, much less had a chance to rest in our comforting cottage after the exhausting afternoon on the river. Instead I was being carted off into the unknown, bruised and afraid. Separated from Brantley.

I was perilously close to drowning in self-pity. *Don't swim in those waters, Carya!* After all, Saltar Kemp and the dancers were working hard so that we could make early contact with the collection of islands. And here I was, in contact with them.

But this wasn't the plan. I had never intended to meet with them alone.

I swallowed and shielded my eyes against the last gleam of subsunset. As we traveled around a bend of Meriel's rim, the light from scattered fires flickered in the distance out in the ocean. Vague floating shapes coalesced into a collection of islands that rose from a hazy blue glow coating the water between the lands. Smoke rose from a few of them.

Wizzle whooped and shook his fist in the air. "Looks like our clan took some plunder while another foeland was busy foraging. Mander was right. Perfect chance." Then he snarled. "And we missed it."

"Dip," Ratinger ordered. Wizzle pulled me down seconds before the frame holding the curtain swung around. It would have knocked me into the sea or crushed my skull.

"Thank you." I sat up slowly, making sure I still had all my limbs. Both men ignored me, adjusting ropes on their craft. Our direction shifted, taking us even farther from Meriel and toward one of the islands.

My chest constricted as the rim of my world pulled away. The last of the subsunset extinguished, and darkness shrouded us. If I were Brantley, I'd leap into the water and swim back toward Meriel. Or I'd whistle for my stenella. Or I'd overpower my kidnappers and sail their veskal to Windswell. Neither of us had ever seen a vehicle like this, but he'd built rafts to tow supplies, so I had no doubt he'd be able to figure out how to navigate.

But I was just Carya. A crippled dancer.

No. I lifted my chin. A dancer who served the Maker, no matter where He led.

"Watch out for the sail. Dip." Ratinger's sharp order cut through the night air. This time I didn't need Wizzle to push me down. I bent in time to feel the beam brush past. When I poked my head up again, we glided up to a wooden platform.

Wizzle leapt out and tied up the veskal. "Out."

I moved awkwardly to the edge of the rocking craft and crawled onto the floating platform. My cane had fallen in the woods when they'd grabbed me, and without that support I hop-limped along the platform toward the mat of tangleroot on the shore.

"Lookie there. She can barely walk." Wizzle sneered.

Ratinger laughed. "Mander don't need her to walk. 'Sides, she'll be easier to manage."

My resolve to remain calm drained to my toes. *Maker, protect me!*

Wizzle sniggered. "Don't remind him of that foeland gal that got away. Mander near killed her guard."

With nowhere to go, I didn't resist when they dragged me inland. But if this Mander had the dark intent their conversation implied, I'd fling myself into the ocean first.

In the faint light of the stars, I couldn't absorb much of my surroundings. But I could feel the land. It should have been buoyant, rocking gently with each surge of waves. Instead, it was as still as the very center of Meriel.

Our narrow path opened to a huge circle of torchlight. A two-story barricaded structure stood in the center of the clearing. Sharpened sticks poked out in all directions. Four men with bowed sticks, swords, and haphazard pieces of armor stood guard.

Rough shacks rimmed the clearing, and rough-edged people lounged by campfires. To one side, long tables held men and women guzzling from large tankards. Spilling, laughing, jostling each other, they bragged about their day's exploits.

A man and woman approached, carrying a crate piled high with sparkling stones similar to those on Wizzle's tunic. The four guards straightened to attention.

The woman spoke. "Good raid today. Got these back again."

One of the guards opened a door in the prickly structure and placed the crate inside, then handed a token to the woman. "Fair theft. Take this to Mander."

Ratinger jerked me forward. "Fair theft indeed, Bonty. But lookie what we've got for him."

The woman crossed her arms and eyed me up and down. Her lips curled. "I'll wager he'll be happier with my find."

Wizzle poked my belly. "Look closer. She ain't barren."

Bonty's eyes widened, a glimmer of starlight flickering in them. She sketched a mock bow toward my captors. "Very fair theft. Best deliver her before others notice."

We'd already drawn attention. Some of the drinkers at the long table had stopped bantering and watched us with speculative gazes.

"No fear there." Ratinger hefted his bowed wooden weapon with his free hand and snarled. The others turned away. Still, his grip on my arm tightened. He wasn't as confident as he tried to appear.

Bonty laughed and headed around the storehouse and farther inland. Ratinger tugged me toward the guards, and for a moment I thought he planned to toss me inside the storehouse. Instead, Wizzle held out his palm, and a guard gave him a round wooden token.

Without further explanation, my captors pulled me around the building and in the direction Bonty had gone. A row of torches lit the path inland. Leafy limbs overhead erased the starlight. Detritus crunched underfoot. My pulse pounded in my skull. *Maker, protect me. Protect my babe.*

Ratinger shoved aside a prickly bush and we emerged into a new, smaller clearing. A large cottage, covered top to bottom in thorns, dominated the space. Surly guards manned each corner. The narrow door was edged in gold, with sparkling stones set into the broad surface, creating a pattern in the shape of a veskal like the one that had brought me here.

"Keep her here." Ratinger released me. "I'll go tell Mander."

Wizzle let go of my arm and stepped in front of Ratinger. "Oh, no you won't. We caught her together. Ain't letting you go in alone and claim the reward. Give me that."

He snatched for the wooden token, and Ratinger lurched out of reach. "My plan. My bounty."

As the men argued, I slid quietly toward the cover of the trees. The door to the cottage opened, and Bonty emerged, hefting a sack. As she watched my captors argue, she grinned and shook her head.

The men began to scuffle, the guards ignored them, and Bonty seemed distracted by the commotion. No one was paying attention to me. This was my chance.

I ducked under a branch and ran. The underbrush tore at my tunic and tugged my hair from its braid. The sounds of conflict faded behind me, and I aimed away from the large clearing where we'd landed but hopefully toward the near shore.

Floundering in the darkness, I crashed against a trunk, knocking the wind out of my lungs. A hand grabbed me. "Fair theft," said a light voice. Bonty.

I strained against her grip, but the woman had the strength of my former captors combined. In only seconds, she pulled me back into Mander's clearing. It was disheartening to see what little progress I'd made. But at least I'd tried.

Ratinger and Wizzle had come to blows, and Bonty snatched up their wooden token from the dirt and guided me to the building.

"Hey!" Ratinger turned, face red in the torchlight.

"Fair theft, men. Good night." She hustled me into the cottage as the two men raced forward. The door slammed in their faces.

"Back so soon, Bonty?" A bearded man, presumably Mander, sprawled in an oversized chair and stacked more tokens on a low table at his elbow. "And which foeland is this creature from?"

The room was unremarkable. A typical hearth, table, chairs, shelves, and doors leading to back rooms. The walls held various armaments. Knives, swords, and bowed weapons like Ratinger had used.

Unlike the room, Mander was not unremarkable: thick dark hair pulled back in a tail, dark beard that gave him the menace of a predator, teeth that flashed as he assessed me, and eyes that displayed intelligence and cunning.

"She ain't from a foeland. Ratinger took her from the newland." Bonty shoved me forward.

I stumbled and caught myself just before sprawling into his lap.

The man stood, crossing his arms, gaze still fixed on me as he spoke to Bonty. "Brave work. Why didn't you bring her with the rest of your haul?"

She shrugged and handed him the token that apparently gained her entrance for bartering. "Took her off the others."

He chuckled, then barked, "Servant Thirty!" A woman scurried into the room, head bowed. He barely glanced her direction. "Two bags of supplies for Bonty here. With straps to carry it all."

"Three bags." Bonty tossed her head. "Look closer."

In the dim firelight, his perusal sharpened and focused on my belly. "Three bags it is."

I wrapped protective arms around myself and edged back. I didn't appreciate being bartered like a sack of grain. Everyone seemed fascinated that I was with child. Would that grant some protection? Or did I need to fear for my baby?

A slow smile curved his lips, as if he read my thoughts. When the servant returned with Bonty's payment, she reached for the wrapped packages.

Mander grabbed her wrist and twisted it, wringing a hiss from her. "Fair theft, but don't think to push my patience."

She dipped her chin. "Never, Commander." The note of fear in this bold woman's voice made my nerves hum. But I had once faced down a high saltar and an evil Gardener. I wouldn't cower now either.

He released Bonty, and she hefted all her bags and left. After the man added the token to the stack on his table, a flick of his hand sent the servant dashing away into the back again.

We were alone. The walls of the room seemed to close in, and a log in the fireplace crackled with menace.

He grabbed my chin and tilted my head, studying my eyes. "I'm the 'Mander, lord of this island. You belong to me."

When I didn't react, his grip tightened.

"Do you understand?"

I wrenched away from his hand and glared. "I'm Carya of Meriel, and my only Lord is the Maker."

11

"YOU SPEAK?" MANDER'S EYEBROWS LIFTED. "WE DIDN'T expect that of newland creatures." He settled back into his large chair and rested his feet on a stool but didn't offer me a seat. "Or are you in truth a foelander sent to spy?"

Poor manners aside, at least we were communicating. For the moment, no one was restraining me, dragging me, or chasing me. A hopeful sign.

I smoothed my braid and lifted my chest the way I prepared for a challenging dance pattern. "Of course we speak. I represent our high saltar, and we are willing to negotiate trade with your islands."

His eyes narrowed, glinting amber. "Not islands. Island. One. The others are foelands. And if your people think to raid us, you'll regret the attempt."

A wave of exhaustion washed over me, and my knees struggled to hold me up. "We have no wish to raid you. In fact, some of the leaders thought it best to steer our world away from your islands. But the currents drew us together."

A wolfish grin answered. "Your leaders did well to fear us. Tell me, are there many more unbarren on your island?"

I didn't like the avarice lighting his expression, or the speculative way he watched me. I didn't like carrying the responsibility of speaking for our people. I didn't like his fascination with my "unbarren" state. Whatever his intent, peaceful trade negotiations didn't seem likely. Yet I had to try.

"May I sit? I've traveled all day."

His fist pounded the arm of his chair. "Answer my question."

I sagged. "If you plan to treat our people as you've treated me, I have no more to say to you."

He shot up and grabbed my arms, his face inches from mine. The force of his anger burned through his fingers. "Where is your storehouse? What weapons do your people use? How large is your army? Where are the unbarren kept?" He shook me.

I refused to wince and met his stare. "If your people think to raid us," I said, repeating his earlier threat, "you'll regret the attempt."

He released me abruptly and barked a laugh. "Full of surprises."

My stomach growled, and I wrapped my arms around my middle again. He'd seemed fixated on my pregnancy, so perhaps that could be turned to advantage. "It's been a long time since I last ate. My babe needs food."

He gave a sharp whistle, much like a herder summoning a stenella. The servant I'd seen earlier shuffled into the room. "Bring her a chair. And a meal."

Once settled by the hearth and nibbling from a plate of familiar fruits and saltcakes similar to those made on Meriel, I attempted to steer our conversation toward a diplomatic exchange rather than a prisoner interrogation.

"So these islands are at war with each other?"

He rubbed his hands near the fire—callused and scarred hands that could snap my neck in an instant. "We raid. If they mine gems we want, we take them. If they see an unbarren in our midst, they steal her." He shrugged. "Fair theft. Are your people so different?"

Under his fierce scrutiny, I chewed mechanically, forcing my dry throat to swallow. "We don't mine gems. And each village tends its own fields and orchards. We don't need to raid." I decided not to explain about the recent shortages and struggles that Meriel was still recovering from. Or the internal factions feuding over control. In some ways, our world sounded sadly similar to the life on this cluster of islands.

I swallowed a slice of persea and licked my fingers. "At heart, we humans are all tempted by fear and avarice, aren't we? On our world, we forgot all about our Maker. We set our own course, which nearly destroyed us." I leaned forward, praying silently for wisdom. "Do you know about the Maker?"

Mander hooded his eyes, making him look even more dangerous, if that were possible. "Our legends tell of a bridge builder who will unite the foelands." He snorted. "You've seen the foelands."

I nodded. "From a distance."

"No one could build bridges to span that far. And no one will stop the raids." He waved his hand as if brushing away a fly. "It's of no matter. We take what we want."

"Are you short on food? Do you work with stenella to herd fish?"

"Stenella?"

"The large sea creatures. Surely you've seen them when they float above the waves."

His eyebrows shot upward. "The sea creatures? Only the bravest dare kill them. They can upend our veskals or hover over and smash them. And their flesh is far from tasty."

Kill them? These people even chose to be enemies with the gentle stenella? I swallowed back nausea, fighting to hide my horror and shock. "Are you short on crops for your people?"

"Crops? We have plenty." His arm swept open. "But more is always better."

I shook my head. "Not if it leads to endless battle. I don't know the Maker's plan for your world, but I know He offers His love to all."

Darkness glinted in his eyes, and he smirked. "I'm never one to refuse an offer of love."

Bile burned my throat. The walls of the room closed in. I'd held my fear at bay as long as I could, but reality pressed in on me. I was a prisoner. A prisoner of a man with total control over his island. No one knew where I was. If Orianna had escaped, she would have told Brantley only that men had captured me. Even if Brantley approached these islands, he'd have nearly a dozen to search in an effort to find me.

"Let me see what I've purchased in this barter." Mander pulled me to my feet and moved me closer to the torches over the fireplace. He paced slowly around me, his scrutiny burning over my skin. Then he pointed to my bandaged ankle. "Did your former master do that to keep you from running? Or as punishment?"

The reminder of the high saltar's brutal knife pierced me. He was more accurate than he knew. But that was my old life.

I lifted my chin. "I have no master, save the Maker."

Almost casually, he backhanded me across the face.

I stumbled, grabbing a chair to keep from falling against the hearthstones. Shock stung more than the blow.

"Know your place, servant." He turned toward the back room. "Thirty!"

The servant scurried in, her expression forlorn and devoid of life as she stared at the floor. Was this to be my fate? Owned, abused, broken? *Maker, help me!*

"Clean her up and bring her to my room. And prepare a pallet in the servants' room for later."

I rubbed my stinging face and flexed my jaw. My tongue tested to be sure all my teeth were still in place. Out of ideas, I straightened slowly. "I cannot stay here. I have important work on Meriel. And I'm married."

He shrugged. "Then your man should have protected you. His loss."

The insinuation that Brantley had failed in any way torched through me like a blacksmith's forge. Insults, threats, and blows were one thing. But this tyrant would not speak ill of my husband. I spun and grabbed a longknife from the wall—the one weapon Brantley had taught me to wield.

The servant gasped, wide-eyed.

"Thirty," Mander said calmly, "go prepare her pallet."

She threw a terrified glance toward me and backed out of the room. I rounded on Mander, pointing the shining blade his way. I was pleased that my hands didn't even shake. "I do not belong to you, and I never will."

Mild annoyance flashed across his brow. Then his hungry gaze traveled over me as if I were a roasted game bird, and he licked his lips.

"You think being unbarren protects you. I have no need for stolen children now that we've found a new world to raid. I care not for the babe's safety." His voice darkened, and he grabbed a sword from behind his chair. "But you should. Will you risk the babe's life to defy me?"

My lungs constricted. An impossible choice. The longknife weighed heavier in my grip, but I'd do anything to hold him at bay. *Maker! Where are You?*

He lifted his weapon and stepped closer. I batted away his steel with my knife. "I have more of worth to offer than my body or my child." Even I could hear the thread of desperation in my throat.

He feinted a jab at me and laughed when I flinched. "I doubt that."

Frantic pounding rattled the door. "Mander! We have news!"

The commander sighed, knocked the knife from me with a sharp rap that bruised my wrist, shoved me into a chair, then bellowed. "Enter."

A hunched older man slipped into the room. Tattered layers of clothing covered him, as if when each article wore thin, he'd simply placed another threadbare garment atop.

Mander's grip on my shoulder warned me to stay in place, even as he addressed the man. "Vertco, it's past time for reports."

The man shook, bits of bark falling to the floor from his tangled hair. "Yes, Mander. I know. But the news is important. I ain't disturbing you for no purpose." His gaze cut toward me but darted quickly to the floor.

"Well?" Mander barked, his patience stretched too taut.

"The windward dock. It's burning."

I felt Mander's rage as his fingers squeezed deeper into my shoulder. "Impossible."

The man's trembling increased. "Saw it myself. Ran all the way back."

The commander became a blur of movement, grabbing weapons, adding them to his belt, shoving past Vertco, and tearing out of the cottage. Vertco slunk out behind him.

I tiptoed to the open door and peered out. Acrid smoke carried on the breeze, stronger than the scent of the torches around the clearing.

Guards still manned their posts. One of them noticed me and glared my direction, so I withdrew. No escape, unless I could find a back exit.

"Psst." The hiss barely reached my ears. It took me a moment to find the source. Servant Thirty cowered in the shadows of the backroom doorway. "Your place is prepared," she whispered. "You don't want to be in this room when he returns."

I picked up the longknife and tucked it in my belt. "Where is the windward dock? How long will he be gone?"

She hunched even lower. "Depends. This way." She guided me to a tiny back room, where six pallets lined the wall. Two other women slept under threadbare blankets, and a young boy whimpered in his sleep beside one of them. Only one tiny window broke up the far wall, too small to offer escape from here. I would need to keep searching.

Servant Thirty lowered herself to one of the empty pallets and motioned for me to take another. "Why are you called Thirty?" I whispered. "Are there other servants' quarters elsewhere?" Perhaps I could convince them to rally against their master. That many of us could easily overpower one man and a few guards.

Dark rings drooped beneath her eyes, revealing ages of suffering. "Twenty-seven came before."

"And escaped?"

"If death is an escape, then yes." Seeming weary of my questions, she lay down and turned away. "Best get some rest while you can."

When it was clear she wouldn't answer any more questions, I tiptoed from the room to explore. A hall led deeper into the building. To one side I discovered a cooking area, embers dying under a large caldron. Across the hall, I nudged open a door to a room that could only be Mander's. More weapons studded the walls, and haphazard chests of all sizes filled much of the floor space. The chests that were open revealed gems, tableware, candles, and more robes and tunics than any person could use in ten lifetimes. Avarice glinted from every surface. A large bed with a crimson silken spread dominated the room.

My throat constricted, and nausea roiled in my stomach. I withdrew, continued down the hall, and discovered a few more storage rooms—most containing more practical items. At last I reached the end of the building. A small door made my hope rise. I tried the handle, but it was locked. Using the longknife, I tried to manipulate the lock, but soon realized I'd need a key.

I hurried back to the commander's room, limping as silently as I could. If he returned while I was searching, I knew I wouldn't survive the night. I worked fast, running my hand under pillows, pushing aside jewelry in chests, and rummaging through the pockets of any clothing.

Ready to despair, I turned in a slow circle, scanning the room again. Behind me, hanging on a peg near the door, was a key ring. Stupid! If I'd searched thoroughly instead of rushing around, I wouldn't have wasted so much time.

I grabbed the keys and raced to the back door, pulse pounding in my ears. My hands fumbled as I tried each key. At last, the lock turned.

I eased the door open. It creaked, and I froze. Taking a deep breath, I opened it enough to stick out my head and peer around.

The first thing I saw was the back of a guard's head and several more men pacing the clearing. I stifled a gasp and pulled back inside, silently closing the door again. The soldiers had been intent on guarding the house from intruders, so they hadn't seen me. But my heart pounded against my ribs at nearly being discovered.

A part of me wanted to sink to the floor and give in to tears. No time for such an indulgence. When I trained as a novitiate, my brain ached from memorizing combinations, and my muscles quivered from strain. When the saltar asked us to repeat a rigorous pattern yet again, I would swallow the tears, never showing weakness. I rallied that training now. Mander hadn't returned. I hadn't exhausted every option. I just needed to think creatively. *Maker, You created all things. Please send me ideas.*

I limped to the servants' room and studied the sleeping forms. I could ask Thirty for help, but that would only endanger her once Mander discovered I'd fled. However, I could borrow her cloak. The guards must be used to seeing Mander's servants going about their duties.

I slipped the hooded cloak from its peg over Thirty's pallet and put it on. In the kitchen, I took a basket, so I'd look like I was on a mission to gather herbs or fruit. I had no idea if servants typically went out after dark, but if I moved with purpose, perhaps the guards wouldn't stop me. That brought up another problem. I couldn't move quickly.

A fireplace poker was about the right height to become a makeshift cane. I took a few steps with it and almost managed to hide my telltale limp. If the guards stopped to think, they'd wonder why a servant was using a poker as a walking stick. So many flaws in this plan. Brantley would have come up with far better ideas. But he wasn't here.

I drew several deep breaths to steady myself, hobbled to the back door, yanked it open, and stepped out into the night.

SMOKE CURLED THROUGH THE AIR, MASKING THE STARS.
The odor was stronger than the last time I'd poked my head outside.
The guards paced restlessly. A soldier near the door turned to watch me.
I huddled under my hood and held up my basket in silent explanation
while my heart fluttered in my throat. If he challenged me, my ruse
would be discovered. I was mad for trying this.

"Above the trees," a guard near the side of the house called to his
comrades. "You can see the edge of flame."

The man closest to me stepped away for a better view. "Cursed
foelanders. I wager we'll be on a counter raid tomorrow."

While the men were occupied, I limped across the clearing and
reached the woods.

My breath came in tight gasps, but once I was out of sight of the guards,
I wanted to shout in victory. Rash as it had been, my plan had worked.

Which direction should I go? Not back toward the dock and village
where my kidnappers had landed. Not toward the smoke where another
dock was burning. Mander was certainly there.

Making my best guess, I pushed deeper into the undergrowth, using
the fireplace poker to push aside bushes and then to support me as I
limped forward. How large was this island? When I'd viewed the cluster
from the Order, none had seemed very large, but there had been no
way to judge.

I'd caught glimpses of shoreline as we traveled here but had been more
focused on the sight of Meriel drawing away from me. As I fumbled in the
darkness, I realized I had no plan. I stopped to catch my breath. Perhaps

I should find my way back to where Ratinger and Wizzle had first brought me. At least I knew there was a craft there. Could I convince some kind soul to sail me over to Meriel?

Or if Mander's enemies were battling him in the location where hints of amber tinted the dark sky, perhaps they would rescue me and be open to trading with the Order.

Possibilities flitted like gnats until I went cross-eyed trying to sort them out. Brantley would say to make a plan and then commit to it. Once he chose a course, he didn't waver. I needed that sort of resolute courage now.

Deep in the trees, I lost all sense of direction, but I pushed onward toward what I hoped would be the rim—and a deserted section of it. I'd figure out my next step once I could see the precious ocean again. Darkness concealed tree branches until they rose up and smacked my forehead. Thorn bushes hid in blackness until my ankles felt them scrape. Wandering a strange forest in the middle of the night was painful. Was I even making progress?

I fought my way forward because I could think of no other option. Each inch that distanced me from Mander was worth the struggle. Crashing, tearing, limping, I felt like I was battling the entire forest. At last I glimpsed a break in the trees. The darkness tried to choke me, and I coughed. The thickening scent of smoke should have warned me my direction was flawed, but all I could think about was seeing the ocean.

I pushed aside a thorny bush that clawed my cloak and twisted the hood around my face. I pulled it away and stumbled onto a path.

Two soldiers stared at me, silhouetted by distant flames.

"It's one of the raiders!" one of the men shouted. "They didn't all escape."

The other whistled sharply.

I spun and ran with my awkward, lopsided gait, begging the Maker yet again to restore my tendon. Surely there was never a better time for Him to act. My survival depended on speed.

Please, please, please. But the leg still could barely hold weight. *Then at least guide me. They're right behind me!*

Indeed, angry crashing and cracking branches dogged my heels, no matter how fast I moved. Silent sobs shook me with each gasping breath. My dragging foot snagged a root, and I tumbled forward, hitting the ground with enough force to knock the wind from me. *My babe!* Even if I somehow escaped this nightmare, would my unborn child survive the ordeal?

"He's here," said a deep voice that chilled me. "Now we'll learn which foeland deserves our wrath."

The toe of a mud-splattered boot slid beneath my chin and forced my head up. As my gaze rose, I met the blazing eyes of Mander. The smoke above us seemed to swirl out from his rage, as a soldier behind him held a torch aloft.

The commander reached down and pulled the hood away, letting the light hit me full on the face. "You?" He pulled his foot away abruptly and turned to one of his men. "Didn't Bonty say Ratinger captured her from the newland? If he brought a mere foelander into our village, I'll flay him myself."

A soldier stepped forward. "I saw their veskal arrive. They definitely brought her from the newland."

"Bah. Some trick of a foeland. Get her up."

One of the men jerked me to my feet, and I winced. Every part of my body felt bruised and battered. Mander leaned forward, drilling me with his threatening gaze. His clothes and beard reeked of smoke and fury. "Are you working with Rogue's Aerie? Or is it your island that burned my dock?"

"We know nothing of the foelands, and we would never harm you."

He pointed to my belly. "Yet you risk harm to your child by running through the forest at night. Why should I believe you don't thrive on destroying?"

I drew a steadying breath, more to control my anger than my fear. "It is to protect my child that I sought to escape. To return home." In spite of my best efforts, my voice shook. The stolen knife weighed heavy against my waist. I shivered and pulled the cloak forward to hide it.

"If you've conspired with a foeland, I'll send your body back to them in pieces."

"I've told you. Our world is called Meriel, and we mean you no harm."

He stared into me, as if trying to read my soul. I met his gaze, unblinking.

He flicked one hand. "Take her back to my house. I'll deal with her after we finish our search for any more raiders."

My imagination leapt to dozens of ways he planned to deal with me, but I shut those thoughts from my brain. *Maker, You freed our world. I know You can free me. Save me!*

One of the soldiers grabbed me roughly.

I snatched up the fireplace poker. "My leg is injured," I said, forestalling any worry he might have that I would conk him over the head with it.

Disdain flashed over his face before his soldier's blank expression slipped back into place. I tried to engage him in conversation as we wound our way, but he refused to answer. He dragged me along small trails that I hadn't been able to find. In far too short of a time, we emerged into the clearing around Mander's house.

The guards in the back stiffened at the sound of our approach. My captor pulled my hood back and shoved me toward one of the startled men. "Are you in the habit of allowing Mander's servants to wander in the night?"

Nervous excuses, glares my direction, and a few minutes of arguing ensued, while I wavered on my feet, ready to collapse. By the time the man holding me pulled me into the house, I was so exhausted all I felt was relief.

I sank onto a stool by the fireplace embers, one palm pressed against my side, seeking to reassure my tiny child with a gentle touch. I was done with escape attempts for the night. The terror, the running, the battering of branches and the hard fall were dangerous for my baby. Time to eke out a little rest while I could. For both our sakes.

I stood, ready to slip into the servants' quarters and settle on an empty pallet.

"Sit." The guard glowered.

"But I—"

"We wait here for the commander." His sword grated against leather as he slid it halfway from its sheath.

When I settled back on the stool, the knife in my belt pinched my hip. I still wore the borrowed cloak that kept it out of sight. Not that I'd have much use for it. I'd learned to flick a knife in the general direction of a bog rat but had never succeeded in skewering one. Brantley had all the accuracy.

Brantley. My heart ached with worry. What had he done when I didn't return? Had Orianna escaped to explain what happened? *I know you're coming for me, but please be careful.*

Worrying over things I couldn't change only heightened my anxiety, so I turned my thoughts to the Maker. *Lord of my life, why have You allowed me to be here among these people?*

The answer came with my next breath. The Maker created our floating worlds from the outpouring of His love. He formed human souls to partake of it. And the people of this land—as with all others—needed His love.

I tried to strike up a conversation with my guard, but he only responded with grunts and glowers. Eventually I subsided and watched the glowing embers dull to black. As I prayed silently for the Maker's protection on Meriel, Brantley, Orianna, Fiola, silent tears spilled down my cheek. I brushed them aside and shook my head. I had to turn my thoughts from my loved ones and trust they would be safe, or else I'd crumble.

To distract me, I prayed for Servant Thirty and the other wretched slaves in the back room. I prayed for Bonty who profited from my capture. I prayed for the quarrelsome Wizzle and Ratinger. I prayed for anyone hurt by the blaze at the dock. I asked blessings for these "foelands" and the people I'd encountered. There was only one person I couldn't bring myself to pray for.

And then the door crashed open and he entered.

With a jerk of his chin, Mander sent the soldier scurrying away like a field rodent. I stiffened, bracing for a blow.

But the commander dropped into his large chair, allowing his shoulders to sink in a sigh. With his posture collapsed, he seemed smaller, weary. Soot streaked his face. Compassion almost curled up under my ribs, until I thought of how he treated his slaves. I steeled myself.

"Thirty!" he barked.

Rustling and scrambling sounds preceded hurried footfalls. Eyes heavy with sleep and with an even wearier cast to her spine than earlier, Servant Thirty ran into the room and bowed before her master.

"Rouse the servants. I need hot water and a meal."

He seemed to have forgotten me for the moment, so I tried to be inconspicuous as I moved aside for Thirty. She stoked the dying fire and added kindling. Soon the house buzzed with activity, even though dawn was hours away. No one cast me a single glance, their spirits too broken for curiosity. Watching them sent dread deep into my bones.

Mander eventually rose and rolled his shoulders. He carefully removed his sword belt and hung it on a peg near the door. Still ignoring me, he headed down the hall to his room. Thirty scooped a pitcher of heated water from the cauldron over the fire and followed him. There followed the sounds of splashing and murmuring of voices as the commander washed away the night's battle. I took advantage of his absence to crack open the front door. An alert guard quickly pivoted toward me, so I ducked back inside. I knew this wasn't a time to try to flee again, but gathering more information about my surroundings was vital.

I slipped the door open silently a mere slit and peered out again. This time the guards didn't notice me, so I continued studying the area around the house.

"If you are a saboteur from a foeland, you are an odd one." Mander's deep voice entered the room before his footsteps.

I spun, unobtrusively closing the door behind my back as I faced him. His fresh-scrubbed face, combed hair, and clean tunic made me conscious of the bits of dried leaves crumbling and falling from my cloak, and the dirt under my nails. I wished someone had offered me the opportunity to bathe. And sleep. And leave.

"Odd or not, I'm not a saboteur or a foelander. I'm a simple dancer from Meriel."

His lips twitched, making him slightly less a monster and more human. The rings under his eyes, the sigh as he crossed his arms reminded me of Saltar Kemp.

He stepped closer. For a large man, he walked with the quiet tread of a stalking forest hound. "The work of the commander never ends."

"Don't let me keep you," I said bitterly. "Ask one of your men to return me to my island so you can get on with your . . . commanding."

"Give that to me." He held out his hand for the poker, which he used to rearrange logs in the fireplace, stirring up more heat, then propped it against the bricks. "Sit."

I hesitated, unsure what he intended. But since I couldn't oppose him standing any better than sitting, I might as well rest my aching bones. I limped awkwardly to a stool and stretched my throbbing leg in front of me, still clutching the borrowed cloak around my shoulders.

His gaze shifted to my ankle. "You say you have no master but the Maker. Did you come by that wound in battle?"

I pursed my lips. How to answer? Even now, the memory of the high saltar's dagger drew fire across my tendon. "I understand what it is to have enemies," I admitted quietly. Then I hastened to add, "But we have no desire to make an enemy of your island."

"So you say." Instead of sinking onto his large chair, he crouched before me and unwrapped the torn and stained bandage from my leg. His touch repulsed me, and I froze as if stillness could make this all go away.

The skin of my ankle looked sickly and white in contrast to all the dirt that the bandage had blocked. He touched the ugly scar across my tendon and whistled. "Surprised you can walk at all." Was that the tiniest hint of compassion?

Quick as a snake, his hand darted to my hip and pulled out the stolen dagger. With chilling calm he held it so the firelight glinted wickedly on the blade. Then he met my eyes, his voice flat and devoid of any sympathy I'd imagined earlier. "Run again, and I'll do the same to your other leg."

13

MANDER LOOMED, A TOWERING THREAT OVER ME. FLAMES on the hearth cackled, mocking me for thinking I'd found a glimpse of humanity or a point of connection with this man.

I cowered on my low stool. I hated myself for showing weakness, but primal horror had a grip on me. My heart couldn't even form a prayer other than, *Maker, Maker, Maker!*

My tormentor tossed the blade, caught it deftly, then tucked it in his own belt. He pulled his chair nearer the fire and sat. "Now you understand me. Who sent you?"

Even with my heart racing because of his earlier threat, the weight of exhaustion piled on top of my body like waterlogged pallets. I sank lower, all strength leaving my spine. I had already tried to explain, but he hadn't believed me. I studied the floorboards, searching for an answer that would satisfy him.

He scooted his chair closer with a sharp scrape.

I startled, my head coming up. Light from the fire was absorbed and extinguished by his gaze, changing his eyes into two pits of darkness under his black eyebrows. "Answer me. Who sent you?"

Who sent me? Of any question he could ask, this was the one that flared my strength. Dying or living, crawling or dancing, captive or free, I was not my own. That gave me courage to firm my chin. "The Maker sent me."

Mander leaned back and crossed his legs. "At last, the truth. And how many lands does this Maker command?"

A slight smile tugged my lips. "All of them."

He snorted. "Do I need to remind you the price of lying?"

"It's the truth." In a rush, I poured out the heart of the Maker's letter, my experiences of meeting Him, His love and purposes. Mander let me speak, his expression giving away nothing.

". . . and although I don't understand your group of islands and the conflicts you seem to be having, I know the Maker can bring you answers. I'm sure that's why He allowed me to be brought here. So I could tell you."

He barked a laugh. "Allowed? You were stolen fairly—though I doubt your home is truly the large windward island. Clearly one of the foelands sought to rid themselves of an addlebrained cripple and left you there for Ratinger to find. But I'll admit you spin a fine tale."

Frustration laced my tone. "It's no tale. But I don't need to convince you. You'll learn soon enough there is One with far more power than you."

Mander's eyes narrowed. His fingers flexed a few times as if deciding whether to form a fist.

I rubbed my eyes, so depleted I couldn't muster the energy to defend myself.

His gaze moved to my belly. "Go sleep. I've need of every slave I can get, and you've done enough to endanger the babe tonight."

Me? I'd fought to protect my child. He was the one endangering us. But I pressed my lips together, struggled to my feet, and limped to the back room. A pallet welcomed me, the borrowed cloak serving as a blanket. Relieved to still be alive, I imagined the arms of the Maker cradling me as my womb cradled the baby.

A GENTLE HAND BRUSHED A LOCK OF HAIR AWAY FROM MY face. A whisper of sound coaxed me from my sleep.

"Orianna?" I murmured and snuggled deeper under the blanket. Brantley's niece often visited our cottage before anyone else was stirring, ready for adventure.

"Miss? The commander is about his work. This is your chance to eat."

My eyes flew open, gritty with dried tears and insufficient sleep. Memory flooded back, sending my pulse surging through my veins. Thirty knelt beside me, a worried frown twisting her haggard face.

I sat up, blinking a few times while I coaxed my heart to slow. I untangled from the cloak I'd used as a blanket and held out the bundle. "I borrowed this last night. I'm sorry."

She stared at me, impassive. "Makes no matter. Come. Eat quickly."

I rose awkwardly, then used the wall for support as I followed her to the kitchen. "What is your true name? I can't call you Thirty."

She scooped gruel into a flat bowl and handed it to me, along with a saltcake. "It's my only name." A subtle movement of her shoulder could have been a shrug if she'd had more life in her. "To remind me of those who came before."

"I'm Carya of Windswell. The Order where I was raised gave me a different name, but I found my true name again once I was free."

"Free?" She snorted her derision, the most animation I'd seen from her so far.

A scruffy child ran into the kitchen, set a basket of tubers on the counter and scampered back out. Softness like a warm mist drifted across Thirty's face.

I swallowed a mouthful of the bland gruel. "Is he your child?"

Her expression shuttered, and she turned to wring out a rag and scrub the tabletop. "He belongs to the commander, as do we all."

But I noticed the way her free hand brushed her abdomen, that tiny gesture of remembering and yearning. "What's his name?"

She stopped cleaning the table and turned toward me, clearly bewildered by my question. "Mander calls him 'boy.' If he lives long enough, he'll earn a number when he's older. He may even earn the right to join the raiders."

I rested a hand on her thin arm. "What do *you* call him?"

She pulled away as if she'd touched a lanthrus plant. Clearly she believed even thinking a name for her little boy was a rebellion too dangerous to contemplate. I couldn't really blame her. I'd only been here a day, and already I breathed the pervasive stench of fear. What would it be like to be here an entire lifetime?

Perhaps a bit like growing up in the Order. I smiled ruefully. At least they had taught me skills to draw on now: stay alert and unobtrusive until I could escape.

A male servant stomped in from the back door and dropped a pile of logs near a rack. Thirty left her cleaning and began stacking neat rows. I finished my breakfast and moved to help her.

"No!" Her shoulder blocked my reach. "The commander hasn't yet assigned your duties." Then she spared a quick perusal and sniffed. "Although he wants you cleaned up. I'll heat water for you when I'm done here."

I longed to wash away the dirt and soot from my skin and comb the tangles from my hair. But not for Mander. Still, I didn't want to distress Thirty any more than I already had. I'd eat, I'd rest, I'd clean up. All for the sake of my baby and myself. Never for my captor.

With that defiant thought, I allowed Thirty to help me wash and dress in a clean tunic and leggings while mine were washed. She watched, curious, while I braided my hair. Out of habit I felt beside me for my scarf, then remembered I'd lost it. Had Brantley found it? What was he doing at this very moment?

Protect him, precious Maker. He takes too many risks.

"Wait here until Mander returns," Thirty said. A flash of anxiety lit her eyes, and she paused, clearly wanting to be reassured. If I fled again, she would suffer.

I nodded. "I will."

After she went about her duties, the sleeping quarters remained quiet and empty, while the bustle of activity around the encampment hummed like a nest of honeybirds. I nudged aside a torn curtain and peered out the tiny window. Both suns were high in the sky. I'd slept away the morning but still ached with fatigue. I took advantage of this moment of solitude to stretch, rearrange the bandage around my ankle, and talk to the Maker. Every few minutes I returned to the window. As my gaze tracked a bird toward upward branches of a pine, I spotted a platform high in the tallest tree bordering the clearing. A man stood on the flimsy wood with a telescope to his eye, scanning in all directions. From such a perch, Mander's islanders were likely able to watch for danger from any of the nearby foelands. How much of Meriel could they observe? And had the large telescope atop the Order seen last night's fire? What did Saltar Kemp make of these feuding islands from her distance?

Heavy bootfalls invaded the front room. Servant Thirty called softly from the hallway. "Carya of Windswell, the commander wants you in the room for his daily tribute."

A quiver scraped my nerves, but I limped to the front room with rigid calm. Observe. Avoid notice. Watch for opportunities. Reciting my plan over and over, I was able to hobble into Mander's presence without showing my inner trembling.

Men and women, perhaps village leaders, sat on the floor, nearly filling the room. Mander strode toward me and clamped a hand over my belly. "My people! We suffered loss last night, but look. I've captured a victory child!"

Victory child? What did that mean? There was no one to ask. Everyone cheered and pounded the floor with their fists until the entire building shook. I glared at Mander. My baby was not an emblem of the commander's power. *Observe. Avoid notice. Watch for opportunities.*

Leaning against one wall, Bonty crossed her arms. A frown flicked across her brow before she resumed her impassive expression. Perhaps she didn't like Mander taking credit for a captive she'd delivered to him. Perhaps his people weren't as loyal as they seemed.

When the cheering ended, the commander pointed toward a stool in the corner. I took my seat with all the dignity I could muster. The commander settled in his large chair and promptly ignored me, for which

I was grateful. A guard at the door admitted men and women one by one. They brought armloads of cargo: bags of food, boxes of gems, bundles of weapons. Mander calculated value, bartered, and sorted items. Some went to the village's storehouse outside. Choice items were taken to Mander's room. In between the offerings, Mander took reports from soldiers. One of his veskals had been damaged in the fire, so he dispatched a dozen villagers to work on repairs. He sent others—including a handful of children—to rebuild the dock. Unfortunately for me, he didn't send away any of his guards. He had dozens of armed men protecting his estate.

As the afternoon dragged on, my resentment grew. Watching a leader satiate his greed on the backs of his people reminded me too much of the former high saltar, who sent soldiers to steal girls from villages, starved people with forced tributes, and even killed those who opposed them, such as Brantley's brother. On Meriel we'd finally begun to turn away from the senseless cruelty, but seeing it dominate another world broke my heart.

And I couldn't do anything to change it. I hated feeling so powerless. *Maker, let me bring a difference here. Show me what to do!*

The only word I heard in answer was *Wait*.

If it tortured my soul to watch this suffering, it must torment the Maker even more. If this wasn't yet the right time to rescue them, there was a reason beyond my limited understanding.

I met a range of curious and hostile glances from Mander's villagers with a gentle smile. One woman offered a silent nod in return. That small gesture helped me endure the long afternoon. At last the room emptied of everyone but the commander and me. I immediately wished the soldiers, villagers, and servants would return.

Mander stretched, clearly pleased with himself, and pulled me to my feet. Then he paced a slow circle around me. I held my chin high, determined not to let him intimidate me.

He touched my face, and I flinched. So much for my determination. The muscles in my stomach contracted so tightly I hoped I wasn't squashing my baby.

"You're not so bad when you're cleaned up. Time to see exactly what the foelanders have sent me."

Grabbing my arm, he pulled me from the front room toward his bedroom. I dug in my heels as best I could, strained against him to free my arm, and screamed silently. *Maker, now! I need help now!*

In his room, he threw me toward the bed. I stumbled and spun, ready to fend him off with fists and feet and teeth and nails.

"Commander!" A man's call joined the sound of the front door slamming against the wall.

Mander pointed at me. "Stay." Then he stomped from the room.

I lurched to my feet, stole a longknife from his wall, and followed to the hallway so I could hear.

"The watch reports an approaching raid."

Mander swore and shouted for servants. He snapped orders and hurried out without returning to his room. My heart leapt with hope. Was it Brantley? Perhaps with a group of herders? I hoped they were well armed. Brantley would have assessed the threat here before trying a rescue, wouldn't he? Did he know about the weapons they could throw from their bows? Those sharpened sticks they called arrows could pierce a tree trunk, so they would cause huge damage to a human.

The rising hope congealed in my throat. *Maker, protect Brantley.*

Maybe I could help from here. I tiptoed to the commander's window. The storehouse was still guarded, as was the front entry. I tucked the longknife into my belt, then lifted one of the bow weapons from the wall. It flexed slightly but was strong enough to use as a cane.

A servant's eyes widened as I limped down the hall to the kitchen, but she didn't talk to me. My status was undefined. Since I carried a "victory child" valued by the commander, they were likely afraid to challenge me. I offered no explanation and continued on my way with feigned confidence. From the kitchen window I could view the back of the clearing. Sentries still patrolled. The figure high on the watch platform shouted something to them.

One of the soldiers below nodded and raced away.

Still too many guards to attempt an escape, but at least I'd be alert and ready when Brantley and his men reached me.

Heavy feet trampled the step by the front door. "Where is she?" curled a surly and out-of-breath voice.

Servant Thirty left her duties to grab my arm. "Miss? This way. They need you."

I leaned on the bow and accompanied her to the front room. "Why?"

When she didn't answer, I directed my questions to the bulky soldier in the doorway. "Where are you taking me? Have my people negotiated my release?"

He grabbed my arm and pulled me outside. "The 'mander wants you on his veskal."

My mind raced. Was this a good sign? Was I finally to be returned to Meriel? We emerged from the trail at the dock where I'd landed the night before. I scanned the sea. Meriel's forests rocked gently in the distance. Too much open water to swim, but tantalizingly close. But there was no sign of any stenellas, or any rescue. My smile faded. Instead, several veskals darted about. I counted four with white sails, including the large one at the dock where Mander waited. Four other craft bore mottled blue and green sails. They glided with the wind like seabirds, approaching the island where I stood, then angling away. No not like gulls. More like carrion birds circling watchfully.

On board, men shouted, adjusted sails, and jostled for position.

The soldier dragged me out on the floating dock toward the large veskal. Mander shouted orders. "Arrows to the aft!" Three men using lengthy bows let fly the sharp sticks toward the colorful sails. One arrow found its mark, and a man yelped and fell into the water. I gasped, the scene coalescing, and random movements defining themselves. These men were killing each other. Killing each other from a distance. What madness was this?

"Get aboard." The soldier shoved me, and I fell headfirst into the veskal.

"Ha!" Mander glanced at me with a predatory gleam. "Let's show these foelanders from Rogue's Aerie that we've captured their victory child."

With an economy of signals, he directed the craft away from the dock and into the fray. "Stand!" he ordered me.

Rubbing the sore places where this latest fall had battered me, I tried to comply. The deck beneath me listed and the sail swung across. I stumbled, and my guard emitted a disdainful chuckle that made me hate him.

I still had the bow, so I braced myself and found my footing. I raised my chin. Could I say anything to convince Mander to sail toward Meriel? The roiling waves beckoned me. Perhaps I should simply fling myself overboard and take my chances. But I no longer had the luxury of selfish choices. I had to think about my baby.

I stepped closer to the mast, hoping it could protect my child from any arrows shot in my direction. With dizzying speed, we cut across whitecaps toward the largest of the opposing craft. A tall man with full beard and muscled physique stood on a plank deck beneath the sail that mimicked the ocean's hues. His wide stance absorbed the rocking motion beneath him. Like Mander, he shouted and signaled crisp orders. Soon five of his men faced our direction, bows at the ready. And Mander sailed us straight toward them.

14

"STOP!" I SCREAMED.

My cry was cut off when Mander grabbed me and thrust me in front of him. "We have her!" he shouted. "Go back to your pitiful island or she dies, and the victory child with her." His voice was as triumphant as the splashing waves and the rush of wind. His men raced around, pulling ropes, turning rudders, bringing the veskal to only a few yards from collision but then angling it to a stop.

The opposite commander stared at me. A flare of confusion wrinkled his brow, but it was quickly hidden by an arrogant glare. Whiskers drew shadows across his face, and dark tangles of hair framed his face like a forest hound's ruff. He rode the dipping craft under his feet with the same sort of balance Brantley used when riding a stenella. The man drew an arrow from behind his back and readied it. "We've come to reclaim our goods. Return the gems and we'll leave."

Behind me, Mander laughed. "You'll have to kill her first. And all the rest of us."

The lethal tips of several arrows aimed my direction. My pulse leapt in my neck, and my throat tightened so much I couldn't breathe. These men were like greedy children snatching playthings from each other. But this game could end my child's life. For a pregnant moment the wind held its breath. The sea leaned in to hear the outcome of this confrontation. The muscles of every warrior—on our veskal and theirs—stretched as taut as their bowstrings. The men were as eager to bring destruction as those sharpened arrows.

The enemy commander lowered his weapon. "Tack to the leeward," he ordered his men. The universe exhaled. He glowered at Mander. "You can't hide behind a baby forever. We'll return. Count on it."

The enemy leader's determined jawline reminded me of Brantley when he'd faced down the Order. I hoped he could read the gratitude in my eyes across the distance between us. Backing down had cost him status, but it had saved my life.

The man's sharp whistle rent the air, and the three other veskals with blue and green sails followed their commander in a zigzagging path away from Mander's island. He waited until they rounded the coastline and were completely out of sight. Then he rubbed his hands, clearly proud of the encounter. "Well, you've had some worth already. Tell me. Was it his foeland that set the fire?"

I shook my head. "How would I know? I keep telling you I don't know any of these islands. Just take me back to Meriel." I had to ask again, even though I knew my request was futile.

Instead of a sharp refusal, a slow grin pulled Mander's lips into a greedy line. "Perhaps you're right. When we're ready to raid the newland, I'll bring you along. It worked today. If you're truly from the newland, tell me. Will they honor a victory child? Or will they kill you and resist us?"

Nausea curdled the gruel I'd eaten for breakfast. "You can't use me to attack my world." I was proud of how steady my voice and stance remained, even as the waves rocked us on our journey back to the dock. His other, smaller crafts fell in behind, adjusting their sails.

Mander scoffed. He faced into the wind, his long hair pulling free from its binding. His chest filled with the sweet sea air. The white curls of the waves seemed to bow to him. This man was dangerous. He could conquer whole villages with his soldiers and their arrows. He could reach all the rim villages easily with his sails. If he discovered the river toward Middlemost, he could attack the very core of our world. My heart pounded so hard, the sound filled my ears.

Somehow, I had to warn my people.

Eyeing the sea again, I measured the distance to Meriel's shore. I couldn't swim that far and certainly not fast enough to escape pursuit from these crafts.

The next opportunity I had, I'd need to slip away, take a veskal, and use it to reach the nearest rim village. With that new plan—one reckless enough to impress even Brantley—I studied the actions of the men. Mander's craft was large and several men moved smoothly from ropes to other tasks, all too complex for me to manage alone. Some of the other dugout rafts were smaller, but even if I could find my way to one under cover of darkness, I'd have to pray the waves would carry me toward Meriel and not out into the expanse of endless ocean.

We reached the dock, and I was hefted ashore like a bag of supplies. Mander clamped a hand on a soldier's shoulder. "See to the other raid."

I limped away from the dock, trying to distance myself from the commander, who continued issuing orders to his men. His long strides caught up to me before I'd even reached the storehouse.

"So eager to return to my home?" He smirked and offered his arm in mock politeness.

My fingers itched to grab the knife still tucked in my belt and take a stand here and now. But even if I wounded Mander, dozens of soldiers stood between me and escape. Instead I stepped away and glared at him. "How dare you use my baby as a shield?"

He laughed. "I knew he'd never continue the attack if it meant killing a baby. They're too valuable. Especially a victory child."

People kept using that term, but I refused to give him the satisfaction of asking what a victory child meant.

I'd seen so few children in Mander's village. If babies were rare, that offered me some protection. Unless it also meant other foelands would seek to steal me. If I didn't escape, I might face an endless game of capture the banner with myself as the emblem.

A woman in a long brown tunic emerged from the storehouse with a crate in her arms. "Commander, these lenka are overripe."

He shrugged. "Toss them in the sea."

I stared, dumbfounded. "You hoard supplies only to let them rot?" Mander had boasted that his island had plenty of food. His soldiers looked bulky and sturdy as tree trunks. The servants were weary but not malnourished. "Why take things when you have more than enough?"

He growled. "We want. We take. Others take from us." His lips bent in a grim parody of a grin. "Or try. They rarely succeed."

"Is this a daily occurrence? These raids and battles?"

"Daily? No. Although recently it feels that way." A tinge of weariness colored his words. "We want. We take." He rolled his shoulders as if throwing off weight.

A light shove propelled me forward a few stumbling steps. Each one drew me further from comforting glimpses of Meriel. Further from rescue. Further from hope.

"You know the way. Stop stalling." Mander gave me another shove, then slid the longknife from my belt. "And stop stealing my weapons."

The tang of citrus sea air soured in my throat. Would he see the knife as evidence that I was plotting escape and carry out his threat to hobble my other leg? Blood left my face, and my fingers went cold. I cast a sideways glance to gauge his expression.

He winked at me. "Fair theft." His gaze narrowed toward his bow that was serving as my walking stick. "I'll have one of the men carve you a crutch. You'll warp my second-best bow if you keep leaning on it like that."

I took a shaky breath and walked the rest of the way to his home in silence. His amiable mood was far better than his rage. But I couldn't let down my guard. What awaited me when we reached his home?

When we entered his house, a new gleam lit his eyes, and he pulled me toward his bedroom. I was bereft of knives, and my weapon of words had so far failed me.

"Wait." I leaned hard away from his pull and dug in my heels.

His eyebrow lifted.

"If you promise not to touch me, I have something of great worth to barter."

He sneered. "I already have your child. Or will soon enough."

I shook my head, fighting to hide my desperation. "Something else. I've told you I'm a dancer."

His sneer stretched and his teeth flashed. "You want to dance for me?"

I clenched my jaw. "No. On Meriel, our dances help to shape our world. We steer the direction, we adjust the wind and rain, we dance growth to crops and healing to the land."

He glanced around, suddenly wary of being overheard, and pulled me all the way into his room, slamming the door. My heart banged against my ribs, but he didn't push me toward the bed. "Explain," he ordered.

Leaning weight on my good leg, I stood like a novitiate about to recite answers to a difficult test, praying I wouldn't make a misstep with my words. What would get through to him? "It will be easier if I show you."

He smirked and sat on the edge of the bed. "So dance."

I swallowed, needing him to believe my next words. "We dance with our bare feet touching the earth."

He rubbed the back of his neck, watching me speculatively. Then he surged to his feet and grabbed me. His hands ran over my tunic, down my legs. I tried to scream but only managed a squeak.

He released me. "No more hidden weapons. All right. Outside."

With shaky breaths, I allowed him to prod me down the hall and out the back door. The guards on patrol straightened when they saw him, waiting for an order, but he only led me past them and into the woods. A game trail wound toward a small cove. I scanned the area for inspiration. There. A berry bush bobbed its head, wilted and thirsty. The stems of unripe fruit gripped their branches.

"I need space."

His eyes narrowed, but he backed away a few paces. I slipped off my shoes, nestling my feet into the dirt and leaves. The voice of the island approached, but I blocked it from my mind. I couldn't risk being overcome by its call—whatever that might be. After closing my eyes and focusing, the rhythm for rain pattern clattered in my head as if a saltar's sticks were keeping tempo. Awkward at first, keeping weight from my bad leg as much as possible, but then with growing confidence, I invited rain. My strong foot carried me, my foot lifting and lowering sharply. My fingers stretched in small exploding gestures. I was concentrating so hard on the pattern, I barely noticed the breeze pick up. When I opened my face to the sky, clouds had formed. They burst open and rain sprinkled down. As the earth turned to mud under my feet, I transitioned into the fruiting pattern. The movements felt especially satisfying as I performed them with my baby inside. My arms opened outward, my turns welcomed growth. The bush perked up, and each bud of fruit grew and ripened.

I thanked the Maker for the gift of dance, for the rain, for the blessing of fruit. I finished the basic pattern. No need for more variations on the steps. Unless Mander dismissed the rain as coincidence and failed to notice the berries' growth, I'd fulfilled my intent here.

I plucked a few berries and carried them to him.

Water matted his hair and ran down his face, dripping off his lashes and his wide eyes. He didn't even move to brush the rain away. The sight of his stunned expression told me I would yet see this arrogant commander bow before the Maker.

"What else can you do?" The words crept out, tight and restrained.

"I'll be happy to talk to you about it, if . . ." Now was my chance to bargain. I wanted to demand my release, but I knew that wasn't a deal he'd consider. While I'd caught his attention, I could at least protect my baby and myself. "I'll tell you more if you promise to never touch me."

He waved that away as unimportant, tossing the hard-won berries to the ground. "I have my pick of women. But this . . ."

Relief surged through my lungs. If I could trust his word—still not a certainty—he wouldn't assault me. I was safe. Still a prisoner, but safe. My baby was safe.

But then the gleam of avarice settled over his face as if finding its familiar home. "Can you destroy enemies? Can you craft weapons? Can you cause the stones to produce gems?"

I stared at him in dawning horror. What had I done? The patterns were meant to serve. They were a gift from the Maker's hand. Mander had no understanding of that. I shook my head, mute and dismayed. My muscles trembled from the effort I'd expended, and my soul ached.

Mander looked at the sky, where the last wisps of rain clouds scattered. "Do you realize what this means? You control even the weather!"

He took my arm, although his grip was less bruising than earlier. I'd become a more valuable prize now. I carried my shoes, not wanting to slip them on over my muddy feet. With each step I felt the growing hum of the world, its need, its plea.

If I listened, I'd soon be as mad as Dancer Subsun. I halted and tugged on my shoes.

Mander waited, watching me with narrowed eyes. Then he guided me back to his compound. "You will teach my people how to do this. None of the foelands will stand against us now."

I groaned. "You don't understand. The patterns take years of training."

"Not a problem." He grinned. "You'll have the rest of your life to teach them."

15

SHAME BATTERED ME. CONSUMED WITH MY OWN SAFETY, I'D
handed the Maker's power to a monster. I'd failed Him. Moment by
moment since my capture, I'd sought to protect my baby and the people I
loved. At every turn, the dangers grew more tangled. A maze in which I
couldn't find a clear path.

As we reached Mander's clearing, a small whimper escaped my throat.
Mander frowned. "Your wound must cause pain after you dance." He
shouted for his servants and ordered them to care for me, to provide me
with their best herbs and poultices and a hot meal.

My ankle was indeed throbbing, but the true wound was in my soul.
Servant Thirty settled me on a chair in the kitchen and rubbed a potion
into my leg with a skill that nearly matched Ginerva's.

A phrase pulsed through my mind like the center-ground drums. *What
have I done? What have I done? What have I done?*

I slumped under the weight of my choices and their consequences. "I'm
sorry," I whispered, trying to remember the tender arms of the Maker
cradling me in times of pain, or dancing me into the sky with visions of
hope and promise. Those memories felt like a distant sunbeam that I
couldn't quite touch.

Mander returned. The servants all tightened like a sharp inhale, poised
and fearful. He ignored them as if they were no more than plates and
spoons and handed me a staff. He'd wasted no time in finding me a new
walking stick.

I nodded a weary thanks.

He stared at me. "Do these dances sap your strength? You were weak
before. Now you look frail."

Frail? I wanted to harangue him with a description of just how much strength it took to be a dancer of the Order. Instead I nodded. "Dancers need days to recover after they complete a pattern." A small exaggeration. Dancing required massive energy and focus. But if needed, I could perform patterns for hours. However, if he worried that I'd collapse, perhaps he wouldn't push me to perform patterns to aid his conquests . . . at least for a few days. And surely by then Brantley would have found me among the maze of new islands.

"Make sure she rests," he ordered before striding from the room again.

The boy tending the fire, Servant Thirty, and the woman near the pile of persea peelings all released a breath, as if his absence allowed their lungs to function again. Their faces resumed their usual expression of resignation and hopelessness. A seed broke open in my heart. A germ of a wish. I didn't want to merely escape. I wanted to free all these slaves from Mander's tyranny.

"You heard the commander." Thirty stood and rubbed liniment from her hands with the edge of her apron. "Use the free pallet. Go rest."

I didn't need to be told twice.

The sleeping room was empty with all the servants busy at their tasks. My body welcomed the chance to lie down, but even more, my soul welcomed this moment of privacy. I curled on my side.

"Maker, dare I ask You?" I whispered into the waiting silence. "I feel I've made so many mistakes, but would You please help Servant Thirty, and her son, and the other slaves?"

And more. The inaudible words were rimmed with joy and swollen with love. I caught a glimpse of the Maker's heart. Of purposes bigger than I could ever dream. Images that made no sense flickered in my mind, but they didn't rest long enough for me to understand them.

I closed my eyes and prayed silently. *If You can use me to help these islands, I am willing.*

Not an easy prayer, since I had no idea what that might require. And who was I to think I'd be of use to the Maker? I reminded Him of my mistakes, my fears, all my past choices.

He didn't declare that every choice I'd ever made was righteous and wise. I knew better. He didn't argue each point of my self-doubt and order me to stop questioning my past decisions. That would have led to endless introspection.

Instead, He reminded me that He was big. I was small. I didn't need all the answers. He had a plan so huge in hope and mercy and wonder for the people here, I would be content to play whatever small role He asked of me.

I drew peace from His presence, but couldn't fully release my worries. I seemed so prone to missteps, it was possible I'd fail in my part, no matter how small. I tried to push away my doubts, but they pounded like the center-ground drums.

A CLATTER OF WEAPONS, HEAVY FEET, GASPS OF PAIN, AND sharp voices pulled me from my nap. The boy popped his head into the room. "The commander wants you."

Of course he did. So much for his order that I rest. I pushed down my irritation, grabbed my staff, and limped to the doorway of the front room.

A crowd filled the room. Soldiers growling orders to captives. Bruised and bloodied men and women tied with ropes or bound with shackles. When he noticed me on the threshold, Mander beamed from his oversized chair. "My raiders have captured more servants from Ecco Cove. You will begin teaching them your patterns tomorrow."

My eyes widened with horror. "You stole them from their homes?"

"Of course. We've planned to attack their foeland for months, and the wind was favorable today. If any of them gives you trouble, tell one of my men."

Bonty was among the raiders. She pushed past a few of the others and took the floor in front of Mander. "You said we could each keep a slave. My roof needs repair, and I haven't had a decent cook since the last time we were raided."

Instead of standing to confront her, Mander slouched back farther in his chair. His fist tapped the armrest, the only sign of his anger. His face was dangerously flat, like the sea before a huge storm. "Do you challenge me?"

She paled and dipped her chin. "Of course not, Commander."

"We'll soon be raiding the newland, and there will be ample slaves for you all. But this sorry lot"—his smile was potent with evil plans—"are needed by her."

All eyes turned toward me, and I wanted to sink into the floor. Fear and anger etched into the faces of the captives. And something more: blame.

I shook my head, but Mander's glare froze any refusal in my throat. He stretched and stood. "Night approaches. House the captives in the second storeroom and you"—he pointed at me—"begin your training of them tomorrow."

Questioning eyes and threatening glares assaulted me as the men and women shuffled from the building. "Let me speak with them," I blurted to Mander.

He lifted one skeptical eyebrow but waited for an explanation.

"Only a few have the calling and skills to become dancers. If I talk with them, I can find out who to work with."

His eyes darkened. "I want you to train them all."

"That won't work." None of this would work. I'd taught Orianna a few simple patterns, but she had a rare gift. Dancers of the Order trained for a lifetime. And even if I could transform reluctant captors into dancers, I'd never teach them patterns that could be used to harm others. But I'd let Mander believe I was his secret weapon as long as possible.

He flashed his teeth, reminding me again of a forest hound. "You are a demanding servant, aren't you? Very well. Take a guard to protect you."

I nodded and followed everyone outside. One of the soldiers hovered as close as the shadows being cast by the setting subsun. I tilted my head toward him as we walked. "Do your islands raid each other at night?"

For a moment I thought he wouldn't answer. His expression struggled as he tried to discern my status—slave or prize? Worthy of response? Finally he kicked at an unsuspecting twig. "We raid when Mander tells us to. We defend when a foeland attacks."

I stopped and looked him in the eyes. "Sounds like a hard way to live."

A wistful longing washed across his face for a heartbeat. Then he blinked it away. "Did you want to talk with the captives or not?"

"I do." I resumed walking, wishing I could kindle more than brief flickers of connection with these people. Maybe I'd have more success with the men and women from Ecco Cove.

That hope sank when the guard opened the door of the crowded storeroom. "There you go," he said in a tone that showed the folly of my task.

Hostile faces turned toward me from the people huddled on the floor, crowded along the wall, blotting away blood from their injuries, and murmuring darkly among themselves.

Earning the trust of Mander's slaves or raiders was one thing. Convincing these people to hear me was even more impossible. I couldn't tell them I was on their side. Not while the guard hung behind my shoulder ready to report my words to Mander. I swallowed and took a steadying breath. "I'm Carya of Meriel. That's the large island that has moved near to all of yours. Can you tell me your names?"

Stony silence was my only answer. A wince drew my attention to the side of the room. A man was tying a strip of fabric around a woman's arm to brace it against her body. His efforts were awkward, since his wrists were bound with rope. Even in the dark room, purple swelling was evident all along her forearm. I remembered Brantley's advice when we'd first explored the green village on the forsaken island. Look for a stray to leave the herd. Perhaps focusing on one person would be more effective.

I stepped closer, and the woman's eyes widened. I crouched beside her, hoping she could sense my compassion. "You need care. Let me take you back to Mander's house."

"No!" both the man and woman gasped.

"No," my guard barked.

I lightly touched the woman's shoulder. "I won't hurt you." Then I spoke to the man beside her. "I promise you."

His teeth ground together as he directed all his rage toward me. "Your time will come."

The guard stepped past me and backhanded the man across the face, knocking him away from the woman.

"Stop!" I stood to block the soldier, but it was too late. He yanked the woman to her feet, eliciting a yelp of pain.

I offered a supportive arm, but she flinched away. All I wanted to do was talk to her, to help her situation. How had I become the enemy? "Remove her shackles," I ordered. The guard hesitated but finally unchained her ankles.

Silent promises of vengeance glared at me from all the prisoners and rode my heels as we left the storeroom. I couldn't worry about that now. I needed to focus on this one injured woman and her story.

When we reached the house, the guard took up his post at the threshold and left me to lead the woman inside. The front room was empty. In the kitchen, Thirty was cleaning up the remnants of supper. "Where is he?" I whispered.

"Retired for the night."

I blew out a relieved breath, guided the captive woman to the kitchen table, and asked Thirty for help. The servant's bowed head and defeated attitude made her less threatening to the injured woman, and some of the tension left her shoulders. After her arm was treated and wrapped, with a sling to keep it from moving, I poured her a mug of tsalla and settled across from her. Thirty left us, presumably joining the other servants in the sleeping quarters.

"I'm from Windswell. That's a village on the island these people call the newland."

I waited, but she didn't respond, only stared resolutely at a knot in the wood of the table.

I tried again. "The commander's men captured me, too." I nudged the cup closer to her, so the steam rose invitingly.

She licked her lips, watching the tsalla cool.

"Could you at least tell me your name?" I asked.

Her gaze met mine, amber eyes flickering with reflections of torchlight. She drew herself up as if summoning the dregs of her courage and defiance. "Teva of Ecco Cove."

"Thank you." My gratitude blew out on a breath. "I wish we were meeting under better circumstances."

Her eyes narrowed, then her gaze slid to my bandaged ankle. "You're truly a captive? Did he do that to you?"

I was tempted to lie to gain her sympathy but shook my head. "It's an older injury. But yes, I'm a captive here too. Until I find a way to escape."

She drew back and glanced around. "Are you bold or foolish to speak such words?"

I pressed my lips together, then sighed. Brantley would never blurt out dangerous plans. "Only inexperienced," I finally answered.

She rolled her eyes. "So what help are you? Can you provide me with weapons?"

Now I glanced around as if the walls were leaning in to eavesdrop. "I . . . I don't think so. I'm trying to gain his trust."

She stood, her chair scraping against the wood floor. "Fair luck with that. I'll take my chances with my people. Take me back to the storeroom."

I leaned forward. "I could. Or you could stay here, where you can learn more of Mander's plans and perhaps help your people."

She lowered herself slowly onto the chair. "I won't let him use me."

I nodded. "I've made a bargain with him. I can protect you. He won't touch anyone learning the patterns." Was I being overconfident? Could I truly keep her out of Mander's grasp?

One skeptical brow angled upward. "Patterns?"

I nudged the mug of tsalla toward her and poured myself another. "On my world, dancers can use patterns of steps to help our world." While she sipped her drink, I quickly told her about Meriel and the Order. Then I shared what I'd learned about the origins of our world and the heart of the Maker. Passion fueled my words.

She listened. Listened with her whole being. Her lids were hooded, and I couldn't judge her response, but she was weighing everything I said. Weighing me.

"Well?" I said at last. "Will you let me teach you patterns?"

Before she could answer, a door creaked. A woman in a torn tunic and bare feet padded past us from Mander's room and disappeared down the back hallway to the servants' quarters. I shuddered, and Teva blanched at the reminder of our constant danger.

"You spin quite the tale." She leaned forward, her whisper barely audible. "I'll stay. But when we make our move, don't expect us to take you along."

My eyes widened. Here was a complication I hadn't planned on. I should have anticipated that her people would plan a counterattack or an escape. Where would I end up in this cycle of raids and prisoners? And why hadn't Brantley found me yet?

"I expect nothing from you. Escape when you can." I turned the base of my mug in circles on the table. "Before you were captured, did you by any chance meet anyone else from the newland? Maybe a man with blond wavy hair and a brash manner?"

Her lips quirked. "Someone important to you?"

My eyes stung. "My husband. I'd thought he'd find me before now."

Compassion softened her features. "The islands are many. The dangers are many. If he's a worthy man, he'll keep searching."

"He's beyond worthy." Much more worthy than I would ever be. My heart constricted, wondering where Brantley was right now. Riding the seas as the waves darkened into the night? Scouting a distant island, barely avoiding raiders with their lethal arrows? Or back in Windswell, gathering a force to protect his people?

I showed Teva to a pallet where she could sleep, moving silently so as not to disturb the other servants. As I felt my way to my own space in the dark room, I prayed I'd wake in my own lovely cottage and laugh about this strange nightmare.

"WHY DID YOU CHOOSE AN INJURED CAPTIVE?" MANDER
towered over me like the pines on the clearing's edge as I blocked him
from Teva.

As soon as the morning dawned, I had honored my bargain and begun
teaching basic positions to Teva as if she were in the first form at the
Order. When Mander came out to the yard behind his house to see what
I was doing, his face turned the red shade of a rutish tuber, and veins in
his neck pulsed.

Praying for calm, I tucked my trembling hands into my sleeves and
lifted my chin. "She showed the most potential."

"And this?" He waved his hands in a mocking approximation of the arm
motions I'd been demonstrating. "That will conjure us treasure? Power?"

I bit back my sigh. "Dancers don't conjure. We receive the Maker's gift
and pass it along to the land to encourage health and growth and good
weather. And"—I squared my shoulders—"it takes years of study. We've
only begun."

Mander's hand found my throat, squeezing enough to remind me that
an ounce more pressure and my neck would snap. "I won't wait for years.
And why did you only pick one? I need dozens of dancers."

"I understand." My voice rasped. "But I need to evaluate each one so
I don't waste your time on training the wrong people."

He released me with a shove that made me teeter. Teva's hands against
my back steadied me.

The commander's impatience wasn't soothed. "Show me again. Show
me what you can do. Stir a wind from that direction." He thrust a hand
past his home toward the shore.

Teva drew in a sharp breath. She still believed my talk of the dance was a ruse. From Mander's narrowed gaze, he was losing trust in me too. Once again I would need to desecrate the dance to prove its worth.

Forgive me, Maker.

I hated this. Hated taking this precious gift and allowing Mander to conceive of it as his future weapon. Hated abusing something holy and powerful, something to which I'd committed my entire life. But I had a higher loyalty now. My life was no longer committed solely to the rules of the dancers. My life was committed to serving the Maker. Sometimes those merged, but I'd seen that some dancer taboos had to be set aside to put Him first. If giving Mander another glimpse of what the dance could do would serve the Maker's ultimate purpose, I wouldn't refuse. But was this truly the Maker's purpose, or my own?

I handed my staff to Teva. "Give me room, please."

She glanced at the unmoving tree boughs surrounding the clearing and lifted her face to the motionless air. With a sigh, she stepped back, cradling her bruised arm.

I closed my eyes to remember the rhythm used to stir wind. When I heard the drums' pattern in my mind, I took the starting position—a lunge to the right side, arms reaching forward with palms raised. The imagined beats pulsed through me, and my bare feet embraced the dirt. I was grateful that this unfamiliar land didn't resist my connection.

Smoothly, gently, I shifted to a lunge the other direction. Next came a wide pattern of turns that moved inward in concentric circles. *This would be so much easier in the Order's center ground with a whole team of dancers. Or even if I could dance without limping and hobbling.* I drew on my training to shut out every intruding thought and celebrated the freedom of the ocean breeze, the growing swirl of temperatures that met and moved and pushed the air, just as my arms did.

I finished the introduction and prepared for the first variation, but Teva's gasp and Mander's chuckle pulled me out of the work.

Overhead, pine branches whispered. Even down here in the clearing, the sweet scent of the ocean wafted across our skin.

Breathing hard, I straightened from my last pose. "Enough?"

Mander flicked a hand toward us. "Good. Now teach her how to do that." And he strode away to inflict misery somewhere else.

I collapsed to the ground, rubbing my bandaged ankle and waiting for my lungs to recover.

"You weren't lying." Teva settled across from me. Her once skeptical and hooded eyes had opened with wonder. "And thank you."

"For?"

"For shielding me when he came out here. Did you think I didn't notice that you stepped in front of me?"

I lifted a weary shoulder in a lopsided shrug. "He's . . . unpredictable. And I told you I would protect you."

She tilted her head. "I know. But that didn't mean you would." She glanced back toward the commander's house and a watching guard by the back door. "Can you teach me that one?"

"We'll begin with fern pattern. I suppose we better get to work in case the commander returns."

Teva stood and helped me to my feet. "No worries there. He won't be back for a while."

I lifted my bad leg and rolled the ankle a few times. "Why do you say that?"

"Now that you've stirred up the wind, it's favorable for his ships. He'll be out raiding with his men." She gave me a sly smile. "Maybe even your big island."

I gasped. *No, no, no! Carya, you're a naive idiot, and every time you think you're helping you cause more trouble for the people you care about.* "I didn't know . . . didn't think." I cast my gaze upward at the rustling trees. "I have to stop him."

Drained, bloodless, somehow I coaxed my muscles to move again. Teva backed away, studying me through narrowed eyes. *Maker, help me fix this.* I danced a new pattern to quiet the breeze. If the earth and sky were confused by this sudden reversal, at least they didn't resist. As gently as it arrived, the wind died down to a blessed stillness.

When I finished, I sank to the ground, drooping forward over my exhausted legs and throbbing injury. I was vaguely aware that Teva walked to a well set near the back door and drew water. She brought a cup to me and sat beside me as I sipped. Cool seawater, drawn up from the depths, comforted my raw throat.

"Thank you," I whispered.

"Is it always so exhausting?"

"The patterns require effort . . . but they are easier with a group. And for dancers who are whole." I pressed my hand against the bandage. Sure enough, the old wound had begun to seep again. Would it never improve? "And this is an unfamiliar world, so that makes it more difficult as well."

Teva offered me the cup once more, but I shook my head, so she drained it. "You're different from the other dancers."

A cold shock jarred my spine, as if she'd poured the water over my head. I twisted to face her. "Other dancers?"

She pursed her lips, clearly debating with herself about how much to say. "The day before I was captured, a band of dancers visited our island. All in white." She scanned my grubby and mottled tunic and leggings. "They promised our commander bounty and power beyond compare."

That didn't sound like any delegations Saltar Kemp would have sent . . . River! Bad enough that she was turning Meriel's villages against the Order. Apparently she was also in league with a foeland that would like nothing better than to pillage our goods and steal our people. Frustration swirled in my skull. I felt like I was fighting shadows. I'd rather have an enemy I could face down instead of someone who plotted and schemed behind the scenes where I couldn't directly confront her.

"And what did they ask in return?"

"An alliance, of course. They told our leaders of a village ripe for the raiding. Two of our ships went with them. That's why Mander's men found us unprotected." She snarled. "But he'll pay when they come to reclaim us."

I grabbed my staff and lurched to my feet. "What village?" My voice sounded shrill in my own ears. "Teva, where were they going?"

She rose slowly. "A village on the rim of the newland."

Windswell? Undertow? I had no way of knowing how much Meriel had rotated, or if it had rotated at all. Which rim villages were now closest to this cluster of islands? Did River hold so much rage about the changes to the Order that she would truly ally with Teva's clan? What did she hope to accomplish? I bit my lip. There was only one thing she wanted. A foeland army could enable her to move inland. Their veskals could provide a rapid way up the channel to Middlemost and a means to put her back in power at the Order.

I couldn't wait for rescue. I was sick of being a step behind River in every direction I turned. I had to warn my people.

"Come on," I whispered. "We're getting out of here now."

IN SPITE OF MY BOLD PROCLAMATION, I HAD NO IDEA HOW
to mount an escape.

Teva gathered her hair back in a braid as if preparing for battle. She
shot a glance toward the guard near the back door of Mander's home and
turned so he couldn't see her lips. "I won't leave without my husband."

"The man in the storeroom?"

She answered with a firm nod.

I could try to run away again on my own, but I'd seen how ineffective
that attempt had been. Teva or her husband might know how to sail a
veskal. I nodded. "All right. We'll get him out."

But how?

A seed of an idea came to me. I limped toward the house's back
entrance. The guard bristled. "Where are you going?"

"I need to speak to Mander. If he wants me to train the dancers more
quickly, I need to bring them all out here at once."

The soldier scratched the back of his head, struggling with conflicting
orders. He was supposed to assist me but also supposed to keep me out
of trouble. While he hesitated, I walked past him and into the house with
Teva following.

Thirty looked up at our sudden entrance into the kitchen where she
stirred laundry in a boiling cauldron.

"Is Mander nearby?" I asked. "I have to talk to him."

Her eyes whitened. She spent her life trying to stay out of his way. I'm
sure she thought I was mad to go looking for him. "He went to the dock."

We headed through the house and into the front room. "What are you planning?" Suspicion edged Teva's voice, and she grabbed my arm, stopping me before I opened the door.

"Will your people follow you? I think I can convince Mander to release them, but when we see our moment, we'll need them to act. They won't trust me."

A slow grin blossomed, lighting her face. "I can signal them. They may not like you, but they're smart enough to grab a chance at escape."

A fragile alliance, but the best I could hope for right now.

When we emerged from the house, two soldiers near the door whirled and frowned at us, the younger one going so far as to draw a sword. I raised my hands. "I need to speak to Mander. It's important."

The older guard eyed us. "Wait here. I'll see if he's set sail."

He strode toward the dock. Teva only had eyes for the secondary storehouse, which was also guarded. How were the captives faring in that dark and cramped space?

"He'll be all right," I said softly. I didn't dare say more with the alert young soldier standing nearby. If my plan worked, Teva's husband would soon be free.

She crossed her arms. "If he's harmed"—she made no effort to lower her voice—"we'll fill the sea with the corpses of these raiders."

The young guard clenched his sword, fingers white. He glanced around as if hordes were about to advance on the clearing.

All the bristling threats between these groups hurt my heart. I rested a hand on Teva's shoulder and turned an apologetic expression toward the guard. "I'm Carya of Meriel. What is your name?"

"Lutin." His jaw firmed, but I could see the faint boyish whiskers on his face and the youthful insecurity in his eyes.

"Well met, Lutin. Perhaps we can find ways to bring some peace to your islands."

His eyes widened. "So the rumors are true? You think you carry the bridge builder?"

"That's not—"

A bellowing voice from the trail interrupted. Mander stormed into the clearing, past his first storehouse, cast a wary gaze toward his second storehouse, then stalked directly toward me. "Your feeble breeze didn't last long enough to do us any good. So much for your bargain. What's to stop me from feeding your bones to the carrion birds?"

His anger was as forceful as a wind gust, and I swayed back. Then I drew myself up with all the calm of a saltar. "That's why I asked the soldier to find you. I've realized you were right all along." Playing to his pride would surely help win him over. "Just as you suggested, in order to help you, I'll need to train all your captives. It requires many more dancers to stir up the wind and keep it working."

Mollified, the crimson in Mander's face tempered to a dull chestnut shade. "Of course I was right. I'm the commander."

I fought to hide my true emotions and gave a respectful bow. "Please instruct your men to bring out all the captives. The clearing behind your house should give us enough room."

His eyes narrowed. "It will have to wait. When the wind died, I sent a team of rowers to Halyard's Hull. I can't spare soldiers here on Scavengewood."

I fought to keep my expression blank, thinking quickly. "Surely your men are skilled enough to watch a handful of captive servants." I elbowed Teva. "They aren't even warriors."

Teva's stance was every inch the warrior. Anyone paying attention would know to fear her. But at my nudge, she shrank into herself and stared at the ground, making a point to cradle her injured arm.

"I have little trust for you or your ways." Mander stepped so close that I smelled the fermented rutish on his breath. "But I trust you remember what will happen if you cross me."

I didn't need to feign the fear that made me gulp. He would keep me alive until my baby was born, but he'd make sure each moment until then was misery for me. If this plan didn't work, I'd have no further chances.

Lips pressed tight, I nodded. "You've seen what is possible with one dancer. Imagine what is possible with a whole band."

As I'd hoped, the gleam of greed lit his face. "I want a strong wind and no rain. Don't fail."

He ordered his men to bring out the captives. I returned to the back of the house, whispering a few more instructions to Teva. Six guards took up positions around the clearing under Mander's watchful eyes. Twenty adults and a few children shuffled uneasily into the center, still bound with ropes or shackles. "You'll have to free them," I said.

One of the guards barked a low laugh. Mander frowned at him. "Draw your weapons. You"—he pointed to the guard who had laughed—"free them all."

A few soldiers' faces showed surprise, but none dared argue. Once the people were free, I gathered them close. If I were truly going to teach them to dance with the island, I would have asked them to take off their shoes. I would have given them a history of dance. I would have instructed them about the careful placement of their feet. Instead I used a few random movements—not from any true pattern—and asked them to copy me.

Since Teva offered a subtle nod, they all agreed.

Soon the sharp attention of the guards wandered. Mander grew restless. "How long will this take?"

I exhaled a long-suffering sigh. "As I explained, I'm trying to teach techniques that can take years to learn. But have no fear. I sense they will all develop the skills quickly."

He waved a dismissive hand. "Well hurry. I have other things to take care of. I'll watch for the wind to pick up." And he strode away.

Some of the tightness left my neck and shoulders, but only a little. A lot could still go wrong. Repetitive rocking movements lulled the observers even more. Swords and bows dangled in inattentive hands.

I encouraged the captives to spread out, filling the space and getting closer to the ring of guards. Then I explained loudly that the pattern called for them to gather in tightly and back out. After repeating that invented series of movements several times, the soldiers no longer tensed each time the dancers got close to them.

Teva shot me a raised eyebrow, and I nodded. Next time everyone gathered tightly, she hissed, "Attack and head for the dock."

"Wait. First we will need a favorable wind. Keep your pattern going."

As the group shuffled out and then back into a tight clump, I stepped back and began the wind pattern. When breeze tickled my hair, I gestured everyone together one last time. "It's time."

They opened out, arms waving languidly. The strongest men each aimed toward one of the guards—most of whom were slouching and distracted.

"Now!" Teva yelled.

Chaos erupted. Everything happened so quickly, I didn't know which way to look. A man pummeled a guard's unprotected stomach and grabbed his sword when it dropped. Two women ran straight for another guard, knocking him backward, then clocking his temple with the hilt of his own knife. Grunts and clashes filled the air for only a moment. Then silence ruled.

"Let's go!" Teva's people were already racing into the woods and toward the dock. She grabbed my arm and handed me my discarded walking stick.

I limped as quickly as I could. Branches snagged my tunic and slapped my face. A trickle of blood found my tongue from a broken lip. Pain and blood were no concern. I'd soon be back on Meriel.

By the time Teva and I reached the docks, more of Mander's men lay sprawled on the ground, and her people were freeing one of the sailing veskals.

Teva's husband stepped toward his wife as we approached. "Leave her. Time to flee."

My ally shook her head. "This was her plan. Fair trade. She freed us, so we take her with us."

He scowled but helped his wife into the craft and waited for me to stumble on as best I could. The light breeze I'd raised was enough to fill the sail. I craned my neck. The rising hills of Meriel floated in the distance, and I pointed. "There. That's my world."

The man ignored me, and we veered around Scavengewood.

"Wait! That way!" I lurched to my feet, fighting for balance. I couldn't make out how much Meriel had rotated, or which rim village might be nearest. But that didn't matter. I had to get back to my world. I'd figure out how to get word to Saltar Kemp from wherever I landed.

Teva tugged me down. "As soon as Mander discovers our escape, he'll send men after us. We need reinforcements. Once we reach Ecco Cove we'll figure out what to do with you."

Frustration clawed its way up my chest. "No! Please."

She grabbed my face, speaking to me as if I were a child. "Mander sent men to Halyard's Hull, so we have to get past that island before the wind dies. Can you keep the air moving?"

I wanted to sulk. To refuse to help until they delivered me to Meriel. But I read the truth in her eyes. We were all still in danger. The crowded craft gave me no room to move, but I closed my eyes, tasting the breeze, the sweet sea spray, and the freedom of movement. *Maker, please tell the wind to carry us to safety.*

Teva released me, and I continued to pray, but this time with my eyes open. Her husband turned a wooden handle at the rear of the craft and shouted instructions to others who adjusted the sails. We appeared to veer straight out into the nothingness of the ocean, but I soon saw the reason. He guided the veskal in a wide berth around another island.

A craft with no sail was tied to a tree along the shore, and flames devoured a hut nearby. In the distance, raiders clashed. Arrows flew, men and women howled in anger or pain.

I squinted at the sail, willing it to speed us out of harm's way. If any of Mander's raiders noticed us, they were too preoccupied with fighting and lugging crates toward their veskal to react.

Once we glided past the battle, the entire company relaxed. "How far?" I pointed to the tallest island I'd seen yet floating into view. "Is that your land?"

Teva shook her head. "No. That's Rogue's Aerie."

As we drew close, I gaped at the sheer cliffs. Rock faces stretched toward the clouds, taller than the Order tower. Glass from a telescope high above caught the sun and flickered a warning: we see you. We see all who approach. Seabirds shrieked alerts, soaring along the cliff, then disappearing into nests tucked in the crevices.

"People truly live there?" I asked.

Teva frowned at me. "Of course. They dock on the opposite side. Though I wouldn't risk a quick theft on these cliffs. They keep watch in all directions to protect their treasure above."

What an exhausting way to live. Stealing, grabbing, hoarding. I stared out at the waves, hoping for a glimpse of a friendly stenella. A few seabirds glided near the shore, but there were no herders to answer that clear sign of a school of copper fish.

Where are you, Brantley?

"Faster!" Teva's husband scowled as we sailed into the tall cliffs' shadow. A few of his people adjusted sails, others ducked below the hull as if hiding their bodies would somehow make our veskal less visible to the foeland.

No other sails polluted the ocean, and we gave Rogue's Aerie a wide berth.

The subsun joined the primary sun overhead, and their heat brushed my cheeks. I rubbed away beads of sweat. A stronger wave tossed us. A child whooped, but I clutched the side. My gut roiled. When had I last eaten? I rubbed my stomach. *Little one, I'm sorry for all the turmoil. We'll find a way back to your papa soon.*

Teva shot me a sympathetic gaze. "I'll make you tsalla when we reach the Cove."

Her promise coaxed a tired smile from me. "It's been a . . . challenging few days."

Her lips quirked. "For all of us."

"Will your people help me return to Meriel?"

She shrugged. "Depends on the deal they've made with the dancers."

The nausea spun into a cold knot under my ribs. If River and her renegade dancers were still on Ecco Cove, my rescuers weren't carrying me to safety. They were delivering me into the hands of the dancers who wanted to destroy me.

18

MY DREAD DIDN'T STOP THE WIND OR WAVES. OUR VESKAL sailed inexorably toward the next island in sight. After what felt like hours of rocking and leaning into the current, I longed for the smooth sensation of riding a stenella instead. Crafts like these would be good for hauling cargo from rim village to rim village, but nothing could replace the partnership of herder and stenella.

Zigging and zagging, water splashing our faces, at last we reached land. Huddled in the bottom, I gazed at the strange shoreline. Hills of smooth rock held curved openings, like dark doorways. Pebbles covered the earth all the way from the caves to the tangleroot rim.

At the sight of our approach and the Scavengewood sail, armed men and women ran forward, arrows ready to fly. Teva waved her arms and shouted toward them. "It's us! We escaped!"

A whoop went up from the soldiers, and more villagers emerged from the caves to greet us as we glided right up against the land. Some of my fellow escapees leapt out, and jubilant chatter and relieved embraces filled the shore.

A short woman with bare, muscular arms strode forward, her feet crunching on the small stones underfoot. "How did you manage to steal their veskal? Mander isn't usually so careless." Her voice was surprisingly deep for someone barely taller than Orianna.

One of the men helped me onto the shore. Once again I was disoriented by how little the rim rocked underfoot. I stumbled a few steps forward, then found my balance. Teva walked over and stood beside me. "Carya, this is our primary, Larcy of Ecco Cove."

Larcy scanned me, and her eyebrows climbed, disappearing under matted hair. "And you captured us a victory child! Teva, you've outdone yourself."

I waited for Teva to correct the assumption that I was their captive, but she simply acknowledged the praise with a nod. My arms moved protectively over my stomach, and I frowned. *Little one, I will find a way to get you home as soon as I can.*

"I'm from Meriel, and I must return immediately."

Teva rolled her eyes. "She's one of those dancers. Like the ones making deals."

I shook my head. "No, not like them. They aren't—"

"And she helped us escape."

Finally a word in my defense. Too little, too late.

Larcy waved over one of her men. "Take her to the captives' cave."

"Wait! I'm an ally, not a captive. Teva, tell her. Please!"

Teva shot me a look of pity—not pity for my situation, but pity for my foolishness in thinking anyone here would defend me. She pivoted away from me. "Primary, have I shown you I'm ready to be a raider and not merely a servant?"

Larcy stared up at her, lips pursed. "This was a fine theft. You've returned our people, captured a veskal, and brought us a victory child. Yes. Choose arms from storage."

"Thank you, Primary." Teva raced toward one of the caves without a backward glance. So much for gratitude or loyalty. All she cared about was making a name for herself. And River had partnered with these people to attack an innocent rim village of Meriel. All this betrayal burned like bile in the back of my throat.

Larcy frowned at the guard holding my arm, as if surprised we were still there. "Captives' cave. Now." She marched along the shore with stubby strides and began inspecting this latest prize. My pleas were ignored.

As the soldier dragged me to one of the curved openings farther up the beach, I struggled to keep my footing on the loose pebbles. Darkness loomed under the heavy dome of wind-polished granite. Of all the caves that opened toward the shore, this one had the smallest opening. I shuddered at the thought of entering. Perhaps I should refuse—kick, struggle, attempt to run. But that would only risk injury to my baby. Once again, I would need to be patient and watch for an opportunity. Perhaps I'd be able to build friendships here that would prove more productive than my efforts on Scavengewood.

Two guards glared at our approach, and from one of the men, the glare was especially intimidating, coming through a swollen and blackened eye. Larcy's soldiers wore injuries to their bodies and their wounded pride, most likely from the raid that had captured Teva and the other servants. They didn't look in the mood to make friends, so I held my tongue.

My guard stopped at the shadowed opening and pointed. "Inside. Now."

I took a last deep breath of sea air before ducking to enter the dim and musty cave. Limping forward, my eyes struggled to adjust to sparse torchlight and the oppressive low ceiling. At least this cave wasn't as crowded as Mander's storeroom. To one side, an old woman knelt on a pallet, finger-weaving fibers. Her gaze flickered up, then dropped back to her work as if I were invisible.

Hoping to stay near the pale light of the entrance, I aimed for an empty pallet nearby. A man emerged from the deeper gloom. "That's mine! Get away."

"Sorry. I didn't know."

He scoffed and sprawled heavily across the ticking.

I veered around him and headed deeper into the cave. A few captives had settled in side alcoves. I counted seven men and women before I neared a niche that I hoped would be empty. Back here the air was dank, and no natural light penetrated. I angled my body so I wouldn't block the torch mounted on the wall and peered inside.

A shadowy figure slumped unmoving against the cave wall, eyes closed. The rank copper scent of blood hovered around him like a cloud. Had Larcy neglected a wounded captive to the point of death?

"Someone? Anyone?" I called toward the prisoners I'd passed. "This man needs help!"

The lifeless man's eyes flew open, vibrant blue even in the dim glow of torchlight. "Quiet," he rasped. "Don't draw attention."

I gasped. I knew those eyes. That voice. "Brantley?"

He shielded his eyes and squinted against the torch behind me. "Carya?"

I threw myself forward, hugging him. His tunic was wet with the blood I'd smelled. "You're injured. Let me help." I patted and poked him, frantically searching for his wounds.

He grabbed my hands to still them. "No. First tell me. Are you all right?" He pulled my hands toward his chest. "It's really you? This isn't another delirium?"

"I'm real." I squeezed his fingers. "And I'm fine. But where are you hurt? Let me go for help."

He grimaced. "If they think I'm too much trouble or not able to work, they'll kill me."

"At least let me tend to you."

My tug on his arm elicited a hiss of pain, but he allowed me to coax him from the alcove to where we had more light. He pointed to his side, and I gently peeled his tunic away. This time he couldn't suppress a low groan. An ugly raw gash ran across his ribs. "Sword?" I forced my tone to be matter-of-fact, as if I bandaged battle wounds daily.

His lips twitched, acknowledging my efforts to stay casual. "No, it was one of those accursed flying sticks."

"They're called arrows. Yes, it gave you a little scratch, but I'll fix it." I was already tearing a strip from the hem of my tunic. "Is there water nearby?"

"A well farther into the cave." He grabbed my arm before I could leave. "Dancer, it's good to see you."

I kissed him. "I'll be right back." As I stumbled away to find the well, I let my chest contract. The wound looked serious. Brantley's life was leaching out onto the floor of the cave. And when I'd touched his skin, it burned like the primary sun. But he was alive. He was here. I would cling to that blessing. *Thank You, Maker!*

I managed to resume a brave face before returning to him and did my best to wash and dress his wound. "How did you end up here?"

"Rescuing you," he said dryly. Then he tilted his head back against the cave wall and closed his eyes. "Haven't done a good job of it, have I?"

I hated hearing the defeat in his voice. Wiping off my hands, I forced a grin. "Guess it's my turn to rescue you this time." I wanted to burrow against his chest. I wanted to weep for joy that we were together, no matter how dire the circumstances. Our separation had wrenched at me more than I wanted to admit. I wanted to savor Brantley's arms around me, his crooked smile, his chuckle.

But our world was in danger. And judging from the fever raging through him, Brantley was in danger too. I couldn't indulge my desires to simply hold him and pretend nothing else existed.

I offered him water from a chipped clay cup I'd found near the well. "Tell me everything."

He drank, then sighed. "Maybe later." His eyes closed.

If he slid back into unconsciousness, he might never wake again. "No, I need to know. Did Orianna tell you what happened? Did you find my scarf?"

He rubbed his temples but opened his eyes. "Yes. I followed the trail to the rim, where it disappeared. I couldn't believe a herder had taken you. Some from Windswell said if your trail ended at the sea you must be . . ." His voice broke.

I pressed the mug into his hand again. "But as you can see, I'm just fine, and so is your daughter."

A hint of life lit his glazed eyes, and he touched the swell of my stomach. "I should have known. You've always been stronger than you look. And you'd do anything to protect our babe."

"It's more the babe who protected me. When they saw I was with child . . . well, it seems to have some significance to these people." I was about to tell him everything I'd learned these past few days, but his eyes closed. Like water spilling from cupped hands, the strength left him again, and his head drooped forward.

"After you lost my trail, what did you do? Brantley?" With an arm supporting his shoulders, I coaxed him to take another drink. "Tell me everything. We need to make a plan." If I kept him talking, perhaps the fever wouldn't drag him under. He coughed a few times but then began to relate his story. In his own terse way, he told me about searching the shoreline with Makah, and an encounter with raiders not far from Varney's hut. He had decided the only way to learn my fate was to search for me on the cluster of islands—a decision complicated by their veskals, bows and arrows, and constant skirmishes among each other.

"Your turn." He squirmed as if his bones ached but tugged me. "I'm fine. How did you find me?"

I filled him in on the blur of the last few days. I skimmed lightly over the danger, but even so, Brantley glowered as I described life on Scavengewood. Inwardly, I smiled. An angry Brantley was an alive Brantley. Even his posture began to revive as we talked.

"There you are!" Teva stomped toward us. A leather vest covered her servant's tunic, and a quiver of arrows rested over her shoulder.

I scowled at my erstwhile ally. "How did you get in here?"

She grinned. "I've been promoted to raider. The guards had to listen to me."

"I trusted you," I hissed, itching to slap the smirk from her face. "Instead of helping me, I'm just a prisoner again so you can, what? Gain a little status?"

"If your ally gains power, you gain power." Her tone was matter-of-fact, and she didn't seem troubled by my anger.

My fists clenched. "Then use that power. My husband is injured. He needs more help than I can give him in here."

Her eyes widened. "Your husband? Here? What do you need?"

"Broth. Herbs. Clean bandages. A needle and fine thread to stitch the gash."

She hesitated, gaze darting between Brantley and the tunnel leading toward the outside. "I'll see what I can do."

Her stride held a new confidence as she left, and I dared to hope she'd actually aid us. But when I turned back to Brantley as he slumped against the cave wall, helplessness threatened to overwhelm me.

"We have to get back to Meriel," I said, forcing a quaver from my voice. "River and her group of dancers visited here and made a bargain with the raiders of Ecco. She's gathering allies to attack the Order."

That roused him. He pushed himself more upright, but the effort made his eyes roll back, and he passed out. I eased him to the ground, pressed on the inadequate bandage at his side, wishing I knew a dance to stop the flow of blood. Instinct had once helped me create a pattern that healed Navar's spear wound, but right now I felt paralyzed, my mind blank.

A short time later, Teva returned with supplies and even held a torch so I could see what I was doing. With a supreme force of will, I forced my fingers to move. I sewed his skin as if it were a tear in a pair of leggings. I created a poultice and covered the wound and wrapped a bandage around his torso. After I sponged his forehead with water, his eyes finally opened again.

"Carya? Are we home?"

"No, my sweet. Just rest and get stronger. We'll find a way home together."

He turned to his side, braced a hand against the ground, and tried to push himself up. The attempt made him shake, and he collapsed back to the cold cave floor.

Teva sighed. "He's in a bad way. I'll have a servant continue bringing broth until Larcy decides what to do with you."

Worry curved my shoulders so much I could barely force my chin up to look at her. "Thank you."

She nodded and left.

Brantley's fingers crept toward my arm and grabbed me. "Tell me again. What is River doing? What are these islands planning?"

I explained everything again, unsure he was really following anything I said. At least my talk seemed to distract him from the pain of his wound.

When I finished my recitation, his grip on my arm tightened. "You have to escape. As soon as you see an opportunity, you must find a way to reach Meriel."

I nodded. "Yes. As soon as you're stronger, we'll find a way."

"No." His voice rasped with the effort to speak with strength. "You can't wait. Meriel is in danger. When I'm stronger I'll find a way, but someone has to warn them about River before it's too late."

My jaw gaped. "Never! I'm not going to leave you here."

With a groan, he braced on one elbow and touched my belly. "Please. Protect our baby."

Oh, that was not playing fair. I pressed my lips in a hard line.

He reached up and stroked the side of my face. "From what you've told me, they will never let you go while you carry a victory child. Or you'll be snatched by yet another clan. Meanwhile . . ."

He wheezed and clutched his side, unable to continue. But he didn't need to finish the thought. Meanwhile our whole island world was in danger.

"Promise me," he insisted. Torchlight played off the gold in his hair. Fever and desperation brightened the deep blue of his eyes. "Use your dancing, ask the Maker to show you a way. Just get back to Meriel and warn the villages and the Order."

"I can't go without you." I hated the pleading note in my voice, but leaving him in this condition would break me.

"Promise me!" He tried again to sit up.

I feared he'd reopen the gash in his side. "All right. If you promise to heal and take no needless risks."

His body softened against the rock. "My tunic pocket." He waved one hand weakly.

I reached inside and pulled out his whistle. "Do you think Makah is near? Are you going to call her?"

"No. When you get to the water's edge . . ." He panted with the effort of speaking. "No warriors in sight. Call her."

I pushed the whistle back toward him. "I don't know the calls."

He gently shaped my fingers around the holes. "Two low and three high. Try it."

Tentative and breathy, I managed a sound, but nothing like the clear signals I'd heard him use. "This won't work. Let me stay with you until you're stronger."

"You promised. First opportunity." His eyes closed.

My fist clenched around the whistle. Yes, I'd promised. Promised to once again desert the man I loved to protect our people. *Maker, help me!*

19

MY OPPORTUNITY ARRIVED MUCH SOONER THAN I'D expected.

"Where is she?" a gruff voice called from the outer cave. "The bearer of the new victory child?"

Listless voices directed a guard toward the back alcove where I huddled beside Brantley.

"Come with me." The man in a leather breastplate and gauntlets stared down at me and pointed toward the entrance.

Brantley squeezed my arm, eyes burning into my soul. "Promise me."

"Until the Maker reunites us." I wanted to scream, to shake my head, to hold him and never let go. Instead, I picked up my staff, struggled to my feet, and forced myself to leave the cave without looking back. If I saw Brantley's weak and wounded body one more time, I wouldn't be able to carry out my promise to him—the pledge to take the first opportunity to escape and warn the people of Meriel.

The pebbled beach was alive with fires, music, and excited chatter as families celebrated the return of captured kinsmen. The scent of roasting fish made me count how many meals I'd missed lately. Somehow another day had passed, and the primary sun drooped toward the horizon, followed closely by the subsun. As I walked, I again noticed the odd lack of movement underfoot, almost as if I were standing in the paved courtyard of the Order. Under the night sky, the shore seemed rimmed in a blue glow. Perhaps it was the reflection of stars on the black sea, but the eerie effect only reminded me how far I was from home.

I also noticed, as I had on Scavengewood, that there were very few children. Perhaps they were tucked away safely in their homes, or perhaps the people of these islands were no longer being blessed with babies. Was that what led to the strange fixation they had with me?

The guard led me farther inland toward a much larger arched cave opening carved into stone. Beyond it, rock-strewn hills rose, but nowhere near as tall as the cliffs of Rogue's Aerie. The gravelly ground must give way to soil, because dark forests spread across the higher land.

We entered a warren of tunnels and rooms, with brighter and more frequent torches, as well as pools of light spilling from holes that pierced the roof of stone. A group of raiders sat together whittling arrows. As we walked past, Teva separated herself from the others and jumped up. "She was my prize. I'm coming with you." In addition to her new weapons, she wore a new warm cloak, lined in fur.

My escort merely shrugged, so Teva fell in beside me. "If you offer your dancing to Ecco Cove, you'll be well treated. And don't worry, I'll be sure someone brings food and bandages to your man."

"Thanks." My voice was terse. She'd lost no time in profiting from my imprisonment. I wasn't about to trust Teva, or anyone else on this island. All I could focus on was finding a way to escape. "This cave is much deeper."

Teva tugged at her gauntlets, which were bunching around her wrists. "It's a series of caves, with tunnels that lead to other parts of our territory."

My ears perked up. "So this runs clear across the island?"

"Of course not. That side route leads to a secluded section of shore."

"What does it face?"

She shot me a sly look. "The far side of Rogue's Aerie. We always have to keep an eye on them. They took us by surprise once last season, and Larcy won't let that happen again. And there's also a good view of Halyard's Hull."

All I wanted was a view of Meriel. And an opportunity to summon Makah. As we walked deeper into the tunnel, I asked her about other side paths and where they led. Teva pointed out one route past servants' quarters that led to an area less stony and able to produce grain and tubers. A bit of farmland sounded promising. They probably didn't spare many soldiers to watch that. I paused, pretending I needed to catch my breath.

From my side where the guard couldn't see, Teva kicked my walking stick, causing me to lurch.

"Ow!" I'd already felt betrayed by her, but this petty aggression flared my anger.

She wasn't watching me. Teva glared at the guard. "This woman hasn't eaten in days."

An exaggeration, although the hollowness in my stomach agreed.

She crossed her arms. "You can't bring her to the primary when she's fainting from hunger."

The guard sneered. "She's fine. Move along or leave."

"Larcy will have you scrubbing keels the rest of your sorry life if any harm comes to the victory child." Teva stared him down with all the fury of a full-fledged raider. I clutched my belly and moaned, wavering unsteadily. I had no idea what Teva was doing, but ridding myself of a guard could only help.

"Go get her a salt cake and some broth. We can't bring her to Larcy like this."

The guard's eyebrows worked down and up again. "Then you watch her."

Now Teva stepped back. "Hey, she's not my responsibility."

I blinked a few times. What was she doing?

The guard shoved me toward her. "I don't take orders from you. But I'll find her some food if you take charge of her."

She sniffed as if offended. "Fine. And mind that the saltcakes aren't stale."

The guard glared at Teva one more time but then marched back out the way we'd come.

Before I could ask Teva what she was up to, she took my arm and tugged me down the deserted side tunnel. "You heard what I said?"

I nodded. "Past the servants' quarters to the farmland. But—"

Teva glanced at my cane. "You'll have to be quick. Now hit me."

I reared back. "What?"

"Use your staff. Hit the side of my face so it'll leave an impressive bruise."

"I can't—"

"It has to look like you overpowered me. Hurry! And take this." She yanked off her cloak and thrust it into my arms.

Slow to absorb her intent, I tilted my head. As her plan sank in, I gasped in a breath half surprise and half hope. I swung my cane and landed a timid tap on the side of Teva's head.

She made a sigh of disgust but slipped into a side alcove where she wouldn't be quickly found and feigned a fall to the ground, closing her eyes. "Speed!" she hissed.

I used my awkward hopping lope to run down the tunnel. I passed one servant, but she kept her gaze on the ground. A few side passages held living quarters with more people, but I had no idea if they would be friend or foe, so I kept running.

Friend or foe? When I reached the tunnel's exit, I slowed. Could I trust Teva? She'd worked with me to escape Mander but never intended to take me to Meriel. She'd bartered me for status. Was this all another ruse?

Citrus air swirled from the sea. Pale-rose shades dusted the sky as the subsun lowered. A grain field stretched to my right, and an orchard rose on my left. The trees offered more places to hide. I raced among them, skidding on a fallen lenka, stumbling against a trunk, but pushing forward. Deeper into the trees and closer to the shore. How much time did I have? A boulder stood guard along the rim, and I ducked behind it. From here none of Larcy's soldiers emerging from the cave's entrance would see me. At least not immediately. I pulled out the whistle and flattened onto my stomach. I managed a few notes, sending the signal into the water.

After doing my best to send the call several times, I huddled under the rock, straining my eyes for a sign of Makah. This side of Ecco Cove faced into the cluster of islands. There was no glimpse of Meriel. Even if I threw myself into the water and tried to swim, I'd only find myself on yet another of these warring lands.

I pictured the events unfolding within Larcy's domain. The guard would return and not see us. Perhaps he'd continue on, thinking Teva had taken me to Larcy's antechamber. If I was lucky, he'd be too worried about his own reputation to raise the alarm immediately. He'd begin searching for Teva. It wouldn't take him long to discover her sprawled in the shadows of the side tunnel.

Would she give them a story to steer a search in the wrong direction? Or was this all another plan? Would she lead the search and find me, cementing her status? Perhaps this was all a game to her.

I shivered and wrapped Teva's cloak around my shoulders, pulling up the hood. Night was falling, and I hoped the darkness would make it harder for Larcy's soldiers to find me, but if Makah didn't arrive soon, I'd need to find a better hiding place.

I twisted my hands, aching with indecision. Every fiber of my body wanted to go back to the captives' cave and find a way to rescue Brantley. How could I leave him here? Should I risk stepping out from the boulder and use the whistle again, or should I just wait for Makah? How long dare I wait?

Grumbling voices from the direction of the tunnel exit made the decision for me. I peered around the edge of the boulder. Torches held aloft revealed several soldiers fanning out to search. One man shouted something, and the others followed him away from me along the rim.

Heart pounding, I slipped away from the boulder and headed inland. This island wasn't as large as Mander's, but there was still plenty of forest that could provide me a hiding place. I'd worry about connecting with Makah later. Right now I only needed to avoid capture. Although my feet longed to leave the stark pebbled shore and touch daygrass and fallen leaves and warm earth, the woods unfortunately required a climb. Using my staff as leverage, I made my way up the incline that formed the roof of Larcy's enclave, and farther inland to the high forests.

A howl broke the night air, a mournful, haunting sound. I moved that direction. Forest hounds terrified most people, but I'd once danced with one. The memory of Brantley's face on that occasion almost brought a smile to my lips, until the thought of him recalled the terrible heat of his skin, the angry slash of his wound. I forced my attention back to the present.

When I no longer heard the lapping of waves, I listened for any sounds of pursuit or settlements. Reassuring silence welled up around me. So far, so good. I huddled beside a tall tree and drew my knees up. Even with the cloak pulled around me, the night breeze made me shiver.

I was cold, hungry, and alone. Brantley needed rescue. Meriel needed to be warned. How long could I evade capture?

Listen.

The Voice I'd come to love resonated through my bones.

"Yes, I'm listening."

He didn't say more. What did He mean? Wasn't I bristling with tension as I listened for pursuit? Wasn't I already listening to every stray sound in the forest?

Listen to this world.

Oh, no. The cry of Mander's island had threatened to swallow me, even as I held it at bay. When I'd listened to the deep call of Meriel, or the foreign island's mournful pleas, they had shaken me to my core. I couldn't open myself to this land's suffering.

Yet those voices, those connections had shown me things I'd needed to know. Perhaps the Maker would use the land's voice to guide me to safety. I shook my head. Even if it didn't, His plans were His own. My part was to trust Him and follow His leading.

After assuring that no soldiers were heading my direction and that the night provided the protection of darkness, I slipped off my shoes and nestled my bare feet into the broken bits of leaves and damp daygrass on the forest floor.

I rocked my weight side to side, pointing one foot, and then the other. My wound protested, but I ignored it. Bending my strong leg, I traced a circle with my free foot, scuffing along the ground. A tremble rolled through the land. I braced myself, remembering past encounters with other worlds.

Sinking. A fierce and heavy weight drove me to my knees. The island shuddered again, and I pressed my palms against the dirt to steady myself—or to reassure the world. I wasn't sure which.

Maker, lift us. Unite us.

I joined my pleas to those of the island. Images swirled through my mind. Insatiable hunger, violent hues, a grasping and tugging back and forth. And always the heaviness. Sinking, falling, dissolving into the sea. I gasped for air, as if I too were dropping into the depths of the ocean.

This world longed to escape its suffering, and its desire consumed me. I pressed my hands over my ears, trying to shut out the call. No, no, no. I couldn't answer this need. I had a baby to protect. Brantley to rescue. Meriel to warn. I tried to tell the island that I only wanted direction so I could complete my escape plan. Was it the impression of the islands sinking that made me feel that I was also sinking under the weight of responsibilities?

As I'd learned in the center ground of the Order, my will couldn't stand against the fierce need of a world. The ache poured over me, drowned me, screamed through me.

I offered the only help I could. I threw my head back, sending an urgent cry toward the star-speckled sky. "Loving Maker, save this world."

Fragile hope stirred in the depths beneath the island. A melody as pure as birdsong breathed over the forest. The soil beneath me stopped writhing. The island seemed to hold its breath. *Now?* it asked.

Soon. The Voice that called star rain to dance, that guided currents, that whispered of His love spoke that quiet word and gave me a glimpse of His purpose. The Maker's heart swelled with love and ignited my own tiny pulse with a hint of that promise. The song from the Maker built until grace rolled across this world in wave after wave.

I pushed to stand, once again caressing the earth with my feet. Fueled by love, I danced a new pattern. These were steps to reassure, lifting the soul of the island as if gathering up a child who had been flailing in deep water. Was it my imagination? It almost seemed that the mass of land underfoot rose the slightest amount. Images again played through my mind, of a wider pebbled beach, or the island growing as it was lifted from the sea.

Then, my muscles quivering from effort, my heart overwhelmed by the message I'd touched, I collapsed. My vision closed in until even the stars disappeared. Darkness shrouded me. I clutched handfuls of daygrass, letting my gasping breaths begin to slow, drawing in air rich with scents of pine needles and crushed leaves. When I was finally coherent enough to think again, I whispered. "Oh, Maker, yes. Do save these lands."

But in all the swirling visions, I hadn't discovered a way back to Meriel. "But please . . . save us, too."

ONCE AGAIN, THE NIGHT GREW QUIET, AS IF I'D IMAGINED the Voice, the dance, and the island's response. Pulling the cloak's hood further over my head, I tiptoed to the edge of the woods, and I listened for any sounds beyond waves. Had soldiers continued their search while I'd been caught up in my dance with the island? Even now they might be right beyond the trees.

Overhead, clouds moved in to cover the stars. The darkness helped hide me but also made it challenging to maneuver. When I was reasonably sure no one was approaching, I left the sheltering woods, clambered back down the rocky hill, and felt my way toward the shore. Still no sign of Makah or any other stenella.

Would Larcy's soldiers call off the search until dawn? Did I dare stay near the rim? Should I try calling Makah again, or was it too dangerous for the creature to make her way into this tangle of islands? If Brantley weren't bleeding in a prison cave, I could ask him.

Brantley. My dearest love. The proud father of the baby curled inside me. Was he fighting off the fever? Would he survive the night? My worry for him tore at me like clumsy hands shredding thin parchment. Yet this anxiety didn't serve me. And it didn't honor the Maker. So I set my jaw against the fear and tiptoed to the rim. Aiming the whistle into the water, I hoped the noise wouldn't carry through the air and alert any searchers. This time the notes sounded more like the signals I'd heard Brantley use. But just because I produced clear tones, it didn't mean I was signaling the right thing. If I had the pattern of notes wrong, I might be warning Makah to stay away instead of calling her.

I waited a few minutes and tried again. And again. If any stenella were nearby, they were probably confused by the strange repetitions. But I hoped that somehow Makah would be curious enough to respond.

Black water lapped lightly over the tangleroot and onto the stony shore. Straining my eyes to make out any ripples in the stretch of water between the islands, I shivered. The sea held too much mystery already. In the darkness, my imagination conjured all sorts of monsters that might lurk in the depths.

If by some miracle Makah came, I'd be setting out across that water. In the darkest time of night. On a barely trained stenella that I wasn't skilled to command. Alone. I didn't know whether to pray Makah would show up or pray that she wouldn't.

I shifted my position, patrolled the area, listened for approaching soldiers, and returned to the shoreline over and over, my nerves growing more and more taut. When a shape parted the water and chirped a greeting, I threw my hand over my mouth to suppress a yelp.

Then I grabbed Makah's long neck in a hug.

She stiffened, but thankfully didn't pull back and yank me into the water.

"Thank you. Oh, thank you, you dear, dear creature," I whispered.

The sinewy neck remained stiff, and she snorted a low greeting, then pushed at my chest with her muzzle.

"I know. I'm not Brantley. He's hurt. But he wants me to ride you back to Meriel."

She butted me again, forcing me back a few steps. Even in the darkness, her narrow eyes accused me.

"I don't want to leave him either." As I murmured the words to Makah, the truth of them pierced me. Yes, I'd promised Brantley I would escape when I could. I'd fulfilled that promise. But I wasn't leaving him in the prisoner's cave. A new resolve sent warmth through my chest. "Makah, we're going back for him."

Maybe she understood me, or perhaps she was merely curious at my intent, but she stayed still as I hefted myself from the tangleroot to a seated position on her back. She twisted her neck and focused on me, waiting for instructions.

Now what? I swung my fist in the air a few times, mimicking what I'd seen Brantley do. In the darkness, I could barely make out the confused tilt of her head. Makah's huge limpid eyes must have helped her see in the darkness, because she responded to my signal and swam away from shore.

By my calculations, the place where we'd made landfall in Mander's stolen veskal would be some distance along the rim. And Makah was heading the wrong direction. I clenched my legs against her sides. "No, we need to turn. We don't want to get closer to the tunnel I used to escape." I swirled my arms, but she was no longer watching.

"Makah, please. Brantley needs you." I whistled, nudged the weight of my body to the side, and waved my fist again.

She slowed and craned her head to give me what I could only assume was an irritated glare. It was too dark to be sure.

Then her whole body rippled in what felt like a full-body eye roll. But she turned. The clouds shifted, and starlight helped me keep track of the shoreline. Once we curved around more of the perimeter, torches flickered in the distance, marking the dock where I'd come ashore.

"Whoa. Stop here. We need a plan."

It might have been the unfamiliar craft tied at the dock that made Makah uneasy, or perhaps she understood me. Whatever the reason, she stopped propelling her body forward while I squinted at the rocky beach. Pale embers died in scattered campfires, but the villagers had retreated to their cavern homes for the night. No raiders guarded the dock. Perhaps Larcy had sent most of her soldiers to hunt me down. The situation was looking hopeful, until I focused on the prisoners' cave. Two guards still stood on either side of the entrance under tall torches. Both well armed. Swords glinted blood red from reflected flames, and quivers of arrows reminded me they could easily kill me from a distance. I huddled lower on Makah, even though they'd given no indication they'd spotted us.

"Now what?" I whispered to myself. Makah wriggled with a nervous chitter. One of the guards stiffened and looked our way, and I flattened myself along her back. "Shh!"

The men carried out a low conversation. Their reaction to sounds from the ocean gave me an idea. If they could be distracted, I might be able to get past them. Brantley would be furious at the risk I was taking, but I'd rather have him angry and alive than dying by inches in an enemy's cave.

With a subtle tap of my heels against her ribs, I urged Makah forward toward the dock. The guards had slouched back into silence, and I was relatively sure that our low position in the water made us nearly invisible against the black sea. The sail of the captured veskal wasn't raised, but if I freed the craft, the currents of the waves might ease it away and draw the guards' curiosity. When we reached the dock, I leaned toward the rope securing it to one of the dock's pillars. Makah graciously counterbalanced so I didn't tumble off. The knot would have been tedious to untangle, but I was able to lift the whole loop of rope off the pier and slide it silently into the water.

The craft was secured in one more spot. This might actually work. Already the front was pulling away from the dock. Again, we moved close, I leaned in and lifted the massive knot. A wave rocked the veskal, tugging it farther from the dock. Just as I freed the rope from its pillar, it pulled taut and slipped through my hands, burning my palms as it went.

The knot splashed to the sea in an explosion of sound. Makah jerked.

"Hold!" The soldiers started our direction.

I sucked in a breath, my legs reflexively squeezing.

Makah dove. Under the dock, under the veskal, back the way we'd come. My lungs burned. I held on as the ocean swallowed us whole. My arms clung to Makah's neck. My legs curled like a leech circling a reed.

An airless whimper bucked inside my chest. Too long. Too deep. Would the water hurt as it poured into my lungs? Air. Air. Where was it? Did Makah understand I needed it? Pinpoint sparkles danced across my squeezed-shut eyelids.

The pressure fell away in a rush, my ears popped, and I tasted air. I opened my eyes as I gasped in breath after breath.

Behind us, the veskal had drifted from the dock. The two guards were scrambling to reach it without success. One man unbelted his sword and began stripping off his armor, ready to swim after it.

"Call for help!" he demanded, his voice carrying through the still night air.

"We can handle this," his partner's gruff voice answered. "Unless you want Larcy to demote us to scrubbers."

Recovering silently from a near drowning is a difficult feat. My whole body convulsed with relief, but I managed to draw in enough breath to scan the shore, and silently enough to avoid drawing their notice. The prisoner cave was unguarded now. "Makah," I murmured. "I'm going for Brantley. Wait here. Stay out of sight."

I maneuvered her to the edge of the shore. She might not be fully trained to herd schools of fish, and I might only know the most basic of signals, but between us we managed basic shifts in direction, starting, and stopping. When she was right against the rim, I scrambled off. She flattened and lowered herself into near invisibility. I limped to the cave at record speed. The pain meant nothing. My awkward gait meant nothing. The fear of an arrow piercing my back meant nothing. I didn't dare glance behind at the dock to see if the soldiers would notice me. They must have been preoccupied with recovering the veskal, because no cry went up, and I made it through the entrance.

Snores and a few whimpers were the only sounds to meet me. Thankfully a few torches remained lit, so I didn't have to slow on my way through the tunnel. I gritted my teeth as the dull throb of my tendon turned to sharp fire. No time to indulge the growing ache. I ran like the final variation of wind pattern. Had the tunnel been this long before? It seemed to stretch like a piece of honey candy.

There! Brantley lay where I'd left him inside the small alcove. The water mug had been knocked over. He curled on his side, one hand out as if reaching for the elusive cup, but his eyes were closed.

I skidded to my knees and touched his face. "Brantley, we're leaving. Can you walk?"

A bleary gaze met mine, fogged with confusion. He blinked a few times, then propped on an elbow and glared. "You promised. Didn't you find any opportunity to escape?" Even hoarse and thready, his voice held the timbre of a man who braved ocean waves, fought despots, and protected his village.

I smiled. With that strength, we had a chance.

"I did escape. I am escaping. And you're coming with me. Makah is waiting, and the guards are distracted, but not for long. Hurry."

Pushing to his feet, he staggered and stifled a groan.

I pulled his arm around my shoulders and took as much of his weight as I could. His body still burned with fever, and the heat warmed me through my saturated clothes. "That's it," I whispered. "Just a little farther."

Together, we dragged his weakened body forward a few steps. Then a few more. But it was taking far too long. If the guards secured the veskal and returned to their post, we'd both be trapped in here again.

"Really? That's the best you can do? I thought herders were supposed to be tough."

A low growl answered my barb, yet Brantley surged forward, stumbling, but covering more ground.

A woman sat up on her pallet, squinting at us in the dim torchlight. "You there! What are you doing?"

I fought to answer between my panting breaths. "Getting . . . out. The guards . . . are busy."

She grabbed a bundle and a cloak and shook someone else awake. All the better. If more of the captives fled, it would add to the chaos.

Finally, the cramped arch of the entrance beckoned. Brantley leaned heavily on the rock, nearly doubled over. I nudged him onward. "Makah is waiting at the rim."

"How did you . . . ?" He shook his head as if words were too much effort.

I peered outside. The guards were still towing the veskal, one in the water, and the other tugging a rope from the dock. "Ready? This is the hard part."

"Stop yammering. Let's go."

If his irritation fueled him enough to move his legs, I welcomed it. "She's over—"

Where was Makah? The torches by the entrance created a circle of light that kept my eyes from adjusting to the dark. No time to worry now. If she hadn't waited by the rim, our escape would be over before it started. If I guided Brantley to the wrong part of the featureless beach, the guards would spot us before we mounted Makah. I infused confidence into my voice. "That way. Run!"

Running was an overly optimistic word for our loping, dragging, scuffling gait. We probably looked like a lumbering two-headed monster crossing the beach. Small stones grated underfoot.

The guard on the dock turned, a hand over his eyes. "You there! Stop!"

Summoning all my reserves, I pulled my husband the last steps toward the water. Makah's head popped up several feet away. Thankfully, she didn't have to deal with a half-conscious man or a severed tendon. She met us in a flash, and I half threw Brantley onto her back.

Sharp wind whistled past my ear, followed by a splash. My nerves jolted. An arrow. "Go!" I yelled, shoving Brantley down across Makah's back and covering him with my body.

For once Makah didn't give us attitude. Her powerful fluke churned the water, and we slid into the darkness. Occasional torches flickered from distant islands. Only more danger awaited us on those shores. "Brantley, you have to steer her toward Meriel."

Spray coated us both, and I hoped the splash of water would revive him, but his only answer was a moan. I sat up, leaving Brantley draped along Makah's spine. I raised my hand to signal but paused. Which way? Everywhere I turned, darkness shrouded the coasts of island after island. How would we find our way out of this maze and back to Meriel?

At a loss, I let Makah set her own course and turned my attention to my husband. I felt along his side, locating the bandage. It was soaked— whether with blood or seawater, I couldn't be sure.

"I missed you too, wife," his voice grumbled. "But this is hardly the time or place."

I choked out a laugh. "Can you sit up and take charge of this stenella? I don't know where we're going."

"She'll be fine. As long as it's away from that blasted cave . . ." His words trailed off with a sigh.

"Brantley?" Leaning forward, I stroked his face. The ocean spray had at least cooled his fever. The rise and fall of his chest reassured me. Sleep was probably the best thing for him until I could get us to a safe land, herbs, dry shelter.

Now that we were away, my body gave in to strange tremors. The fear and tension that had kept me focused and alert all bled away. When something warm dropped onto my hands, I realized they were my tears. With one arm around my belly, I stretched over my husband again, cradling our little family and creating a blanket with my body. Makah swam us into the darkness with a gait smoother and more mature than I'd felt her use before. "That's right, girl. Find us somewhere safe."

21

STILL ASTRIDE MAKAH AS WE SURGED THROUGH THE
night, I lifted a palmful of sweet water and guided the liquid to
Brantley's lips. "Can you drink?" His mouth didn't open much, but
his tongue moved, welcoming the moisture. "That's it. Wait. I'll get
some more."

It was a challenge to keep my balance on Makah while reaching down
to capture the top of a wave—a battle to hold every drop I could on
its journey to my husband's mouth. Still, the effort was worthwhile. He
began to revive. Until that moment, I hadn't been sure he would. When
the first blush of primary sun colored the sky, Brantley's pallid skin made
my chest contract. He looked as washed out as a copper fish belly, and
the slack lines of his face made him seem as old as Saltar Kemp. No,
older. A whisker from death's door.

Now that I could see more than dark shapes and shadows in the
distance, I was tempted to stand on Makah's back to better find out
where we were. Just then she altered course with a sudden zag to catch a
fish, nearly throwing me off. No, I wouldn't try standing.

Makah stretched her tall neck, chomping contentedly. Our mad dash
into the sea had slowed. We were following a shoreline of what I assumed
to be Meriel. The feuding islands were no longer in view.

Gaze fixed on the island, I smoothed my husband's damp hair, trying
to rouse him. "Brantley, you know the coast better than me. Can you tell
where we are? Can you signal Makah to take us to Windswell? We need
to go up the channel and warn Saltar Kemp."

But he didn't respond. If anything, his skin turned a grayer cast.

My chest contacted. "Makah, we need to go ashore. I have to get help for Brantley."

Her head swiveled, long eyelashes fluttering as she stared at me, violet eyes uncomprehending.

I pointed to the shore. "There. Go there." Was that a hint of smoke in the distance? Hope kindled in my breast, and I almost forgot my exhaustion and the cold morning air against my damp clothes. Smoke meant village cooking fires. I didn't care which village. I blew a short whistle and used the correct hand signal. When Makah angled toward the land, I could have kissed her wet hide. "Yes. That's the way. Thank you." Brantley had been right. Makah had definitely bonded with me, and I was grateful that she understood my clumsy directions.

Brantley's unconscious body shifted with each sharp turn Makah made, forcing me to hold him in place until my arms shook from the effort. After craning her neck a few times to peer at us, Makah smoothed her approach toward land. Maybe she was beginning to care about her new herder.

Leaning forward, I whispered in his ear. "We're almost there. Hold on a little longer."

He stirred. Hands pressed against the smooth hide, and with an effort that hurt to watch, he pushed upright. My arms circled him from behind and I squeezed gently. "You're going to be all right. We're almost home."

He took in his surroundings, twisted to look back at me, then gasped and grabbed his side. He frowned. "I don't ride sitting like an apprentice," he grumbled, and made scrambling movements as if trying to stand.

I pushed my hands against his shoulder. "It's an improvement from sprawling unconscious. You can show off later. For now, stay put."

He twisted again, more cautiously this time, frown deepening. "You did it again."

I leaned back from the frustration in his voice.

He glared, but a twinkle—a blessed Brantley twinkle that I'd thought I'd never witness again—flared to life in his eyes. "I was supposed to be rescuing you, not the other way around."

I grinned, wanting to tease him back. But hot tears surprised me, and my jaw trembled instead. "The Maker rescued us both." My voice broke, and I dashed away an errant tear.

Reaching an arm toward me, even in our awkward position astride Makah, he managed to cup my face in one hand and lean his forehead toward mine. "Thank you." His spine began to sag again, the effort of sitting too much for him.

I steadied him against me. "Rest now."

The only concession he would make to his injuries was to face forward again and use his arms to prop himself up in a sitting position. I wrapped him in my arms and my cloak, drawing warmth from his fevered body and hoping my touch and my love would help him heal—or at least stay conscious until we found help.

"It is Meriel, isn't it?" I asked as we neared the shore a few minutes later.

He snorted. "Do you think Makah swam us to some other huge new island? That's all we need . . ." His locked elbows gave way, and he slumped forward, passed out again. Makah twisted her head, eyes narrowed at me in accusation.

"Go faster. To shore." I waved frantically toward the plumes of smoke.

Makah bent her serpentine neck to nudge Brantley with her nose. Her chirping sounds rose like a worried question.

"He'll be all right. He has to be. Now move!"

Her spine rippled once but then she swam us directly to the tangleroot rim.

I managed to rouse Brantley enough to get him onto shore. I begged Makah to stay near but wasn't sure if she understood me or if I'd used the correct hand signal. I covered Brantley with the cloak, coaxed him to drink a few more handfuls of water, then limped along a path. It would help if I knew which village I was approaching. Not a large one, judging from the small plumes I'd spotted from the sea. Windswell would welcome us with open arms and a skilled healer. But I didn't know in which direction it lay. If we stayed on Makah, we could journey farther from aid. In spite of my travels with Brantley when we'd fled soldiers from the Order and when I'd shared the Maker's letter from town to town, most of Meriel's vast forested shoreline was still a mystery to me. Perhaps this *was* a completely different island.

A thin breeze caught my damp tunic, and I shivered, picking up my pace. Forsaking caution, I stumbled into a clearing. A tiny enclave of just a dozen homes surrounded a pavilion set up for communal cooking. Beyond the cottages, the trees thinned, and grazing land stretched up a gentle rise. Families crouched near a fire, chatting and passing saltcakes and charred fish around.

"A wraith!" One child pointed my direction, voice shrill in the morning air. Instinctively, I glanced behind me, then realized she spoke of me.

I lifted my hands. "Just a traveler, seeking help."

A wiry man stood, gesturing to the others to stay put. His long strides brought him close, where he towered over me. "Seeking help, eh? We've heard that before."

"My husband is wounded. I left him near the rim. Do you have a healer?"

A sneer twisted his face until it looked like an image formed of tree bark rather than skin. "We had a healer, until she was stolen."

"Stolen?"

His gaze took in my belly, full beneath the damp tunic. "She was with child, and the raiders took her."

I staggered back a step, leaning on a sapling for support. "That's why they took me. But I escaped."

Suspicion flared in his eyes. "Escaped? How? Our best protectors followed their trail and saw the raiders take her on a strange raft and across the sea. How did you come to be here?"

Frustration thrummed through my veins. Brantley needed help. How could I convince these people I was not another enemy?

"My husband is a herder. He came after me on his stenella. He was wounded fighting the raiders. Please. He needs care. Is there anyone who could help?"

He frowned, examining my face as if searching for any hint of duplicity.

"Look at me. I'm no raider. I grew up on Meriel my whole life. Raised by the Order. My husband is Brantley of Windswell."

The tight knots of the man's face relaxed. "Aye, heard tell of him. We're precious close to Windswell as the stenella swims."

I should have known that Brantley's name would carry more weight than any of my pleas. "Wonderful. Now will you help?"

He called over to a few other men and told them to bring a blanket. I limped back toward the sea, leading them.

"Name's Willet," the man said, his gaze tracking my limp. "You say you were raised in the Order?"

"I'm Carya of Windswell. I was a dancer until the former high saltar hobbled me." No, that wasn't quite right. *I am still a dancer.* And I didn't want his pitying stare. "Here."

Brantley still sprawled on the ground where I'd left him, gray and limp. Makah hovered close, chittering and circling. Willet's eyes widened as he watched her. Thankfully his men were quicker to grasp what the important focus should be, and gathered Brantley into the blanket to carry him, sling-like, back to their enclave.

Even that didn't rouse him. I walked beside, rubbing life into his hand. "Almost there. We'll fix that bandage and get you some broth. You'll be better in no time."

The men carrying him glanced at each other. One shook his head. Another rested a consoling hand on my shoulder.

They thought he was past hope. No! They would not treat me like a widow. "He'll be fine," I told them firmly.

Willet directed us into one of the homes. I was relieved they didn't just place Brantley in the pavilion. The home was cramped and dark, but the bedding looked clean. They lowered him, and a woman bustled in with a bucket of steaming water and a basket of supplies. She chased the men away, except for Willet.

"This is Ronlee, my wife." His voice lost all its gruffness when he said her name. He lifted the bucket from her hands, and the tender smile he gave Ronlee transformed him. That was the expression I'd often seen in Brantley's eyes when he looked at me. Oh, to see it again. Would I?

I introduced myself while peeling away the soaked and tattered bandage around Brantley's worst wound. A rank odor rose from his flesh. Not the copper tang of blood, but the sickly rot of death that even sweet seawater couldn't mask. Ronlee sucked in a breath through her teeth. "Good thing our healer was teaching me her craft. She'll soon be busy with her babe . . ." Her voice trailed off and her brow pinched. "Or planned to be."

Was it Mander's raiders who took their healer? Or another foeland? How dare they steal women from their families! "Did they take anything else?"

Willet snorted. "There was little they wanted. They asked after jewels and riches. Held me at knifepoint. We offered them tubers and dried copper fish. They took what they could carry and left."

"They didn't harm anyone?"

He shrugged. "They didn't linger. Said something about bigger targets."

A shiver jumped through me.

Ronlee noticed and thrust her chin toward her husband. "Fetch her a dry cloak. Can't you see she's had a rough journey? And open the shutters." Then she resumed her examination of Brantley.

"He's had a fever, but the seawater has cooled him," I offered.

Ronlee felt his skin and frowned. "Ocean water often helps, but see here?" She pointed to the edges of the wound in his side, swollen and inflamed. "It's infection. The fever was helping him fight it, but now it's given up."

I swallowed. "But we aren't giving up."

Her muddy green eyes met mine. "Of course not, child. But we'll need to cut away some of the infection, then pack the wound. It needs lanthrus, but we have none in our village." She faced me frankly. "Do you know an experienced healer? If I can get him stable, you should take him there."

Ginerva would know what to do. And the Order had every herb and plant known on our world. "Will it be safe to move him?"

"It wouldn't be safe not to."

Brantley's lids opened, clouds across the usual vibrant azure of his eyes. "Dozed off," he murmured.

I rested my hand on his forehead. "Yes, dear heart. You can keep dozing while we tend this little cut."

The cottage held no hearth, so after Ronlee washed off a sharp kitchen knife, she sent Willet to hold it in the flames of their village fire. When he returned, she wasted no time. "Hold him," she told us. I leaned my weight onto Brantley's shoulders, though if he began to thrash, I wasn't sure how much good I'd be. Willet held his legs to keep him from turning. Ronlee quickly sliced away the putrefied tissue. The scent of burning skin brought gorge to my throat, but I clenched my jaw.

Brantley stiffened and gasped. His eyes flew wide, then rolled back, and he passed out again. My ankle tendon throbbed in empathy. He remained unconscious while Ronlee finished her work and packed the wound. I was grateful he didn't stir, then terrified that he didn't stir. He was so far gone.

Ronlee wiped her hands and shook her head. "He can't ride a stenella in this state."

"But I have to get him to Middlemost. To the Order. They have the best healers, all the herbs."

Ronlee took her husband's arm. "What can we do?" she asked him quietly.

"Aye, it's a puzzle. Say . . ." The lines on his face lifted. "Remember Jocko?"

"Of course. The saddle."

Willet raced out on long legs.

"Saddle?" I gathered up the strewn bandages. "A pony would take too long, and it's a rougher ride."

Ronlee turned her compassionate smile toward me. "A few years back, we had a lad with a wasting disease who always dreamed of stenella. A herder from Whitecap offered to give him a ride, but his legs couldn't grip the sides. Willet built a tall-backed saddle with straps to hold him in place."

My eyebrows climbed. "Our stenella is barely trained. I don't think she'll take kindly to a saddle."

Ronlee sighed. "You have to try. What choice do you have? I suppose we could try building a raft and constructing a harness to tow him."

"You're not towing me like a load of tubers." Brantley managed only enough force in his voice to sound grumpy.

I spun. "You're awake." Kneeling beside him, I plastered kisses all over his face.

His eyes crossed as he tried to focus on my face. "Did I sleep too late? Cole will tell father. The best fishing will be over. Need to call Navar . . ."

Regret choked me all over again. Would he ever heal from the loss of Navar? And Cole—the brother killed by soldiers of the Order. I'd served that same Order most of my life. So much pain in my husband's life was linked to me. Had the past year really atoned for all the damage caused? I rested my cheek against his forehead. "He's hot again. Is that a good sign or bad?"

Ronlee rubbed her temples. "He needs help fast. How long will it take you to get to Middlemost?"

"How close is Windswell?"

"Not far. Perhaps a half-day's journey on stenella if the seas are good."

Brantley stirred again, muttering fragments of nonsense, eyes closed.

"Then nearly a full day to get to Middlemost. But as you said, what choice do we have?"

When Willet returned, the men carried Brantley to the shore. With a great deal of coaxing on my part, Makah finally allowed the saddle. My husband was the biggest obstacle, raving about how no self-respecting herder would use a saddle, until his head lolled forward, and we strapped him in place.

"One more thing," I said after thanking Willet and Ronlee. "There is a former dancer named River who is building an alliance with one of the enemy islands. She can't be trusted. Warn your people—and any nearby villages you can."

They pointed me in the right direction, and Ronlee pressed a few saltcakes into my hands. "Keep up your strength," she ordered.

After one more worried look at Brantley's pale, sweat-beaded face, I settled in front of him and signaled Makah. A half-day's journey to Windswell. Then several more hours up the channel to the Order. And that's if the weather stayed calm, Makah stayed on course, and no raiders appeared on the horizon.

"All right, girl. Swim for all you're worth."

22

"A DEEP WOUND, AND LEFT UNTREATED TOO LONG."
Ginerva straightened from Brantley and wrapped her plump arms
around me. "You got him here in time. He's strong. He'll make it. But
you . . ." She touched my stomach reverently. "You need to keep your
strength up for your babe."

She was right. The room was tilting. For the sake of my child, I needed
sleep. But how could I close my eyes? How could I stop watching each of
Brantley's labored breaths?

The frantic day's travel had brought us to help long after the subsun
set. A few times, I'd spotted sails in the distance. Huddled low on Makah,
urging her to keep her head down, I wasn't sure if she or Brantley was
more irritated with the journey. Soothing them both, while also coaxing
more speed from the stenella had been exhausting. I hadn't even dared
stop in Windswell. Brantley's shallow breathing had rattled in his chest.
His skin was clammy. My heels had rubbed raw from pressing them into
the stenella's sides, hastening her up the channel.

The wall torch sputtered, then resumed its feeble glow in the stark
dancer's quarters. I kissed my husband one more time before turning
back to my former attendant. "You're sure one of the prefects gave my
message to Saltar Kemp?"

"Yes. She understands the threat. She'll meet with you tomorrow."
Ginerva unrolled a pallet a few feet from Brantley's, set a mug of herb-
laced water within reach, and gathered supplies into her basket. "Here.
Lie down."

A tap at the door made me jump. Starfire poked her head in, tousled mass of auburn hair accenting her worried expression. "I heard you were back. How can I help?"

Ginerva smiled. "Stay with them, and make sure she sleeps. I'll check on you through the night." She slipped away with a graceful waddle, leaving the door open a few inches. I knew she'd be nearby.

Starfire bounded over and crushed me in a hug, then stepped back and frowned sternly. "You heard her. Get some sleep. I'll keep watch."

"Promise you'll wake me if he stirs?"

Her expression softened, and she settled cross-legged on the floor between the pallets. "Of course."

I wanted to sit up with her, staring at Brantley until I was sure he was out of danger. But Ginerva and Starfire were right. I needed rest. The coarse blanket scraped against my face as I curled under it. The scent of calara pulp, used to wash the Order's laundry, comforted me with its familiarity. With a last caress over my baby, I let myself sink into sleep.

"WHAT'S THAT SMELL?" A MALE VOICE DEMANDED querulously.

I shot up, grabbing the edges of the pallet, trying to get my bearings. I was no longer on Makah's back, though the sensation of rolling waves had flooded my dreams. The bare walls spoke an answer to my confusion. Still here at the Order. Each day for the past week, I'd prayed and worked beside Ginerva, longing for Brantley to fight back from the fever that pulled him away. Whenever Starfire could be spared from her other duties, she had come and sat with me, insisting that Brantley would wake.

And now beside me, my husband braced on one elbow, sniffing his forearm suspiciously.

I took my first deep breath in days. He was alive. Beautifully petulant and only inches away. "It's Ginerva's lanthrus cream. She boils the plants and then adds curdled goat milk and lets it ferment. Claims it heals anything."

Bright ocean-current eyes met mine, alive, awake. "I didn't ask for the recipe." He used the blanket to rub the offending ointment off his arm. Then he examined the large bandage wrapped around his ribs. "Ginerva?" His gaze shifted to the smooth pale walls of our room in the Order, and comprehension dawned. "We're back on Meriel? But why does she have me trussed up like a chicken on the way to market?"

Ignoring the rancid odor of Ginerva's cream, I threw my arms around him. All the stress of long nights and fearful days fell away. "You're better."

He squeezed me with satisfying strength and nuzzled the top of my head. "How are you? How's our baby?"

"About time you got to the important topics." I kissed his lips, dry from the fever that had flared again in the night. I handed him the mug of water.

He sipped cautiously, then wrinkled his nose like Orianna when forced to eat a rutish plant.

I giggled, surprised to find I still knew how. I filled him in on our escape and what I'd learned about River's plans to ally with the raiders and take control of the Order.

Brantley shoved himself to his feet. He leaned against the wall, pale and unsteady. I stood, ready to catch him if he fainted again.

He pushed his shoulders back. "We need a plan. How many soldiers are still loyal to Kemp? Let's go speak with her now."

I stepped into his arms, subtly supporting him while also comforting myself with the sensation of his embrace. "I met with her already. She'll welcome our advice when you're able. But now you need to rest." I pulled back and faced him sternly. "You almost died."

He waved a hand. "I'm fine. And I'm not leaving a bunch of dancers to organize a military defense."

I should have felt insulted but was too relieved that his eyes held life today. Besides, I couldn't argue. High Saltar Tiarel had held Meriel in tightfisted control, using threats, lies, and starvation to subjugate the rimmers and midrim villages. The new Order was a fragile entity, rediscovering its original purpose of serving our world. The remaining dancers, saltars, soldiers, and attendants weren't prepared for civil war, or for an attack from these new islands.

"All right." I nodded. "We'll talk to Saltar Kemp together."

I convinced him to give me time to wash and change, and Ginerva helped him do the same, though he grumbled the whole time. After a light breakfast, we headed to the high saltar's office, walking slowly. In spite of claiming he barely felt the deep wound in his side, Brantley hunched slightly and didn't resist when I pulled his arm around my shoulders for support. Ginerva had found me a new cane, and I leaned heavily on it. Our frantic escape had aggravated my injury, and my limp had become more pronounced, even after days of rest.

"We're quite the pair," I said, hoping to coax a chuckle from Brantley.

He was too focused on putting one foot in front of the other to respond.

I stopped. "Maybe you should rest a little longer. I can talk with the saltars and fill you in later."

He growled. "Moving around is good for healing a wound."

"That's not what Ginerva said." But we had reached the doorway, so I aimed for the inner office and toward a chair.

Saltar Kemp came around her desk, helped me lower Brantley into a chair, and then embraced me. "I'm relieved you're safe," she said to Brantley. "Or as safe as any of us are."

I pulled in a stool from the edge of the sparse room, my ankle thanking me as I took weight off of it. A tapestry covered one stone wall, bright with the colors of each novitiate form. Behind us, a tall window provided a view of the center ground where drums kept rhythm and dancers performed a pattern. I cocked my head. Harvest pattern. Good choice. The villages would be more content with the work of the Order if their farms and orchards thrived, and less quick to shift their loyalty to River. Though who knew what tricks she was using to undermine cooperation with the Order?

The high saltar returned to her seat, pushing aside a brass sextant, a stack of leather-bound parchments, and a mug of willow pens. "We only recently discovered River's plots, and now we face this new threat. What terrible timing."

Brantley leaned forward, resting his elbows on his legs. "Those raiders are relentless. I see only one course of action."

I watched him in admiration, waiting for his recommendation. Gratitude filled me. He was alive—alive and ready to help carry the burden of decision-making.

Before he could continue, an attendant raced into the room. "There are dancers approaching the main entrance. Wearing green scarves of truce."

"What?" I hurried to the window behind Kemp's desk. From this angle I couldn't see the front courtyard. "Which dancers?"

The attendant fought to catch his breath. "Don't know." The look he bounced between Saltar Kemp and me was accusatory, as if asking, "Aren't you the ones who keep track of the dancers?"

"Never mind. I'm coming." Kemp rose gracefully. She walked with measured tread, her bare feet rolling with suppleness, a habit born from her many years as a dancer and saltar. Brantley and I fell in behind her as she led us to the entrance courtyard. Starfire emerged from the hallway to the kitchen and joined us, brushing flour from the front of her apron.

Just beyond the courtyard walls, several dancers in white tunics stood in a precise triangle formation, all wearing green scarves tied around their necks. Another row of dancers created a backdrop. Beyond them, ponies stomped, grazed, and shook their mangy heads.

"I don't understand," I murmured to Saltar Kemp. "Are these the dancers who are off shift today? What are they doing out here?"

The high saltar shook her head. "These are not ours. Not anymore."

Then I recognized dancers I had once trained with. The same women who had chosen to leave with River after High Saltar Tiarel died.

Oh, merciful Maker. Was River's band of dancers already so emboldened that they had come to directly oppose the Order? It couldn't be.

River herself stepped out from behind her row of acolytes, gliding from the daygrass and onto the cobbled surface of the courtyard. She stopped a few feet from Kemp. Even here in the center of our world, I felt the earth shift beneath my feet.

Her gaze skimmed over Brantley and me, and a smile that was more of a rictus tightened her face. "How convenient finding you here as well," she said smoothly.

Seeing her like this, I was once again a frightened novitiate, facing the harshest saltar who had ever taught me, desperate to please, hoping to survive one more class. River never bothered to hide her viciousness behind a façade of benevolence the way Tiarel had. Why had these dancers followed her?

Their raised chins and uniform posture gave me a clue. River offered them a way to remain in bondage, and bondage felt safe and familiar.

Saltar Kemp remained calm, but I wondered if her heart, like mine, pounded in syncopation to the drums. "You are not welcome here. You chose to forsake the Order."

I admired her strength and directness. My throat was so dry, I doubted I could have spoken.

Anger sparked in River's eyes but disappeared so quickly I wondered if I'd imagined it. When the former saltar spoke, she used a soothing tone. "Not at all. We only forsook the abandoning of the truth."

Fabric rustled behind us, and I looked back. Word had spread, and several other dancers, saltars, and attendants spread out around the courtyard, eyes full of curiosity.

River widened her smile, opening her arms. "I don't hold it against you. You were deceived by this outcast." She spat the final word and glared my direction, then turned a look of gracious acceptance on the growing crowd. "I know how much you've struggled since then, and I've come to offer my assistance."

With a wave of her hand, several of her dancers advanced, setting down baskets laden with fruit, tubers, and mounds of bresh. Enough to make my mouth water.

Whispers rose from the onlookers. If River had stormed in demanding a place for herself and her band of dancers, the Order's soldiers would have been called to escort them away to Middlemost. But an offer of help? Everyone in the Order had been suffering. The lack of tithes, smaller teams of dancers required to work more shifts, and danger from the raiders all made River's overture appealing.

Brantley, one hand on his longknife, gave a respectful nod to Saltar Kemp. "Permission to respond?"

I stood taller, heart full at his show of honor. Kemp needed to look strong in front of the rest of her people.

"Of course." Kemp tucked her hands into her wide sleeves, standing serenely, but the sleeves trembled slightly. So did I.

Brantley filled his lungs and spoke loudly. "We know you've allied yourselves with the raiders who are attacking our rim villages."

Murmurs rippled through the crowd of onlookers, a subtle turning of the tide. That should stop them from being sucked in by River's duplicity.

But she only dipped her chin, then lifted her face with another beatific smile that sat poorly on her sharp features. "We are aware—more than those secluded up here in our world's center—of the serious needs in villages throughout Meriel. After all, we have traveled widely. Of course we sought to trade and obtain vital provisions for those in need." Her gaze narrowed on Brantley and me. "How does that differ from the negotiations you had with the last island that crossed our path?"

"No." I winced at how shrill I sounded. She was right. We had sought out alliances and provisions, but for genuine motives. I couldn't let her spin these lies. "I was in Salis and Foleshill. I learned what you did. How you convinced them to burn the Maker's letter."

Starfire edged closer to me and planted her fists on her waist, raising her voice to the watching crowd. "It's true. I was with her."

Gasps rose behind me. The dismay of the onlookers encouraged me. More dancers had made their way to the courtyard, some rubbing sleep from their eyes. Soon her audience would include all but the drummers and dancers in the center ground.

River's eyebrows formed a concerned and sympathetic expression. "I had no idea. We certainly would never have encouraged that. I have nothing against the Maker's letter. It is lovely and poetic. But let's not argue the finer points of history and philosophy. You need help, and we love our world and the true Order. Let us join together in serving Meriel."

She sounded so sincere, a kernel of longing burst inside me, sprouting roots. It would be so lovely to have the full complement of dancers working together again, to stand united. My face softened.

"What is your purpose here?" Saltar Kemp asked, seeming calm but for the hint of strain in her voice.

River paced, again encompassing the growing audience. "I told you. We've come to offer our service. To join you. Together we will heal our land and protect our shores." Her supple dancer's form moved back and forth across the cobblestones as she spoke.

Brantley growled low in his chest. "She wants control of the Order." He spoke in an undertone meant only for my ears.

But River paused directly in front of him. "I would never challenge the high saltar's leadership." Her words were as smooth as bresh dough, able to stretch and form into any shape needed. She sounded so reasonable. "If you hold such animosity toward others and wish us to leave, we will. I only hoped we could help the villages more if we worked together. Doesn't the Maker's letter speak of unity?"

Saltar Tangleroot moved closer to Kemp. "Think how it would help to have more dancers. And they could bring in the missing tithes."

River smiled. "Of course. We could send out a small band from the Order to visit the villages. Some from your people, some from mine. I have fostered strong friendships with village leaders and have no doubt the scarcity you've suffered will end with my help."

No more murmurs or whispers floated around the courtyard. The tide had more than turned again, washing over every person in earshot. Onlookers held their breath, waiting for Kemp's answer.

EVEN THOUGH I HAD SEEN FIRSTHAND THE DAMAGE RIVER caused in midrim villages, I wanted the lovely, hopeful image she painted to be possible.

When Kemp didn't answer, River crossed her arms. "We must work together to protect our people. The raiders plan to bring their veskals up the channel."

I blinked. The spell River had been weaving suddenly broke, and my fingers clenched my cane. "*You* told the raiders about the channel. How else would you know what they're planning with their veskals? If you truly want to help Meriel, stop damaging crops. Stop intercepting tithes meant for the Order."

River stiffened but ignored me as if I were an insect underfoot. In her eyes I was a hobbled outcast. Worthless. Instead she watched for Kemp's response.

Saltar Kemp sighed. Then she did something odd. She stepped up beside me and rested a hand on my shoulder. "The Maker has shown us truth and freedom. We will never go back to the lies that controlled the Order and caused so much damage to Meriel." She made a graceful gesture toward the ranks of dancers. "You may go."

A command from a saltar automatically triggered movement. Some of them turned to leave without waiting for River's instruction. Veins pulsed along the temples of her angular face as harsh color spread across her skin. Then she forced a smile and gave a small bow as if the response didn't faze her. "I'm sorry you won't accept our help." She spoke over Kemp's head to the novitiates and dancers. "But we are not so hard-hearted. If any of you want to avoid the coming attack, you are welcome to join us. I will keep you safe."

Surely her honeyed voice wouldn't deceive anyone.

But footsteps pattered lightly across the courtyard. Two of the older novitiates and one of our precious dancers ran to join River's group. The novitiates tossed an apologetic glance toward High Saltar Kemp, but the dancer avoided looking at us.

A cold, heavy stone sank deep into my stomach. I pressed a hand against my lips, fighting a rising nausea. Would more leave?

River's smile grew, and she waited. When no one else moved, she gave a last nod. "We'll leave Middlemost in the morning. Come find me if any more of you are ready to leave the failure of this place." She turned on her heel. Her dancers floated back, creating a passage for her. Then they filled in behind her as she descended the slope toward Middlemost.

I bit my lip. She was leaving, taking her deception with her. But eddies of anxiety swirled in her wake. I saw it in the faces of the saltars, the dancers, the attendants. I felt it in my own heart. One part of River's claim was true. The raiders would come up the channel eventually. They would attack. How could we hope to defend the Order against that?

Starfire shook her head. "Don't worry. No one else will listen to her lies. I'll remind everyone that these baskets of supplies don't make up for all the tithes she's convinced villages to withhold. Every bit of lack we're facing is of her doing." She stormed into the Order, her determination putting my worry to shame.

Saltar Kemp's face was grim. "Carya, Brantley, let's return to my office. We need to continue our planning."

I glanced at my husband. His skin was waxen again. He'd been on his feet far too long. I draped his arm over my shoulder, and he didn't protest, letting me bear a little of his weight and steady him. To a casual onlooker, we'd simply look like an affectionate couple. Only I knew how much he relied on my support to walk to the high saltar's office.

Once the three of us were near her desk, Brantley straddled a chair, resting his arms across its back. Kemp unrolled a map, weighting its corners with simple gray stones. "Our only option is to move our world away from the raiders' islands as quickly as possible. Do you think we can outrun their—what are those huge rafts called?"

"Veskals," I answered. "But I don't—"

"I agree." Brantley straightened, nodding at Saltar Kemp. "Because of River, we can't count on the loyalty of the towns. Some would rally to protect our core from the invaders, but we know she has already made alliances with some of the raiders. The sooner we can get away, the better."

They were so quick with their foregone conclusions, as if we'd learned nothing in the recent months. Forcing our world into paths by our own efforts had nearly destroyed Meriel. We were still learning how to let the Maker guide our path in the currents of His design.

I thumped my cane against the floor. "This is wrong."

They turned to me as if they'd forgotten I was there.

I frowned and tried to infuse my voice with confidence. "On our way here, we sought help in a small enclave. One of their women—a woman with child—was stolen. We can't just flee."

The sides of Kemp's mouth drooped. "We've had reports of attacks on several other rim villages. At least a dozen women have been taken. But how can we stand against their weapons? Their veskals? Better to save the rest of our world."

That was the thinking of a saltar. One person had little value when balanced against the good of the Order, the good of Meriel. In the short time I'd been acquainted with the Maker, I'd learned His mind didn't flow in that sort of channel.

I sucked in a breath. Of course. The channel! "I understand your fear, High Saltar. Larcy's clan knows about the channel, which is a danger. But we don't have to steer our island away immediately. I have another idea"

Brantley raised an eyebrow but waited to hear me out.

I stood and pointed to the map. "We can have the dancers rotate the mouth of the channel farther from the raider's islands."

Saltar Kemp's face puckered as if she'd bitten a sour lenka. "But their veskals—"

"They'll still make their way to Middlemost eventually," Brantley finished for her. "And the rim villages that move closer to the cluster of islands won't thank you for endangering their people."

"We can't just flee." I wished I could just agree with them. I hated this conflict. But there was a deeper plan at work here. I could share the vision the Maker had given me, but I could picture Brantley's response to that all too clearly. I felt my way slowly, unsure how much to say. "We might be able to help the foelands."

"Help them?" Kemp's voice went shrill. "They've needed no help in attacking our shores."

I turned a pleading gaze toward Brantley. *Support me. Stand up for me.* But his eyes had the glassy look of fever. He blinked a few times. "Carya, she's right. There are battles we can't win."

"You said that when the Maker asked me to challenge the Order."

He lifted his hands in a placating gesture. "That's different."

"No, it's not. We need to ask the Maker how He wants us to respond."

Brantley grimaced. "I haven't heard Him say anything, even with a fever that made me hear all sorts of things. You?" he asked Kemp.

Her face softened. "Carya's right. We need to seek His guidance."

Brantley snorted. I brightened, but Kemp shook her head at me. "Brantley's also right. Discerning His will isn't always easy."

Was she coming around? I pressed my point. "We know the Maker guides our world. We didn't encounter these foelands by accident. I can't believe the Maker wants us to abandon the kidnapped women and their unborn babies."

"I know. But if we don't set a new course, more could be taken. We don't have much time to debate this. I'll gather the saltars. We'll read from the Maker's letter and seek His guidance. Meet me back here at primary sun's peak."

"I can come with you," I offered.

Affection rimmed her eyes. "Thank you, but you've made your opinion known. The Order must learn to manage itself in this new era."

I should have been relieved at responsibility being lifted from my weary shoulders. Instead I felt as if I were sinking deeper into the sensation of being useless, unwanted. I waited for Brantley to make a snide comment, especially after how often the Order had requested my help in recent weeks. But he had stopped listening and seemed to be struggling just to stay upright.

Saltar Kemp noticed too and rang a bell that rested on the corner of her desk. An attendant scurried in. "Care for your husband," she said to me. "I'll meet you after the saltars' discussions."

As much as I wanted to insist on being included in the decision-making, my priority was caring for my little family. With the way we seemed to draw trouble, that alone was enough challenge. But what did this mean for the call I'd heard at Ecco Cove? Did the Maker have no more use for me? Was my gift as a dancer no longer needed?

Against Brantley's protests, the attendant and I guided him back to the room we were using. Ginerva scolded him for aggravating the wound. She tended him briskly, while also reassuring me he would be fine if he rested. I was grateful for her reassurance, because Brantley had stopped complaining about her poultices and herb-laced drinks. He tried to hide it, but pain etched tight contours in his face. I held his hand as he dozed, until Ginerva lured me away to eat.

The dining hall was a colorful bouquet of novitiates, each at the table of their form. The tiny scarlet girls giggled and whispered, then straightened under the stern frown of their prefect. The older blue-form girls waved to me. The saltars' table was empty. They must still be in deliberation, so I took a seat with the blue form, the girls so close to their testing day. Relaxed chatter circulated with the baskets of saltcakes as they discussed a particularly difficult class, a new variation to the storm pattern, and the handsome young landkeeper they'd seen working in the courtyard.

When I'd been a novitiate, we'd barely risked brief whispered exchanges, silenced by the tension of constantly being observed, evaluated, judged. The pressure to be worthy had crushed our spirits even as the training honed our minds and muscles. I stiffened. Old habits. Wasn't that exactly what I had been caught in? I drove myself, criticizing each choice I made, each poor result, trying to please the Maker as if He were the harshest of saltars. But I should know better. Just as the Order had discovered joy, I needed to find a way to serve without all the fear and striving.

I looked around the room. Despite the struggles our world had faced recently, the changes here gave me hope. The teams in the center ground were smaller, because some dancers—given the choice—had left the Order. But the classes hadn't shrunk as much as I'd feared they would. New dancers would join soon, and the patterns would continue to support Meriel, but in a spirit of love and joy instead of fear. That is, if we could prevent River's schemes. I shuddered to think of how quickly she'd send the Order back into a place of lies and terror.

I stood and moved past other tables. Young women in the green form murmured in low voices and stopped speaking when they noticed my approach. One girl jutted her chin upward, even as her friend tugged her arm to stop her from speaking. "Was River right? Will the foelands be attacking? What is the high saltar doing about it?"

My throat tightened. "It's true that the foelanders are a danger, but so is River. And the saltars are making plans right now." I gave what I hoped was a reassuring smile. "You've seen how powerful the Maker is. You were here when He freed Meriel and carved the channel. Trust Him." Saying those words infused renewed confidence into my own heart.

I excused myself and went to find the saltars. They might not want me to join their discussion, but it was midday and time for me to meet them. Brantley would want to be part of the planning, but he needed to rest.

The saltars had gathered in the larger rehearsal hall, the room where I'd once done my testing before a gimlet-eyed panel. Strange how their formal robes and stiff postures no longer intimidated me.

Saltar Kemp beckoned me forward, the silver embroidery on her cuffs catching sunlight streaming through the tall windows. The cool marble floor eased the ache in my bare feet, and my good foot rolled through each tendon appreciatively as I walked in. The other saltars sat in a circle on the floor, hands tucked into the wide sleeves of their white robes. Several copies of the Maker's letter sat before them.

With my cane for support, I lowered smoothly to the floor. I wanted to cajole, persuade, argue, and insist, but my new resolve to cease striving in my own strength dried my words to one question. "How can I help?"

Saltar Tangleroot smoothed the edges of her headscarf. "We agree that forsaking the rim women who've been taken seems . . . wrong."

"But we can't find a solution that doesn't make us vulnerable to more damage." Saltar Kemp sighed. "Even our original plan to flee won't work if River has taught them enough of the patterns to move their islands. They could pursue us forever."

"I can set your mind at rest about that, at least." I stretched my legs out in front of me, flexing my foot to relieve a cramp. "They know we shape our world with dance, but—"

"But it doesn't work on their worlds?" Saltar Furrow, face hopeful, clasped her hands together near her heart, her wide sleeves falling back to expose the thin bones of her arms.

The privation of the recent months hid in plain sight here at the Order. *Maker, we have so little. Protect the little we have from being stolen away. Help us!* I reached for one of the bound parchments. My fingers traced the precious and hopeful words. "I'm sorry. It *does* work on their world. But they know little about the patterns. River couldn't have found potential dancers and trained them in so little time."

"Unless . . ." The high saltar lifted her head heavily. She gazed across the grand hall as if picturing the days not long ago when Saltar River taught here. "If her band of dancers returns to one of those islands, they could guide it through the currents."

Worried murmurs rose from the women in the circle.

I pursed my lips. "We agree we need to rescue the women they've stolen. So for now, let Meriel stay in the current."

"And turn our world so the channel is farther from them?" Kemp asked.

I shook my head. "Brantley was right. That only exposes more rim villages to the danger. They would reach us eventually."

The drums altered their pattern. Leeward wind. A tree in the courtyard rustled, leaves bobbing at the shift in air current.

"That's it!" I rose to my knees. "There's our answer."

"HAVE YOU LOST YOUR MIND?" HOURS LATER, BRANTLEY glared at me, propped against the wall on his pallet. The nap had reduced his pallor but done nothing for his temper. He was furious to learn he'd slept through an important strategy meeting. And apparently my idea didn't meet with his approval.

"It will succeed. If the herders and dancers work together."

He squeezed his temples. "But you want to purposely lure them here!"

I offered him a mug of tsalla, which he ignored, so I set it down and settled beside him. After months of marriage, I'd learned our discussions went better when we sat side by side instead of across from each other. "The more time we give River, the more villages she'll manipulate to her side. And if the raiders send their veskals up the channel, our herders can mount a rescue when the prisoners are less protected."

"And when the raiders reach Middlemost?" He raked a hand through his hair. A few curls flopped back over his eyes. He needed a haircut, but this didn't seem like the time to suggest that.

"They won't," I said calmly.

"You can't know that."

"It's a challenge navigating even a stenella upriver. Their largest veskals won't fit."

"But some of the raiders have small, maneuverable crafts. They'll sail to the heart of our world. What sort of plan is that?"

"You've seen how the sails work. When the raiders try to progress up the channel, the dancers will change the wind's direction and push them back. It's the advantage we have by using stenella."

Brantley sighed. "There aren't that many herders. And they aren't soldiers. You can't rely on a few herders and stenella to find and rescue the stolen women."

I touched his bristly face. "You rescued me."

"I think we've established that *you* rescued *me*. Again." He slouched lower against the wall, a storm cloud hovering over his features.

If only I could create a dance pattern to chase away *those* clouds. "Why does that upset you so much? We're a team. You helped me escape the Order when you barely knew me. You gave me courage. Held me when my mother died. Stood alongside as I brought the Maker's letter to village leaders. Built our home." I placed his hand over my belly. I still hadn't felt our child move, but the little lump seemed to have grown in the last few days. "Given me a baby."

His lips parted. He seemed taken aback by my outburst. A rueful smile surfaced. "It's not just about you. I failed to protect Orianna—"

"But you rescued her."

"—and I wasn't there to fight for my brother."

He rarely spoke about Cole. I held very still, hoping he would tell me more so I could understand the remorse that often threatened to pull him under. He reached to put his arm around my shoulder, then winced as the small movement aggravated the wound in his side. Dark skies returned to his face.

Brantley wasn't the type to enjoy sitting around. "Is the pain worse? I can get more poultice. Poor man."

His growl was like a low roll of thunder. "I don't want your pity."

"It's not pity. It's compassion."

"I'm a herder. Do you have any idea how humiliating it is to not be able to stand on my stenella? To be carted here like an infant? In a harness? To have to rest while others plan the protection of our entire world? You don't understand."

I flexed my ankle. "I don't understand? Me? A crippled dancer?"

At least he had the decency to flush.

"*Your* wounds will heal—if you let them. Mine—unless the Maker intervenes—will be a battle for me to face every day."

He blew out a breath, took my hands in his. "I'm sorry. I wasn't thinking." The worried gaze he turned on me overflowed with tenderness. Dangerous tenderness.

"Stop. No pity, remember?"

"It's not pity. It's compassion."

I snorted. "No fair using my words."

His crooked grin lit his eyes like a rising subsun. Warm and gentle. "They were good words." He kissed me, then struggled to his feet.

"Where are you going?"

"Someone has to coordinate the herders. I'll take Makah down to the rim and . . ."

I shook my head. I didn't want to dampen his spirits, but there was no use pretending he was fit to travel. "Another herder was upstream trading at Middlemost. He's gone to notify Teague, and they'll spread the word among all the nearby herders."

He ground his teeth, ready to argue, but then swayed. Braced against the wall, he slid down to sit again. "Maybe I'm not a hundred percent yet. But as soon as I can stand for more than a few minutes, I'm heading to Windswell to oversee this scheme. Are you sure the raiders don't have stenella? If we push back their veskals, they could still invade up the channel."

"They fear stenella. The 'sea creatures,' as they call them, can glide over their veskals and crush them or lift from beneath and overturn them."

Brantley rubbed his jaw, raising a rasping sound. "A stenella would never do that."

I smiled. "They wouldn't. But the raiders think otherwise. So that's one less thing to worry about. Now, if I have an attendant bring some supper, are you able to eat?"

"Anything but broth," he grumbled. "And where's my longknife? I need to shave."

OVER THE NEXT FEW DAYS, BRANTLEY FOUGHT OFF THE remaining infection and continued to heal. His wound threatened to tear open when he twisted or reached too suddenly, but in spite of his disregard for the injury, I had to admit he was growing stronger. Working with Saltar Kemp, he sent pony riders to villages still loyal to the Order, warning of a possible invasion—although if my plan worked, it wouldn't come to that—and counseling them to set scouts in place and bolster their local soldiers. Watchers were placed along the upper banks of the channel. From the telescope atop the Order's structure, I spotted stenella swimming along the coast, their herders coordinating plans for a rescue. I reviewed wind patterns with the dancers, taking a few turns in the center ground, helping rotate Meriel so Windswell would once again be close to the raiders' islands. We also stirred up storms that kept the raider's veskals at bay until we were ready.

In spite of my limitations, dancing with colleagues was exhilarating. Bare earth spoke to my feet and infused me with hope. The breeze carried energy, even past the towering walls. The thunderclouds provided protection. The Maker's world did His bidding. If only His human creation served so faithfully.

I knew rescuing our people wasn't all that the Maker intended, but since His plans to help the cluster of lands remained a mystery, I locked those thoughts deep in my heart, resolving to follow His currents wherever they led.

"I'M READY," BRANTLEY DECLARED ONE MORNING. HE pulled out a whetstone and rasped it across his longknife.

I frowned. "For?"

"To return to Windswell. The Order is fortified—as much as possible. The villages have been warned. Windswell is in more danger than any other village since it's near the mouth of the channel. That's where I need to be."

Did he resent that the plan put Windswell in harm's way? "But we had to—"

"I understand the strategy. But I have to be there. I'll organize an evacuation and coordinate the herders." He slid his longknife into its sheath with force, as if burying it into an enemy's chest. "I've been to the islands. I can direct the herders. You'll be safe here."

"Oh, no, you don't."

He raised an eyebrow. "You can't believe I would hide here while my people are in danger?"

I pursed my lips. "Of course not. But you can't believe *I* would hide here while my people are in danger either. I'm coming with you."

The mix of expressions splashing across his face would have been comical if we weren't both so dead serious. His chest filled when I called our village "my people." But soon a glower darkened his brow. With his carefree hair and sea-blue eyes, how did he manage such a thunderous appearance?

"You have no reason to put yourself, and our baby, in extra danger. You're a dancer. You help the cause by dancing."

Crossing my arms, I leveled a steely gaze at him. "The others tolerate my encouragement and new patterns, but a crippled dancer is very little use in the center ground. I'm coming with you."

Brantley cocked his head, then sank to his pallet and gestured for me to join him. He entwined his fingers with mine. "I know you want us to stay together, but it makes no sense for you to ride down to Windswell only to hide in the forest while we mount our rescue."

"I wouldn't hide . . ." My stomach churned. How could I convince Brantley that I wanted to—*needed* to—return to the islands? That the Maker had unfinished business with the people there? That He had once again given me a vision, a way to serve?

Brantley squeezed my fingers. "What are you thinking?" He kept his tone calm and even.

I stared resolutely at the floor. Of course, I should tell him. But if he knew my intent . . .

"Carya?" Confusion, worry, and love blended on his face like different colors of wax on a chandler's bench. Braided, melded.

"When I was on Larcy's island . . ."

When I faltered, he tugged my hand. "When you were rescuing me."

I sniffed. "Yes. Well, the Maker spoke to me through the land. Those islands need Him. There's more for me to do there."

The air left him in a sudden huff, his posture collapsing. I waited for the argument. The rolled eyes. The "not again."

But he didn't speak. Instead, he stood and moved slowly to the door, as if sleepwalking.

"Brantley?" My plea for understanding came out in a near whimper. Once again I was causing him pain—the last thing I wanted to do.

Back to me, he braced one hand against the doorframe. "I need to talk to someone." The words squeezed past a constricted throat. Then he was gone.

I wanted to run after him, but he clearly needed time. Instead, I went in search of Saltar Kemp. Saltar Tangleroot informed me she was at the telescope. I labored up the flights of stairs. My hand traced the fine cracks in the stone wall. As I neared the upper floor, the youngest voices carried from a classroom, full of laughter and energy. I smiled. Even if rations were tight, at least tiny girls were no longer locked in storage rooms. Dancers were no longer punished with shackles. Novitiates were no longer cast out or hobbled. The Order had seen many positive changes. We couldn't let River take us back to the bondage of the past.

When I emerged from the stairwell, Saltar Kemp turned from the telescope. She tucked her hands into her full sleeves. Worry painted lines in her face, much like the tiny cracks in the Order's wall. But the walls still stood firm, and so did she. "The extended lens design Brantley brought back from your explorations has made a huge difference," she said. "We can see in much greater detail."

"Good. You'll need to know when to direct the dancers to change their patterns." The Maker brought treasure from trials. That was exactly the reminder I needed. I'd felt hopeless more times than I could count while trapped on the island with the strange villages, but not only had the Maker brought us home, we'd returned with supplies and gifts and new ideas. I could—I must—trust Him in the midst of our current danger.

Saltar Kemp updated me on what the telescope revealed. "There's been a great deal of activity. The stenella and their riders are staying out of sight of the veskals. One group of raiders moved farther along the shore past Windswell. Almost to Undertow. When the last storm died down, a few larger craft made their way along the rim and closer to the channel entrance. We don't have much time."

I nodded. "We'll send the signal to the herders today. May I?" I gestured to the telescope.

Saltar Kemp nodded and backed away.

When I peered into the eyepiece, a blur of color met my eyes. I blinked a few times and played with a small dial until the focus cleared—sharp enough for me to spy a harrier bird perched on a tall pine that bordered a midrim village. Amazing. I attempted to glide the scope sideways, but it jerked and bobbed, losing focus again. I hoped Saltar Kemp or one of the prefects was better at using this tool than I was. I managed to shift the telescope's gaze to the mouth of the channel, then over to the cluster of islands. Docks stood barren. Clearly the raiders' veskals were in full use. I located two large crafts facing off and imagined I could feel the air snip and bite as arrows flew. If they continued to battle each other, it would give us more time to rally our forces. We needed at least a half day to reach Windswell, ensure everyone had evacuated, and signal the Order to launch our plan.

I squinted as I moved the view to the woodland between Windswell and Undertow, hoping for a glimpse of Orianna or Fiola or Bri, but everyone from Windswell was well hidden by foliage—hopefully well hidden from raiders as well. The scope bounced again, and a new image flared into focus.

I jerked back from the telescope.

"What's wrong?" Saltar Kemp asked.

One hand to my chest, I peered in again, hoping my eyes had deceived me. No. There it was. I couldn't bear to tell her what I was seeing. "This is bad," I managed in a strangled voice.

ALTHOUGH THE BENCH BENEATH ME WAS SOLID, I GRIPPED
the edge of the dining hall table, trying to steady my erratic heartbeat.
Every saltar who wasn't busy teaching or supervising huddled around
the table, joining Saltar Kemp, Brantley, and me. Clattering kettles and
attendant voices floated from the kitchen, almost soothing me with their
normalcy. But there was nothing normal about this day.

Brantley stood with one foot on the long bench. "How can this be
more dangerous than the raiders?"

I brushed a bead of sweat from my forehead, turning to the others who
were waiting for my report. "You don't understand. River is starting a
whole opposing Order. I saw the clearing near Shadowswell—a different
center ground. And even novitiates in red tunics. She's recruiting—
training more dancers."

Saltar Kemp winced, the horror of the news squeezing her voice.
"River will only grow in power."

"And she's holding a strategic position. Other than Windswell at the
sea, Shadowswell is the only village along the channel, and it's partway
upriver. From there she can watch any travel on the channel and try to
control the winds. And there's more." My head throbbed. "We spotted a
veskal heading upstream already. It's making slow progress against the
headwinds, but if our storms die off, more foelanders will follow. The
invasion is beginning."

Brantley rubbed his temples. "Carya is right. There's no more time
to debate. I'll head downriver on my stenella and try to scare the veskal
away. We know they fear the stenella. And we just have to move faster
with our plan before River's group can do more damage."

I shook my head. "You can't risk them hurting Makah. Not after . . ."

Brantley's hand closed over his longknife, and his eyes blazed into mine. "I couldn't protect Orianna or my brother or the other villages that suffered under the Order. But this is something I can do. I must do. No more time to waste."

Saltar Tangleroot drummed her fingers on the table, seconding his words.

I rose and stood beside him. "I'm coming with you."

He frowned. "I'm not feeble. I'm almost over the fever."

"Of course you're not feeble. But it might be useful to have a dancer along." And I would do all I could to protect Makah as well. I couldn't face the guilt that would come if another of Brantley's mounts were harmed.

The group around us murmured agreement, but Brantley glared toward my middle. "Can't you just wait in safety? For once?"

Suddenly self-conscious, I smoothed my tunic. Did he think I didn't care about our baby's safety? But I had to balance that against the safety of our entire world. More than that, my loyalty to the Maker. He had proven Himself faithful time and again. If He insisted on calling me to tasks beyond myself, who was I to refuse? Why couldn't Brantley understand that?

Saltar Kemp's gaze darted between us, and she raised a hand. "Brantley is right. We need to move ahead. We have to rescue our people from the raiders' islands before River becomes more powerful. But Carya is also right. Her dancing may help the plan."

Brantley's gaze moved to a window and beyond, and his jaw tightened. He gave a tight nod as if he'd won an argument with himself. Now he wasted no more time on argument. He rested a hand on my shoulder, the way I'd seen him interact with village soldiers. "One step at a time, right?"

I gave him a soft smile. He really was trying to understand. He knew the conflict I felt between the Maker's call to serve other worlds, to serve Meriel, and to serve my family. I looked at the saltars. "We need to carry word to every village, warning them about what River is trying to do. We don't want any families sending their daughters to her."

Saltar Tangleroot frowned. "We only have a few harrier birds to carry missives. It will take weeks to send word to all the villages."

Saltar Kemp sniffed and leveled her gaze at Tangleroot. "So begin sending word out today. The message should explain that River has allied with the foelands and can't be trusted. Begin with the villages closest to Shadowswell."

"But not Shadowswell," I said quickly. "It would let River and her people know we are getting word out against her."

"Not to mention that she might harm one of my birds," Tangleroot muttered.

Brantley helped me up and addressed the saltars. "Fair winds for the channel, but not until after we've made sure Windswell is evacuated and the herders are ready. Then let the ships make it partway up before changing the patterns."

Saltar Kemp squared her shoulders. "I understand the plan," she snapped, her tone conjuring echoes of High Saltar Tiarel, or Saltar River before she'd donned a benevolent façade. My stomach clenched.

Kemp stood slowly. I could almost hear the creak of her joints as she struggled to straighten. "Forgive me." With a deep breath, her expression softened. "Go with the Maker's blessing and ours."

All the saltars drummed their fingers on the table like a rainfall of good wishes, and it filled me with a swell of camaraderie and refreshed hope to see this reformed Order willing to serve the Maker with courage and humility.

Minutes later, Brantley and I made our way down the rocks toward the end of the channel where Makah splashed playfully.

"Who did you need to talk to?" I asked, pausing to catch my breath.

"What?" Brantley tightened his grip on my arm, guiding me past a steep drop off.

"When you left our room. You said you needed to talk to someone."

He ducked his head, but I saw the flush crawling up from his neck.

"Watch your step here."

"Brantley?"

He guided me down the last rocky bit and to the water's edge. "I needed to be alone to talk to the Maker."

My eyebrows lifted. "And?"

He cleared his throat. "I . . . expressed my concerns." Like a boy caught stealing a saltcake, he sent me a worried glance. "Do you think that's all right?"

Warmth bloomed from deep inside my chest, and I smiled. "I don't think He rebukes us for our questions. I often remind Him that the choices He is making seem . . . improbable."

Brantley laughed, a free and open sound that stirred my love for him even more. "That's one word for it." He shrugged. "I tried to be respectful, but I did tell Him my frustrations. Then I remembered everything I've seen Him do."

"Did that help?"

His face puckered. "Some. I don't mind Him sending me into danger. It's a lot harder to watch someone you love face a battle you can't rescue them from."

I rested my hand on his ribs, where a fresh bandage hid beneath his tunic. "I agree."

He kissed me, then rested his forehead against mine. "I know your plan goes beyond just bringing back our people and thwarting the raiders. I'll get you onto one of the islands while the rescue is going on. I'll stand guard. Beyond that . . ."

"Beyond that, we'll trust the Maker to guide us."

Makah chittered impatiently, and we both laughed. I settled onto the stenella's back, while Brantley stood behind me and signaled. Soon we were rushing down the channel. Makah's movements lacked the steadiness of Navar. She still dodged obstacles with sudden jerks that made me wince. But she followed Brantley's signals better than before.

A strong breeze pushed us from behind, making me wonder how the veskal I'd spotted from the telescope could possibly make any headway upchannel. I hoped they would give up and retreat before we reached that point in the river. When I twisted my head to talk to Brantley, the wind stole my breath. "How many herders will help?"

"Teague sent word of at least a dozen. They'll wait at Windswell. Their stenella will stay out of sight until we're ready."

He sounded gratified at that number. Herders were usually solitary folk, though carting supplies from the strange island we'd encountered last year had given them an opportunity to practice working together. I pressed my lips together. With nearly a dozen warring islands to search, the task still seemed impossible.

As if reading my thoughts, Brantley reached down and squeezed my shoulder. "They'll find the captives or die trying."

I shivered. *Maker, don't let me be responsible for more deaths.* This plan had seemed so inspired, so ordained. What if I was as misguided as the Order had been for so many years? Doubts assailed me. Perhaps I was again trying to save the world in my own strength instead of trusting the Maker. Why was it so often difficult to discern the right path? *Guide me, dearest Maker. Protect me from myself. Show me when to move and when to wait.*

We neared an outcropping with a stand of trees blocking our view. Brantley nudged me and pointed inland. "Shadowswell is just beyond that ridge."

Soft spray from the river misted my face as I turned again to look up at him. "As soon as we're done with the raiders, I'll need to confront River there. I can't let her keep deceiving people."

Brantley's affectionate smile for me was shaded with worry, and his hand settled over the longknife at his hip. "I know."

We continued down the channel, wind at our back. Suddenly, my husband jerked as if hit by an arrow. His sharp whistle pulled Makah to an abrupt stop, nearly unseating me.

A veskal loomed ahead, almost filling the channel. Its massive mast stretched, empty, to the sky, like a desolate pine stripped of needles.

The foelanders I'd spotted from the telescope had maneuvered farther up the river than I'd realized.

Brantley crouched low and pushed me forward as if staying down would make us invisible.

Raiders on one side of the craft held long poles, which they jabbed into the shore to edge their veskal forward against the current and the wind. Watching their efforts from the front of the craft, the captain shouted a command, then shook his head as if frustrated by their tedious progress. When he turned to face upriver, he saw us. His chin lifted. The wind tangled his long hair and tugged his open vest aside, revealing a sword at his waist. He was the same captain who had confronted Mander's veskal but backed down rather than kill me and my babe to get to his foe.

Brantley sprang to his feet on Makah's back. My gaze flew over the raiders, hoping they were all too busy with their poles to fire arrows at us.

Instead of turning Makah, Brantley whooped and waved.

"What are you doing?" I yelled over the rush of the wind. Even Makah twisted her head and shot him a confused look.

Brantley only waved again, arm swinging wildly, face jubilant.

The veskal moved closer. I could see the storm gather on the captain's face. "Brantley, we need to go—"

My husband shouted one eager, hopeful word. "Cole!"

26

COLE? MY BRAIN SCRAMBLED TO MAKE SENSE OF Brantley's shout. Then it hit me. "Your brother? But you told me—"

"The Order's soldiers ran him through and tossed him in the sea. How can this be?" Wonder clogged his throat, and he signaled Makah to move even closer to the veskal. He drew a deep breath. "Cole! It's me. Brantley."

I watched Cole's face for answering jubilation. No wonder my first glimpse of the man had made an impact on me. Now I could see the similarities. Same strong jawline. Same adamant posture. Same tousled curls. But where Brantley's eyes lit like the sparkling sea on a clear day, Cole's eyes were hooded, boring into us. He squared his shoulders and called to his men. "Raise sail!" His men stowed their poles and raced to new positions. Soon a huge curtain of fabric unfurled, catching the wind and propelling the veskal away from us, down the channel toward the sea.

Brantley's breath left him in a rush, as if he'd been hit in the chest. The hurt and confusion on his face tore at my soul. I squinted into the distance. "Maybe it's not him. It's easy to mistake people from a distance."

He sank to his knees on Makah's broad back. "It was Cole."

"Then let's follow him. Find out what happened."

Brantley stroked Makah's hide, his touchstone for all that was normal and right when the world was reeling. "No," he choked out, eyes downcast. "He recognized me. And he chose to go."

"Maybe he withdrew his men because of you. To protect you. Don't assume the worst."

He gave a low growl of pain. "Is that another axiom of the Order?"

Any words I would offer him now would only sound hollow to his ears. Instead, I carefully turned around and wrapped my arms around him. I held on until I felt his heartbeat slow, until his sighs were less ragged, until his arms softened around me as he remembered that love and tenderness and loyalty still existed.

Still Brantley didn't give Makah the signal to move. He tore his fingers through his tangled hair, letting his hand stay pressed against his head as if trying to push the painful thoughts from his mind. "How could he? He would have passed Windswell. Wouldn't he have looked for Bri and Orianna? For our mother?"

And for his brother. The thought went unsaid. Too painful to voice.

"The village was evacuated. The channel is new and changed the shape of the coastline. He might not have recognized Windswell or even realized this is Meriel. And maybe it's a good sign that he turned back when he recognized you. His clan of raiders was planning to attack, and when he saw you, he retreated. He's protecting you."

Brantley shook his head but then raised his chin. "We have work to do."

HE WAS RIGHT. AS SHOCKING AS COLE'S APPEARANCE WAS, and as many questions as it raised, we still had to coordinate the herders and lead the search. And I had my own appointment with those islands. If the Maker had a new dance to teach me, I wanted my heart to be ready.

I repositioned myself in place on Makah, Brantley stood, and we were soon making our way downstream again. Because of the strong wind, each time we caught a glimpse of Cole's veskal, it grew smaller and more distant.

In the Order, although many lessons were twisted with falsehoods, I had learned at least one valuable truth. Distraction was a temptation and a danger. Brantley and I both needed to focus on the plan. The herders would be facing peril as they searched the various foelands. And I would be facing . . . what exactly? Why couldn't the Maker paint His plans in vibrant colors like a map of Meriel?

I trust Your love. Help me trust You more. I prayed that simple prayer over and over as the water splashed over my bare toes and the green foliage on the banks blurred past us. I sat up taller. He may not have shown me every part of His plan, but the fact that the Maker had a plan would have to be enough.

WHEN WE REACHED WINDSWELL, THE DESERTED VILLAGE felt ominous. Wind kicked up brittle leaves and howled under eaves. Subsunset cast long shadows of the bouncing branches, creating a parody of dance on the ground.

We stepped off of Makah and quickly hid in the woods near our cottage. Teague found us there. "The herders and their stenella are around the outcropping on the Undertow side of the village. One craft entered the channel but gave up."

Brantley frowned grimly. "Yes. We saw it."

Teague's eyes widened. "Did they see you? Did they shoot those sticks at you?"

My husband's jaw clenched. "Did you see which island they retreated toward?"

Teague shot me a questioning look but then turned back to his mentor. Crouching behind underbrush to stay hidden, Teague pulled out a small scope. "That one. The tall island with cliffs just behind the smaller one."

"Rogue's Aerie," I whispered.

He passed the scope to Brantley, who peered into the distance, letting no emotion show. "Time to rescue our people."

Teague edged farther inland, only standing when he had reached the cover of trees. "We aren't waiting until morning?"

"Go tell the herders to be ready. Once the raiders move up the channel, we'll hit the islands. I'll go raise the signal for the Order now."

"What if the raiders have gone to bed and don't notice the fair winds?" I asked. "Wouldn't it be better . . ."

"No." Brantley stared out toward the islands. "Cole knows about herders and the abilities of trained stenella. We have to move fast before he spreads the word."

"He wouldn't."

Brantley snorted.

I tugged his arm until he faced me. "I mean it. He wouldn't share information with foelands. Those clans are all enemies to each other. So even if he could guess at your purposes, our plan will still work."

"Let's see if the foelands react to the wind change." Brantley strode boldly to the border of Windswell and raised a huge red banner to the top of the tallest tree. Even in the dimming light, the Order would be able to catch sight through their rooftop scope.

"Now what?" asked Teague.

"Stay hidden and wait." Brantley led me into the forest, following the shoreline away from the foelands and staying far enough inland that we wouldn't be spotted by any observation platforms. When Brantley felt we were clear, he led me to the shore. We could no longer see the raiders' islands. Just beyond this outcropping of land, at least a dozen stenella swam in idle circles. Huddled around a small fire, herders roasted fish and talked in low tones. I recognized several of them from the trips they'd made to gather supplies off the barriered island. Their presence made me smile. The villages might be rebelling, the Order struggling, and River causing chaos, but this union of herders was a rare and beautiful event.

"Put out the fire," Brantley snapped. One of the men hurried to obey.

"What news?" another asked.

"Mount up. I'll signal when their veskals are well up the channel. Watch for torchlight. That will guide you to the villages. Carya?" He nudged me forward.

My optimism fled. These men would still find armed guards and lethal danger ahead. "I only saw two of the islands, but they both had special huts or caves where they keep prisoners. If you don't find our women there, look for the commanders' homes." I tried to keep my voice level, as if this were as simple as moving supplies from one coast to another. But I knew better. "Spread out and coordinate so you're each searching a different island."

These gruff and brave men, some old enough to be my father, nodded with respect and strode to the shore to call their stenella in. Their trust made my stomach tighten even more. I rested a hand over the fluttering I felt. Then I gasped.

"What's wrong?" Brantley turned from answering a herder's question, instantly alert.

I paused. There it was again. Not nerves. "Our child. I felt her move."

His eyes widened, then his jaw hardened with more resolve.

Joy sang through me at the babe's fleeting touch. Though perhaps this wasn't the best time to remind my husband of just how much was at stake. He would be even more reluctant to let me come with him now.

Overhead, the sky was dull. There would be no brilliant star rain to illuminate the herders' ride. Then the wind changed. Stronger. Whipping in from the sea. The waters stretched dark and menacing, boiling like poison in a cauldron. The men nodded to each other and Brantley grinned. "Kemp saw the signal."

He was eager, relieved that the plan was moving forward. Yet I could only feel dread.

"Don't lose faith now," Brantley said quietly, his breath warm against my ear.

I drew my shoulders back. "Let's ride Makah around the point to stand watch."

He patted my back, and his approval put strength back into my limbs. Brantley sat behind me, not wanting to create a tall silhouette, even though it was doubtful anyone would see our dark form against the dark waves. In no time we were in sight of Windswell and the mouth of the channel.

Makah liked waiting even less than I did. Brantley had to remind her several times to hold her position. She flicked an impatient fin and chittered a few times, but the strong gusts pulled the sound away into the night.

I tightened my head scarf as the wind mounted and threatened to tear it away. When I shivered, Brantley wrapped his arms around me. Time hovered, uncertain, all around us.

My muscles couldn't sustain their tension indefinitely, and soon I relaxed back, my spine molding to my husband's body, even as the babe curled into the safety of mine. "What if they don't risk the channel at night?" I murmured. I wasn't sure if I felt frustration or relief. "Even if River gave them information, they won't know how narrow the way is or what obstacles they will face."

"The wind will be too tempting of an opportunity. Watch and wait." Calm. Resolute. Whatever torment Brantley had felt when he watched his brother command a raiding veskal and sail deliberately away from him, he had been able to set that pain aside. How did he do that? How did he store away his emotions and focus on the task of the moment?

I wished I had that skill. Instead, my heart danced in worried rhythms. I hurt for Brantley and feared we'd never find answers that would satisfy his questions about his brother. I feared for the women we needed to rescue. I feared for the herders waiting beyond the outcropping. I feared I wouldn't have the strength for whatever the Maker asked of me. The mysterious glimpses of His love and His plan to manifest that love to the foelands were undoubtedly good things, yet I'd learned He would bear any cost to offer that love.

And I feared I'd wear myself out with the waiting and wondering.

Then something moved. In the distance, faint as a gull's wing as it hovers, a striped sail pulled out from behind one of the islands, lanterns dangling from the front and lighting its way. "There."

"Yes. Stay low."

And the waiting continued. Even with the strong wind, it seemed to take forever for the veskal to maneuver past foelands and find the channel. We huddled low on Makah, even though it wasn't likely they'd see us at this distance. Besides, they wouldn't be watching the sea. They wouldn't expect people to be floating on the waves the way their veskals did.

Brantley shifted, finally revealing some of the same impatience I'd been battling. "This will only work if the others send their raiders too."

I turned my face into the wind, forcing myself to look away for a few moments. Staring toward the menacing islands had made my eyes ache and my head throb.

"Even if the others follow, if they're spread out too far, the plan won't work," Brantley said, half to himself.

"I know." My legs tensed, and Makah splashed forward until Brantley eased her back into place. "Sorry."

Brantley rested a hand on my shoulder. I assumed he meant to reassure me, but when I glanced back, he was so intent on the foelands, I realized he had done it absently. "There!" he said, still focusing on the distant shores.

I turned and squinted. Sure enough, a medium-sized veskal wove through the gap between two other islands, bedecked in Mander's white sails. Soon a parade of veskals aimed for the channel, some jostling for position, all moving with growing speed as the steady wind drove them along. My muscles throbbed as I thought of the dancers in the center ground working so hard to sustain this strong wind.

"I counted twenty so far. About ten mid-size crafts, the rest small. Sound right?"

I pressed a hand over my mouth. I'd never thought to keep count. "I don't know. I saw sails from Ecco Cove, Halyard's Hull, and Scavengewood. I don't know the others. River probably does," I added bitterly.

Brantley wheeled Makah, and we darted through the choppy water to where Teague sat astride a borrowed stenella. At Brantley's signal, he raced back to let the herders know it was time.

No more opportunity for instructions, warnings, or advice. The rescue was underway.

Maker, save Your people. On Meriel and on these foelands.

Makah leapt forward with so much vigor, I had to cling to stay on. Rogue's Aerie loomed ahead. Brantley's eyes burned in the darkness. I fervently hoped that Cole was with the convoy in the channel. It would be hard enough to locate and rescue the captives. A confrontation between Brantley and his brother would be disastrous.

SPRAY FROM THE WAVES MISTED MY FACE. OVER MY shoulder, I glimpsed a few other herders and stenella. As soon as the last sail disappeared up the channel, they had come out of hiding and surged toward the foelands. Even though I knew to look for them, I could barely see the ripples of their approach. The wind had blown away the dusting of cloud cover, and though the stars were muted and dull, they offered more light than I preferred. As we drew close to Rogue's Aerie, I worried about sentries spotting us.

Brantley apparently had the same fears. "Hold on," he said. "We're going to dive."

"What? No—"

Too late. I held my breath as the water swallowed us. My eyelids had reflexively squeezed closed, but a blue glow coaxed me to open them. Instead of the inky blackness I expected, azure crystals cast light far into the depths. Between and under the small islands, a stretch of land connected the foeland that we were approaching to another one. When we surfaced, I forgot to complain about how little warning he'd given me before the dive. "Did you see that?"

Brantley's eyes were wide, even as water dripped from his hair and ran down his face. "I've never seen stones that give light. What are they?"

"I don't know. Did you see the path? Connecting this island to the next? The people here have a legend about a bridge builder. It looks like they already have a bridge—at least between those two lands. It's just hidden by the sea. No wonder the foelands felt different underfoot."

"Very strange. I'd love to get a sample of that glowing rock, but we don't have time now." Brantley shook water from his head and guided Makah to the shore of Rogue's Aerie, some distance from their empty dock. "Wait here with Makah until I scout ahead."

I'd prepared for this. In spite of his promise to help me seek the Maker's purpose for these lands, I knew he'd try to find ways to keep me back. I understood the desperate need to keep a loved one safe, but when he leapt from Makah to the shore, I climbed onto the tangleroot after him. The steady wind that was luring enemy veskals up the channel tugged my wet tunic and dried my face.

"What are you doing?" he demanded.

I pulled a cloak from my pack and wrapped it around my shoulders, ready to blend into shadows. "I'm safer with you than alone in the darkness."

He sighed but offered me his arm. With my cane in one hand and Brantley beside me, I moved forward with a silent tread. Tangleroot gave way to a stretch of soft dirt. Only a short distance forward, the surface changed underfoot to hard slate. Rogue's Aerie rose starkly upward, presenting us with a rock face that felt as impenetrable as the hearts of the foeland commanders.

Perhaps I should go back to Makah. I'd never be able to scale this natural fortress and would only hinder Brantley. "Maybe we should try a different island," I whispered.

"This way." For now at least, the plan didn't seem to include scaling the heights. Brantley moved swiftly but cautiously along the rock face toward the dock. There had to be a way inland from there, or the raiders would have no way in and out of their settlement.

Hugging the deeper darkness of the cliff, we neared the dock and found a crevice that opened into blackness. If Brantley were a forest hound, his fur would be standing straight up. The fine hairs on the back of my neck rose as we entered. My bare feet sought clues from the earth, but the unrelenting stone didn't speak the way soft soil could.

Maker, what am I supposed to do in this place?

Flint scraped. Light flared, blinding me. Squinting, I saw a man holding a torch.

"So we meet again, little brother." Cole's voice held a twist of bitterness, as if his soul had been scarred like my tendon, no longer able to support the weight of hope or love.

Under my hand, Brantley went rigid, muscles bunched and hard. He didn't speak, so I eased forward. "I'm Carya, Brantley's wife."

In the flicker of flame, Cole's gaze raked me. As he took in my sodden leggings and headscarf, his lip curled. "What's a dancer doing so far from the Order?"

I drew back from his disdain, pressing closer to Brantley, who finally found his voice. "What are you doing raiding your own people?" Even as he demanded answers from his brother, he scanned the dark passage through the rock, undoubtedly searching for Cole's men.

Cole noticed and snorted. "Scared? If I'd wanted to kill you, you'd already be dead." His dark brows pulled downward. "How could you marry one of the accursed people who stole my daughter?"

I was grateful Cole's hand was occupied holding the torch, because I was certain if he had both hands free, he'd draw one of the arrows stored in his shoulder pouch and send it through me.

"Orianna is safe," I said quickly.

He glared at me. "No child is safe in the Order."

Brantley stepped in front of me. "Carya helped Orianna escape."

That was stretching the story a bit. I'd merely tagged along on his rescue of his niece.

Cole's death-glare toward me eased slightly. Yearning, hope, skepticism all warred in his eyes. "Orianna is free? Safe?" Then his free hand grabbed a fistful of Brantley's tunic. "Are you lying? What about Bri?"

Instead of knocking Cole's arm away, Brantley stood still, matching his brother's searching gaze. "They live in Windswell. Mourning you every day. As does our mother." Then my husband scowled. "And you sent a veskal to attack us."

Cole released his grip and shrugged. "It's what we do."

At Brantley's growl, Cole held up a hand. "Don't get your breeches in a tangle. I didn't know this was Meriel."

"But after you saw me, you knew. Admit it. You. Knew. And still you let your raider friends attack again tonight."

"Let them? I'm in command here. I *sent* them. I guessed you would come. Didn't need an audience for our reunion." His sneer made my mouth sour.

Brantley's shoulders tensed. I edged around him to smile at Cole. "I'm sure you both have a lot to explain to each other. Is there somewhere safe where we can talk?"

Cole continued to ignore me. "Take me to Bri and Orianna. Now."

"Do you think I'll let you break our mother's heart again? Bringing a wild, murderous raider to her door? I won't even tell them you live until I'm sure of you."

Cole grinned—the same crooked, boyish grin I'd see so often on my husband's face. "Wild and murderous, eh?" Then the humor fled. "You won't keep me from them." Two bristling forest hounds, and I had no dance to calm them.

I wedged between the brothers. "We're here to rescue the women stolen from our rim villages by these foelands. Are any of them here?"

"I don't encourage the stealing of a potential victory child." He still watched Brantley, refusing to look at me, but at least he answered my question this time.

"Then will you help us find the others? Can you protect us while we search?"

"My little brother doesn't need protecting, do you?" He poked Brantley's ribs, and in spite of his effort to look fierce and strong, my husband winced.

I shoved Cole back a step. "Don't touch him. He's injured. Could have been an arrow from one of your men, for all we know."

Cole lifted the torch and studied his brother more closely. "Are you healing?"

"He will." I threw my shoulders back. "If he stops ripping open the wound. He almost died. Now will you help us? There's not much time."

Brantley shook his head. "She's right that time is short. If you swear none of the women from Meriel are here, we need to move on."

Cole cocked his head. "So it *was* a trick. I suspected as much. What's the next stage of the plan? Change the wind to push the veskals back?" He shrugged. "The foelanders will fight among themselves and return to raid each other's lands. Another day, another battle." A current of weariness wound through his words.

Brantley's anger seemed to fade, replaced by confusion and hurt. "What happened to you?"

"I don't owe you an explanation. If you won't take me to Windswell, I'll head there myself when my veskals return."

I rolled my eyes. "All right. You don't owe an explanation. But we want to hear about your experiences, don't we, Brantley?" I nudged his uninjured side gently, willing him to stop bristling. "And we can tell you about your family."

Cole shook his head and scanned me again, his loathing pouring over me like a rainstorm. "A dancer? Really, Bran?"

"Not just a dancer. A woman who carried the Maker's letter to our people, confronted the Order, and danced Meriel free. That's when the Maker carved the new channel across our island."

"Quite a tale." Cole reached for a pack hidden in the shadows and slung it over his shoulder. "You won't be safe here much longer. Let's go."

Brantley shifted his weight, indecision making him dance side to side.

A rodent rustled in the weeds at the cliff's base. Wind howled up the crevice. Danger taunted my nerves. We couldn't stay here. "Brantley, whatever has happened to him, he deserves to see his wife and daughter."

"Makah can't carry all three of us."

No, but she could carry the two brothers. Clarity sent a wave of peace through me. "Cole, is there a clearing where I would be safe until Brantley can return for me?"

Cole rubbed his jaw. "I could assign a few trusted guards to watch you. What are you up to?"

"You might trust your men. We don't." Brantley turned to me. "I promised to guard your back."

I touched his face. "Let the Maker do that. It's time." He knew what I meant. It was time for me to dance for these lands, to raise the bridge, to bring hope and change to all the foelands.

Brantley groaned and raked a hand through his hair. Then he jabbed a finger at Cole. "Safest place you can think of where she can touch the earth of your island."

"No. She's not dancing on my island." Cole's mouth cut a grim channel through his face.

Brantley's chin rose. "That's the price of passage to Windswell. A safe place where she won't be interrupted. Where no one will see her."

"All right," he drawled at last. "You don't ask for much." A hint of humor laced Cole's tone, reminding me achingly of Brantley when he was feeling sarcastic. Oh, how I hoped these brothers could find their way back to each other. If Cole only knew how many days Brantley had searched for his body. And I could only guess what Cole had endured to survive the Order's attempt to kill him. Perhaps they would both find compassion for each other's pain. And while they worked out their differences, I could fulfill my calling to raise the foelands and reveal the bridges.

"This way." Torch aloft, Cole led us deeper up the crevice and to an intersecting ravine. "Not far." He shot a questioning look at my cane.

I lengthened through my spine. "I'm fine. Lead on."

Brantley reacted at every sound, head snapping this way and that, eyes scanning for danger.

Maker, I'm prepared. I'm coming. I'm ready to help these lands.

"Here." Cole waved the torch in a wide arc. We emerged from the towering rock face near the sea. The clearing ahead was secluded, with only low shrubs and daygrass dotting the earth.

"This will work. Thank you." I offered Cole a grateful smile, but he just narrowed his eyes, lips pressed in a speculative line.

Brantley pulled me into an embrace and whispered against my ear. "I'll be back as soon as I've brought Cole to the Windswell people in hiding."

"Are you sure you can trust him?"

"No," he said flatly. "But if he intends to bring harm to his own family, I'm not sure I'd want to be alive to see it anyway."

I squeezed my husband, careful of his bandaged ribs. "Hurry back." We rested our foreheads together, breathing the same air, tasting the citrus wind, hearts bound forever in a desperate but joyous love.

Then he stepped away, following Cole and his torch back into the darkness. My eyes adjusted to the night. Overhead, red stars were swelling, near bursting. There might be a star rain tonight after all. A night bird cooed from somewhere on the cliffs overhead. The sea splashed as the wind continued its forceful push against the water. Time to focus on a new world that needed help. The Maker had used me in the past, and I was ready to save these islands as well. I tossed aside my cane, nestled my bare feet into the daygrass, and began to dance.

28

THE SURGE AND RETREAT OF WAVES BECAME MY DRUMBEAT.
I knelt, arms sweeping the ground before me, then arched back with
hands open to the stars. I swayed, listening for the call I'd heard before.

Heaviness invaded my bones. The sensation of sinking pulled me toward
the earth. With huge effort, I staggered to my feet. *Lift!* I spun on my good
leg, creating pictures of lightness and beauty with the line of my body.

The sorrow of the broken lands seeped through me, and I cried for
them. I cried for the slaves, I cried for the raiders trapped in greed and
endless cycles of theft. I cried for the women snatched away from their
homes because they carried a child that another clan wanted. And as I
cried, I danced.

Overhead, the red stars burst and fell, lifting my spirit. This had to be a
sign of favor. A sign that my efforts would succeed.

Swirling in place, then moving outward in concentric circles, I waited
for the earth to stir, to tremble, to rise. My chest heaved, sweat joined the
tears on my face, my muscles trembled. Still I danced, springing upward
again and again. When all strength was expended, I collapsed back to the
ground, limp as wrung-out laundry.

The Maker would answer now. I'd done all I could. I touched the earth
to feel the rumble, brushing aside the sand left from the brief star rain.

Nothing happened.

This didn't make sense. The Maker had sent me here. I knew it. And
I'd heard the cry of the land, heard the legend of a bridge builder, knew I
had been called to return to these dangerous islands to help them. Even
Brantley saw the truth of that and brought me here when everything in him
wanted me safe on Meriel.

Maker, I'm here. I'm trying to build the bridge, trying to lift the land. What am I doing wrong?

I wiped sweat from my forehead, shook out my throbbing legs, and stood doubled over. Years ago, after a long and brutal class at the Order, I'd felt this way. And when the saltar demanded another pattern, somehow I had found the strength. After a few deep breaths, I closed my eyes and threw myself into another round of wobbly turns. I stretched, bent, swung my leg high and let it hover. I tossed star rain residue skyward, watching it glitter then die again. The lack of response from the island made it feel as if I were flinging my body against a cold marble wall over and over until my bones would break.

The next time I crumpled to the ground, I sprawled forward, my face tucked in one arm, the other stretching forward, palm up and pleading. *Maker, do something!*

That was how Brantley found me. "Carya?"

The alarm in his voice motivated me to stir. "I'm all right. But . . ." I didn't have to tell him I'd failed. The evidence was all around us.

"We need to leave. The wind has changed."

I let him help me up and attempted a few unsteady steps. "Did it work? Did the herders find all the women?"

"I'll fill you in on the way. Here, jump on my back."

Brantley had found many creative ways to carry me in the past, but doing so now would tear open his wound again. "I can walk."

"Hurry!" With his arm supporting me, he led me back into the rock canyon. Here the stars barely cast any light, and Brantley hadn't brought a torch. Yet he seemed confident of the direction, so I concentrated on not stumbling over my leaden feet.

"What happened?" Brantley asked as we emerged from the canyon and headed toward the shore.

Nothing. I shook my head, not trusting myself to speak. Clearly, I'd failed.

Brantley helped me settle on Makah and crouched behind me. "Stay low," he cautioned.

I nodded, still mute, and Makah sped away from the foelands. As we neared Meriel, the wind scoured my face. Had the dancers allowed enough time for our team of herders to rescue everyone?

Brantley patted my shoulder. "Cheer up. The plan is working. As soon as their veskals withdraw, we can pull Meriel away."

My eyes burned, too dry from the wind for tears. We hadn't helped these foelands. The Maker had given me a glimpse of His heart for the people of these islands. I was sure of His plan and my part in it. And I wasn't good enough. Not strong enough, skilled enough, wise enough. Confusion and humiliation battered me with the same searing pressure of the downstream wind. My heart contracted into a tight ball. At least I hadn't proclaimed my secret intentions to anyone besides Brantley.

At a whistle from Brantley, Makah veered, pulling farther out to sea and giving the mouth of the channel a wide berth. No retreating veskals appeared yet, but better safe than sorry. We traveled well past deserted Windswell before approaching the shore. Soon we'd be reunited with Brantley's family where they hid in the woods.

"How is Cole?" I asked when I finally trusted my voice.

"Bri and my mother welcomed him with open arms." He didn't sound happy about the glad reunion.

"That's wonderful."

"We'll see."

I twisted to look at him. "Brantley, give him a chance. We need to hear his story." I'd much rather give him advice than confront my own failure. Grateful for the distraction, I pressed my point. "His return is a miracle."

Now that we were nearing shore, Brantley straightened, his stance adjusting subtly to Makah's surging movements. He glared at the shore as we approached. The tight line of his jaw didn't bode well for a quick reconciliation between the brothers.

As we stepped onto the shore and headed into the forest, I tried again. "Why are you so angry? It wasn't his fault he was speared and cast into the sea."

Brantley stopped dead, his incredulous expression clear in the starlight. "Have you forgotten how these foelanders live? Think what he's become." His arm wrapped absently around his ribs.

I had no answer for him and felt far too defeated to argue. If I hadn't been able to raise a bridge between islands, I doubted I could create a bridge between brothers. Subdued, I followed Brantley silently until we reached the encampment.

Under the cover of the spreading limbs of tall pines, joyous and whispered conversations circulated, melding with the rustling of wind-tossed branches. Most of the rescued women had gone straight on to their own rim villages once the herders had freed them. But a few herders from a greater distance away were letting their mounts, and their village's women, rest for the night.

A group of men brought Brantley the latest reports. Veskals had been pushed back down the channel, and some were already visible near the mouth of the river. Rim villages were prepared to defend their land if the foelanders attacked before Meriel could be moved to safety. As far as the herders could tell, most of the stolen women had been rescued. A few injuries, but no deaths. Brantley headed out to check with some of the outposts, ready to signal the Order again once he was sure everyone was accounted for.

Not wanting to dampen the celebratory mood, I searched among the tree trunks for family. I found Fiola sitting on a blanket, her back braced against a tree, cradling a sleeping Orianna. Beside her, Cole sat with his arm around Brianna. She nestled against him as if she wanted to burrow into him. He kept touching her face, her hair, her hands. Both trembled with the wonder of no longer being lost to each other.

Brianna glanced up. "Where's Brantley?"

I settled near them, exhausted, famished, and relieved to sit. "He's getting reports. Finishing the mission."

Brianna squeezed Cole's hand. "What will your men do when they return and find you gone?"

He shrugged. "They'll be too afraid to question my absence for a time." A hint of arrogance colored his voice.

Brianna frowned, perhaps noticing it too. Cole had become a different person. What would that mean for the two of them?

But when he turned his head to watch his sleeping daughter, my worries on that score eased. Tenderness washed over his expression. Longing, regret, and even hope.

"How did you come to survive when everyone thought you were dead?" I asked.

Brianna shook her head. "Before he tells that story, he wants Brantley here."

"If he cares to hear it," Cole said. "He made it clear that he despises what I've become."

Brianna stroked his face. "And you turned away from him when you first saw him. He's hurt." Bri would build the bridge.

I stretched out, leaning back on my elbows. I wasn't needed here either. None of my efforts seemed to make a difference, not for the foelands, not for Meriel, not for the people I loved. I let the cushion of pine needles take the weight of my tired muscles. Although part of me wanted to hide my shame and confusion over my failure on Rogue's Aerie, another part of me longed to talk to Brantley. Maybe he could help me figure out what I'd done wrong. But that would have to wait.

"There you are." Brantley took in the scene and frowned but then handed me a bundle of fabric. "I brought you a dry cloak."

My tunic and leggings were almost dry, but the added layer was a comfort. "Thank you." I sat up and patted the ground beside me.

He lowered beside me, stiff and bristly, ignoring Cole.

Brianna rolled her eyes, shaking her head. "Brantley, I won't let you ruin this miracle. Cole was lost, and now he's back. We should be laughing with joy."

Neither man looked close to laughter, but Brantley sighed and actually turned his gaze to his brother. "What will the foelands do next? If we move the island away, will they pursue us? Did anyone explain our plan?"

Fiola spoke quietly from her place against the tree, stroking Orianna's back. "We've already told Cole about the changes to the Order and the fact that the dancers no longer have our island locked in place."

"I saw some of the changes for myself. Didn't even recognize that this world was Meriel because of the channel. Just another island ripe for plunder." Cole laughed, a bit of the clan captain showing through.

Brantley stiffened beside me, and I took his hand. "Just *talk* to him," I whispered.

"Fine." Brantley leaned forward. "When you saw me. When you knew who I was—*where* you were—why did you sail away?"

Cole leaned forward as well, and the space between the two men crackled with suppressed fury. "Because I didn't trust myself. I've hated you for so long, I wasn't sure what I'd do."

Brantley recoiled as if Cole had punched his pierced side. Fiola gasped. Brianna stared at the ground.

"But why?" I choked out.

Cole never took his eyes off his brother. "Tell her."

A LAD APPROACHED OUR HUDDLED CONVERSATION. "IS IT safe to build a fire?" he asked Brantley. "Word's come that the veskals are returning to their lands."

"No," Brantley snapped. The boy's eyes widened, and he scurried quickly away.

Around us, the steady wind continued. Cole's chest filled with the arrogance of a clan leader. "Go on. Tell them the truth."

Brantley glared at his brother. "You know I would have done all I could to protect Orianna." My husband spat out the words.

"Right. If you'd been there." The venom in Cole's voice was directed at Brantley but was angry enough to sting all of us.

I tried to catch Brianna's eyes. I wanted to slip away into the woods and leave these two men to have this bitter conversation in private. But she had eyes only for Cole. If she wasn't leaving, I wasn't either. I only hoped Orianna slept through it.

"Brantley risked everything to rescue her," I said gently.

"She wouldn't have needed rescuing if he'd stayed home that day."

I sat up taller. "If he had been in the village then, there would likely have been two of you run through by the Order's soldiers. There would have been no one to rescue Orianna. How would that have done any good?"

But neither man was listening to me. Brantley tightened up again, as if ready to fight. But then he gave a deep sigh, and his whole body sagged. He rubbed the back of his neck. "You're right. It's my fault."

"What? Don't say that." I clenched his hand more tightly, drawing it to my heart. Even in the shadows of night, despair was clearly written across his face.

He tugged his hand away, refusing my comfort. "I was stupid and proud. I wanted to bring in fish, and the gulls were circling far out to sea." He raised his chin only enough to meet Cole's gaze. "I didn't believe your story about soldiers from the Order being nearby. When I got back and they told me a soldier had driven a spear into you, and they'd thrown you into the ocean . . ."

"He went mad with grief," Brianna said. "He searched day and night for your body, still believing that somehow you'd be alive."

Cole's shoulders softened a fraction, and he tilted his head. At least he was listening now, instead of hurling accusations.

Brantley's voice broke. "When I couldn't search anymore, I bundled my rage and headed inland to find Orianna. I hadn't been there to help you protect her, but at least I could try to save her."

I knew that part of the story. We'd met during his rescue campaign. I took his hand again, hoping he would feel my love through that simple touch.

Now that both men's postures seemed softer, I dared to speak again. "Cole, how did you survive?"

He scratched his head. "That's a strange tale." He kissed the top of Brianna's head. "I waited until you were all here, so I only have to tell it once."

She looked up at him, adoring. In whatever ways Cole had been changed by his experiences, whatever he had done to endure, it clearly didn't matter to her. Brantley, however, still narrowed his eyes in suspicion as he waited for Cole to explain.

Cole gave him a rueful smile. "Glad to see you've learned a little about being careful who you trust, baby brother."

Brantley snorted. "You think you're going to convince me to trust you? I've seen how you raiders live."

Brianna straightened. "Brantley, I've never known you to be cruel."

Cole pulled her closer. "No, he's right. I have a lot to account for." A deep pool of regret swirled in Cole's eyes.

Bri gave murmured reassurances. My husband studied his brother, searching for signs of—what? Betrayal? That hardly seemed likely. My husband's own false guilt was keeping him from embracing Cole.

"Tell us," I urged, hoping Cole would talk before their animosity escalated again.

He sighed. "There's a lot I don't remember after the attack. I wasn't going to let them steal my daughter, but we were outnumbered."

A tiny flinch of Brantley's arm under my hand showed me he was still blaming himself. It was probably easier for him to hate Cole than to face the weight of that blame. I stroked his arm.

"It felt like the spear cut me in half, and the next thing I knew two soldiers were dragging me to the rim. I remember Bri screaming and Orianna crying. Then the water buried me, and all sound fell away. The world darkened. I was sinking into the deep unknown . . . or else I was passing out. I didn't know. I told my limbs to swim, to go back, to grab the tangleroot. But I couldn't move."

I shivered, remembering the terror of sinking into dark water. Under the tree, tears glistened on Fiola's cheeks as she cradled her granddaughter.

Cole cleared his throat. "Strangely, a peace washed through me. It was over. No more striving. And I closed my eyes." He rubbed his forehead. "After that, I don't know what was real and what wasn't. I opened my eyes once and was on the surface. Something beneath me pressed me upward and held me above the water. But breathing hurt so bad. No matter how hard I tried, I couldn't stay awake. I had lost so much blood everything was weakness and darkness and sparkles across my vision like black star rain."

Brantley shifted beside me. Was he recalling his own arrow wound? He'd felt that same leeching away of life, the same tug toward death that Cole endured.

"I don't know how much time passed," Cole continued. "Glimpses of the suns. Sips of water. The touch of milky waves. The sound of splashing. One time when I woke, I heard the chittering of a stenella, but that made no sense." He looked at Brantley. "You know I never went near the creatures."

Brantley managed a tight smile. "You can't deny their usefulness after tonight."

Cole pressed his lips together, but then nodded. "Not just tonight. I suspect it was a pod who saved me. When I finally woke, I'd been tossed onto a tangleroot shore. But I soon learned I wasn't on Meriel."

I shivered. Until recently, none of us had known there were other worlds floating on the vast sea. Wounded, cast adrift, in torment for his wife and daughter. How had Cole endured it?

Brianna snuggled closer to him. "But you are now," she whispered.

Cole's brow furrowed, as if not quite believing it himself. "A woman found me. Bonty was her name."

I stiffened. "I met her. She sold me to Mander."

Cole narrowed his eyes my direction. "We have something in common, then."

I waited while he gathered his thoughts.

But Brantley shifted impatiently. "That doesn't explain how you came to be the captain of a veskal attacking our people." A fair question, and I noticed less accusation in his tone.

"I told you. I didn't know this newland was Meriel." He shrugged. "Once my wound healed enough, I was a slave. I was captured by the commander of Rogue's Aerie during one of the many skirmishes. He soon saw that I would have more value as a raider, so I was promoted."

Sorrow welled up in my chest. Cole adapted. He survived. But what had it cost him to change into a violent, thieving foelander? From the gravel in his voice, the pain was near the surface, especially now as he held his wife and watched his sleeping daughter.

Cole lifted his jaw, daring Brantley to mock or chide.

But my husband only nodded. "I'm glad you didn't die."

Cole barked a surprised laugh. "Nicest thing you ever said to me, brother."

Brantley ducked his chin. "That didn't come out the way I meant. It's just . . . I understand. You found a way to build a life."

His brother sobered. "I didn't know if I was in some strange afterlife. I soon surrendered any hope of seeing this world again. So I . . . yes, I built a life. Of sorts." He raked a hand through his snarled hair, so similar to Brantley's, but even more untamed. "I defended my clan. I fought to be sure the servants weren't abused. And when my commander was killed in battle, the other raiders called on me to be their new captain."

"Of course they did," Brantley muttered, but without animosity.

Cole chuckled. "Still jealous of me? Seems like you've become quite the leader yourself. Getting herders to work together, forming armies to take down the Order."

Brantley sat a little taller, but he shook his head. "It wasn't our fighters who took down the Order." He wrapped his arm around my shoulders. "It was this dancer."

Now I shook my head. "Not me. The Maker freed Meriel."

Cole raised a skeptical brow.

Time enough to explain all that later. Yet the words echoed in my heart, calling to me. *It wasn't me.* I needed to think about that truth more deeply. But for now I had questions of my own. "I've had a little experience with the foelands," I said. "At least with yours and Mander's and Larcy's. But there's something I don't understand."

Cole's eyes narrowed, but he didn't cut me off.

"The raids on Meriel. They've been different from the raids among your clans."

He shrugged. "The raiders value gems and weapons. They didn't find much fair theft in the rim villages they reached."

"And they value pregnant women." I touched my belly, the longing to guard and protect welling into my throat.

He dipped his head in acknowledgement. "That's the tradition."

"Except they take all sorts of captives from each other; so why only take pregnant women from Meriel?"

Brantley straightened. "Did they take anyone else? If so, our mission is far from over."

Cole shook his head. "Capturing each other's servants is a show of strength. No clan wanted to bother with more mouths to feed from the newland—especially as they didn't come across warriors who would be much use."

"Then why the women about to bear children?" I persisted.

He sighed. "It's an old myth among the foelands. They believe that a victory child will one day create a bridge. A time will dawn without all the conflict and raids. The foelands will be united."

Tingles lifted the hair at the back of my neck. "And they think that by capturing pregnant women . . ."

"They've proven a victory—thus a victory child. And you may have noticed, there are few successful births and few children among the foelands. So each commander hopes to be the one to gain a victory child and see it born—in case it is the foretold bridge maker."

"Horrible," Brianna said.

Cole squeezed her shoulders. "As I said, I didn't join in that pursuit."

Brianna elbowed him. "Good thing."

Brantley stood, still favoring his side. The ground was rocked by a gentle wave, but overhead the branches had stopped rustling now that the wind had died. "Only one runner has yet to report back. I'll go to await his news and make ready to signal the Order."

We couldn't steer Meriel away. Not yet. The work wasn't done! I stood as well. "I'll go with you."

We limped slowly toward the sea and then along the rim to the watchpoint. From behind the cover of trees, we watched the mouth of the river, where yet another veskal emerged and sailed toward the foelands, barely limping along in the faint breeze that remained.

"Teague is supposed to bring me news here. If you're worried that we'll leave someone behind—"

"Not someone. Everyone," I blurted.

Brantley studied me. We were both in pain from our injures, both exhausted, both pushed past our limits. Whatever he saw in me worried him. "You tried."

"And I failed."

"Maybe the vision you saw was just a glimpse of something the Maker will do ages from now. They have a legend of a bridge maker."

How I wished that were true. It would be so much easier to divorce myself from all responsibility. After all, guidance from the Maker was often subtle and sometimes difficult to discern. Perhaps I had mistaken His intent.

I shook my head. "How will they know about the Maker if there is no one to tell them?"

He turned me toward him, holding my arms. "Carya, you've done all you can. Whatever the Maker intends, He'll find another way."

"But—"

"You think of yourself as special . . ."

I bristled. I'd never said that.

Brantley's grip on my arms tightened. "Of course you would. You stood alone against the entire Order.

"It wasn't me. It was the Maker." Those words again. They confronted me. Held up a reflection. Heat rose to my cheeks. I had acted as if I, and I alone, needed to save the foelands. Glimpsing my arrogance shocked me. My eyes widened. "That's it, isn't it? I've carried a weight to prove myself, to be worthy, to save others. But I've been sinking. Sinking like the foelands."

Deep, caring eyes met mine. "You don't need to prove anything. Only the Maker can save us—and others. You don't have to carry that burden."

When had my husband become so wise? I nodded, relief buoying me like a gentle wave. I touched the soft lines furrowing Brantley's brow. "And your burden. You don't need to drown in guilt either."

His frown deepened. "Fair point, but I'll think about that later. Now about the dancing. Perhaps the desire that the Maker stirred in you needs the work of many, not just you."

My eyes widened. "You're right. There may be times we're called to stand alone, but other times, we're called to dance in community."

My pulse sped up. Brantley had managed to organize solitary herders to work together and rescue our people. Why couldn't we also gather a team to dance?

"That's it!" I bounced up and down.

Brantley released me, his eyebrows lifting. "What are you thinking?"

"If we brought a team of dancers to Rogue's Aerie, we could dance together. We could restore the land bridges. And we could leave the people the Maker's letter."

"How would you bring a group of dancers to the foelands? There aren't enough stenella and herders left here—and you wouldn't convince most dancers to ride a stenella anyway." Even as he objected, Brantley rubbed his jaw. "Of course, now that villages know about the raiders, they could protect the women we rescued—at least for a few more days."

I nodded eagerly. Recognizing that I was no Maker, I felt a new freedom to trust Him to provide. A new plan began to form. "But we still have the problem of how to get a group of dancers to the foelands safely and quickly."

Another veskal sailed away into the night.

Brantley grinned, his teeth a white flash in the dim starlight. "A veskal would work."

"What?"

"Cole could sail upriver to the Order and take the dancers back to his island. *If* he promised dancers safe passage . . . *if* his foeland will still follow him, can you convince enough dancers to come with you?"

I was already mentally designing a new pattern. Perhaps a dozen dancers. Starfire would come. Iris. Maybe Furrow and even a few saltars. Yes. Yes, this could work. With favorable winds, the veskal could reach Middlemost and take us back within a day or two. Then a new problem struck me. "But with favorable winds, all the foelands would send crafts. We'd be back to the same problem."

"Cole's people used poles to travel even against the wind."

"But that will take too much time."

"We'll figure something out. Maybe no wind. Then the other veskals won't try the journey, but Cole's people can. Then the dancers in the center ground can whip up a gale to send the craft back to the sea quickly. But will the dancers trust a veskal full of raiders?"

I pressed my fist against my mouth, deep in thought. Finally, I looked up. "Maybe. I think if I explain, they'll risk the journey. But as you said, will Cole's raiders still follow him? If he travels upriver and doesn't raid, won't they rebel against him as their leader? And if they know he's been here with us, will they see that as a weakness in him?" I'd seen the way raiders grappled for advancement and power. A hint of weakness from Cole, and the plan would crumble.

Brantley grimaced. "We don't even know if Cole will agree to this. He's just returned to his wife and daughter, to his whole world. Why would he risk everything to bring a group of dancers to the foelands?"

He was right. But the image of the islands lifting and uniting burned in my mind. If we did nothing, the foelands would continue to fight each other, the land might well continue to sink, and soon there would be no one left to save.

30

"ABSOLUTELY NOT." THE PRIMARY SUN GLEAMED ACROSS the water, highlighting Brantley's angry glare.

"It's the only way this will work." Cole leveled his hard gaze at me. "How much does this matter to you?"

How much was I willing to risk in order to help all the strangers of the foelands? His plan was crazy. Dangerous. But so was mine. To have any hope of success, we had to trust each other. I swallowed. "I'll do it."

"No!" Brantley said. "I'm not putting her in your hands."

"If I return empty-handed after my absence, my people won't follow me. Especially not in another journey up the channel when Rogue's Aerie has made two attempts that have failed." He dropped a heavy hand on my shoulder. "Bringing them a victory child will consolidate my power."

I didn't like the sound of it any more than Brantley did. But I could think of no other way to transport a large group of dancers quickly and safely to the foelands. I clutched my husband's hand. "We have to move fast. If we keep Meriel near much longer, there will be more raids. We won't be able to defend our villages forever."

"So let me signal Meriel's move away. Problem solved."

I crossed my arms. "And ignore the Maker's call? The people of those lands are miserable. They need our help."

Brantley dug his fingers through his hair, the gesture of exasperation that I'd become so familiar with. "Makah can't carry Cole, you, and me all at once."

"You worry too much." I stepped closer to brush an errant lock out of his eyes, and fondness warmed my chest. "After Makah has dropped Cole and me at Rogue's Aerie, she can return to you, and you can follow his veskal." I turned to Cole. "How soon can we leave? Will your raiders be willing to attempt the channel again today?"

Cole grinned, seeming amused at his brother's distrust. "Go ahead and summon the creature while I say goodbye to my wife and daughter."

As soon as he was out of earshot, Brantley handed me a newly carved whistle. "If anything feels off, signal Makah. On the foeland, on the channel. If you feel the slightest bit uncertain, Makah and I will be near."

I frowned. "Do you really think Cole would betray us? He's thrilled to be reunited with his family."

"Maybe. But none of us know who he has truly become. And I know he has no fondness for dancers." Brantley's grim tone made my stomach tighten. The baby squirmed in protest, a tiny kick startling me.

My arms cradled my belly. "Believe me. I know what's at stake. Besides, rallying a whole group of dancers was your idea."

"It was a hypothetical," he protested. "I only meant that you don't have to save worlds on your own. Recruiting a team from the center ground was your idea."

I clasped his face and drew it down to meet my lips. My deep kiss may not have reassured him fully, but it distracted him. As we separated, his eyes flared with a better emotion than worry.

"You do keep life interesting, dancer," he said.

Brantley signaled for Makah, who must have been hovering nearby. She appeared like a vegetable bobbing up in a kettle. I fussed over her and stroked her floppy ears, while my husband watched, bemused.

In no time, Cole returned. "You first."

I positioned myself behind Makah's neck. Cole stumbled awkwardly onto her and sat behind me, his feet drawn up to avoid her tucked-in side fins. It felt strange to have this commander of raiders crouched behind me, rather than Brantley's agile form standing and directing.

Makah must have thought the same, because she chittered anxiously. I circled my fist overhead and pointed. For a moment I thought she'd ignore me. She spun and tilted her head, eyeing Brantley on the shore.

He repeated my signal, and she gave a very human-like snort but obeyed. Soon we were cutting through the smooth sea straight for Rogue's Aerie. I didn't need Cole's help to find the way, since its cliffs loomed higher than the other islands.

I glanced back at Cole's tense features and hid a smile. I shouldn't laugh. I'd been every bit as uncomfortable riding a stenella at first.

We skirted one of the other foelands.

"Down!" Cole shouted, shoving me hard.

Makah swerved, and I struggled to keep my seat.

Arrows whistled past. I spotted a watchtower on a small foeland, from which several archers scanned the sea and probably attacked anything that moved. We quickly outran their weapons and neared Rogue's Aerie. I wondered if we'd receive a similar welcome there.

"Guide her straight to the dock," Cole said through gritted teeth.

He seemed as worried as I was—or else he was still unnerved by only his second ride on a stenella in his life. Makah balked at drawing too close to the three veskals tied to one side of the dock, but eventually I coaxed her near.

A watcher at the rim shouted a call, and by the time Cole climbed off of Makah, several raiders emerged from the cliffs and canyon. I scrambled onto the flexible wooden platform while Cole drew a length of rope from his tunic. "Give me your hands," he hissed.

Another wave of doubt washed over me. I'd told Brantley to trust his brother, but what if Cole used my "capture" to raise his status? Too late to back out now. I held out my arms, and he quickly tied my wrists. With a swagger, he pulled me up the dock toward his people.

One man, wearing a breastplate, gauntlets, and more weaponry than the others stepped forward. "We feared you'd perished."

Cole sneered. "You mean you hoped to take over command, Danless. Sorry to disappoint."

The raider dipped his chin in submission. Cole ignored him and strode forward, tugging me along.

"He's brought us a victory child!" someone shouted.

"He rode in on a sea creature. No one has ever done that!"

"Captain, how did you conquer it?"

My unease grew. Cole's scheme to impress was working. But would he follow the plan?

He drew in a deep breath of sea air. "With this one"—he tugged the rope—"we will have the means to conquer the channel and raid the newland's innermost town."

I stiffened. I was supposed to be the decoy to keep his people from questioning his earlier absence. We'd never talked about—

"How?" Danless kept his gaze respectfully low, but his voice held a strong thread of challenge. "You forced us to withdraw the first time. Our last attempt—made after you deserted us—left us battered by infernal winds. Yet now you claim to know a way?" As he spoke, his chin lifted.

Cole drew his sword. "You think you can lead our clan better?"

What was he doing? Armed combat would only lead to disaster, no matter which of the men won. I pressed my lips together.

Danless glanced behind his shoulder, gauging the mood of the clan. He must have seen their eagerness to follow Cole on yet another raid, because he lifted his hands in appeasement. "I ain't opposing you, Captain. Just wanting to hear the plan."

"Load the mid-veskal. A dozen raiders and six of the best polers."

A few of the watching men groaned. Pushing the craft with staffs on their first attempt must have been exhausting. But the others cheered. Cole sent a runner up into the cliffs to spread the orders. As soon as everyone dove into their tasks, I rounded on him.

"What's this about conquering Middlemost? That wasn't the plan—" Too late, I noticed Danless had stopped behind me, arms full of empty baskets for plunder. Had he heard?

Cole's gaze landed on his second-in-command, and his nostrils flared. Then he backhanded me across the face. "Hold your tongue. Victory child or not, I won't tolerate insolence."

My cheek stung, and I had no trouble feigning the role of frightened captive. It seemed that was exactly what I'd become. I rubbed my face and seethed. Brantley would kill him when he heard about this.

"When do we set sail?" Danless asked. "Ain't no wind."

Cole bared his teeth. "There will be."

What was he thinking? He knew Brantley would be following us up the channel and that he'd do anything to protect me. Cole wasn't plotting to actually raid Middlemost or the Order, was he? He tugged the rope again, guiding me to a plank that provided a bridge onto the medium-sized veskal. The main sail hung slack, but once the men and women boarded and the polers pushed us away from the island, a smaller sail was raised and coaxed a bit of movement from the craft. Sweet spray coated my skin, and I glanced upward, reminding myself that the Maker didn't need my help to fulfill His plans. He could save and protect, and I could rest in that truth.

"Ready to earn your keep?" Cole said loudly, pulling the ropes away from my wrists.

I rubbed the chafed skin and glared at him. "What are you talking about?"

He waved an arm skyward. "You're a dancer. So dance. We need a strong wind—just for us so it won't draw the other foelanders."

That was his strategy? I shook my head. "I dance with bare feet on an island's earth. You're better off using your polers."

The frown he leveled on me reminded me of Mander, and my throat constricted. Poor Brianna. She had no idea what her husband had become. And Cole's betrayal would break my husband's heart all over again.

He leaned toward me and said in a low, mocking tone, "Where is your sense of adventure, dancer?"

I sighed. For now, Cole and I had the same objective. Reach the Order. "Give me space."

I removed my shoes and stood in the widest part of the veskal's low floor. A few inches of water sloshed across my toes. Closing my eyes, I prayed for guidance. I had danced in unconventional ways before. I'd swum around Navar and her wound had been healed. But later, to my great sorrow, nothing I'd done could save her. Dance didn't give me control over every circumstance. It connected me to the One who held all things in His merciful but sometimes incomprehensible hand.

Soft murmurs rose in my mind. Where in the past I'd heard the deep voice of the Maker's call through the earth of Meriel, now I heard His gentle whisper.

Ever and always. Ebbing and flowing. Carrying My people.

I rocked side to side, arms overhead, reaching toward the elusive wind. I didn't want to use a gale pattern or create a breeze that other foelanders might use. But I couldn't find a way to stir up air just around our sails.

The waves whispered again, wafting in a new idea. Not a wind pattern. A current pattern. The veskal lurched, and I fell to my knees, but stayed there. There was no way to perform the standard current pattern here. Instead, I gathered water from the deck into my palms and flung in overhead, then splashed my hands again and again. Rocking back and forth, my whole body became a wave. Deep beneath the surface, I sensed the sea's response.

The next time I looked up, the sails remained slack, but the craft soared along, pushed by a strong current, carrying us directly to the mouth of the channel and the still-vacant village of Windswell.

Cole had moved to stand at the prow, one foot on its lip, a hand shielding his eyes. He looked back at me, eyes wide. Then, masking his shock, he showed his men a smile that was more a satisfied sneer. "Raiders! Who still harbors doubt? You're welcome to disembark now."

A few men and women, all heavily armed, leaned over the sides to watch the ocean fly past. Their faces were pale. Two raiders near me backed away, as if I could fling them overboard with a wave of my hand.

Cole pointed at me. "Continue your dance until we reach Middlemost."

Still kneeling, I glared at him. If his goal was to win back the confidence of his clan, he'd succeeded. But if he had any desire to win my trust—or Brantley's—he was failing magnificently.

I reached into my tunic pocket. Was it time to signal Makah? Had she retrieved Brantley by now? Would she be able to slide into this powerful current and keep up with us? I pulled my hand away, empty. I needed to see this through. Once we reached the Order, I knew I could convince some of the women to accompany me. Together, if the Maker asked us to, we could lift the islands. The legend of the bridge builder would be fulfilled, and the commanders would no longer have a reason to capture and recapture the increasingly rare pregnant women like some child's game of hide the lenka. My palm rested on the rise of my belly. "Little victory child, hang on. The Maker wants to heal these people. We have a small part to play. Let's see what He does."

Sinking back to sit on my heels, I leaned forward again, letting the deck water wash over my legs, dancing my hands through each drop. The sea offered no resistance to the rushing veskal. It seemed to exult in concentrating this current into an eager push with a greater speed than even a stenella could manage. If it continued within the channel, we'd approach Middlemost before midday.

I spared another glance toward Cole, whose broad chest again reminded me of Brantley riding the seas. Untrustworthy raider or returning son of Windswell? I still had no idea. Surely if the Maker was allowing the sea to serve us this way, the path wouldn't lead to betrayal.

ONCE THE WATER'S PUSH WAS WELL ESTABLISHED, I TOOK A break from dancing to stand and look around. One of the raiders shouted and pointed. A veskal flying the colors of Ecco Cove slid between the islands, catching the tiniest puffs of air in their smaller sail.

If they found the current, would they be able to follow us? How far back did it extend? Cole's veskal entered the mouth of the river. Its tree-lined banks slid past in a blur. Cole wore a satisfied grin. He set his polers on either side of the craft in case the forceful upstream waters edged us too close to either side. Although the veskal was large, it was streamlined enough to slip through, even when the river narrowed near Middlemost.

I clambered over a coil of rope and a few empty crates and made my way to the back, hoping to catch a glimpse of Brantley and Makah following us. Part of me wished he wouldn't attempt the journey. He could tear open his wound. He should be resting and recovering from the fever that nearly took his life. Still, I shielded my eyes and scanned the river. But the frequent bends and outcroppings made it impossible to see a great distance. The raiders stayed away from me, and once I'd had my look, I returned to the center of the craft, sitting on a bench seat with my bare feet in the puddle that pooled in the bottom. Eyes closed, I listened for the rhythm of the coursing water but didn't coax it any further. In fact, I wasn't sure what would happen when we reached the rock cliffs by the Order. If the current didn't slow, we could be smashed against the stones.

Your heart finds new worries with every turn.

The gentle voice of the Maker seemed tinged with humor. He knew my tendencies. He knew me. But instead of rebuke, I heard His invitation to trust Him more deeply. Ignoring the rough, heavily armed people around me, I closed my eyes and lifted my arms. "Thank You for guiding us," I whispered. "Thank You for caring for each person, including those on the foelands and on this veskal."

A short way up the channel, as near as I could tell, we passed the outcropping where Brantley had mentioned the village of Shadowswell, where River's group was recruiting and training new dancers. I hoped that Tangleroot was making progress sending messages of warning to other villages. *Maker, help families see the truth. Open their eyes so they don't surrender their children to a life of striving and abuse.*

A flash of white drew my eye. A dancer perched on a ledge above us, scanning the channel. When she spotted us, she turned and ran inland on light feet. Off to inform River, no doubt. Would the opposing dancers ruin this whole precarious plan?

For the rest of the trip, Cole kept his distance from me, apparently satisfied with my performance. His back-slapping and animated conversations with the men and women of his raiding team showed me that if they had doubts about his choices until now, he'd won their respect today. And Cole's fondness for his people was evident in his manner. He crouched to help a young soldier bind feathers onto an arrow and eye whether it was straight. He passed a cup of water to a woman standing watch with a pole.

I rubbed the sore spot on my face that still stung from his blow. Ally or enemy? Brother or foe? The thoughts sloshed through me like the water moving forward and back with each tilt of the deck. I didn't know. Couldn't know. Time would tell. I turned my thoughts to trusting the Maker and made my way forward to Cole.

"Captain," Danless said sharply, warning him of my approach. Not that an off-balance, limping pregnant woman was able to arrive stealthily.

Cole's expression flattened, and he waved Danless away. "How much farther, dancer?"

I'd forgotten. He didn't know much about the center of our world. Cole was a rimmer, born and bred. And in his time, there had been no river to hasten travel inland. He'd probably never ventured far from Windswell.

Instead of answering his question, I gripped a railing near the prow for support and lowered my voice. "How will you keep your men onboard while I recruit dancers? They can't be allowed to raid Middlemost or the Order's storerooms. You'll need to keep them on the craft."

Cole gave a grin—almost as disarming as Brantley's, though I was far from ready to trust it. "You certainly do like to give orders," he said. "Does Brantley know that about you?"

I paused. I'd never seen myself that way. If anything, I was overly compliant from all my years as a novitiate. But he was right. Since discovering the Maker's letter, I'd sometimes been insistent on a path, zealously demanding my own way. Too much so?

There had been times when the Maker's purpose was clear, when He had guided me on a specific, if implausible, path. Sometimes that path included pain and loss, but He had been faithful, and the blessings He unfolded made the struggle worthwhile. But there were also times when I'd leapt into action only to find the way blocked. I'd been sure I was meant to raise the foelands and that it would bring peace to the people— until Brantley pointed out that I was wrong to believe the work rested solely on my shoulders.

Cole cleared his throat. "How much farther?"

I blinked and looked at him. His mouth slanted in a hard line, but his eyes held a bit of a twinkle. Unless I was imagining that. I sniffed. "At this speed, we'll arrive soon. But you didn't answer my question. How will you keep your people on the veskal? You can't allow them to raid. I promise I'll have the dancers bring supplies. We don't have gems or weapons to offer, but we'll bring food, cloth, salves." I was already making a mental list. Ginerva would help me collect spare items quickly. A peace offering of sorts. Enough to get us back to Rogue's Aerie without Cole's raiders deciding to completely pillage the Order or Middlemost.

Any humor I'd imagined in Cole's eyes disappeared. His hand clenched over the hilt of his sword. Another gesture that brought a pang, as it reminded me so much of Brantley. "My clan will follow my orders. Just don't let on that the Order is offering gifts freely. They need to believe it's a raid."

"Fair theft," I murmured.

Now Cole grinned in earnest. "You're learning."

Far from reassured, I returned to the center of the veskal and immersed my feet in the water again. The soothing rhythm of the voice of the waves dragged my eyelids down. When had I last slept? A tiny rapid beat joined the chorus. What other piece of the world was I hearing now? Not the trees that we swept past. Not the stony ridges that rose as we went farther inland. Not the birds flitting away at the sight of the strange craft.

I gasped. Deep within, I touched the bouncing, joyous beat of my baby's heart. My own pulse speeded, although it could never match the pace of hers. I sat taller, strengthened by awe and wonder. I longed to shout my thanks to the Maker, but instead I whispered. "You create worlds and people. Your gifts are amazing. Help me remember Your love when I'm afraid. Help me trust."

WHEN WE REACHED THE LARGE POOL, RIGHT BEFORE THE final bend, I dipped my hands into the shallow deck water and let my arms move in a soothing, calming rhythm. But there was no need. The current had already slowed, and we glided to a perfect stop right before the channel ended. Cole's people threw more glances my way and muttered darkly, distrustful and afraid.

Fear echoed in my own heart as I squinted up at the sliver of sky. Our arrival had not gone unnoticed. Soldiers from the Order lined the cliff above us, swords drawn, shields reflecting glaring sunlight. I glanced at Cole. With no way to let the saltars know the plan, how would we avert disaster here without dropping our mask of animosity before Cole's raiders? The soldiers on the ledge feared a real invasion.

Around me, a few of the Rogue's Aerie raiders raised their bows. They also expected an armed battle, welcomed it, even. I took a halting step toward Cole.

He faced his men and raised his arms. "Stand fast. No need to attack. We have a different weapon here." In a quick, smooth motion, he slid out his longknife and pressed the blade against my throat. "They'll give us anything we ask while I hold this hostage. I'm going alone to demand tribute. Just be ready for my return."

"What are you doing?" The whisper escaped, although I dared not move my throat against the sharp edge. My darkest fear was realized. Betrayal. Not only against me, but Brantley. His brother's evil would break his heart.

Cole signaled two raiders to place a plank from the side of his craft to a large boulder that marked the rocky climb upward.

One of the young raiders stepped toward him. "Sir, you can't go alone."

Danless jutted his chin, a cunning gleam in his eyes. "Let him. Far be it from us to question our commander."

Cole and his second-in-command deserved each other. Plots within plots. I strained against the knife, fighting to slow my uneven breathing.

"Guard the veskal. No one—" Cole raised his voice. "No one sets foot on shore."

Danless crossed his arms. "And if you don't return?"

Cole laughed. Did it sound forced? "Oh, I will. And I'll bring treasure. Count on it."

With Cole's knife never far from my neck, I limped across the plank, glad for my years of balance training in the Order, then began the arduous climb up the ravine. Behind me, Cole sauntered, swaggered, and waved back at his raiders. However, once we reached the top, he gripped me tightly, blade once again pressing my skin.

"Make way, or this dancer's blood will paint your stones." Cole's grim voice chilled my soul. The soldiers inched toward us but held back, unsure. Many of them knew me. Most had seen me confront the Order and dance as the Maker freed Meriel. Cole was smart. I was a useful hostage.

The standoff stretched, until a flurry of movement from the Order courtyard drew everyone's attention.

Saltar Kemp emerged, followed by other saltars and attendants. "Don't harm her. What do you seek?" Her voice carried authority but held a shrill edge that hinted at her panic.

Cole drew in a satisfied breath. "Inside. And keep your men away from the cliffside."

"Yes," I squeaked. "They'll fire arrows—weapons—if they feel threatened. Please keep everyone back for now."

At the entry of the Order, Cole's grip on my arm tightened. He breathed against my ear. "Can you guarantee my safety?"

"As much as you can guarantee mine. You're the one holding a knife."

That made him look even grimmer. "Lead on."

We made our way inside and into a small rehearsal room near the front door. "We'll speak with you alone," Cole demanded of the high saltar.

She waved away the hovering soldiers and attendants, then drew herself to her full height and glared at Cole. "What do you want?"

Once he was sure we were alone, he withdrew the knife from my throat. I sagged with relief and stumbled away.

He pointed the tip my direction. "This dancer of yours has a plan."

Perhaps I wasn't a hostage after all.

Saltar Kemp's brow knit together, and she looked at me. "What's happening? We haven't seen the signal to move Meriel away. Then we saw this veskal traveling against the wind."

I spared an uncertain glance at Cole, still half convinced his treachery hadn't been an act. He crossed his arms and raised an eyebrow. "Get on with it. My men won't wait forever."

I faced Saltar Kemp. "High Saltar, this is Cole of Windswell, Brantley's brother who we thought dead. It's a long story. I'll fill you in, but while we talk, could you ask the attendants to gather supplies?"

"So this was a ruse?" Kemp clearly distrusted him as much as I did.

"Cole is a son of Meriel. He's helping us."

"So why hasn't Brantley given the signal to move Meriel away?"

I took her hands. "The captive women from our rim villages have been rescued. But before we go, there's something else I believe the Maker is calling us to do. I want to bring other dancers to the foelands."

She stared at me as though I had become a stranger. "You want to risk dancer lives . . . risk Meriel itself . . . for what? What do you hope to accomplish?"

Maker, help me explain. Choosing my words carefully, I told her of the voice I had heard, of the underwater land bridges, and of the suffering I'd witnessed. It took precious time, but she listened without interrupting. Hope swelled. She had once danced in the center ground. Perhaps she'd heard the voice of Meriel during those years—why had I never asked?

When I had finished, Saltar Kemp walked to the window overlooking the gardens, still not speaking. After an agony of moments, she shook her head, and my heart sank. Still, I prayed silently and waited for her to speak. I'd said all I could say.

She turned to face Cole. "How will it help their situation to lift their islands and bring back the land bridges? Would not access by land simply make it easier to raid each other's villages?"

He scratched his head. "I never fully understood the legends. But my sense is that all the foelands are dying. The land grows smaller each year—even in the time I've been there we've lost shoreland. And there are fewer and fewer children."

I huffed. "Probably because they harass every woman who gets pregnant by kidnapping her back and forth between clans."

Cole shot me a glance. "I think it's more likely that with raids being the only interaction between isolated islands, most marriages occur within the ever-shrinking clans. And even those don't often produce children."

I tilted my head. "So perhaps the bridges will forge new relationships and make intermarriage more likely." I shrugged. "We can't really know all the answers. For me, it's enough that the Maker stirred this in my heart and the people clearly need help."

Saltar Kemp frowned. "Enough for you, but we can't spare dancers."

"Move aside! I have to see Carya." A familiar voice rang from the outer hall. Kemp rubbed her temples but opened the door. "Let her pass."

Starfire raced into the room and hugged me. "I was so worried. Rumors are going crazy. Someone said you were held captive." She held me at arm's length and scanned me.

"I'm fine."

Her gaze shifted to Cole, and she released me to stride over and confront him. "And you are?"

I hid a grin. Starfire's voice held all the arrogance of a high saltar but with none of the decorum. "He's Brantley's long-lost brother. It's a complicated story. But we're here to gather volunteers to dance on the foelands."

"And I just explained we can't spare anyone." Saltar Kemp's rigid posture hadn't softened.

"I'll go. And I'm sure some of the novitiates who aren't yet working in the center ground could be spared. Or you could promote them now to replace dancers you send."

Kemp's lips parted, momentarily taken aback by Starfire's outburst, but I saw the thoughts playing behind her eyes as she considered the possibility.

"You truly believe the Maker has called us to aid these people?"

"Yes, but we have to move quickly. Cole's men are held back by his orders, but if we don't return soon, they'll attack. Even if the Order's soldiers hold them off, blood will be shed."

She nodded slowly. "It might be possible. But I won't ask any dancer to join you in this plan unless she understands the dangers and chooses freely."

Starfire tossed her head. "Of course. We won't have a problem recruiting dancers willing to help Carya."

I gave Starfire another grateful hug, then turned to Cole. "Let's get your spoils of war onto the veskal."

He grinned. "Too bad I didn't have you along on my other raids."

With Saltar Kemp's agreement, things moved quickly. Several dancers and advanced novitiates agreed to accompany us to Rogue's Aerie. Cole oversaw the delivery of supplies to his people but kept me close, making sure his men could see him on the clifftop still leveraging his valuable captive. As we gathered at the top of the path and stared down at the waiting veskal, I nibbled a fingernail.

Dancer Iris stepped close and touched my shoulder. "This will work. And if it doesn't, we've lost nothing in the attempt."

"Unless"—Starfire edged closer to me and lowered her voice—"Cole doesn't plan to let us leave."

The threads of doubt in my mind wove themselves into an ugly tapestry. What if? I had to admit I'd questioned his motives each step of the way. "He's Brantley's brother," I said firmly. "He won't betray us. We just have to make it appear that he's conquered us so his raiders won't challenge his leadership."

A few other dancers shook their heads, uneasy.

"If any of you don't want to come along, please speak now." I looked around the group. Faces glowed with the dancers' typical earnest desire to serve. Eyes met mine, bright and determined. Familiar fear pressed down my shoulders.

Oh, Maker, I don't want to lead others into danger. Is this the right path?

His quiet voice reminded me that I was not doing the leading. I was simply called to follow Him.

Starfire squeezed me. "It will work. We'll be back here before you know it. Oh, and I asked a friend to join us." She nodded toward the outer courtyard.

A young drummer hovered shyly on the steps, carrying his instrument and a set of rhythm sticks. He cleared his throat. "Starfire thought I could be of assistance."

Starfire scampered to him and pulled him closer to the group. "Carya, this is Pondin."

The lanky lad hunched his shoulders, freckles dotting his already-rosy skin. Auburn hair spiked from his head. He offered an awkward smile. "Happy to help if you can use me."

"Of course!"

He nodded, full of eagerness and then directed his smile at Starfire, looking for her approval.

"I've also asked Aanor to come along," Starfire said.

Pondin's grin drooped, and I turned from his crestfallen face to hide my smile. Did Starfire know the turmoil she was causing? Probably not. We'd been so immersed in the belief that affection was not allowed to dancers or those attending them. But that was the old Order. Starfire would have some new issues to navigate in the coming days.

"Star, we can't bring Aanor. Cole needs to convince his people that he can use dancers to help his clan, but they won't trust him if he brings along enemy soldiers."

Cole had been shouting instructions down to his men, who were packing the veskal with loads that attendants had carried down. Now he turned to the cluster of dancers. "Ready? Make it look good. You're terrified captives that I'm going to use to control the winds."

I'd explained our ruse, but even so, when we made our way down to Cole's veskal, they hesitated. Cole's men looked just as hesitant.

Cole stepped aboard, grasping a rope near the mast and addressing his men. "I told you she was a valuable hostage. To avoid harm to the bearer of the victory child, they've surrendered all this bounty and these dancers."

Danless planted fists at his waist. "We have enough mouths to feed. And none of these others look to be carrying a victory child. Why would we want these scrawny slaves?"

Cole's jaw hardened. "Another challenge, Danless? I don't explain my plans to you." But he took in the hard faces of all his raiders and raised his voice. "Larcy made an alliance with a group of dancers who can shift the winds to her command. Do we want to allow Ecco Cove that advantage?"

As understanding dawned, the raiders raised their fists, grinning their approval of Cole's plans. Danless jutted his jaw but muttered, "As you say. Captain."

Danless's reluctant obedience made me glad that Cole only had a short time left with Rogue's Aerie before returning to Meriel permanently. At least I assumed that was Cole's plan. Or did being a commander hold too much appeal?

He directed his men to lift the main sail. The dancers remaining in the Order would keep the wind blowing toward the sea as long as they could— although there weren't many women left to work the center ground. High Saltar Kemp had even allowed the advanced novitiates to assist. A plan I approved of, although some of the saltars were worried about lowering standards. I sighed. Would I never escape conflict and disagreements? The new freedom of Meriel had brought a whole new set of questions and challenges to be resolved.

I settled among the other dancers, murmuring reassurances to them as they crowded together on the few benches. Thankfully the raiders were too excited by the convenient wind to harass them. They coaxed every bit of speed from the sail, while polers watched the shoreline and warned of protruding branches and submerged outcroppings.

Cole stepped onto a small crossbeam midway up the back mast, squinting downriver and holding the mast as his body adjusted to each sway of the veskal. His balance reminded me of Brantley. He seemed meant for the sea as much as his brother. I frowned. Perhaps Cole planned to bring Brianna and Orianna to Rogue's Aerie, where he could continue to command his people and ride veskals across the waves. I shook my head. Brianna would never agree to that. Would she? Would I, in her place?

Sometime later, the sail slackened suddenly. Where was our wind?

Before I could make any guesses, Cole shouted a warning. I stood, but a sudden lurch of the craft nearly tossed me overboard. The polers abandoned their long staffs and drew bows, fitting arrows to them.

I wanted to see what was happening, but even if I could keep my footing, I couldn't push my way past the crowd of dancers and the agitated raiders.

"Everyone down!" Cole yelled.

Around me, dancers adjusted awkwardly, some crouching, and others sitting in the water that sloshed around the bottom of the veskal. My heart clenching, I spared one more glance to see what the threat was. Another craft blocked our passage. Ecco Cove. The same foelanders we'd seen trying to follow us when we'd first sailed for the channel. Larcy stood at the bow, signaling her people. And we'd lost our wind.

A whistle of air brushed past, inches from my face. Arrows! I ducked, calling to the dancers to stay low. My schemes had led them into danger. And how could we even reach Rogue's Aerie now to attempt our dance?

A man near us gasped and fell on top of two of the dancers, blood splashing across his tunic. The dancers screamed. I looked for Cole, who stood stubbornly directing his people. If he was killed, not only would we have no opportunity to raise the foelands, but I would have delivered a group of trusting, dedicated dancers into the hands of either Danless or Larcy.

Or worse, River.

32

HEAD SWIVELING, COLE'S HARRIER-BIRD GAZE TOOK IN every detail. His orders were terse and specific, and soon his archers had forced the Ecco Cove raiders to duck down into their veskal where they couldn't fire at us—some injured, some perhaps dead.

Crouching as low as I could, I tore off my head scarf and tended to the nearest fallen raider. Blood pulsed from the deep gash across his neck. At least the arrow hadn't lodged in his windpipe or sliced the life-carrying artery. I wrapped my makeshift bandage around his neck. It seemed to stem the bleeding, but he was unconscious. We eased him to the bottom of the veskal, careful to keep him propped out of the standing water there.

"Carya!" Starfire gasped, looking at the injured man and then at me.

My hands were coated with blood. More had splattered my tunic. A vivid reminder of the cost. Restoring the foelands could yet cost everything. Should we retreat? Pole our way back to Middlemost?

"Swords!" Cole shouted. Blades whisked from leather scabbards answered him immediately. "Carya! We need the current."

What was he thinking? If we had a current, Larcy's craft would have it too. "But they'll—"

"Now!" He stepped close, pretending to threaten me with his blade, then hissed through a clenched jaw. "We've lost the wind. Unless you give us a current toward the sea, we'll be forced to stay here and fight."

Another quick glance at Larcy's veskal revealed that it was tied to a huge tree that jutted out from under a rocky ledge. My gaze darted over the surrounding banks. This was the spot where I'd seen one of River's acolytes standing guard earlier. Shadowswell was a short way inland. A terrible suspicion began to dawn. Could it be this was no fluke? Had River's dancers changed the wind exactly when it would endanger Cole's craft the most?

In the space of a breath I understood Cole's intent. "Current pattern," I said to the young drummer, Pondin. Pale, shaking, he gaped at me. "Now!" I took a page from Cole's show of authority. It worked. Pondin beat out the pattern. The other dancers left me as much room as possible while remaining below the lip of the veskal's sides. I swished my hands side to side, praying, listening. Red stained the water, wicking up the fabric of my tunic. I closed my eyes against the ugly stain of violence.

The water beneath the veskal stirred.

I was vaguely aware of yelling, the clash of swords, the whiz of arrows, Cole's bellowed commands. I shut it all out to coax the ocean to push our craft. *Steer us, Maker. Propel us past danger. Let Your waves carry us.*

Eventually the chaos stilled.

"You can stop now." Cole's voice recalled me to my surroundings.

I opened my eyes and straightened. Cole stood over me. Two of the raiders were hoisting the sail again. Larcy's veskal shrank behind us. A few injured men groaned. The sail cracked and snapped as a renewed wind hit it. Timber creaked. But other than that, there was blessed quiet.

Cole crouched to check on the man with the bandaged neck. "Thanks for your help," he told me without looking at me. "I hope this will be worth it." Distrust and anger still threaded his voice.

"So do I," I said simply.

He snorted and moved away, inspecting each part of the veskal, talking to each of his raiders. Then he jumped back up to a crosspiece of the mast. "You acquitted yourselves well in that small skirmish. Larcy will be slow to tangle with us again. And we didn't lose our cargo." The men and women of his clan cheered, although with muted enthusiasm. Small skirmish? The man before me might be dying. Others carried new wounds and would bear new scars. And the dancers—the shock of being flung from their sheltered life into raw danger painted all their faces white.

"Will we face more attacks?" Starfire asked me quietly from where she huddled low against the side of the craft, holding her arm.

"I don't know. We didn't expect to face that one." I pushed up to sit on the bench and whispered to all the huddled dancers. "Be ready to dance as soon as we land. We don't know how long we'll have."

"But these . . . people . . . will bring us back to the Order when we're done, won't they?" Iris tucked her trembling hands into her sleeves. Instead of disguising her fear, it only made her whole body vibrate with the same uncertainty we all faced.

I braced my shoulders, ready to comfort them. Yet I couldn't reveal more. Cole's people had to believe we were spoils of war. I leaned forward and lowered my voice. "We will get home. If not on this veskal, then on stenella or ponies. Brantley and High Saltar Kemp won't abandon us."

They nodded, eyes trusting, earnest. Their faith in me broke my heart. I managed a reassuring smile, but when I looked up, I spotted Danless hovering nearby. Had he heard me? One of his eyebrows raised, but then his face closed off, and he turned away.

A wave of dread threatened to drown me, but I stood against it. It battered me but didn't knock down my spirit. Just as when learning a complex new pattern as a novitiate, all I needed to focus on was the next step.

Seeking the comfort of a friend, I turned my attention back to Starfire. She still gripped her upper arm in a strange way, and the freckles across her face stood out more than usual. Her skin had paled. "Star? Are you all right?"

She shrugged and winced. I edged over to her. "What happened?"

She pointed to an arrow lodged in the mast. "That one nearly pinned me. Just a little scrape."

I eased her hand away. Another ugly wound. I gently removed Starfire's scarf and tore it, using part as a bandage and part as a sling.

"I'm sorry," she whispered. "I won't be much help dancing like this. And this is my own dumb fault."

"What are you talking about?" If anyone was to blame, it was me for getting them into this reckless scheme.

"I thought I saw something, so I stood up for a better look."

"What did you see?"

She rested a hand on my shoulder, worry subduing her spark. "Carya, there were dancers on that other veskal."

Blood drained from my face. Either Larcy was kidnapping River's dancers for her use, or River was volunteering them. Bad enough that River's group had established a point on land where they used dance to oppose the plans of the Order. Bad enough that we'd suspected River of conspiring with Larcy, but this . . . this was proof of her treachery. Larcy's veskal might be heading farther up the channel with plans to attack the Order even now. Or they might follow us and hinder our efforts. But if they had dancers on board, it considerably cut any advantage we might have once possessed.

I brushed Star's auburn hair from her face. "Rest. I need to talk to Cole."

With the veskal racing toward the sea, I managed a quiet conversation with the commander. He seemed unconcerned by what Starfire had witnessed. "We'll be on guard. My raiders are used to watching for foelanders on the water." His confidence did nothing to reassure me. As far as I could tell, we were rushing toward an impossible task that would only make us vulnerable to enemies—whether River's band of dancers or foelanders or Cole's own men if they discovered he hadn't actually "conquered" us but was helping us.

I gnawed the side of my thumbnail, stood to scan the channel ahead, sat, stood again, and continued that restless pattern again and again.

BY THE TIME WE REACHED THE CHANNEL'S MOUTH, THE subsun was setting. Deep violet streaked the sky, and the horizon stretched into darkness.

"Time for the second phase of my plan," Cole announced to the whole crew, catching my eyes. "There's an empty village nearby. From our recent raid, I learned the cowards who lived there have fled before rumors of our might."

How dare he refer to Windswell's people—his own family—as cowards with a straight face? I bit my lip.

He continued. "We'll raid it tonight and rest there. Then we'll bring home even more plunder tomorrow."

I wanted to shout "No!" but held my tongue. There had been no sign of Brantley. Perhaps Cole wanted to coordinate with his brother. Perhaps he feared we couldn't fulfill our special dance in the darkness. It would certainly be a challenge to guide all these dancers to an open stretch of land in the night. And we could all use rest before attempting to raise the land bridges.

Turning to reassure the dancers, I found them staring at the sea with expressions of wonder, horror, or disbelief. I smiled. Even the women born in a rim village had no memory of the sea. They'd been cloistered in the Order all their lives. My first glimpse of the ocean that carried us had stirred all the same reactions in me.

"The Maker set us upon a wide sea, but He guides us in His current of love." I infused all my faith into the words. Some of the women nodded and offered tentative smiles, but others continued to stare wide-eyed at the play of starlight on the vast emptiness stretched before us. I let the truth soak deeply into my soul. I could not meet each need, just as I couldn't create this endless sea. But the Maker could and did.

The veskal was soon tethered along the shore of Windswell. We filed along the plank onto the tangleroot, dancers clinging together as they adjusted to the rolling movement underfoot—so different from Meriel's center. The raiders cheered and ripped through the homes but returned with little in their arms.

"No gems."

"Scarcely any food. We brought what we found."

"At least we'll have shelter."

Cole directed his men to build fires, then sent the dancers to rest in one of the cottages, posting a guard at the door. However, he kept me beside him. Once everyone had eaten and shifts were assigned for the watch, he took my arm and guided me toward the shore. Putting distance between us and the activity in the main village, we soon neared the cottage Brantley had built.

"Are you still determined to go through with this?" Cole asked. He dropped all his bravado and feigned hostility. "I've been thinking about what you said about running into Larcy midway up the channel. Ecco Cove is up to something."

"Yes, and if Larcy is working with the Shadowswell dancers, the ones who follow River, she might try to stop us."

Cole shook his head. "I agreed to this scheme because before I return to Meriel I'd like to offer my clan a better life on Rogue's Aerie. The legends say the bridges will bring peace. But if it's a fool's errand, tell me now."

"So you do plan to return to Meriel to stay?"

He drew back. "Of course." He raised a hand toward me.

I flinched.

Carefully he touched my cheek where he'd struck me earlier. "Sorry about that," he said ruefully. "I had to convince my people I hadn't grown soft."

I shrugged. "It worked. They seem very loyal to you."

He snorted. "Until a stronger commander comes along. To answer your question, of course I'm well ready to return home. To Brianna, to my mother and daughter. Even to Brantley, as annoying as he can be. I'll be glad to see the foelands carried away in a different current. If we survive tomorrow."

I glanced back toward Windswell. "Are we far enough away from your men? I want to signal Makah and find out where Brantley is."

Cole nodded, so I crouched at the rim and blew a quiet whistle, hoping any raiders would mistake it for a night bird's call.

After we waited for what felt like half the night, although it was probably only an hour, Makah glided toward us. Brantley's silhouette hunched low on her back—a worrying sign. His spine slumped. He clambered to the tangleroot beside us instead of springing lightly. "Where have you been?" he demanded. "I've been circling Rogue's Aerie, trying to stay out of sight."

I ran to hug him, subtly supporting him at the same time. "Have you eaten at all today?"

Cole crossed his arms, rocking back on his heels. "We ran into a bit of trouble. One of my men needs care, and I figured the dancers would do better if they could see what they were doing."

Instead of bristling or scolding, Brantley nodded wearily. "Good thinking."

I had to check Brantley's bandage and make sure he had something to sustain him. "I'm taking him to our home. It's just beyond the willow." A night's sleep would benefit us all.

Cole nodded. "I can stand first watch here so no one approaches, then I'll put my most trusted man on second watch."

"Thanks," my husband said with no hint of rancor.

Cole frowned. He clearly understood, as I did, that Brantley would only be this agreeable if he was seriously ill. I knew he had been doing too much too soon. Stubborn man. Stirring up irritation to help me avoid my anxiety, I threw Brantley's arm over my shoulder. "Stop wasting time. I'm ready for some rest, even if you aren't."

He managed a weak chuckle as I led him to our cottage. The familiar hearth was so welcoming I almost cried. The letter from Saltar Kemp still rested on our table. It seemed that eons had passed since her request had arrived, and all our lives had changed.

I settled Brantley onto our bed, stirred up a tiny fire, and slipped outside to fill a bucket with fresh seawater. While the tsalla brewed, I unearthed a few saltcakes and two persea. I set several candles nearby and examined his wound. Infection had returned, and his skin burned beneath my hand. "You've made it worse," I scolded. "What were you doing today?"

"Mostly worrying about you. I tried to stay close, but then that other veskal started following you up the channel, and there was no way to stay out of sight. I tried diving, but . . ."

"Diving? You and Makah are both crazy."

He ignored my protests and reached out to rest his hand on my stomach. "Are you all right? And our little one?"

I smiled as the baby shifted, pressing my skin up and down under Brantley's hand. "I'm fine. The baby's fine. And I think Cole is sincere about helping."

Brantley tossed his head back on the pallet. "He had better be. I don't have it in me to fight him."

I sniffed. "All you need is a good night's sleep. Here, drink your tsalla. Did you bother to eat today?"

My husband relaxed under my fussing, and we ate, then eventually he drifted into a feverish slumber. I nestled beside him, far less confident than what I'd tried to project. Nothing was going right. I had no idea what tomorrow would hold. And I could scarcely bring myself to focus on plans with Brantley slipping back into fever. *Maker, here is another need I can't meet in my own power. Please, please, please heal him.* Admitting my emptiness and helplessness apart from my Creator had a strange effect. The despair melted away and peace enveloped me. Trusting in myself made me flail and drown, but trusting in Him helped me float.

With my ear against his chest, the faint rhythm of Brantley's life beat a soothing pulse until I also slept.

DARKNESS AND EXHAUSTION AMPLIFIED MY FEAR AND torment, but they lost their grip as rosy dawn peered through the shutters. We'd both slept deeply all night. Brantley's eyes were still glazed and red-rimmed, but he sat up with only a small wobble.

He took my hand and kissed it. "Ready to dance the foelands into their future?"

I stared at the floor. "Am I wrong about this?"

He chuckled. "A little late to ask that now." After a pause, he tilted my chin up and met my eyes. "If the Maker has asked this of you, He has a good reason."

"But He could just raise the islands with a touch of His hand, or a word."

Brantley smiled. "And He could have shaken Meriel free from the grip of the Order without your help. But He asked you to be a part of it."

I lost myself in the blue of his eyes. "But I still worry. I didn't tell you. Starfire was wounded on the journey down. And one of Cole's men was nearly killed."

My husband pressed his forehead against mine. "Seems that every adventure carries a cost."

My heart twisted. "Like Navar. That was my fault too."

He gripped my shoulders and held me away, capturing my gaze. "Stop. I've seen you do this far too often. You've been taking on guilt that isn't yours and letting it eat away at you. We've been over that, and you have to stop. I've been doing the same thing. I wasn't there when Cole was attacked and Orianna taken. I hate myself for that. But bearing that weight won't change the past or help us move forward. Navar gave her life, and because of her, that strange island has hope. We can honor her sacrifice by helping the foelands, continuing her legacy."

His tone, his gaze, even more than his words, helped ease the ache in my chest. "You're right. Thank you."

After a quick breakfast, I checked on Brantley's bandage, coaxed broth into him, and pressed him back down on our bed. "There's no need for you to come with us. Once we've danced, Cole will bring us back here."

Brantley brushed my hands away and stood, wavering even though the ground beneath wasn't rolling at the moment. "That's just it. You don't know what you'll need. Makah and I will stay near Rogue's Aerie so you can signal if you're in danger."

I wanted to make him promise to stay far from the foelands and their veskals. "Our child needs a father. You're injured. You're sick. What if you pass out in the sea?"

I'd said the wrong thing. His eyes narrowed, glazed with fever and determination in equal measure. "I'll be on the water with Makah until your work is finished."

Instead of further useless argument, I hugged him, praying that my husband wouldn't have to bear any more of the cost of this endeavor. Then I pulled myself away and limped quickly along the rim to Windswell.

Cole's people were already ushering the dancers onto the veskal as he supervised. The dancers cast wary glances at the raiders. The raiders threw questioning looks toward Cole. He stepped over to me. "We only have to deflect suspicion for a few more hours. But you and your dancers will have to work quickly. My raiders are uneasy about my strange directions, and Danless will use any opportunity to lead a revolt."

I nodded. "I'm doing this because I believe the Maker has asked me to help the foelands. But why are you helping us?"

He rubbed his chin. "I've led my clan for many months. I care about them. I'd like to see change come to the foelands. If the legend of the bridges can be fulfilled . . ." He shrugged. "I'll leave them that gift before deserting them. And an alliance between River and Larcy would cause disaster to Meriel, even if we moved away."

I tilted my head. This man felt torn between two duties, much as I grappled with the needs of the new Order and my role in Windswell with my family. Maybe I could trust him. Maybe. "That's my hope too. An answer for both worlds."

One of the men called from his position near the mast. "Time to go," Cole said, features hardening, once again playing the role of commander. He guided me onto the veskal, and his people set a small sail to harness the morning breeze. I shielded my eyes and caught a glimpse of Brantley and Makah, riding low in the distant waves.

AT THE BASE OF THE CLIFFS OF ROGUE'S AERIE, COLE ordered his raiders to bring the crates and baskets of "plundered" supplies up to their settlement. He personally led our team of dancers along the ravine path to the site of my failed dance. Danless of course objected, but Cole swaggered and brandished his sword, accusing his second-in-command of insulting him by doubting he could control a group of frail dancers and a scrawny drummer. Once more, Danless backed off, but Cole's ability to control his clan was slipping. We had to hurry.

Shaking out cramped and stiff limbs, the dancers rolled tension off their shoulders, clearly relieved to be free of the raiders. We spread out across the ground, and I told them again about the bridges deep underwater that connected the lands. "I know you haven't all heard the voice of the land as you dance in the center ground, but you've read the Maker's letter. His promise of love, His longing for relationship is just as true for these people. Let His love flow through you as you dance." I tapped out a rhythm, and Pondin quickly nodded and began keeping time on his drum. The dancers followed me, and our bare feet caressed the earth of Rogue's

Aerie. As before, I was quickly caught up in the heavy weight of greed and turmoil these lands had suffered, and the sensation of sinking. I danced against that downward pull, lifting, jumping on my good leg, while the other dancers were able to leap fully and powerfully. My puny effort and my gestures of love were still feeble. I limped awkwardly, wishing I could fly through the air instead, as the rhythm called for.

But I was no longer alone.

The ground trembled, but even with all of us dancing, it barely rose. Yet slowly, I sensed the Maker's voice calling to the worlds He had made. Drawing them to Himself. Calling them to unity, to a new way. The others felt it too. Leaping with a new freedom, spinning in the air, white-clad dancers moved as one, filling the clearing. Coating the earth with blessings.

I joined as much as I could, but I continued to be the weak link. My jumps were mere hops. I sometimes stumbled as I landed. But I could hear the land straining to be free, much as I'd once heard Meriel.

"That's it! Keep going!" I spun toward the shoreline.

Pondin's eyes were wide, staring at the shivering cliffs behind us, but to his credit, he kept the rhythm. Some of the dancers shot nervous glances toward the rumbling earth underfoot. But years of novitiate training kept them focused.

"Carya! Look!" Starfire's shout was no joyous call of success. Fear burst from her throat.

I paused and followed the direction she was pointing.

Larcy's largest veskal raced into view, red sails full. They moved close so quickly I immediately spotted the white tunics. At least a dozen dancers on board. They stood, fearless. Would Cole order his raiders to fire arrows at them from watch points on the cliffs? These were women of Meriel, no matter their allegiance.

Other dancers stopped, gathering around me.

"What's happening?" Iris asked.

"River and her dancers." I smoothed my tunic. "We can't be distracted."

"What if they dance in opposition?" one of the younger dancers asked, brow wrinkled.

Starfire made a broad, graceful arm gesture with her free arm, even as the sling held her injured arm still. "We keep dancing."

"Did you feel it?" I asked her quietly.

She grinned. "Look at the rim."

Tangleroot stretched much farther along the shore. Already the land had shifted upward enough to expand the area of the clearing.

I grinned, too. "She's right. Keep dancing!"

We resumed our dance. But a sudden wind gust made me stumble. I limped to the rim. Another sail glided into sight from behind this island. Another craft wearing the colors of Ecco Cove. Then another. They moved in the direction of the dock, just around a jut of land from where we danced. A full invasion? Could Cole's people hold them off long enough for us to finish our work here?

On Larcy's broad deck, River guided her dancers in the percussive jumps of the windward storm pattern. Indignation brewed in my chest. River claimed to want the Order to return to old ways, yet here she was dancing away from the center ground—or any ground at all. I saw more clearly than ever that she made her own rules and chose when to break them. Clouds rolled in like an army and shadowed the islands and the sea. We were running out of time, and River's interference would only make things worse.

I spun to rejoin the dance, but my ankle buckled. The shore rocked underneath me, and I fell. I tried to stand, but my leg wouldn't support me.

"Maker, not now!" I whispered.

Even on my knees, I heard the groaning, yearning, stretching of the islands.

They will carry the dance. You take to the sea.

The voice I so often begged to hear with greater clarity now spoke simply and firmly. The sea? But the dancers needed my guidance and encouragement, didn't they? I shook my head. They needed the Maker's help. And they already had that.

No time to wallow in frustration about my limitations. No time to debate with the Maker. No time to explain. I pulled out the whistle and signaled Makah, praying Brantley could find a way past Larcy's veskals without becoming a target.

"What's wrong?" Starfire broke formation and approached me.

"Keep dancing," I called over my shoulder. I pressed my hands to the earth. A tortuous tug-of-war pulled the earth up, then back down. Waves lapped the rim more fiercely. I squinted, River's people were dancing under her direction, tight, contained steps on the deck of the large craft, but effective nonetheless. More dark clouds scudded overhead. Whitecaps built around us. The foelander veskals bobbed crazily. I saw Larcy gesturing, shouting at River. The former saltar crossed her arms, looking down her arrogant nose at the small clan commander. Then she pointed to us. Their argument was fierce with as many wild waves as the ocean. I wished I could hear what they were saying.

Makah suddenly surfaced, Brantley sputtering, knees gripping her sides.

"You shouldn't be diving," I shouted over the sudden rush of a violent downpour.

He ignored that. "What do you need?"

I reached for his hand, and he helped me onto Makah. "The Maker told me to take to the sea."

Makah turned her head to stare at me. Rain dripped from her long lashes. She squeaked, then chittered firmly. Without a signal from Brantley, she wheeled around, heading out to sea.

Larcy must have won the argument, because River's dancers stopped stirring up storms, though they continued to dance. From what I could tell, as I wiped rain from my eyes, they had switched to a current pattern.

Makah gave the veskals a wide berth. A few arrows flew past as she swam between two of them, but they landed harmlessly to be swallowed by waves.

"Where are you taking her?" Brantley wrapped his arms around me.

"I'm not." Makah seemed to have taken on a mind of her own. I looked back. Rain slashed across my vision, and the churning sea made everything seem to bob. I couldn't be sure, but the islands did seem to be lifting, but far too slowly and too little.

Makah stretched her long neck and dipped her head beneath the water. A sonorous sound rolled from her throat. Then she craned upward, scanning in all directions. The fiercest winds passed by, and the rain calmed to a light shower.

Unsteady, Brantley pulled his legs in and launched to his feet, shielding his eyes. The two, herder and stenella, searched the horizon together, but I didn't know what they hoped to find. We were getting too far from the foelands. Too far from my mission.

"We need to go back and help the dancers!" I yelled, but a last gust of wind tore away the words.

Brantley pointed. Whitecaps rose from the sea and took to the air, then joined the sea again. No, not waves. Stenella. They caught the wind and glided.

"Did you rally more herders?" I asked.

He crouched, his mouth close to my ear. "No. The herders all returned to their villages with the captives they rescued. Those are wild stenella."

My heart caught in my throat. Terrifying, breathtaking, the creatures sailed like giant gulls, into the air then plunging under water, then shooting upward again. Screams rang from Larcy's veskals, her sailors' terror of these creatures throwing the crew into chaos. Even River's dancers stopped.

On shore, my dancers continued to race in bounding leaps. Reaching low and skimming the ground. Exploding into the air. Even out here, I heard the drum. The very air vibrated with the joyful call to rise.

Makah suddenly lurched, propelling herself into a gust of wind, her side fins fanning out into glistening wings.

I gasped. The wild stenella were following her. We wove up and down, the same rhythm as the dancers on land. The band of sea creatures had joined the pattern! They were dancing!

34

WATER SLAPPED INTO MY FACE, AND I HELD MY BREATH AS
Makah dipped beneath the surface before launching into a glide again.
The panic on Larcy's veskals crescendoed, but I couldn't spare them
much attention. Something more remarkable was happening.

Dancers and stenella flung themselves skyward in joyful response
to the Maker's presence. Like a father lifting a child's head above the
water when teaching him to swim, He gently raised the islands. Perfectly
coordinated, the foelands rose together.

From our vantage I could see part of Mander's island, his dock
becoming landlocked with the spreading width of his land. A bridge
appeared, connecting him to Rogue's Aerie and to another foeland in a
different direction. Glowing blue stones lined the sides of the path.

Makah now swam at a speed I'd never experienced before, rapid enough
for us to circle the cluster of islands, the isolated towns. I glimpsed the
charred remains of the dock where I'd once fled from Mander's raiders.
We flew past other, smaller lands and then passed Ecco Cove. The caves
were set much farther inland now. I glimpsed villagers gathered on a land
newly resurrected, while some hovered near the cave entrances, clinging
to the security of the stone.

We passed through the narrow gap of ocean between Meriel and the
foelands. Water surged in gasping sprays upward as the lifting foelands
grew in size and their expanding dimensions slid away from Meriel.
Makah sailed above it. The air moved like a strong gesture of a dancer's
arm, coaxing us ever higher. Makah chortled. I stared down at the
dizzying sight beneath us. The Maker had once caught me up in His arms

and given me a glimpse of Meriel in the vast oceans. Now I saw our world again. And all the foelands beside it. I tasted the Maker's love for these worlds, and it was sweet on my lips. My heart swelled with His yearning for all to be restored.

Brantley let out a low whistle. His arm wrapped my waist, and I felt his hand tremble. I hoped the tremor was from the awe-inspiring sight and not his fever.

As the islands lifted and connected, some veskals tied to docks now rested on their sides, landlocked. Bridges appeared as water poured away from their emergence. Broad stretches of land linked the fragments that were now much closer to each other. The last of the rain dissipated, and the primary sun flooded light over the scene, while the hint of subsunrise colored the glistening new land with rainbow hues and the blue glow of the strange luminescent stones.

We curved, still hovering overhead, and neared Larcy's veskals once again. The sloshing of the sea had capsized her smaller craft. Small figures bobbed in the water, frantically paddling toward shore—any shore. A finger of land rose beneath the large veskal that held River and her dancers. Her craft canted sharply, wedged half on land and half in the water. A handful of raiders and dancers were tossed into the sea.

The dancers, cloistered all their lives in the Order, didn't know how to swim.

"Makah, we have to help them!"

A sigh rolled through her, but she angled her glide down toward the sea, taking us again into range of swords and arrows. I expected a protest from Brantley, but he was silent.

I twisted to look back at him. His eyes were unfocused, his face constricted in a permanent wince, as if every breath hurt.

"Brantley? What's wrong?"

He blinked a few times, then squeezed me in an effort to be reassuring. "Not a thing."

He was lying. What should I do? I wanted to steer Makah straight to help for Brantley. In his condition, he shouldn't be riding, let alone diving. Yet there were dancers who would drown without our help. Enemy dancers, yes, but still women the Maker cherished.

"Can you hold on? We need to get them out of the sea."

"I told you. I'm fine." Brantley pointed to one of the women thrashing in the waves. "I'll go after that one, you grab whomever you can."

Before I could protest, Brantley dove—while we were still several feet above the water. He disappeared, but then surfaced and struck out with strong strokes toward one of the dancers needing help.

Makah landed heavily near the capsized veskal. The raiders had swum for the land bridge, and a few dancers had reached it and were sprawled on the ground, coughing. On a promontory, Cole directed six of his men who raced toward the sea carrying a small veskal. They rowed out and hauled dancers into the craft, one soggy bundle after another.

Farther out from the land, a lone white-clad woman splashed furiously, as if angry at the water that struggled to support her.

"There!" I signaled with a circle of my fist. Makah swam to her.

The dancer's face lifted as we approached, revealing hard features unsoftened even in her terror. River. The saltar who had tortured me during my novitiate days in the Order. The woman who well may have hastened High Saltar Tiarel to her death. The saboteur who had stirred up the destruction of the Maker's letter in village after village.

And still loved by the Maker.

Gripping Makah's back with my legs, thankful that my thigh muscles still held a dancer's strength, I leaned over and reached out my arm.

"River! Here! Take my hand."

Her eyes focused past me, widening at the sight of the lifted islands. "What have you done?" she sputtered as she thrashed. When her gaze met mine, raw hatred flew across the short distance like a foelander's arrow.

I stretched farther, trying to grab her shoulder.

"Never!" She wrenched away in a sharp, decisive movement and sank beneath the surface.

A wave tossed Makah back a few feet. My heels dug in, and she inched forward again. She even dipped her head into the depths, searching.

River was gone, drowned rather than be rescued by me. I sat back, stunned.

"Carya. Over here." Brantley treaded water nearby, then dove again, swimming urgently toward another person who was choking and flailing.

I stiffened my spine. I had to help the people who wanted rescue. Makah circled and reached another of River's floundering acolytes. Dipping her head, she supported her and pushed her to shore . . . much as a wild stenella had once rescued Cole. Then I lost myself in the chaos of racing to help each choking, splashing person to shore.

At last, the sea was quiet. Bits of broken planks floated nearby, but we'd helped all the people we could. I directed Makah to Cole's clearing—now farther inland—where Starfire, Iris, and the other dancers waited. Cole was inspecting his large veskal, which looked ungainly, resting on its side on the new land. It would take the whole village to drag the thing back to the water's edge. At least he'd saved the smaller veskal, which had been so useful in rescuing swimmers. His men had hefted it onto the shore, since there was no place to tie it. His dock had become a strange wooden walkway resting in the middle of the much larger clearing.

I stumbled off Makah and onto the tangleroot and collapsed. My ankle still wouldn't hold me. Starfire raced across sodden earth toward me. "It happened! Did you see it? Of course you did. What am I saying? Is this what the Maker wanted? Will it help these people stop fighting all the time? Look at Cole's veskal! How will we get back to Meriel? I don't think I'm brave enough to ride a stenella, but so many of the veskals are broken. Although I suppose they could row us home in that little one. We won't all fit."

Her cheerful chatter breathed new strength into me. I reached up, and she hoisted me onto my one working foot. I embraced her but then scanned the clearing for Brantley. Dancers, raiders, and clan families milled about, but I couldn't see my husband. "Cole!" I called. "Where's Brantley?"

He strode toward me, also examining the area. "Last I saw, he was towing one of my raiders in." He shot an uneasy glance toward Makah, who had spread her side fins and basked in the sunlight, relaxing in the water near the new shoreline. The wild stenellas had disappeared as mysteriously as they'd arrived, but Makah seemed to wear a smug smile. I spared another moment to marvel at the way they'd joined the dance, but then my concerns rose like a rebellious wave.

Leaning on Starfire, I shielded my eyes and searched the sea. Could Brantley's fever and injury have rendered him unconscious? He might have sunk into the depths. I breathed in a tight gasp. "Where is he?"

Cole's brow knit, but Starfire patted my back. "Don't panic. I'm sure he—"

"It's true!" The short figure of Larcy marched across the clearing followed by several of her raiders. "The legend is true. But who holds the victory child? Where is the baby? Which clan?" Her clothes dripped, and she still bristled with weapons.

Cole stepped beside me, his hand closing around his sword. "Carya of Windswell heard the islands' call. Her babe yet unborn is the victory child of legend."

Larcy drew close to me. She knelt and laid her bow, a dagger, a longknife, and a quiver of arrows at my feet. One by one, her other raiders did the same.

"What are you doing?" I asked, limping away a few steps. Starfire supported me so I wouldn't fall. I didn't want their weapons. Was I supposed to acknowledge their surrender? Surrender to whom?

Larcy threw her arms toward the sky and laughed. "The victory child has come at last!"

Cole smiled at me. "Larcy is right. The legend says that when the islands are united, all will lay down their weapons." He drew his own sword and added it to the pile. "The bridges have come. And with them, peace!"

Every foelander in hearing cheered.

A few of River's soggy dancers watched from a distance. What did they make of this strange spectacle? I glanced around. I'd figure out the appropriate response later. Right now I wanted my husband. Where was he?

Other foelanders crossed one of the land bridges and made their way to this stretch of Rogue's Aerie. Several pointed and headed toward me. The pile of discarded weapons grew. Enemy foelanders interacted with each other, laughing, studying the changes of the land, chattering about the sight of the stenella they had seen dancing around their worlds—now a united world. The atmosphere turned as giddy as a party.

A splash pulled my attention to the rim past the broken remnants of Cole's veskal, the only part of the shoreline I couldn't see from here. "Help me," I whispered to Starfire. She wrapped an arm around my waist and guided my painful steps toward the flotsam.

Cole stepped in on my other side, supporting me as well. Until now his assistance had been given grudgingly. But the lifting of the islands had brought a lift to his spirits as well. He chuckled as he waved his free arm toward the cliffs. "This clan had to cling to the crevices and cliffsides, scratching out a life. Look at all this new land."

His jubilation was infectious, but I couldn't celebrate yet. Not until I knew Brantley was safe.

When we made our way around the angled hull, my lungs froze, unable to release my breath. Brantley's forearms rested on a patch of tangleroot, his head down. Droplets in his fair hair caught gleams from the suns. *Maker, no!*

Cole let me go and jogged to him. "Taking a nap?" he chided, almost masking the worry in his voice.

I held my breath, hoping against hope for my husband's response.

Brantley lifted his head wearily and shot his brother a crooked grin. "Someone had to save your inept crew."

The air in my lungs released in a whimper of relief.

Cole helped him onto land, and Brantley swayed. The shadows beneath his eyes had darkened. His skin was as pale as a dancer's tunic.

Starfire and I caught up to the men. I hugged Brantley with desperation, willing the last ounce of my strength into him. "We have to get you back home."

He nodded. "Good plan." The words were slurred.

Cole could no longer hide his worry. "Better take that beast of yours. I'll help you get him—"

"Look at the damage you've done our clan." Danless strode up to us. "And our veskals. You invited these enemies"—his gesture encompassed the dancers, Makah, Brantley and me—"to harm Rogue's Aerie."

The last thing we needed was a quarrel. Brantley needed help.

But Danless, intent on his purpose, lunged at Cole, a dagger glinting in his hand.

"No!" I reached forward but only collapsed to my knees.

Brantley was faster. He propelled himself between Cole and the approaching blade.

A scream tore from my throat. Time slowed and fragmented.

Cole hit the ground. Brantley fell beside him. The impact rocked the ground beneath me. A man's voice roared in surprise and pain. Danless drew back, his dagger glinting with blood—but whose? Starfire raced from my side and threw herself into Danless, her surprise attack knocking him over and sending his blade flying.

In the space of a blink, the celebrating foelanders converged, clamoring, and restrained Danless.

But my only focus was the two brothers. I dragged myself over the wet tangleroot. "Brantley?" My throat was so tight, the word could barely squeeze out. I reached for his shoulder and tugged.

He pushed himself up. Beside him, Cole sprawled on his stomach, his body motionless. "I'm fine," Brantley said. "Cole? Cole!"

I crawled alongside my husband and helped him roll Cole over.

"Is he . . . ?"

Cole's eyes popped open, and he winced. "You couldn't have reacted a little faster, brother?"

Brantley sagged back in relief, then growled. "Faster than you did. Did his puny blade find you?"

"Just a scratch." Cole surged to his feet. Blood stained his front, and a gash in his tunic showed the shoulder wound that had landed far too close to his heart.

"Hm. Looks to me like I saved your life." A wide grin spread across my husband's face. "I'd say you owe me."

Cole laughed and offered his good arm to Brantley, pulling him to his feet. "Don't get a swollen head."

Brantley helped me up, and Starfire grabbed an oar from the broken veskal and passed it to me. Using it as a cane, I wrapped my arm around Brantley's waist.

"Shall we run him through?" One of Cole's men pointed at Danless, who was held between two loyal raiders of Rogue's Aerie.

"Or feed him to that sea creature?" A woman waved toward where Makah basked not far offshore.

I laughed, imagining Makah's reaction to being offered a violent mutineer for lunch.

Danless paled.

Cole stepped closer to him, ignoring the blood that continued to flow from his shoulder. "Today is not a day for vengeance. Peace has come to the foelands."

Indeed, more people continued to arrive, crossing islands and land bridges. I glimpsed Servant Thirty. Then Mander stalked into the clearing. He caught sight of Makah and shuddered. Seeing me, he clenched his jaw. Then with great deliberation, he removed his weapons and added them to the pile.

He stalked toward me. "The tale was true. You carry the victory child and your dance created new land."

I shook my head. "The Maker lifted the islands. He is the One Peacebringer. We will tell you about Him."

Cole refused to let anyone tend his wound until he'd appointed a new second-in-command and demoted Danless to servant status. Then he gave orders to his people to transport the dancers back to Meriel in his small veskal.

I was ready to whack him with the oar by the time he finally returned and helped me get Brantley onto Makah. "I'll ride back with him and hold him," I said. "But promise me you'll follow us in your veskal. Brianna would never forgive me if I left you here to bleed your life away."

"Don't need help," Brantley mumbled as we hoisted him onto his stenella. This time I sat behind him, my arms struggling to hold him in place. Makah swam toward Windswell with the smoothest gait she'd ever used. As we traversed the sea that still rocked from the lifting of the islands, Brantley sagged forward. With a quiet exhale, he drooped over Makah's neck. She twisted to look at me, giving me an anxious chirp.

"He'll be all right. He has to be," I answered. My baby kicked as if echoing my words.

We reached the rim of Windswell, but the village was still vacant. Thankfully one of Brantley's watchers spotted us and carried my husband to the nearest cottage—Fiola's. Then he ran to the hiding villagers for help.

Kneeling beside the pallet, I began to redress my husband's wound, wincing at the angry inflammation and fresh blood. How had he been able to rescue anyone? It was remarkable he'd been able to get himself back to shore.

Fiola entered, and I longed to leap up and hug her, but my ankle still didn't support my weight. Would she blame me for Brantley's condition?

Instead she knelt beside me and placed a quick kiss on my forehead. "Let me help."

"I'm sorry. He wanted to rescue people that fell in the ocean after the islands rose and—"

"Shh." She touched my face gently. "No one can stop Brantley from helping others. Besides, seawater is wonderful for wounds. Now let me mix up some lanthrus before you bandage him again. And you look like you could use some tsalla."

Her kindness broke the last of my control, and I sipped in a tiny sob. She gave me time to compose myself as she bustled around. I should be the one serving her, but my body betrayed me.

Instead, I stroked damp curls from Brantley's temples. Suddenly his vibrant eyes opened. "Now what?" he mumbled.

Now what, indeed? I smiled. "Now the foelands find their way to peace, Cole comes home, and you and I recover and wait for our tiny herder to arrive."

He sighed, a grin tugging his lips. "Or our little dancer." He started to say more, as if he had more questions, but then let his heavy eyelids close.

After Fiola and I redressed his injury and coaxed some broth into him, I finally changed into dry clothes and sipped my tsalla. Outside her window, conversations rose and fell, doors creaked open, and the sounds of the villagers moving back into their Windswell homes soothed me.

No veskals would be attacking. No weapons would target our rimmers. And River would no longer turn villages against the new Order. With Fiola's reassurance that Brantley would recover, gratitude swelled my heart. I could scarcely process the wonders we'd experienced on this day.

"How many copies of the Maker's letter do we yet have in Windswell?" I asked.

"Plenty to share." Fiola settled into her rocker, which shifted gently as the earth rolled beneath us.

I nodded. It was good to know the foelanders would move forward into a better future. I'd wanted to serve them . . . at least part of me had. Another part of me wanted to protect my baby and flee. Putting my own life in danger was one thing, but risking the child—I stroked Brantley's forehead—or my beloved husband, that had torn me in two. That's what came of trying to carry the weight of the worlds on my small shoulders.

Brantley's eyes slitted open, and his lips twitched. "Can we get back to normal life now?"

I laughed and hugged him. "Normal? That's a high mark to reach. How about just relatively safe?"

His chuckle ushered him into a deeper sleep, and I curled beside him on the pallet. Fiola stood and drew a blanket over us.

"One thing I don't understand," I whispered to Fiola.

"Hm?" She folded the edge of the fabric down and tucked it in place.

"The foelands were waiting for a victory child, but how can my baby fulfill that legend? She or he isn't even born yet."

Fiola touched my belly reverently. "The Maker was able to use this little one, even before birth, to bring healing to a world. None of us—no matter how small—can know what amazing things He will do through our lives. Rest now."

I closed my eyes. Images swirled of weapons and raids and veskals. Of storms and villagers tossing the Maker's words to the floor. Of lean and weary dancers longing for support. Of rimmers hiding their people. But as sleep took me, the picture that lingered in my mind was of the wild stenella diving and sailing joyously over the waves, dancing for their Maker.

EPILOGUE

"WHERE IS HE?" MY TOES CURLED INTO THE TANGLEROOT as a surge rolled under the rim. I shielded my eyes to watch the horizon. With the support of my cane, and a special stiff bandage to support my ankle, I was once again able to stand. And I'd spent far too much time in this spot, waiting for Brantley and Makah to return home from herding trips.

Beside me, Cole laughed. "He'd better be home in time for supper. Bri made her special stew, and she'll kill him if he's late. She's looking forward to having you both over." He stared toward a smudge, barely visible beneath some wispy clouds far out to sea.

"Do you miss them?" I asked cautiously. I still found Brantley's brother difficult to read. Fiola, Brianna, and Orianna had never doubted that Cole had returned to them fully and eagerly. But I'd seen the depth of the ties he had with the men and women of Rogue's Aerie. Now that the foelands were sailing out of sight, I wondered if he felt that tug. I had certainly felt torn when Cole's one undamaged veskal had transported the dancers up channel to the Order in the days following the lifting of the islands. I traveled with them in spirit. Part of me would always live there. Messages from High Saltar Kemp kept me informed. With River gone, some of her band had returned to the Order. Others had disappeared. Along with letters sent by harrier, messengers were sent to villages across Meriel revealing River's ruse in damaging and then "healing" their crops, and her part in conspiring with the foelanders. Animosity toward the Order had quickly melted, and trust was being rebuilt.

"They're in good hands. And I'm satisfied that the peace will last. I belong here." He shot a puzzled gaze toward me. "Are you worried about the foelands?"

I shook my head. We'd had months to meet with each clan and teach them about the Peacebringer. "The Maker's letter will help them. *He* will help them."

Cole rubbed his chin. "Ah, yes. The letter. Brianna read it to me."

"And?"

He paused. In the distance, children laughed. Women hummed while tending firepits. A hammer pounded as a family built an addition on their cottage. Windswell was thriving. Meriel was once again riding the current.

"It's a lot to take in. And I don't understand why a Maker would let those words be lost." He shook his head, tossing aside weighty thoughts. "See you later. I know Bri told you not to bring anything, but if you have any bresh left from the last shipment, I wouldn't complain."

I chuckled and agreed. After he left, footsteps squished on the moist tangleroot behind me, and I turned.

Starfire and Aanor stood holding hands, wide stances helping them adjust to the ever-rolling ground. "We head upchannel tomorrow," Star said. "I wish we could stay longer, but Aanor is needed in Middlemost."

He nodded, but his besotted gaze remained fixed on my friend. She smiled up at him, with a similar glow tinting her skin. They were both smitten.

Then Starfire shook herself and poked me. "Promise to send word when this little one arrives."

I hugged her. "I promise."

I'd miss her. A hint of melancholy floated upward in my chest, but Star distracted me by pointing out toward the ocean. "Here he comes."

Framed by the lowering primary sun, Makah mounted a gust of wind and floated, her side fins shimmering like mirrored scales. Brantley stood proudly on her back, chest lifted and arms cast out as if embracing the sky. After a few weeks of tender care, he'd recovered fully. Occasional itching along the scar was the only lingering reminder of all he'd endured.

Starfire and Aanor slipped away, leaving me to savor the view.

Makah glided closer and settled onto the sea again, and Brantley's knees softened to keep his balance. They were a team now. With the Maker's help, I'd stopped blaming myself for Navar's death, for Brantley's wound, for losses I couldn't prevent. Instead, I focused on caring for my husband every way I could and nurturing the baby that continued to grow within me.

Brantley waved, but didn't steer directly toward me. Makah was herding a large school of copper fish, and together they drove them toward the shore of Windswell. Even out of sight, I could picture the children running with baskets to catch the bounty. Whoops and cheers carried on the breeze.

I walked slowly back to our cottage, rubbing my back. It had been aching for weeks now, but today the pain went deeper. Fiola had made me a wider tunic, but already my belly strained the seams. It wouldn't be long now, and our little dancer or herder would join the family of Windswell. I grabbed a lenka from the basket on the table. Beside our bonding cup, a glowing blue stone rested—a precious reminder of the light the Maker could bring, and a token that warmed my heart with its reminder of the people of the foelands.

Just after I settled into my chair by the hearth, Brantley bounded in. "No messages from Saltar Kemp today?"

I giggled. "She knows I'm not going to travel like this." Then I sobered. "If she does need help later, I won't be able to go. I won't leave our babe."

Brantley leaned against the doorframe, arms crossed. A twinkle lit his eyes like a flicker of subsun on the sea. "I've been thinking about that."

He pushed away from the doorway and rummaged in a lower cupboard— one I'd stopped using since bending had become too difficult lately. He pulled out a bundle wrapped in fabric and thrust it toward me. "Here. I made you something."

Puzzled, I pulled away the fabric and held up a leather pouch with straps and buckles. "A new backpack?"

"No." He took it from me and shook it out, showing me the design. "It's for the babe. If you need to ride Makah up to Middlemost, this will carry our child against your chest."

I lifted my gaze to his face—all eager and hopeful and awaiting my reaction. My vision blurred as tears filled my eyes. "But you . . . but I . . ."

I lurched to my feet and hugged him.

He kissed me soundly, then stroked my face. "The dancers will always be part of your life. Did you think I didn't understand that? We'll find a way for you to help them."

"I love you," I said simply. Was there anything as precious as the support of a good man?

He rested his forehead against mine. "You stole my words." He kissed me again, but I pulled back and gasped.

"Brantley, I think you'll need to let Brianna know we'll miss her dinner."

"What? Why?"

From the table, the blue stone winked a flicker of added brightness. I rubbed my back again. "I do believe we'll be busy tonight."

His eyes widened, and then he gave a shout of joy.

As another wave of cramping rolled through me, I grinned. I had the feeling that the adventure that was about to begin would be the most exciting and fulfilling yet.

THE END

GLOSSARY

ALCEA FLOWER — Delicate, sweet-scented blossoms.

ATTENDANTS — Servants who work in the Order.

BOG RAT — small rodent that lives in low-lying areas.

BRESH — A flaky, buttery roll. Luxurious treat eaten by dancers.

CALARA REED — Well-rooted, supple reeds growing near water. (Calara pattern is one of the most complicated.) The pulp is used as a gently scented soap for linens.

CENTER GROUND — The huge open field in the very center of Meriel, where the dancers of the Order perform the patterns that keep the island turning around its core.

COPPER FISH — Small, glittery fish that swim in large schools and provide food for rim villages.

DAYGRASS — a soft, mossy grass that springs up overnight.

ECCO COVE — One of the foelands; under Larcy's leadership. Their veskals have red sails.

FERN PATTERN — Includes curling frond shape with arms, turns moving from center "stem."

FOELANDS/FOELANDERS — The term used by clans on the cluster of islands to refer to other islands in the group or their people.

FOLESHILL — A midrange village; one of the villages refusing to support the new Order.

FOREST HOUND — A wolf-like beast almost as big as a pony, usually with amber eyes; a feared predator.

FORMS — Various levels within the Order's school. First-form children are generally around seven years old and work up through the ranks to the fifteenth form (twenty-one years of age) and if successful can join the Order as dancers. Some dancers later become saltars.

FOUNTAIN FISH — Pink-and-green-striped bronze fish, kept as pets or in fountains.

HALYARD'S HULL — One of the foelands.

HERDER — One who herds fish from the ocean waters so they can be gathered by rim villagers.

HONEYBIRD — Tiny, nervous, bright red bird.

LANDKEEPER — A person who gardens, farms, cares for plants.

LANTHRUS — A plant with prickly leaves that cause blisters and fever, but when dried is useful for pain.

LENKA — A small, yellow, tart and sweet fruit with a small oval pit inside.

LONGKNIFE — Common long-bladed tool and weapon used by herders.

MAKER, THE — The Creator of the oceans, the island worlds, and everything in them.

MEADOW BLIGHT — A serious illness that causes fever, trouble breathing, and often death; frequently lingers for weeks.

MERIEL — The name of Carya's world (the island floating in a vast, featureless ocean universe).

MIDDLEMOST — The largest city, in the center of Meriel, surrounding the Order.

NEWLAND — The term used by the cluster of island people to refer to Meriel.

NOVITIATES — Girls training to become dancers of the Order.

ORDER, THE — The organization of novitiates, dancers, saltars, prefects, and attendants that direct the course of the world through the dance. Located in the very center of Meriel, in a large edifice that encircles the center ground. They pass down the patterns through the generations. Recently reformed.

PATTERNS — Precise dances and formations named for various natural elements or plants.

PERSEA FRUIT — Knobby-skinned, meaty fruit with a pit.

PREFECT — Support staff for the Order school, they enforce rules, help saltars, etc.

RIM — The undulating outer edges of the island worlds.

RIMMERS — Sometimes derogatory term for those who live in rim villages.

ROGUE'S AERIE — The tallest of the foelands; under Cole's leadership. Their veskals have blue and green sails.

RUTISH PLANT — A tuber that has a pebbly green skin and is good in stews.

SALIS — A midrim village that protected castoff dancers in the past; one of the villages refusing to support the new Order.

SALTARS — The leaders and top teachers of the Order.

SALTCAKES — Dry, crumbly biscuits.

SCAVENGEWOOD — One of the foelands; under Mander's leadership. Their veskals have white sails.

SHADOWSWELL — A midrim village near the channel.

STAR RAIN — A periodic magical occurrence on evenings when stars burst in the air and glittering light rains down.

STENELLA — Dolphin-like sea creatures with long necks and wide spreading side fins that can glide over the water as well as dive under.

SWEET WATER — Ocean water that tastes sweet and citrusy. Loved by the rim villages, but feared and filtered by those in the inland towns.

TANGLEROOT — The matted, intertwined vines that form the outer edge of the islands.

TENDER — Someone who cares for domesticated animals, especially ponies.

TSALLA — Sweet ocean water brewed with herbs.

UNDERTOW — Rim village where Carya was born.

VESKALS — The sailing crafts that the raiders use to travel between islands.

WHITECAP — A rim village Carya visited in the past; one of the villages refusing to support the new Order.

WINDSWELL — Rim village where Brantley herds/leads and lives with Carya; located near the mouth of the channel.

ACKNOWLEDGMENTS

HEARTFELT THANKS TO MY AGENT, STEVE LAUBE, WHO encouraged this series and fights for a place in this world for unusual stories. Eternal gratitude to my editors, Reagen Reed and Lindsay Franklin, who bring so much care, respect, and wisdom to making my stories stronger. Huge appreciation to Trissina Kear and Jordan Smith for all their hard work helping readers find these books. And cheers to Kirk DouPonce for bringing images to life with remarkable covers.

My love to the friends who have prayed with me as I work. I am blessed by every circle of support. The "church ladies," Bible study small groups, writing retreat buddies, the Dancing Realms Facebook group, my Book Buddies, family, and so many dear friends. This series exists because of all of you. Special thanks to critique partners who gave input on various chapters, and to Chawna, Patrice, and Michelle for in-depth feedback on the full manuscript.

Ted, you continue to believe in me when I'm plagued with doubt, and your example of faith and integrity inspire me every day. Every good thing in each character had its inspiration in you.

Above all else, thank you to our Maker who lifts us up. May we rejoice each day in knowing His love.

AUTHOR BIOGRAPHY

SHARON HINCK WRITES "STORIES FOR THE HERO IN ALL OF US," novels praised for their strong spiritual themes, emotional resonance, and imaginative blend of genres.

She earned an MA in Communication (with a major in theatre and thesis in dance) from Regent University and spent ten years as the artistic director of a Christian dance company. That ministry included three short-term mission trips to Hong Kong to teach and choreograph for a YWAM dance/evangelism team. She taught classical ballet and liturgical dance for twenty years, and led workshops on dance in worship.

She's been a church youth worker, a dancer/choreographer, a church organist, a homeschool mom, and an adjunct professor of Creative Writing for MFA students. One day she'll figure out what to be when she grows up.

When she's not wrestling with words, she enjoys speaking at churches and conferences and has taught at Minnesota Christian Writer's Guild, the national conference of the American Christian Fiction Writers, and Realm Makers.

A wife, mom of four, and grandmother of three, she lives in Minnesota and is a member at St. Michael's Lutheran Church.

She loves visitors at sharonhinck.com.